The Monsignor

by

George Banks

The Monsignor
By
George Banks

The Monsignor
Copyright © 2016 George Banks. Produced and printed
by Stillwater River Publications. All rights reserved. Written and produced in
the United States of America. This book may not be reproduced or sold in
any form without the expressed, written permission of the authors and
publisher.
Visit our website at **www.StillwaterPress.com** for more information.
First Stillwater River Publications Edition

ISBN-10: 0-692-64929-8
ISBN-13: 978-0692-64929-9
Library of Congress Control Number: 2016934940

 2 3 4 5 6 7 8 9 10
Written by George Banks
Cover Design by Dawn M. Porter
Published by Stillwater River Publications, Glocester, RI, USA.

Publisher's Cataloging-In-Publication Data
(Prepared by The Donohue Group, Inc.)
Names: Banks, George, 1952-
Title: The monsignor / by George Banks.
Description: First Stillwater River Publications edition. | Glocester, RI,
USA : Stillwater River Publications, [2016]
Identifiers: LCCN 2016934940 | ISBN 978-0-692-64929-9 | ISBN 069-
264929-8
Subjects: LCSH: Catholic Church--Clergy--Fiction. | World War, 1939-
1945--Underground movements--Fiction. | Ardeatine Caves Massacre,
Rome, Italy, 1944--Fiction. | World War, 1939-1945--War work--
Catholic Church--Fiction. | Vatican City--Fiction.
Classification: LCC PS3602.A55 M66 2016 | DDC 813/.6--dc23

One

The Meeting

The day had been dark and dank, the effects of a continuous drizzle. It had been this way all day long. Rome was a city of light, bright sunlight. The night reflected the mood of Monsignor Liam O'Reilly. It reminded him of his native Galway, Ireland.

The cleric was deep in thought. Not only about his religious duties and obligations, but his increasing role in the escape organization that he was an intimate part of. It had begun in September 1943 with an American lieutenant. John Corliss had escaped from an Italian prisoner of war camp near Anzio. He had been assisted by Italian civilians that were a part of the Ambrosia Network. The American had arrived in Rome and had been hiding in the ancient ruins near the Colosseum.

1

O'Reilly had been avidly following the course of the war from his Vatican post. When the war had begun in 1939, he had had no great love of the British. Great Britain had long ground its heel into the Irish citizenry. He had personally witnessed the bitter poverty in Galway, the utter destitution to what the people were consigned to. Nevertheless, the Monsignor had always considered himself an open-minded person. Nazi Germany and its legions were a scourge upon the world and upon Rome. His Rome, he had come to idolize and worship the city. From his vantage point on the steps that led to the Basilica of St Peter' Cathedral, O'Reilly could look out onto the entire square.

"Excuse me, Monsignor?" asked Father Damian Lillard tentatively. O'Reilly's assistant had been hovering in the background.

"Yes?" replied O'Reilly.

"You have an appointment with Hauptsturmfuhrer Krieger tomorrow morning at 9:00 AM."

"Yes. I have not forgotten. Let us retire to my office, Damian," said the Monsignor.

The two men retreated to O'Reilly's office in the German College. The room was Spartan in appearance, rather utilitarian, but it suited O'Reilly perfectly. At first, neither man spoke.

"I suppose I must meet with the man, but I really cannot stand him or any member of the SS," said the Monsignor.

"Do you think he suspects something?" asked Father Damian.

"Of course, he must suspect something. Why would he ask for this meeting? I don't think he wants to discuss Canon law."

Damian stood nervously. He, too, was a fellow Irishman and he had gotten to know O'Reilly rather well in the two years he had spent as his assistant. Lillard had been born in 1921 in

Belfast, in what would become Northern Ireland, following the partition from the Republic of Ireland. He had been raised in a strict Catholic household. His mother was devoted to the Church and attended mass daily. His father was less doctrinaire in his devotions.

O'Reilly glanced over at Lillard. "Sit down, Damian, you're making me nervous."

"Thank you, Monsignor. Err, I'm sorry if I have made you nervous, said Damian as he sat before O'Reilly. "Do you actually believe that Krieger suspects anything about our… group?"

"Yes, I do. I am sure that he believes there is something most suspicious about us, the question is what?," mused O'Reilly. "We know Herr Krieger is insanely jealous of his boss, Colonel Kammler."

"This could be a dangerous game, Monsignor," said Father Damian.

Kammler, Obersturmbannfuhrer Helmut Kammler had long been a thorn in the side of Liam O'Reilly. It had been that way since the German had first arrived in Rome. But now he was becoming the face of the German occupation. The man was in his late thirties with crisp blue eyes, cropped blond hair, and a dueling scar on his right cheek. The ideal Aryan of the Master Race. Kammler was chief of the Sicherheitsdienst, the SS security service.

"Yes," thought O'Reilly, "it could well be dangerous for him and all concerned within the escape network." No. It had become far too dangerous. He knew that he had been getting the better of Kammler and his sycophantic lapdog, Albert Krieger. "Very well. I will meet with Krieger tomorrow," O'Reilly said aloud.

"Maybe, it would have been better to have had the meeting here in the Vatican, Monsignor. What is the expression the Americans use? Home turf?" said Father Damian.

"No! Damian, no! I would never defile the sacred ground of the Vatican with the presence of Nazis, especially one like Krieger!" bellowed O'Reilly. "I will meet the Hauptsturmfuhrer as we agreed for coffee at Prato's Bar."

"Will there be anything else, Monsignor?" asked Father Damian.

"No, I think that will be all for now. Thank you, Damian. You have always been a most trustworthy and devoted priest. I don't know what I would do without you," said the Monsignor.

"Thank you, Monsignor. Please be very careful tomorrow morning. I trust you will be wearing one of your more creative disguises."

"You can count on it, my boy," replied O'Reilly in an accentuated Irish brogue.

After Father Lillard's departure, O'Reilly sat back in silent contemplation of what confronted him. How had it come to this? Liam O'Reilly had been born in Lisrobin, County Cork, to James and Margaret O'Reilly. His love of golf undoubtedly stemming from having grown up beside a golf course, where his father had worked as a steward. He had been set to become a teacher, but then felt a calling from God. In 1918, Liam O'Reilly enrolled in a Jesuit college. He was older than most of his fellow seminarians, but had been allowed admission by Bishop Cornelius O'Flaherty. Father O'Reilly was ordained in the Bishop's diocese amidst a time of fierce conflict throughout Ireland. He was posted to the Holy See in Rome in 1922. O'Reilly remembered his serving as a Vatican diplomat in such far-off places as Egypt,

Haiti, and Czechoslovakia. The great pride he had felt when he was appointed Monsignor in 1934.

Giuseppe Prato was thinking of what would take place in his establishment on the following day. Prato, owner and sole proprietor of Prato's Ristorante and Bar was fearful of what might result from the meeting between Monsignor O'Reilly and a German SS officer. The bar was a small and non-descript affair, offering a wide array of simple foods and beverages. It was not fancy or pretentious, as he felt toward Harry's American Bar. The bar catered to a modest, working-class clientele that reflected the surrounding neighborhood. Customers were more often than not laborers, shopkeepers, street sweepers

Prato was proud of his establishment, which he had acquired from his uncle many years before. The bar consisted of six or seven tables and a likeminded number of barstools.

Prato, himself, was approaching middle age and he had never been involved with anything of this magnitude before. He had always lived a safe life, keeping his mouth shut, doing the right thing. But times had changed. He could not sit back and, yet, he could not bring himself to speak out. He could, however, act in some small way. His serving as host to this meeting would, perhaps, be his small contribution to the eventual liberation of Rome.

* * *

Meanwhile, at the Vatican, Monsignor Liam O'Reilly was considering what disguise he would use for his meeting with Albert Krieger. He had a wide array of costumes from which to choose. There was a Waffen SS officer's uniform, replete with an Iron Cross medal. This he would not use. O'Reilly could select the stonemason's woolen shirt and corduroy pants, or he might use the street sweeper's simple clothing. Yes, he would select the street sweeper. They were common enough and non-descript, and ubiquitous throughout the streets of Rome.

O'Reilly had been preparing for this moment in a surreptitious way. He had been effecting a beard for the past several days, so that he would be in keeping for the part he would play. These men were, after all, not bankers or businessmen, and with the war they were usually even more slovenly in their appearance. He would arrange to join a detail through his good friend, Mario Casso. The man had been cleaning the streets of Rome for more than thirty years and he knew them like the back of his hand.

It would have to be done quickly, but he could not contact Casso directly. O'Reilly would have word sent to the man through his good friend and fellow conspirator, Contessa Rosanna Vallone. The Contessa would be able to contact Casso and have conveyed to him O'Reilly's request. The Monsignor could then be filtered into a street-sweeper crew. Casso could also arrange for the sweepers to be near Prato's Bar. It could be easily accomplished as the Germans had been rather lax in their supervision and oversight of some of the city's operating departments. The Nazis may have seen themselves as the "Master Race", and seemingly devoted to every possible detail. There were, however, priorities that had to be attended to first and foremost. Procuring work labor to send back to Germany for their factories. Then, there was the surveillance of leading Italians, former military officers, doctors, lawyers, aristocrats, the clergy…. But the biggest priority was centered squarely on the Jews and how they had to be squeezed for every possible lira, jewelry, and property.

O'Reilly called in Father Damian to his study.

"Yes, Monsignor?" asked Damian, "you sent for me?"

"Yes, Damian, please come in. Sit down. I need you to contact the Contessa within the hour. Can it be done?"

"Yes, I believe so," replied Damian. "She should be available at this time."

"Good. Please see that she is sent in through the special passage to my office."

"Yes, Monsignor."

"That will be all, Damian." The priest backed out of O'Reilly's office quietly to get in touch with Rosanna Vallone.

Contessa Rosanna Vallone was 41 years old and had been the wife of Maggiore Giuseppe Vallone. The major had been a member of a Bersaglieri detachment in Libya in the western desert. Vallone never returned to Italy, having been killed in action in Libya in 1941. The Contessa had lived in Rome all of her life, now, with her two children, Ariana, age 19, and Gaetano, age 17. Her apartment was located near the famous Spanish Steps.

Upon receiving word from Father Damian, she had immediately dropped what she had been doing for the past several hours. Gazing at pictures of herself with Giuseppe and the children. Ordinary, everyday pictures of themselves in their home or on holiday at Lake Como, the Alps, and so on. She had never seemed to have appreciated what she had had, what they all once had, until this moment.

The Contessa put away the photos and quickly tidied up the room. She checked herself in the mirror. She did not want to appear too ostentatious while walking through the Roman streets. Satisfied, she set out for Monsignor O'Reilly's office in the German College.

"You sent for me, Monsignor? "Rosanna asked upon entering O'Reilly's enclave.

"Yes, Contessa. Please, come in. Sit down. I have asked you here because I have a special request to make of you."

"Yes, Monsignor," she replied tentatively.

"I need to arrange to get word to Mario Casso. I will be assuming the role of a street-sweeper. The purpose of this is that I am to meet with an SS officer tomorrow morning at 9:00 AM. I do think it may well be a good role for me to play," said O'Reilly.

"An SS officer you say. Might that be a bit risky, Monsignor?" asked a now mystified and slightly alarmed Rosanna.

"This meeting is important. I may be able to pick up something of value from this SS man," said O'Reilly.

"Well... I suppose you know what you are doing. I shouldn't have asked. But, I am alarmed when I hear you say in a cavalier manner about playing a role. I think that you sometimes look upon roles as a joke," Rosanna went on. "There is nothing funny that I can see anywhere in Rome these days."

"No, no, I realize that, Rosanna. Believe me, I do, but this is very important to our cause, or it may be."

"I see. When do you need me to have Casso contacted?" the woman asked with increasing concern in her voice and in the expression upon her face.

"It must be by early this evening," responded O'Reilly. "I need to be placed in his sweeper crew by 8:00 AM tomorrow and near to Prato's Bar."

"All right. I will see that word gets to him. Is there anything else, Monsignor?"

"No. That should cover it. Thank you, Rosanna. You do not know how much I appreciate this," said the Monsignor as he gently padded the woman's hand.

"I am always glad to assist you and the organization in any way that I can. You know that, Monsignor."

"Yes, of course. I realize that," responded O'Reilly.

Rosanna leaned forward in her chair and said," Please, be careful, Liam. I still think this meeting sounds risky. You have already taken several risks, that I am aware of. I remember the time you pretended to be a clown. Those big red shoes and that bulbous red nose made you look ridiculous, in my opinion," she chided.

"Ha-ha-ha… Yes…. That was quite comical, I have to admit," replied the Monsignor laughingly.

"Monsignor, you must be careful. I beg of you."

"I will be careful. I assure you," O'Reilly replied with an earnest look on his face.

"All right, Monsignor. I will do as you have asked," said a slightly mollified Contessa,

"Good, good, Rosanna. I believe that will be all for now," said O'Reilly.

"Good-bye, Monsignor," said Rosanna as she left the office. She would now make her way to having Mario Casso contacted.

It was approaching late afternoon in Rome by the time Rosanna Vallone emerged from the Lateran offices. She thought of how best to get word to Casso. "Yes!" she thought to herself. "I will need to see Genevieve." The young woman would be the one to make contact with the sweeper chieftain to convey O'Reilly's request.

Genevieve Alviano was the perfect courier in the Ambrosia Network. This girl was unafraid and possessed stunning looks.

Tall and lithesome and well proportioned, she cut quite the "Bella Figura" so enamored in Italy. Genevieve liked to don low-cut, revealing blouses which showed off her fulsome cleavage. German troops often gave her a wide berth in their admiration of her as she moved through the city.

Alviano also had a personal stake in the cat and mouse contest between O'Reilly's network and the Nazis. Her twenty-year-old brother, Pietro, was at that moment, languishing in a German prisoner of war camp near Hammelburg, Germany. Genevieve, as nearly every Italian did, came face to face with the German domination of their city and their country every day.

At this time of day, Genevieve could usually be found at the Children's orphanage on Via Locarno, assisting the staff with the neglected youth of the city. Since the war, there had been no shortage of their services being needed. The Contessa set off immediately for Via Locarno and, with any luck, could be there within the hour. She only hoped that the young woman would still be there.

Rosanna was at last approaching the orphanage when she observed a contingent of German soldiers, SS men, outside on the street. She wondered if anything ominous could be afoot. No, probably not. The Germans liked to show off their presence, their power to the Italians. Oftentimes, they would drive their tanks through the city, just to make the people cower in their powerlessness. The Contessa made her way by the SS men and entered the orphanage in search of Genevieve Alviano. She spied Sister Mariana at a classroom entrance. Children of all ages were running about through the hallways.

"Hello, Sister. Have you seen Genevieve?"" asked a hopeful Rosanna.

"No, not recently, Contessa," replied Sister Mariana. She noted that the Contessa seemed rather agitated, which was quite unlike most of the time.

"I need to find her. It is most important. Do you have any idea where she might be?"

"You might try the auditorium, the children have been rehearsing a play."

"Grazie, Sister," said Rosanna as she practically ran off away from Sister Mariana. The sister nodded as the woman had run off with a bewildered look on her face. Rosanna ran up to the auditorium and was quietly relieved to see Genevieve surrounded by a horde of young children. Alviano saw Rosanna and immediately understood that something important was up. The Contessa would not show up unannounced unless the matter was most important, or even urgent. The young woman excused herself from her young charges and went to greet Rosanna.

"How nice to see you, Contessa. This is an unexpected pleasure," said Genevieve.

"It is good to see you, Genevieve. I was wondering if I could have a word with you in private?"

"Of course, let us go to one of the secretarial offices."

They soon located one that was unoccupied. "The reason I have come to see you is because of an important matter," said the Contessa with a serious expression. "'Golf' needs to arrange it so that he can join Mario Casso's sweeper crew by 8:00 AM tomorrow morning. Can you get word to Casso?"

Genevieve nodded her head and said, "It can be done. That's it? Our friend wishes to be a street sweeper?" she asked querulously.

"Yes. Casso will understand that our friend has a legitimate and plausible reason to be in this role, for whatever purpose," continued the Contessa. Rosanna looked into the eyes of Genevieve Alviano and knew it would be done. Alviano, looked, at times, to be too youthful, inexperienced, vulnerable. But she also well knew that this young woman possessed an iron backbone and nerves of steel. She would arrange for things with Casso.

Genevieve had always admired Rosanna and had come to look upon her as a surrogate mother. Her own mother had passed away several years before of rheumatic fever. Her father had resettled in the coastal town of Anzio. Genevieve had always worried about him, especially since the Allied invasion there in January. A great battle had erupted there between the Americans and British on one side and the Germans on the other. There had been great loss of life and much destruction. As far as Genevieve knew, her father had survived and was living amongst the ruins, huddled with his equally suffering neighbors and friends.

"Okay. I will visit Casso later today. I am scheduled to complete my day by 4:00 PM. I will go see him then," replied Genevieve.

"Bene," said Rosanna. "Please be careful, Genevieve."

"I always am. At least, I try to be."

"I will take my leave now. I have got to get home to prepare dinner for Ariana and Gaetano," said the Contessa. And with that, she left quietly.

Genevieve sat there thinking of what Rosanna had just told her, of having to prepare dinner for her two grown children. Spoiled children was more like it. She herself would have liked for someone to be at home for her and preparing a meal, as well.

Instead, she was alone in a big city like Rome and in the middle of a war. She quickly put these unpleasant thoughts out of her mind. The Contessa was a good woman with a big heart. Genevieve had always been very grateful to her.

To the matter at hand, Genevieve thought about how she would go about it. Another assignment, another risk. The Germans weren't stupid and there were those Italians who had chosen to sell their souls to the devil, just to be able to get by. It may have been for food or shelter, whatever.

* * *

Later that day, Genevieve Alviano prepared to leave the orphanage and proceed to Mario Casso's residence in the Piazza Navona section of Rome. It was, in fact, not far away, just across the Tiber River. She did not come into contact with very many people along the way, especially Germans. Genevieve arrived at Mario Casso's building around 4:00 PM and went up the stairs to his second floor apartment. The building was a common, stone-faced type. The kind seen throughout the city. The hallways were in a somewhat tattered condition. Chipped and cracked plaster was plainly evident. The place had long since needed a fresh coat of paint.

Genevieve crept through the hallways and approached Casso's door. She knocked lightly. She did not employ a secret knock code, that was only seen in the cinema. It usually never worked. There was no reply. It was possible that Casso might not be at home. Perhaps, he had not returned from work. She knew that he usually was at home by this hour. She knocked again, this time more firmly. She waited. The door opened slowly and Mario Casso appeared before her. He was unshaven, the growth of an, at least, two-day old beard present.

"Ah, please come in," Casso greeted her in a jovial manner. He did not use her name, one could not tell who might be listening.

Genevieve stepped inside. Casso closed the door. She came straight to the point of her visit. "It needs to be arranged for the golfer to become a member of your street sweeper crew tomorrow morning. Your crew is to be in the neighborhood of Prato's Bar by around 8:00 AM or so. Can you arrange this?"

Casso stood and looked at Genevieve Alviano. He could not help but notice how lovely this girl really was. Even without make-up, which had virtually disappeared on Roman store shelves, the girl was mesmerizing. He looked around at his disheveled apartment and was ashamed. The furniture was old and worn, if not outright broken. The throw rug in the center of the room was fraying around the edges.

"Can you do it?" Genevieve asked again.

His reverie broke and Casso replied, "It should not be a problem, but why on such short notice?"

"I do not know," the girl answered. "I am only conveying the message I was given."

"Very well, my dear. I think I can arrange for this assignment for our friend."

"You think you can do it or you think you can't!" Genevieve answered somewhat challengingly.

Casso looked pensive. "It will be done as you have requested. Keep in mind that although the Germans and Fascist bootlickers have been rather lax in their oversight on common tasks, such as street-sweeping, one cannot just move from one end of Rome to another at the drop of a hat. Luckily, for you, my crew has been assigned to an area that is fairly close to Prato's. It should be easily arranged to be there by the appointed hour."

"Bene, I will pass this on. And Mario, you will be careful," Genevieve replied softly. She had not meant to sound abrupt with the older man. It must be that her nerves were finally starting to get the better of her.

Casso seemed to understand. Everyone was under a great deal of stress these days. It had been only natural for the girl to have acted this way. "I am always careful, my child. Things have been getting more intense of late."

"I know that, Mario, but..." she seemed to hesitate.

"It is all right. I will do as you and 'Golf' have requested."

"Grazie, Mario. Ciao. Go with God." Genevieve left the older man. He would now need to make arrangements for the following day.

* * *

Meanwhile, Monsignor O'Reilly had been sitting in his office. He had just completed his daily ablutions and was finishing up some clerical details. He had eaten little that day, likely because of his upcoming meeting with Albert Krieger on the morrow. Tonight, when he sank to his knees in prayer he would ask his Lord God for strength and support for his task. O'Reilly had to find out what Krieger was up to and, by extension, what his boss, Helmut Kammler, might have up his sleeve.

* * *

Tuesday dawned bright and clear with a sparkling sunlight. This was, indeed, Rome. The Monsignor took this as a good omen for the day ahead. He drank some tepid, ersatz tea and consumed a slice of bread, dabbed in precious olive oil. He reminded himself that he would have to be clear-minded and alert at all times with Krieger.

O'Reilly began to dress as a Roman street-sweeper. He briefly recited some prayers, the Our Father, the Hail Mary, and an Irish devotion. He looked at himself in the mirror and pronounced that he looked satisfied. He set off for Via Ezio and Prato's Ristorante/ Bar.

Mario Casso was awaiting O'Reilly's arrival when he observed the Monsignor alighting along Via Ezio just before 8:00 AM. Few people were seen about. Rome had become a completely different city since the German occupation from the one that had normally been seen before the war. The Monsignor was handed a broom, or what was left of one, and a long-handled dustpan. It was the kind that was hinged at the base of the shaft to allow for debris to be swept in.

"All right, let us look sharp!" Casso called out to his crew. "This may seem as if we are only lowly street-sweepers, but we have a job to do." His words were terse and authoritarian sounding, but Mario Casso's men knew he had not really meant it that way. He was one of the best supervisors his men had ever worked for. Some of the managers acted like pretentious, preening Fascists, who enjoyed pushing their charges around. But not Casso.

O'Reilly bent to his task with enthusiasm and was actually outworking the other members of the crew. Casso approached him and said, "Slow down, Monsignor…, err Aldo," referencing the affected name O'Reilly had taken for his role. "You are working too diligently and will soon become exhausted. After all, we have to make the job last."

"Yes, of course. I did not realize," said O'Reilly. He had elected to assume the role of one, Aldo Rossi, for his sweeper role.

"That is quite all right, Padre," replied Casso, again realizing that he had made a slip in how he addressed O'Reilly. He would have to be more careful. After all, one could not be too careful should any Germans be lurking about. "You are doing a fine job. One would think you are a natural."

"So, I look the part, you are saying?" O'Reilly asked cautiously.

"Yes. I may have to promote you soon," Casso jested back.

"No, not at all."

O'Reilly kept on with his work for the next two hours. Around 9:45 AM he noticed a fairly well-dressed man loitering along Via Ezio. The man was about six feet tall, blond-haired, with a rather straight-backed gait as he walked. He wore a grey sport coat and tan slacks. The shoes were chocolate brown and shined to a high luster. Obviously, the man was trying to effect a casual nature, but he stood out like the proverbial sore thumb. This was O'Reilly's mark. The Monsignor continued to watch the stranger out of the corner of his eye, all the while continuing with his street-sweeping duties.

At 10:00 AM, the blond-haired man paused outside the door of Prato's Bar, furtively looking about. O'Reilly thought this contact had a lot to learn concerning undercover work. The man entered the bar. Krieger looked around the establishment and took in the clientele. Two old men, shabbily dressed, were gathered at the bar sipping espressos.

Giuseppe Prato was serving at the bar, busying himself with various cleaning tasks he had already done several times. He was nervous. He only hoped he did not look nervous. He noticed the stranger. Their eyes met and Prato gave a slight nod, as if bidding the man welcome. Albert Krieger gave no sign of acknowledgment to Prato and sat down at a table in the back of the room. The German placed himself so that he was facing the door. Prato glanced at his watch and saw that it read precisely 10:00 AM. "Right on time," he thought. Germans were always on time.

Prato made no attempt to approach the stranger as he would have had it been one of his regular customers. To be tardy in greeting a customer would have been considered a sign of disrespect. He knew that Romans, in general, were considered rather diffident, aloof, in their manner, at least, by other Italians. Nevertheless, he would be required to display some degree of cordiality during the course of their upcoming business.

At about ten minutes after the hour, O'Reilly cautiously entered the bar and glanced around. He took in Prato behind the bar, the two old men, and the nattily attired gentleman at the back table. Krieger observed the street sweeper, but gave no sign. O'Reilly approached Krieger and said, "Excuse me, sir. May I join you?"

Krieger looked up at the lowly man before him and replied, "Of course, why not. I think that would be rather splendid."

"Grazie," O'Reilly replied in brogue accented Italian.

Neither man spoke for several moments. Prato had been observing this exchange and decided it was time for him to greet his two new customers. "Buon giorno, gentlemen. How may I be of service to you on this glorious morning?" he beamed.

Krieger acted as if he had never heard one word that Prato had just spoken. O'Reilly took a quick look at the barkeep and just as quickly looked downward again.

"Yes, yes, you may," hissed Krieger. "I believe that two Café Americanos should be sufficient to start with."

"At once, kind sir. And may I say that you have made an excellent choice. We at Prato's take great pride in our establishment, service, and products," gushed a now perspiring and excited Prato.

"Please, please, just get on with it, man. I have not come here to be fawned over by an obsequious tavern keeper!" flared a now irate Krieger.

"Of course, sir. Your order will be taken care of immediately," said a taken aback and startled Giuseppe Prato. He quickly sped off to the bar for the coffees.

O'Reilly had watched the whole scene and it once again confirmed his complete and utter contempt and abhorrence of the Nazis. They always had to be on-stage, domineering, treating all others as sub-humans. They were the Master Race. They just couldn't help themselves. It was in their genes. O'Reilly could practically envision them goose-stepping as they emerged from the womb.

Krieger glanced over at Prato and surmised that the man was probably in league with O'Reilly. Why else would the Monsignor have suggested this place for the meeting. He made a mental note to have the bar watched in the future. "Well, Monsignor, err, how do you refer to yourself, if I may ask?" questioned Krieger.

"I am called Aldo, signore, or should I say Herr Krieger?" shot back O'Reilly.

"Aldo? Not very original if you ask me, but whatever," said an amused Albert Krieger. "So, what shall be talk about on such a fine day here in Rome?"

"The weather?" O'Reilly tentatively replied. It had just come out. It was all he had been able to come up with. He felt as if he were panicking, but why? He was in safe place. He was among friends. He had to remind himself that Krieger was nothing, just a pretentious guttersnipe

"The weather, yes, why not," laughed Krieger. The German had opened his mouth so wide that O'Reilly could see the gold fillings in his teeth. "The weather, indeed, yes. Look, I did not suggest this meeting to merely discuss pleasantries and banalities. What do you want?" A hardness had crept into Krieger's voice as he practically bit off his words.

"Agree? Want? My dear Hauptsturmfuhrer. Oh, excuse me, I did not catch your name?" mocked a now angry O'Reilly. "You sent word to me suggesting this little coffee klatch. I should ask you what it is that you would like to discuss," he replied amiably. It wounded him trying to appear polite and calm with this cunning and conniving individual. It was hard to picture Krieger, or any SS man, as a child of God. "Indeed, I did. I was wondering that, perhaps, we might be able to mutually help one another." said Krieger.

O'Reilly did not respond, but he wondered, "What game is this man playing? How much does he know about us? And, by extension, how much does Albert Krieger's boss, Helmut Kammler know?" The Monsignor was sure he was here with the knowledge and consent of the senior SS man. Krieger would not be doing this on his own, or would he?

"Well?" prompted Krieger.

"I would expect that you would have to provide something. By the way, I never did catch your name."

"I never mentioned it to you, priest!" Krieger hissed back at O'Reilly. He was becoming infuriated with the man. "Names are not important for our purposes. Let me be clear. I know that you know about certain things that are going in Rome at the moment. We both know that the German High Command has been considering invading the Holy See. I could provide to you and others advance word of such an action, should things become finalized. What did you say to that, Herr Aldo-o-o?" leered Krieger.

"And what is it that you may be seeking?" O'Reilly asked as his comfort level was decreasing by the minute. "What you have just revealed to me cannot be simply largesse on the part of the Germans."

"Why do you assume there is a price tag?"

All of this time O'Reilly had been holding his tongue, desperately trying to maintain his composure while engaged with Krieger.

Krieger leaned in close to O'Reilly and quietly said, "All right, Monsignor, let us leave it that. Take your time while you consider what I have proposed. Perhaps, you can discuss it with your friends in the Vatican. You may even want to drop a word with His Holiness. Maybe even Sir D'Arcy. Ah, here are our coffees."

Giuseppe Prato walked over carrying a tray with the coffees, along with some sugar, and milk. Sugar had become increasingly rare, almost non-existent, in Rome these days. Krieger wondered how Prato had procured this scarce item. Prato set the tray down between the two men. "Your coffees, gentlemen. Due Café Americanos. Is there anything else you should desire?"

"Nein, err, no. That will be all," stammered Krieger.

Prato silently bowed and left the men. Krieger took it upon himself to prepare the coffees. "I do believe that you prefer one sugar in your coffee. Is that not correct?" asked the German.

O'Reilly absentmindedly nodded his head, lost in thought. He quickly regathered himself and took hold of the cup presented to him.

"I do hope that the coffee is to your liking, Herr Aldo. I am so glad that we could spend this time together. Do you not agree?"

O'Reilly remained silent. He felt his skin beginning to crawl over his body. He could not even bring himself to look at Krieger.

The SS man continued prattling along. "Well, I have certainly enjoyed myself. During the course of my work in the SS I don't often have the opportunity to indulge in such a simple, yet worthwhile activity. A leisurely cup of coffee on a lovely day." Krieger proceeded to finish his coffee and, then, stood and bowed slightly toward O'Reilly. "I bid you good day, kind sir. Please, carefully consider what we have discussed this morning. I can really be of help to you, I can. I know we will be in touch in the future. You know, in a way we both have the same opponent."

The Hauptsturmfuhrer rapidly left the bar and disappeared down Via Ezio. The Monsignor did indeed have much to think over.

Two

Kammler

Obersturmbannfuhrer Helmut Kammler stood at the large-scale map of Rome in his office at SS Headquarters on Via Wolkonsky. His interest was focused on the Castel Sant'Angelo area along the Tiber River. The main thoroughfare, Via Della Conciliazone led directly to St. Peter's Basilica in the Vatican complex. Kammler was concentrating on the warren of streets lying between Via Crescenzio and Via Cola de Rienzo, Via Plinio, Via Visconti, and so on, presented a labyrinthian network of passageways. Many men, many desperate men, could be hidden within the many buildings along these streets and alleys. From his intelligence sources, there was more than a strong suspicion that this area was a nexus of activity for an escape operation right in the heart of Rome.

All indications were that direction and guidance were being provided by a group of individuals working from within the very walls of the Vatican. And all signs pointed to one man, Monsignor Liam O'Reilly. The genial Irish priest of the open and beguiling personality. As Kammler continued to stare at the map, he realized that his mission in Rome had become more than just carrying out security tasks on behalf of the Third Reich. This priest had become his "bette noir" in every sense. He was quite sure that O'Reilly was at the core of this so-called "escape network" being conducted under the very noses of the Germans.

"Steiner!" bellowed Kammler. "Steiner," he repeated.

"Yawohl, Herr Obersturmbannfuhrer," stammered Scharffuhrer Hans Steiner, as he ran into Helmut Kammler's office.

"Steiner, where is Hauptsturmfuhrer Krieger?"

"I believe he should be in office, sir."

"I did not ask you about your beliefs. What I have asked is something that you should know," hissed an increasingly angry Helmut Kammler. "He is not in his office. In fact, he is not even in this building at all!"

Steiner stood in front of Kammler, but remained silent. He was long used to these outbursts from Kammler, and Krieger, and almost every SS officer he had ever dealt with. It was a part of their nature, a fiber of their very being.

"Well? Don't just stand there, like some dummy! Find out where he is and, when you do so, have him report to me immediately," said Kammler, in a more civil tone.

"Yawohl, Herr Obersturmbannfuhrer." Steiner clicked his jack-booted heels and threw out the obligatory stiff-armed Hitler salute.

Kammler merely cast off a half-hearted casual heil back at Steiner. Turning back to the map, he wondered, indeed, where is Krieger? He had suspected, for some time, that his underling might be up to something. Kammler had never trusted the man and had taken an almost instant dislike to him from the first moment they had met.

The SS man again turned to the map, but this time in a more detached manner. Kammler had been conducting searches of various sections of Rome in his on-going attempts to locate the hidden caches of this network, but with varying degrees of success. A more and intensive search of the Castel Sant'Angelo neighborhood would be in order. He would have Krieger see to it at once. That is, when he was finally located. "The scheweinehund. The dumbkopf!" he thought to himself. To Kammler, Albert Krieger was a boot-licking toady. Someone who would do anything to advance his own career, even at the expense of Kammler himself. He would deal with him in due course. What was most important at the moment was to pin down and locate these cells Kammler knew must be operating within O'Reilly's network.

Scharffuhrer Steiner knocked on Kammler's door. "Herr, Obersturmbannfuhrer, your wife is on the line and wishes to speak with you."

Kammler took the news and thought. "This must be another crisis of my empty-headed wife." He let out a long breath and reached out for his French-styled telephone that sat on his desk. "Yes, Angela?" he asked with trepidation and dread in his voice.

"Helmut, dear. I was wondering if we could have dinner together this weekend. We never seem to have any time to go out anymore," she cooed.

Kammler had cringed at the way she had pronounced weekend, heavily accentuating the second syllable, in the English manner. "Angela, I am a very busy man. I have many things to do. My job is very demanding," he stated directly. The two of them had been through this many times before. His wife had never been able to get into her vacuous head that he was an SS man. His duties to the Reich came first and foremost. All Angela had to worry about was what dress she would wear each day. Also, to try and manage their two undistinguished children.

"I know, Helmut, I know, but still... We should try once and awhile to have some entertainment. I would bet that even the Fuhrer finds some time to unwind and relax."

"Angela. Do not speak of the Fuhrer in that manner. He does not have the time to relax and fritter about. You have no idea of the many burdens this man has," he replied. Kammler had had this same discussion with Angela countless times in the past.

"But, Helmut, please. Just this one weekend," Angela pleaded.

"I suppose that could be a possibility. I will have to check my calendar. I cannot promise you anything, Angela," he finally relented.

"You are always working, Helmut. I sometimes think that you work too hard. You should really take some time off."

Kammler raised his eyes to the ceiling. This woman would never understand. How could she. Angela was a spoiled woman. Someone who had always had everything handed to her. She had never had to concern herself about anything, except for having to make herself look presentable. He had to admit that when she wanted to she could look ravishing. And her body was still pretty good. When he could bring himself to admit it he could even enjoy having sex with her. That activity had been steadily diminishing over time. It had directly correlated with his ever increasing promotions. "I am not on holiday, Angela," he finally answered.

"I know, but really, you must get some relaxation. I hear that Herr Kaltenbrunner has taken holidays to such places as Paris and the Riviera."

"I do not care what Kerr Kaltenbrunner does with his spare time, Angela. You must be more careful on whose name you throw around. Someone could be listening." Kammler was growing tired and increasingly irritated with this conversation. "I must return to my work. These Italians, even those members of the Church, must realize that we Germans are in charge," he continued on somewhat more stridently.

Angela Kammler had heard this line of thought more times than she cared to remember as well. Her husband was always more concerned about his all-important work. His work as a policeman, in her opinion. She would never tell him this directly. Still, grudgingly, she would admit that he was much more than a policeman. Yet, she could not recall the last time Helmut had spent some real time with her or their two children. Well, she would keep trying.

"Helmut, I am not asking you to quit. I just thought we could spend a little time together. To enjoy a little intimate dinner."

"All right, Angela. I will think about it. I won't promise anything."

"All right, darling. I will leave you to your work, liebschen. Auf wiedersehn."

"Good-bye, Angela. I will see you tonight," and with that Kammler was finally able to ring off from his tiresome wife.

The German then went back to his little project. He would order Krieger to begin a dragnet operation to try and shake loose some of the Roman churches that he was certain were an integral part of that infernal "escape" apparatus. And it would begin in the Castel Sant' Angelo district. He would have Krieger cordon off segments of the neighborhood. For example, one sweep could be directed toward the section between Castel Sant' Angelo and the Vatican. Another would be just to the north, encompassing the area between Via Crescenzo and Via Otaviano. Kammler figured that he each sweep could be completed within one day. That is, provided he could get the necessary manpower. There were his own SS detachments, plus the Fascist units of Mussolini's rump Republic of Salo state. But, he well knew he would need the assistance of Wehrmacht army units. For this he would need the cooperation and acquiescence of General von Vietinghoff's Tenth Army. And, of course, by extension, his superior, Field Marshal Albert Kesselring, commander of all German Army units in Italy. These army men had always given lukewarm support to the true National Socialist ideology of Adolf Hitler. They spoke as if they were true believers, but Kammler had always felt that this was just a front. He was probably going to have to secure support and manpower from his own superior in Italy, SS General Karl Wolff. The general was the head of all SS operations in the country. Wolff, in turn, would go to the chief of the SS, Heinrich Himmler. Kammler was sure Himmler would go for it as it would give him another opportunity to stick it to the

Wehrmacht. He would have to get moving himself as time was growing short. It would be his very next order of business, as soon as Krieger was located.

Despite the business at hand, Helmut Kammler thought about his wife and two children. He had first met Angela at a Sunday outing in Munich in 1926. He had been twenty years old and she was eighteen, but presented herself as an older, more mature woman. At least to him, while he saw himself as little more than an adolescent. Angela had golden hair that she allowed to hang straight ending in a bouncy curl. Not the old-fashioned hausfrau type so favored among most German women. She was of medium height and possessed very good figure. Kammler could see that, despite, the flowing shift she had on, Angela was fairly well-endowed. So much the better he had thought at the time.

At that moment in his life, Kammler had been studying electrical engineering at a technical college in Stuttgart. He had no real plans and was merely worried about his future. This was a time during the troubled Weimar Republic years. Germany's disastrous experiment with western democracy. Jobs were scarce and Germany found herself digging out of the harsh economic reparations imposed on her by the Treaty of Versailles. The Allied nations, victorious over Germany in World War One, were determined to squash the country for having started the war.

That spring day, Kammler summoned up his nerve and decided the time had come to approach Angela Wagner. She was receptive to his advances and they were soon seen strolling about Munich hand in hand. The relationship turned serious and they were married in 1927. It hadn't hurt Angela's chances that her father was a top executive in The Krupp-Thyssen steel empire. This was the second endowment of his wife that Kammler was most appreciative of.

The couple located themselves in Stuttgart and the children soon came along. Their son, Peter, was born in 1932, and daughter Marisa arrived in 1934. Kammler had been able to only obtain work as an electrician laborer at the time. The Great Depression had hit Germany especially hard. Bitterness and disillusionment could be found everywhere throughout the country. The German mark had collapsed, leading to the story of someone having left a wheelbarrow filled with money on a Berlin street. Upon returning to the site, the unfortunate person found the wheelbarrow gone. The money was fluttering about along the ground.

Adolf Hitler's ascension to Chancellor of Germany in January of 1933 provided someone like Helmut Kammler with an opportunity to finally be able to make something of himself. He had already joined the Nazi Party in 1931 and had become a member of the SA (Sturmabteilung) as a stormtrooper. He left the SA in 1933 when he was sworn into the SS.

Helmut Kammler remembered the look on his father's face when he had told him the news of his joining the SS. The man had only been a stonemason and barely provided for his family. Helmut's mother never seemed to possess any new clothes. His two brothers and his sister never had any new clothes, either, merely exchanging hand-me-downs. Kammler's father had once threatened to disown him and had him banished from the family home.

No matter, he was now an SS man, a member of the most elite group in the entire German military establishment. He, Helmut, would prove himself to his superiors in whatever tasks were assigned to him. In 1936, Kammler found himself promoted to the rank of Scharffuhrer (Sergeant) and was assigned to the Gestapo main office in Stuttgart. He was soon noticed by his superiors and was even introduced to Reinhard Heydrich, the cold-blooded right-hand man of SS chieftain, Heinrich Himmler.

The German knew how to move up in the ranks. Kammler was made Untersturmfuhrer in 1938. He was briefly deployed to Poland, following the German invasion of the country in September 1939. He also participated in several Einsatzgruppen actions. It was true that he had found the group's murderous killings, mostly of Jews, and other undesirables, somewhat distasteful, he had told himself that he was a German officer and it was his duty to obey all orders. The Fuhrer demanded it from every man.

By June 1941, Helmut Kammler had risen to the rank of Sturmbannfuhrer and was sent as a liaison officer to the Fascist government of Benito Mussolini. He was fluent in Italian, but knew that his connection to Heydrich had given him a boost as well.

On September 8, 1943, Italy formally dropped out of the war on the side of the Germans. It had been a doomed marriage for the two countries. She soon became allied to Great Britain and the United States. Kammler was ordered to serve as the Chief of the Security Police for all SS police units in Rome. His promotion to Obersturmbannfuhrer was forthcoming with his new assignment.

Kammler liked serving in Rome with its rich and vibrant history, ancient ruins, its gastronomic delights, and perhaps, best of all, its glorious and blazing sunshine. How different it was from the seemingly perpetual overcast and freezing conditions found in Germany for far too much of the year. There were drawbacks, of course, what with the duplicitous and deceitful nature of the Italian people. This was especially true for the underachieving and pathetic military forces of Il Duce, and the Catholic Church. Added to this, was his unhappy and empty marriage to his once beloved Angela. His son, Peter, was a twelve-year-old brat. Only his daughter, Marisa, provided him with a reason to return home at night.

* * *

"You wish to see me, Herr Obersturmbannfuhrer?" asked Albert Krieger, upon entering the inner sanctum of Helmut Kammler's office. He clicked his heels together and threw out a straight-armed Hitler salute.

"Yawohl, Krieger. I have been seeking an audience with you," Kammler spat out. "I understand you have been gallivanting about Rome. I remind you that we are not here as tourists or have you forgotten?" Kammler had never even bothered to respond to Krieger with any type of salute at all.

Krieger stood and thought he would break out into a cold sweat. He dreaded the possibility that Kammler had learned of his little rendezvous with O'Reilly. "Nein, Herr Obersturmbannfuhrer," replied a chastened Krieger. He couldn't dare mention a word about his recent, secret meeting with the cleric.

"Come here, Krieger. Have a look at this map. I have been giving some thought about conducting a more thorough and intensive search of certain Roman neighborhoods. That is, based on a more organized system. Not just a helter-skelter kind." Kammler swept a hand over the large-scale map of the city. The map showed every street, alley, monument, church, everything.

"We've been doing that already, haven't we, sir? We have had some success, as you well know," said Krieger.

"Yes, we have, but not enough has been done so that we can trap that insufferable and infuriating priest," Kammler responded defiantly.

"You mean Monsignor O'Reilly, sir. These Romans are a diffident sort of people," Krieger continued in a more relaxed manner than from just a few moments before.

Kammler knew that Krieger was referring to the well-known phlegmatic reputation of the citizens of Rome. "An operation of this type would be something these Italians have never seen before, and, likely, never forget. I want to create flying squads of troops quietly working through these neighborhoods. We should begin with the Castel Sant' Angelo area. We are to work discreetly during nighttime hours. I was thinking of utilizing several detachments. I want you to begin organizing these detachments immediately, Krieger. I also want to see an organized plan by tomorrow at 1200 hours. Is that clear?"

"Yawohl, Herr Obersturmbannfuhrer!" said Krieger. He always maintained his tone and manner formally. He would never think to address Kammler in a conversational manner. Krieger realized that he and Kammler did not like one another and, probably, never would.

"I am determined to catch this priest and his merry band," said Kammler, referring to Monsignor O'Reilly.

"Priest? Sir," asked Krieger in a halting voice.

"Don't be coy, Krieger. You know I mean the Monsignor. I swear these churchmen have been up to something and I will find out what it is, and how high it goes. Who knows, this may well reach up to the Pope himself. He tries to portray himself as this most pious of individuals, but I am not deceived by him, or by his coterie of Cardinals. And when I do get the goods on this operation, when I finally nail It down, then, I will crush it!" Kammler slammed his right fist down on his desk as if to punctuate his diatribe.

"I will begin work on your orders at once, sir. Is there anything else that you want me to do?"

"Nein, I do believe that will be all for now. Krieger, do not forget about our other on-going tasks regarding the Jewish situation. Another bunch of holier-than-thou individuals. They are even more contemptable than that Catholic gang. All of them are against us Germans," screamed out Helmut Kammler. Perspiration had now formed on his upper lip and along his forehead. He could feel his blood pressure rising as it always did when the discussion was about Jews and Catholics.

"The Chief Rabbi is scheduled to report to you in two days, sir" said Krieger.

"Yes, yes, he is and I do hope that he has made some progress in securing the gold and silver that his 'chosen' people have in their possession. The swine think that they can hold onto their precious valuables. Most of them probably stole it from hard-working and honest Germans," Kammler continued on in an hysterical manner.

"I do not think that is the case here, sir. These are Italian Jews and would not have had the opportunity to steal from us Germans."

"Krieger, Jews are Jews! I do not care whether they are from Germany or Italy or from Mars," roared Kammler. "And another thing. I was only referring to them stealing from Germans in a figurative sense."

"I only meant...."

"I do not care what you meant. Don't you ever question me or my orders. Don't even question me about my philosophy of life. Do you understand, Krieger?"

"Yawohl, Herr Obersturmbannfuhrer," saluted a mollified and shaken Albert Krieger. He then hurriedly left Kammler's suffocating office.

Albert Krieger soon summoned his subordinates to his office to brief them on the operation just proposed by Kammler. He would have the planned operations written up later that night. The four men he commanded stood at attention in front of his desk, waiting. Hans Gunther was his most reliable man, upon whom he would lean heavily for the success of the mission. Gunther was of medium height and possessed a solid build. He never questioned any orders given to him.

Heinrich Klemper stood next to Gunther with a diffident and distant expression on his face. He was also of medium height, but displayed a marked scar on his right cheek. It was not obtained as a result of a dueling competition. The scar had been courtesy of having been attacked as a result of his being surprised by a woman's husband while he had been in the midst of bedding her.

The next man, Reinhard Mannheim, was an interesting figure to Krieger. There was nothing distinguishable about him and most people would not stop to think that he possessed sufficient National Socialist ardor. They would be fooled. Mannheim was a true leader, a natural, but he was too new to Krieger's command. He would have to be watched, though, as Krieger suspected Mannheim of a deceptive cunning. One who might do anything to advance his rank. In other words, a man much like himself.

Finally, Krieger settled upon Willy Kemp and he was still aghast at how this youth had ever been selected for the SS. Kemp was only twenty years old and looked as he were always afraid of his own shadow. He always seemed to have the air of someone who was continuously mystified at his station in life.

"Well," thought Krieger," this is the hand I have been dealt with." He would have to make do.

"Gentlemen," he began, "we are to embark on an important mission. It is of the highest priority of Obersturmbannfuhrer Kammler. He will be observing our actions very closely." With that, Krieger turned and directed his right hand at the wall-mounted map of Rome. It was a duplicate of the one he had gazed at in Kammler's office a short time before. He paused for a moment for effect. "We have been tasked with a most important assignment here in Rome. We are to mount an intensive house to house search, beginning in the Castel Sant' Angelo district next to the Vatican. This will be gradually extended to the north. I envision us swinging down to the Ghetto district between Campo de Fiori and Teatro de Marcello," he expanded. The men looked on with blank, impassive expressions on their faces.

Krieger stared at his subordinates as if trying to discern what was going on in their minds. He continued, "Untersturmfuhrer Gunther and myself will develop a comprehensive plan and accompanying operational orders."

Hans Gunther knew what this meant. It would be left up to him to draft the plan. Krieger would never immerse himself in details, but would always try and take credit for anything done by one of his subordinates.

"Any questions?" Krieger asked, not actually expecting any.

It was Willy Kemp who cleared his throat and spoke up, to Krieger's surprise. "What are we to be searching for exactly, Herr Hauptsturmfuhrer?"

"An excellent question, Kemp. We are to turn up the heat on the "Escape Network" that we all know has been operating under our very noses here in Rome. Herr Kammler has made it quite clear that this operation is to be located and shut down. He considers it an embarrassment for the SS that this group or gang has been able to operate almost, at times, with impunity," he responded. "In a general manner, I envision that each of your forty man units being broken down into ten man squads. We will not be engaging in a loud and demonstrative action. There will be no overt practices of having people thrown out into the streets or being thrown out of windows and then placing them in the Circus Maximus holding area. All right, gentlemen. That will be all. You are dismissed Heil Hitler!"

The four men struck their heels together in unison and threw out the mandatory Hitler salutes with their right arms back at Krieger. As they were leaving, Krieger said, "Gunther, a moment please. I would like a word with you. Close the door," Krieger sat down in his chair. "Gunther, I want a detailed plan drawn up based on what we discussed just now. Is that clear?"

"Yawohl, Herr Hauptsturmfuhrer. When do you want this plan completed by, sir?" asked a not surprised Gunther.

"Tomorrow morning by 1000 hours," replied Krieger.

Hans Gunther nearly openly blanched at this news. It would be nearly impossible for that deadline to be met. Yet, he could not indicate this to Krieger. "It will be done, sir. Heil Hitler!" Gunther clicked his jack boots together and left the office. The sooner he was out of there, the better. He couldn't stand to be in Krieger's presence any longer than was absolutely necessary.

Helmut Kammler was finishing up some paperwork by mid-afternoon, when his mind began to wander. He began thinking again about his empty and depressing personal life. He and Angela were rarely intimate anymore. Whatever spark they had once had had long since been extinguished. Of course, he occasionally dabbled in finding romance with some of the selected and reputable Roman women of the evening. This was done very discreetly on his part. After all, an SS officer had to maintain a proper appearance and image. It then struck Kammler that there was one woman he had recently come across. He couldn't recall her name. It was there on the tip of his tongue. He was pretty sure she was a contessa. "Contessa, contessa… damn!" he thought in frustration.

Kammler was straightening out his desk when his Eureka moment finally hit him. The woman's name was Contessa Rosanna Vallone. Now, he remembered her distinctly. This contessa was an elegant and rather regal full-figured woman. He had thought she stood at about five foot six or seven. Her hair was golden in color and was done up in a curly, frizzled style. She possessed, what he thought resembled, hooded eyes, as if they were concealing something. Beguiling was how he had perceived her. He had found out that she was a single mother of two children, one boy and one girl. The Contessa's husband had been killed in action in North Africa.

Kammler had been introduced to the woman at a reception at the German Ambassador's residence some two months previously. It had been a small, private affair for some of the remaining leading citizenry of the city, and Fascist collaborators, and German military personnel.

The German had spied this intriguing woman from across the room while he had been engaged in light conversation with the Ambassador. Kammler now quite clearly recalled the Contessa in a clinging black dress that vividly revealed her figure. The front of it opened to reveal a magnificent deep cleavage. Kammler had found himself selfconsciously beginning to harden. He had had to meet this gorgeous woman. He had asked the Ambassador as to who the woman was.

"Let me introduce you to Contessa Rosanna Vallone, Herr Kammler," had said the Ambassador. Kammler was then led across the floor until they were standing in front of Rosanna. She had been talking to a minor level Fascist functionary at the moment, but noticed the two men patiently waiting. She had discreetly excused herself from the Fascist and faced Helmut Kammler. The Contessa knew who he was and, inwardly, she shuddered, as the man's reputation had definitely preceded him.

"Contessa, I would like to introduce you to Obersturmbannfuhrer Helmut Kammler," said the Ambassador smoothly. "Herr Kammler it is my distinct pleasure and honor introducing Contessa Rosanna Vallone."

Kammler stood before Rosanna and executed a deep bow while simultaneously clicking his jack boots together. He took the woman's right hand and bestowed, what he hoped, was an elegant kiss upon it. "It is my pleasure and honor to meet you, Contessa. You are truly representative of the best Italy has to offer."

Rosanna was trying her best to compose herself while, at the same time, trying to keep her skin from crawling. Before her stood one of the biggest monsters of the German forces occupying Rome. She knew that this man had the blood of many people on his hands. Some of the victims she had known personally. An unknown number of them had been the victims of hideous and tortured deaths. Nevertheless, as loathsome as it was she had to maintain her cool and greet the SS man as if she were really pleased to do so.

"Herr Obersturmbannfuhrer, how nice to meet you. I have heard so much about you," replied Rosanna. It had pained her deeply to have had to utter the words. She felt, for a brief moment, as if she might faint.

"Contessa, please. Call me Helmut. There is no need for such formality," Kammler answered in an unguinous tone.

"Well then, please call me Rosanna. How are you finding things here in Rome? It is such an interesting city, don't you think? Of course, I am biased, having lived here all of my life," she replied smoothly. "Oh God!" she thought. "Help me get through this." She knew that she was at the reception to see if she could pick up any information that might be of help to Monsignor O'Reilly and the "Escape Network." But, there had to be limits as to what duty called for.

"I have been enjoying myself immensely during my stay in the Eternal City. There is so much history and scenery that is simply breathtaking. I am afraid, though, that my duties for the army have prevented me from completely appreciating all that Rome has to offer. I am curious about something you said only a moment ago."

"Really? Obersturm… excuse me, Helmut. I did not realize that I had said anything profound," answered a now worried Contessa. She was struck by the man's fluent Italian.

"Oh, it is just that you said you had heard some good things about me. Of whom would have been speaking of?"

"Oh that. Well, that was just a figure of speech, Helmut. I did not mean anything by it. You understand?" Rosanna offered cautiously. She knew she had to be careful. This was one of the most dangerous individuals she had ever faced. He was cunning and devious, and treacherous. Perhaps, he was trying to lure her into a trap whereby she might reveal something. Something about the Monsignor or the escape organization.

"Of course, Rosanna. I do understand," Kammler replied. His gaze had fallen upon her impressive cleavage. He seemed to be mesmerized by her ample breasts. The way they stood out. He had thought he had discerned a presence of her nipples, as well. How he would love to caress those spectacular breasts and, then, take her to Valhalla.

Rosanna could see that she had clearly stirred the fancy of this Nazi and, perhaps, she could use it to her advantage.

"I was just thinking that, maybe, when you might have the time, you could show me some of the sights of Rome. You know, some of the hidden treasures that the average tourist is not aware of. Things. Things that are off the 'beaten path.' I believe is the expression. I do realize that I might sound presumptuous and that you are undoubtedly very busy with your day to day activities. Well, it was just a thought."

"I suppose that something could be arranged. I would have to check with my family. You know it is not easy trying to raise two adolescent children in the middle of a war," said Rosanna, again carefully. She knew she could never or would never do what Kammler had asked. Yet, she did not want to appear abrupt and, perhaps, make him angry He said he liked the people. Indeed. The only thing he probably liked about the Italians was locking them up and torturing them. She also knew that the Monsignor and the Network were engaged in an almost personal duel with Kammler and his SS henchmen. Rosanna was well aware of the harsh and inhuman treatment of the Jews. She had seen it for herself throughout the city. Nevertheless, she would have to extricate herself from the Obersturmbannfuhrer as delicately and discreetly as possible.

Fortunately for her, the Contessa was able to avoid this with the entrance of General von Vietinghoff, commander of the German Tenth Army. He had been heavily engaged with military matters due to the Allied landing at Anzio for some time now. Evidently, matters were in hand and the general was allowing himself some light entertainment for the evening.

Upon the general's arrival, Kammler hurriedly bid good-bye to Rosanna and scurried over to von Vietinghoff.

Helmut Kammler now recalled the evening quite clearly and once again he found himself stirring beneath his waist. He would arrange it to see this Contessa Vallone that very afternoon, In the days following his introduction to the Contessa he had found out about the location of her home. It was on a side street off of Via Cavour. Kammler had also had his underlings dig into the personal background of the woman, and her family.

He reached for his phone and spoke into it, "Himmel, I have an assignment for you."

"Yes, Herr Obersturmbannfuhrer?" asked Franz Himmel.

"See to it that my car is ready for 1500 hours this afternoon. I will be going to Via Cavour," Kammler continued.

"Yawohl.! Your car will be ready, sir," said Himmel. It would only be a short drive of a couple of kilometers and, with virtually no civilian traffic, would take practically no time at all. Himmel thought to himself that Kammler was, in all probability, going after some more Italian tail.

Helmut Kammler stood on the sidewalk outside Rosanna Vallone's stone-faced apartment building on Via Frattina. It was precisely 1530 hours. The building had remained neat and tidy, as had the neighborhood in general, as far as Kammler could see. Many areas of Rome had taken on a worn and seedy appearance since the war had begun. He entered the building and strode up the stairway to his right. The interior had begun to show some of its age, as some paint was faded in places along the walls and pieces of plaster had flaked off the walls as well. A tenant on the first floor had opened her door and upon seeing Kammler had suddenly shut it. The German smiled to himself. "Ah, the feeling of unbridled power and control," he thought to himself.

Helmut Kammler continued his walk up the stairs until he came to a foyer. He moved through the hallway until he stood before apartment #210. He knocked on the door lightly. The Contessa had been updating some of her files on the Network. Upon hearing the knock, she stood up suddenly. She had not been expecting anyone at this hour. Her daughter, Ariana, was sitting on a nearby settee in the room. Rosanna motioned to her. To the door she said, "Who is it?"

"Herr Kammler, Contessa," was the reply.

Rosanna quickly gathered up everything in her hands and ran to a cedar chest along the far wall. "Just a minute, Herr Kammler," stuttered a frightened Rosanna. She and Ariana tried to straighten everything out the best they could. She nodded to Ariana to go and open the door.

Kammler was just about to knock again when the door opened. He was greeted by a young woman with short brown hair and lustrous brown eyes. He knew this must be young Ariana. She strongly resembled her stunning and attractive mother. Ariana was dressed in a plain blue dress, one of the best pieces of clothing she had left in her wardrobe.

Kammler gave a slight click of his heels and said, "Buon giorno, signorina. Is your mother at home?"

"Si, she is, sir," replied a near trembling Ariana. The girl thought she might faint dead away.

"Ariana, please, let our guest in. You should show proper manners," scolded a shaken Rosanna. She wondered what Kammler could want of her and at this time of day. Then, she remembered the German Ambassador's soiree and the way Kammler had practically leered at her, her dress, her breasts. "Yes," she thought. "He probably wants to seduce me." Well, that would mean that he probably did not suspect her as being a part of the "Escape Network" of Monsignor O'Reilly. Still, she would have to be extremely careful with this German. This Nazi.

"Please, come in, sir," Ariana was finally able to find her voice. Her face had started to color with an increasing shade of crimson.

"Grazie, signorina. My, I must say you are a most considerate and attractive young woman and your name is Ariana. A beautiful name. It suits you perfectly," said the SS man.

"Grazie, sir. That is most kind of you."

Rosanna had been watching the exchange from her position on her couch and thought to herself that if Kammler could avail himself to her he would just as easily try to bed her daughter.

Kammler nodded at Ariana and stepped further into the room and saw Rosanna. He was immediately taken with the Italian noblewoman. Although, she was now wearing only a plain white blouse and a black skirt, he thought of her as positively breathtaking. Again, the woman's blouse was open and revealed a tempting glimpse of her magnificent cleavage. She certainly was not a shy and unassuming person by any means. The exposure was not to the degree as she had displayed at the Ambassador's reception, but more than enough to titillate any man. He also noticed that she was wearing only light make-up and, yet, she was still radiant.

Ariana stood nearby, but had said nothing as she had observed Kammler making the move on her mother. She shuddered with a cold revulsion. "May I go to my room, Mother?"

"Of course, dear," said Rosanna. She knew this was as painful for her daughter as well as for herself.

"Herr Kammler. It has been my pleasure to have met you," Ariana addressed the man as calmly as she could manage.

Kammler stood and bowed toward Ariana, "It has been my pleasure Ariana, I assure you."

Ariana bid good-bye to her mother and left for her bedroom.

"So, Contessa. You are probably wondering what I am doing here sitting in front of you in the middle of the day. Hmmm. I must apologize as I should have called on you before, but, as I just happened to be in the neighborhood, I thought, I must just drop in. You will forgive me?" Kammler had continued smoothly.

Rosanna was continuing trying to fight to maintain her self-control and just sat, muted. Finally, she said, "There is no need to apologize, sir" She almost blurted out that she was used to receiving visitors at all hours of the day.

"Please, Contessa, call me Helmut. When I am always addressed by my title it gives off a rather stiff appearance, don't you agree?"

"Then, Helmut, you must call me Rosanna. Contessa is just too formal, don't you agree?"

"Indeed, I do Con... Oh, there I almost went again."

Rosanna had started to feel more relaxed, but she did not want to convey this to this Nazi. Nor did she want to convey any kind of receptivity to his clear advances toward her, and her body. She knew she would have to flirt a little with him, but she would maintain that fine line. Rosanna could easily see that the SS man had amorous intentions on his mind. After all, he wouldn't have stopped by merely to discuss the weather.

Kammler glanced around the room and took in the numerous paintings and sculptures. The living room was quite neat and tidy, although, he did notice that some of the furniture was beginning to show its age, but not too much. "I am impressed, Contessa, with the way have been able to maintain your home. And, the artwork and the sculptures are most impressive. I must say. Even with a war on."

"Thank you, sir. It has not been easy. I have received a great deal of help from my children," said Rosanna.

"I have met your daughter. So lovely. I believe you also have a son. Is that not correct, Rosanna?"

Rosanna could feel the oiliness oozing out of this supercilious German. "Si, yes, Helmut, I do."

"And where may he be, if I may ask?" Kammler had tilted his head to one side as if trying to gauge the truthfulness of Rosanna's response.

"I am not sure where he is at the moment. I think he must be with one of his friends," Rosanna said, as she felt the hackles on the back of her neck rise.

"Of course, a young man should be with his friends and not with his mother, just sitting around. Contessa, excuse me,

Rosanna, I was most intrigued by our meeting at the Ambassador's residence some weeks back. I had been beginning to enjoy our little conversation when General von Vietinghoff arrived. And, I just had to go and greet him. It was protocol. I hope you didn't think that I had been giving you short shrift. I have been hoping that we could expand upon this and have dinner some time."

Rosanna had sensed that this was coming, but still, "Good God!" she thought. "This Nazi swine is asking me out. Never mind that the man is married and has children." "Helmut," she began slowly, "I have been living rather like a recluse since the death of my husband. I do hope that you understand," she concluded softly.

Kammler looked at the Italian woman and thought, "A recluse? With the way you were dressed at that party." Instead, he said, "I do understand."

The two of them had unconsciously slipped into English, even though Rosanna had been impressed by Kammler's Italian. Her German was not very good. Kammler, himself, loved hearing the woman's lilting Italian accented tone. The words just seemed to roll off her tongue. Speaking of which, he would have just loved to have been French kissing at the moment. Well, who knew? Perhaps, there would be a chance at that in the not too distant future. "I am impressed with your English, Rosanna. Wherever did you learn it?"

The question was almost delivered in a sinister manner. What could she say that would not arouse any suspicion with Kammler. "Well, you see," she began haltingly. "I have done work, charity work, that is, for the British Legation here in Rome. Sir D'Arcy Osborne has been a true friend to me and to Italians. And so, I have picked up a good deal while working with him and his staff." She fervently hoped that she had sounded convincing.

"Of course, Contessa. A most reasonable reply. Now, Con… err Rosanna. I was not trying to be too forward with you a moment ago. I was just thinking that it might be nice to enjoy one another's company. A simple affair."

"It is just that, at this time, I am still not comfortable with being seen with a man at dinner,' let alone an SS officer like Kammler.

"Rosanna, I, too, have lost someone close to me," Kammler began again. "You see, my mother was killed in a British bombing raid last year."

"Oh, I am so sorry, Helmut," Rosanna said with some feeling of true empathy. "I did not know."

Kammler nodded his head demurely. "Of course, you wouldn't have known. The point is that we have both suffered great personal losses at the hands of a common enemy, the British. Perhaps, dinner would be too much at this time. What would you say to an afternoon coffee at a local bar, say Harry's American?"

"Well? Perhaps we could arrange something, but do allow me to think about it. Is that all right, Helmut?" Rosanna asked with a tilt of her head and an imperceptible wink

"Of course, it is. I do not want you to feel pressured in any way," said Kammler, with his own added wink.

At that very moment, Rosanna noticed a small brass button on the floor next to Kammler's chair, but completely under it. It must have fallen from Robert's uniform while they had been engaged in some passion. In a panic, Rosanna wondered if the German had noticed it. He had not given any indication that he had. Somewhat abruptly, she suddenly stood up and said, "Helmut, let me show you some of our artwork."

"I'd be delighted to have you show me, Rosanna. Simply delighted," enthused Kammler as he shot up out of his chair.

"Most of the paintings were done by my late husband, Giuseppe," she said.

"They are most lovely," he said, "most lovely."

Although, to Rosanna, Herr Kammler hardly seemed to be paying any attention to the paintings and had again directed his eye toward her. Undoubtedly, trying to obtain more peeks of her breasts. "My husband was a most talented man. I still miss him very much. This one here,' she pointed to an Impressionist style painting depicting two young women in a canoe, surrounded by swans. The scene was light and airy, the blues in it rather soft and muted. "It was his first attempt at this style of painting."

"I am not an artist, Rosanna, but if that was his first attempt, the man was more than extraordinary," said Kammler. He secretly wondered if he was laying it on a bit too thickly.

To Rosanna, he was being exactly that. The painting was good, she had to admit, but not that good. No matter, she had to get rid of this German as soon as possible.

Perhaps sensing this, Kammler said to her, "Rosanna, I want to thank you for your hospitality today. And your art collection is most magnificent. However, I fear I have taken up enough of your time. I will take my leave. I would like for you to seriously consider my offer for coffee. Would you?"

"I will, Helmut. Thank you for the invitation.' Rosanna said this as she nodded while looking down at the floor.

"Good. I must now return to my work. A German officer's work is never done."

Rosanna nodded her head slightly at the incongruity of Kammler's words. Did he not see the irony of his statement? His work was never done. And the Italian people would see him to Hell.

Kammler nodded and gave a slight click of heels. He turned to face Ariana, who had come from her room, and was standing off to the side. The girl had noticed the brass army button by the side of the chair and had picked it up. She went to the door and opened it for Kammler.

"Danke schoen, Ariana. Contessa? Au revoir," he said as he turned away from them and left the apartment.

Three

The Beginning

"What do we do now, Majah?" drawled Sergeant Louis Durval.

"We wait and trust in Doctor Narduzzi," came the reply from Major Robert Matthews.

"Yeah, but can we trust him?"

"Sergeant, we just have to trust him. What else can we do? We are, I think, near Frascati, which is very close to Rome itself," continued Matthews.

"I don't know, sir. I mean, what if he turns us in?" countered Durval in his Cajun accented English. The sergeant was from Baton Rouge, Louisiana, and he had never felt so far from home. In fact, he had never been past the Deep South in his entire life. But, he trusted Major Matthews and always had from the time they had escaped from the Italian prisoner-of-war camp near Battipaglia.

"I don't think he will, Sergeant. I have usually thought of myself as a pretty good judge of character and I have a good feeling about the Dottore," Matthews went on.

Privately, he did not, but he couldn't reveal this to Sergeant Durval. He knew Durval was a good man, a good soldier, and loyal. He did seem to possess a rather simple view of the world. He had hardly ever left his native Louisiana, that is until the army had drafted him. Now, it seemed as if fate had thrown the two men together. One, the Ivy League educated officer and, the other, the plain spoken common GI.

"How much longer, sir?" asked Durval to Matthews.

"By my calculations, just a little bit longer."

It was just past midnight and the two men had been huddling in a bombed-out shell of what had once been a factory building on the outskirts of Frascati, some ten miles from Rome, by Matthews' rough estimate. It had just started to drizzle lightly, when Durval noticed a shadow moving along in the distance. It was hard to tell if it could be that of a man or just an animal flitting about.

"P-s-s-s-t, Majah, sir. I think I just seen something movin' out there," stammered Durval.

"Where?" asked Matthews.

"Outta there, sir," Durval pointed off to the right of their position, just passed a collapsed chimney.

"I see it, Sergeant. Perhaps, that is Doctor Narduzzi. I surely hope so."

"I sure hope so, too. I mean, if it's the Krauts or the Eyeties, well, then, we're fucked. Excuse me, sir. I mean we'll be in trouble."

"That is all right, Sergeant. As you said, we will be surely fucked. We have to stay calm," eased Matthews in a lowered tone of voice. "It has to be Narduzzi," thought Matthews.

The next moment, Dottore Luigi Narduzzi appeared right in front of them. "Buon giorno, buon giorno, gentlemen. Or should I say buona sera? Oh well, we cannot stand on such formalities now, can we gentlemen?" greeted Narduzzi effusively. "I am so sorry that I took so long to get back to you, but the Germans have set up many roadblocks and checkpoints in and around Frascati," the Italian began. "It has become very dangerous."

To Matthews, Narduzzi sounded somewhat rattled, which would be natural for any man to feel, let alone having to move about in the midst of roving German patrols. "You do not have to apologize to us, Dottore. We appreciate all that you have done for us," replied Matthews.

"Maggiore, it will be arranged for you and Sergeant Durval to be taken into Rome. Transport will be secured within the next day or so. The car we will be using will bear Vatican plates," continued the doctor. He was now speaking at a reduced pace from moments before.

"Vatican?" questioned a surprised Robert Matthews.

Doctor Narduzzi held up his palm, "Si. Please let me explain, Maggiore. This is the best way for us to move you two men. The Germans will ask fewer questions when they see a vehicle of the Vatican. Do not worry as you will be hidden… safely."

Matthews almost imperceptibly shook his head as he asked, "But how? I still do not understand, Dottore."

"Do not worry. That is for us to do. Trust me, it can be done. For now, though, you men are to remain hidden within these ruins. I have brought with me some food and water. It is not much, but all that we could spare. It will provide you some sustenance."

"All right. Thank you, doctor. I suppose we can hang on here for another day or two," conceded a somewhat disappointed Matthews.

"It is curious, is it not? You men are from a country that is very far from Italy and I am an old doctor. I never imagined that one day I would end up in this line of work. It is indeed strange how our paths have met."

Matthews did not have the heart to inform the good doctor that he had mixed his metaphors. He decided this was a time to let it go. After all, the man was in imminent danger for what he and his colleagues were doing. "Yes, Dottore, it is, perhaps, not so strange at all."

"You know, I was doctor in the last war with Germany and Austria. I was a much younger man then, full of ideas about the world. Everyone thinks of the famous Battle of Caporetto as the singular moment of Italy's war. But my involvement took place further to the north, right in the midst of the Alps. It was a cold and frozen tableau, with poor, desperate men living day to day in mud and squalor. Living from one day to the next, just trying to survive, trying to hang on. Well, I have done too much talking, Maggiore. I did not mean to bore you two men. I have a tendency to reminisce about the old days. It seems to go along with growing old," Doctor Narduzzi extemporized.

"You have not bored us, Dottore. I would like to know more of your story. Perhaps, one day, there will be another time," Matthews replied graciously. Both he and the doctor realized that the time would never actually come to pass.

"Maybe, when the war is over you and the sergeant can return to Frascati and we can share a bottle of my home-made wine. It would be from my family's wine cellar. We have a long tradition of crafting our own wine. It is a secret recipe. There, I am rhapsodizing again," said Narduzzi.

"No, no. sir. It is quite all right. We understand."

"I must go now, but I will return after we have obtained our vehicle. Please, you and Sergeant Durval must stay hidden. The Germans have been quite active with their patrols in the last several days.," said the doctor. With that, he turned and left, vanishing into the night as mysteriously as he had arrived.

Major Robert Matthews would never have described himself as a warrior. He considered himself as a modest, law-abiding, somewhat Christian man. He had experienced a hard and trying upbringing in western Pennsylvania. Matthews grew up in a town called Clairton, a steel-making suburb of Pittsburgh. Robert had been the third of six children of Robert Senior and Marjorie Matthews.

Matthews Senior had always worked in a steel manufacturing firm in the great steel combine of US Steel, but when the Crash of 1929 hit, the family was devastated. The elder Matthews was thrown out of work, along with thousands of others. The Matthews family was forced to scrape along as best they could, but there was never enough for the eight members of the family.

Robert Matthews or "Bobby" as his family and friends called him, took on various odd jobs. He once worked as an apprentice to a blacksmith. He could well remember the sparks of flame that would splash against his body, many leaving a burn mark or welt. The thing that Matthews had working for him was a desire to never give in, to never quit.

In high school be developed into a star halfback on the football team and a dependable point guard on the basketball team of the Clairton High Hawks. Matthews burned with the hope this might lead to a college scholarship, because he well knew his family could never afford a college tuition.

There was the small problem of classwork. Matthews was not a dullard, as he possessed a keen mind, who quickly grasped onto new things and ideas. Explain something once to him and he knew it.

Bobby Matthews' grades could be described as average, but he dearly loved history and literature. He would devour history books on the Civil War, the Wild West, and the Great War, as World War One was then referred to. It was this facet and his football coach's connection to Princeton University that would secure for him his ticket out of Clairton.

Bobby Matthews thrived at Princeton, enjoying a great career on the Tigers football team. He even made first team all-Ivy League as a halfback in the devastating single-wing attack of the team, and as a vicious hard-hitting linebacker on defense. He also managed to participate in the school's reserve officer training corps, or ROTC army program.

It would be this membership which secured for Matthews his next station in life. Upon graduation, while thousands of other young men found themselves drifting along on the fringes of society, the Great Depression still had its grip on the country, Bobby Matthews signed up with the army as a Second Lieutenant.

Upward movement was slow, almost dinasaurus, in the peace-time US Army, but, at least, Matthews had a home, a roof over his head, and plenty of food for his stomach. He managed to be promoted to First Lieutenant by the time of the Japanese surprise attack at Pearl Harbor on December 7th, 1941.

Bobby Matthews was now a member of the First Armored Division, when an Allied expeditionary force landed on the shores of Morocco in November 1942.The division's first engagement was a brief skirmish with Vichy French troops still loyal to Marshal Philippe Petain. After this, First Armored would find itself up against the battle-tested, veteran German soldiers under the command of General Jurgen von Arnim.

The battle of the Kasserine Pass in Tunisia in February 1943 was a moment of disgrace and supreme humiliation for the men of the First Armored Division, and for American troops as a whole. The Division commander, Major General Orlando Ward, acted as if he had been over his head from the first hours of combat. Many of the American field commanders had been found wanting as well. These men were quickly replaced by the overall Allied commander, General Dwight Eisenhower. Men would be found who possessed the needed courage, ardor, and leadership that would be needed in the upcoming, desperate battles ahead.

It was during the Kasserine action that Robert Matthews, having by this time been promoted to the rank of major, was taken prisoner by the Germans. His unit had found itself quickly overrun by the fast-moving German panzer units of the German Tenth Panzer Division. Confusion everywhere had reigned on Matthews and his desperate men. The entire division had been in turmoil, units were not in their proper positions, radio communications had been patchy or non-existent and, perhaps, most telling of all, many of the soldiers had acted as one might have expected during their first combat action. They had been just plain scared.

Following his capture, Matthews was held in a holding pen in northern Tunisia. Once., he had even taken sight of the great German commander, Erwin Rommel, the Desert Fox. Rommel had been driven by the camp Matthews was in on his way to boarding a Luftwaffe transport plane that would take him to Berchetesgaden, for a conference with Adolf Hitler. Bobby Matthews was then passed on to Italian control, which was how he ended up in Battipaglia, and meeting up with Sergeant Louis Durval. It was 1943 and Matthews and Durval languished there until September. They were then hurriedly moved because of the recent Allied invasion of Italy at Salerno. Their route north took a circuitous and dangerous course, as the prisoner convoy had to avoid Allied airpower and ground action. The convoy had at last been able to gain access to the famous A-1 motorway and proceeded onto Formia.

The prisoners were finally deposited at a makeshift camp near Bertipaglia. Italian authorities had hurriedly set up a primitive barbed-wire enclosure. Matthews quickly deduced that an escape would be feasible, the chance well worth taking when the time presented itself. He told no one, not even Durval.

By this time, Italy was out of the war. Interim president, General Pietro Baddoglio had assured the Germans that Italy would remain loyal to the Axis cause. Benito Mussolini, meanwhile, had already been arrested, at the authorization of King Victor Emmanuel. Adolf Hitler believed differently and ordered a virtual German invasion and lockdown of the country.

Robert Matthews chose a dark and snowy night in December to make his escape. Louis Durval had learned of Matthews' planned escape and had been able to finally persuade him to take Durval along with him. The camp, by that time, was staffed by Fascist loyalists, but under German supervision.

Security had always been rather lax, which immeasurably aided the men in their escape. From that moment on, Matthews and Durval had surreptitiously made their way toward Rome. And this was where they had first encountered Doctor Narduzzi.

The good doctor duly returned the next night and briefed Matthews and Durval on the proposed plan of action for their movement into Rome.

"Buona sera, greetings, gentlemen," the doctor enthused.

"It is good to see you again, Dottore," replied Matthews.

"I have good news and, not such good news. The good news is that we will move you two men at 0800 hours. The bad news, if you could call it that, is that you men will have to be hidden in the car," Narduzzi explained.

"That is not bad news, sir. We are in your hands," said Matthews, "but, isn't it dangerous to be traveling in daylight?"

"No, and I will explain. Nighttime motor traffic is almost expressly forbidden by the Germans. I can assure you the journey will be safer in daylight when one can expect to find other transport on the roads," said Narduzzi.

Matthews nodded and said, "I understand. We will be ready. Is there anything else that we need to be aware of?"

"No, that is all for now. I must go. Do you still have sufficient provisions to last you through the night? asked the doctor.

"We are all right. We will manage," said Matthews.

"Oh, there is one more thing I should mention and it is rather important. The vehicle we will be using will be a black Lancia sedan with the aforementioned Vatican plates. When the vehicle stops the driver will get out and wave a white handkerchief. If you fail to see this, do not come out from hiding, remain hidden. You can assume something went wrong. If that should happen I will try to contact you with new instructions. Is that clear?" asked Narduzzi with a most serious expression.

"We understand, Dottore, and grazie for all of your efforts," said Matthews.

"You and the sergeant are most welcome, Maggiore, but this is something I must do to help you and for any Allied soldiers who are in trouble."

The doctor then quietly moved off into the night, ghostlike, vanishing within moments.

The next morning at precisely 8:00 AM Matthews and Durval observed a black car slowly approaching their hiding place. The vehicle stopped and the driver got out and paused for a moment. He slowly reached into his coat pocket and removed a packet of cigarettes. The driver selected one and lit it with a butane lighter. Matthews watched this with a growing sense of alarm. He wondered whether something in fact had gone wrong. Very wrong. Narduzzi had not mentioned anything about a cigarette being a part of the sign. The driver was next seen again reaching into the breast pocket of his jacket and removing a purple colored handkerchief. The man paused for a second or two and, then, waved the article in the air. It was not white, but it was a handkerchief.

Matthews and Durval cautiously emerged from their lair amongst the ruins and walked toward the Lancia. Both of the men looked around the landscape furtively, but did not see anyone else about. As they were about to reach the vehicle, Doctor Narduzzi emerged from the passenger side.

"Buon giorno, gentlemen," he gushed as he was genuinely glad and relieved to see them. "Now, we will have to move quickly this morning. If you please, Sergeant Durval. You will be placed in the boot behind a concealed panel. You, Maggiore

Matthews, will ride in style inside the vehicle. I must caution you that you will be placed under the rear seat. I hope this will be with your approval."

"It looks as if we will have little choice, Dottore. It will be fine.," said Matthews. Durval stood by shaking his head. He was not sure which of them would endure the tougher ride.

"Good. Oh, this is our driver, Alberto. He is a most excellent driver. Before the war he was a test driver for Alfa Romeo. Alberto knows all of the best roads we will need to take on our journey to Rome.

Matthews looked at Alberto and nodded to him in recognition. Alberto smiled back, but said nothing.

"Well, then, gentlemen, without further ado. Let us get underway," said the doctor.

Matthews and Durval proceeded to take their respective positions in the Lancia and Alberto slowly drove off. Once they were underway, Narduzzi turned in the direction of the back seat and said to Matthews, "Maggiore, can you hear me?"

Matthews could understand the doctor quite well, "Yes, I can, Dottore.'

"Bene! I am responding to a request from the Vatican. It seems as if Cardinale Imperiale has developed an upper respiratory infection that requires immediate attention. I am, of course, duly responding to this request as I am a qualified physician. This is the excuse we will provide to any German checkpoints that we may encounter along the way. I have in my possession the necessary paperwork which should clear the way for us through to Rome and the Vatican."

They had traveled approximately ten miles, by Matthews' estimation, when they approached their first German roadblock. Alberto slowed the Lancia. They were third in line behind a commercial truck and another non-descript weather-beaten sedan. Narduzzi noted that the checkpoint was manned by Waffen SS men. He would have to handle their situation most carefully. These Germans might well be a tougher nut to fool than ordinary Wehrmacht troops certainly tougher than an Italian minded post. The car in front of them was directed to drive off to the side of the road, perhaps, for a closer inspection. Narduzzi hoped this might be a "good sign." Maybe this would allow them to proceed right through without having to answer too many questions.

As SS Scharffuhrer stood at the driver's side and said politely in passable Italian. "Good day, gentlemen. Your papers please?"

Narduzzi handed Alberto the Vatican issued papers, who in turn passed them to the German. The SS man carefully scanned the false letter and said, "It seems as if the Cardinale is in some distress, Dottore... err Narduzzi.

Narduzzi leaned toward his left so as to get a better view of the German. He addressed the SS Sergeant, "Si, that is correct, sir. I have been requested to provide medical treatment to Cardinale Imperiale as soon as I can get there," said a nervous Narduzzi.

Two SS sentries stood a few feet behind the SS sergeant, gripping Schmeisser MP-40 submachineguns. Narduzzi was fervently hoping, silently pleading, that he wouldn't be asked to step out of the vehicle and allow the Germans to inspect it. They could well discover the hidden Americans. It would also mean, undoubtedly, the almost immediate executions of Narduzzi and Alberto.

"Yes, yes, I understand, Dottore," the SS man responded ingratiatingly to Narduzzi. "It is just that we authorities must be ever vigilant about our security tasks. What with the Allies attacking Italy and causing all of the destruction you see around you," the German replied.

Narduzzi did not reply to the sergeant's observations on the war. He could feel a cold, damp sweat start to build within him. A sheen of perspiration had formed just under his nose. He hoped the German would not notice.

"Very well, Dottore… Narduzzi, your papers appear in order," said the man as he kept looking down at the letter, as if he were contemplating whether these Italians were in fact telling him the truth.

Maybe a closer inspection would be warranted. Instead, he said, "You may proceed."

"Grazie, grazie, sir. And now we must on our way to the Vatican," exhaled a near fainting Narduzzi.

The SS man took a step back and nodded to Alberto to proceed. The Lancia started to move forward, but, then, stalled. Alberto calmly attempted to restart the engine. All that came out was a whining, sickening sound. He tried once again. No luck. Doctor Narduzzi was quite sure that now he would faint dead away. The dark wool suit he wore was beginning to feel like a suit of medieval armor that was slowly squeezing his body.

Finally, on the third try, just as the SS Sergeant was about to approach the car, Alberto succeeded in getting the vehicle moving again. Matthews and Durval, from their respective hiding places had both died several deaths as a result of the recent drama at the checkpoint. Each started to breath just a little easier once again.

Narduzzi and company were forced to endure several other checkpoints on their journey, but at each one they were virtually waved through, with only perfunctory glances at the paperwork. Soon, they were in the main ring that encompassed the city of Rome.

"Maggiore Matthews, it is my distinct pleasure to announce that we have now entered the city of Rome. The Eternal City. But, please, you must remain hidden. We are not quite in the clear, as they say in the movies,' enthused rhapsodically Doctor Narduzzi. The man never seemed to tire of the thrill he always felt whenever he found himself in Rome.

From his cramped position under the backseat, Robert Matthews allowed himself the opportunity to breathe at a more normal pace. He could have sworn that his heart had stopped, at least, twice, during the group's trek through German controlled territory. He assumed that he and Durval would now be taken to a hiding place within the city. "Rome must have a million places where two men could be hidden," he silently thought to himself. What would shortly be revealed to him would be that, yes, two men could easily be concealed. but what about several hundred men being hidden at the same time.

* * *

At 3:00 PM the black Lancia pulled up to the gate at the Vatican Museum along the Viale Vaticano. The Swiss guard on duty gave a cursory look at the authorization letter Narduzzi handed him and waved the party through. Alberto Famigletti guided the sedan carefully through the warren of streets which ran inside the Holy See compound. He stopped the car in front of a spare, non-descript two story building. They had arrived at the German College, the residence of Monsignor Liam O'Reilly. Narduzzi turned round in his seat and spoke to Matthews, "Maggiore, we have arrived, but, please, I ask you to remain where you are for just a few moments in the vehicle. I will see to the arrangements."

"Yes, of course, Dottore," came a muffled reply from Matthews.

Narduzzi exited the Lancia and proceeded into the building. He rapidly made his way to O'Reilly's office. He saw Father Lillard seated at his desk and said, "Buon giorno, Father Damian, how are you? Is the Monsignor in his office?"

Father Damian looked up at Narduzzi and nodded, "Yes, he is expecting your packages. "Although Lillard's Italian could, at times, be characterized as fractured, the doctor was usually able to understand it. He wondered why Father Damian seemed to insist on using Italian when he could just have easily conversed in English, which Narduzzi spoke very well.

In any event, Narduzzi replied, "Grazie, Father, grazie!" Lillard got up and went to knock on the Monsignor's door.

Yes? Come in."

"Monsignor, Dottore Narduzzi has just arrived and with his two packages."

"Good, that is good. Send him right in, Damian,' said O'Reilly as a broad smile broke out across his face. He could stand to receive some good news. It had been that kind of day.

Father Lillard stepped back out and motioned over to Narduzzi to enter. The doctor did so and stood before O'Reilly.

"How good it is to see you, Dottore, and with two packages. It has been a few weeks since we last saw one another, has it not?" O'Reilly go up from his chair and went around to embrace the doctor.

"Yes, it has, Monsignor. I am glad to see that you are well." Narduzzi replied back with equal effusiveness. A smile had creased his face. The two men were conversing in English, Narduzzi knew O'Reilly would not use the occasion to practice his own version of the Italian language. "Monsignor, is it all right if I now bring the men upstairs to your office. It has been a long and trying day for them. I think they may be a bit cramped up. Signore Matthews has been hidden under the rear seat and the sergeant has been in the boot of the vehicle."

"Of course, man, of course. Bring them right up. I cannot wait to finally meet them," O'Reilly answered.

"Bene, Monsignor."

"By the way, Dottore, how did you manage to transport the men from Frascati?"

"Cardinale Imperiale had a letter drafted which stated that he was in immediate need of medical attention for an upper respiratory infection."

"Yes. Yes, Dottore. That was excellent, I must say," as O'Reilly allowed himself a small chuckle. "All right, let us not delay any further. Have the men brought in." O'Reilly then stopped in mid-sentence and said, "No, wait. I have a better idea. Return to your car and drive out to Via degli Scipione. There is a petrol station on the right hand side of the road. Wait there for Father Damian to arrive. I will provide you with written authorization, which should satisfy any curious Germans who may be about. I know this will be an added inconvenience to our new guests, but I think it is the best course of action for the moment."

"Si, I understand, Monsignor."

"Good. Then, God be with you, Dottore. And, thank you having brought these men here safely."

"Grazie, Monsignor, I will now be on my way." Narduzzi quickly left O'Reilly's office and made his way back to the waiting Lancia, and to Robert Matthews and Louis Durval. He worried that they might explode at the sudden change in plans. Well, they would just have to accept it. Once he was back in the car,

Narduzzi gave instructions to Alberto on where they were to proceed to on Via Scipioni.

Meanwhile, O'Reilly called in Father Lillard to give him his instructions.

"Yes, Monsignor?" asked Father Damian.

"Yes, Damian. I need for you to, as the Americans say, "get on your horse and hightail it" to the petrol station on Via Scipioni. You will then contact the Contessa and see whether she can accommodate our new guests. Is that clear?"

"Yes, Monsignor. I do believe she should be at home at this hour. But what, on the off chance, she is not. What should I do?"

"Damian, we will cross that bridge when we come to it. In any event, if she is at home, contact her by telephone and inform her that you are about to deliver to her the two packages of fruit she ordered. Something to that effect. Also. I will need to contact Sir D'Arcy Osborne. After you have returned from your assignment I would like you to send word to Sir D'Arcy. Convey to him that I will need to speak with him in the immediate future. We are going to be in need of additional help and funding with the way the situation is developing."

Father Lillard left the German College and proceeded on to Via Scipioni on his trusty old bicycle. He had had it in his possession from the moment it was given to him on his sixteenth birthday.

Liam O'Reilly sat down at his desk once again and reached for his telephone. He was about to ask the operator for the number to Rosanna Vallone's home, when he suddenly put down the phone. He thought to himself," What am I doing? I have just dispatched Father Damian to make contact with the Contessa." He felt the pressure must, at last, have gotten to him. It was getting to everyone, of that, he was well aware. Who wouldn't have been aware. A person would have to been rendered practically unconscious.

O'Reilly shot up out of his chair and ran out of his office in search of Father Damian, hopefully, before he had left the building.

The Monsignor had just emerged from the College when he spotted Lillard. Just starting to wheel his way on his journey.

"Father Damian!" he shouted. O'Reilly waved his hands over his head. Father Damian turned his head and nearly toppled over on his bicycle. He saw O'Reilly frantically waving at him. Lillard managed to gain control over his bike. It hadn't been easy for the poor man. He well knew that he would never be regarded as a natural athlete. He had always remembered the taunts he had had to endure on the soccer pitches of his native Ireland. Lillard moved about as if he always had two left feet.

An out of breath O'Reilly soon reached Lillard. "Father Damian, a word…. I was just thinking about when you call the Contessa. You remember the code sequence we are all supposed to employ?"

"Yes. Monsignor. I remember. Do not worry. I know what to do," Father Damian said as he looked on his now somewhat harried looking mentor. The Monsignor had been showing some signs that he was under great pressure and stress in the last few weeks.

O'Reilly nodded. "And I did mention to you about contacting Sir D'Arcy very soon?"

"Yes, Monsignor, you did."

O'Reilly nodded again and turned to go back into the College and to his office. He began to think about Sir D'Arcy Osborne and what he would need from the British statesman and his trustworthy and professional staff at the British Legation in the

Vatican. The Brits had been providing significant funding and material support to the Ambrosia Network's escape activities. At first, the level of processing had involved one or two escaped prisoners. O'Reilly and his subordinates had been able to accommodate these limited numbers in their various hideouts and blinds located throughout Rome and its surrounding environs. But now, the numbers of men seeking protection and provision had been steadily increasing. It brought to mind for O'Reilly the thought that perhaps the "Escape Network" had met its capacity, its ceiling had been reached as to what the "Network" could do without compromising the whole operation. "No. I will have to find a way, perhaps, with Sir D'Arcy's assistance, to pull this off.," he silently thought. The British and Americans and Canadians, and others, were desperate men and were absolutely dependent on O'Reilly and his associates.

Father Lillard found himself making good time on his trek from the German College to Via Scipioni and his rendezvous with Doctor Narduzzi. He arrived at the station, really just a couple of gasoline pumps along the side of the street with an accompanying small hut of a building. Lillard parked his bicycle by one of the hut's walls and looked over the area, furtively. He spotted the black Lancia with the Vatican plates. Lillard walked around and entered the hut. To his surprise, it was bigger from the inside than from what he had imagined while he had stood on the outside. "Scusi, signore, may I use your phone?" asked Father Damian to the man he assumed was the proprietor of this establishment.

"Si, Padre, you may use it," the man responded quizzically. The proprietor was dressed in a grease stained shirt and displayed several days of beard growth on his near glowering visage.

Father Damian nodded, "Grazie, signore," and went to the dust-laden telephone. He was almost immediately in contact with the Contessa. This was a surprise to him as Rome had been known as being lacking in the capability of its communications services.

"Hello? Whom may I ask is calling?" asked Rosanna Vallone.

"Signora, I am Damianello, and I am to deliver the two packages of fruit you ordered. I anticipate being at your address within the hour. Will this be satisfactory for you?"

"Oh yes, I had almost forgotten…. about the fruit. Of course. Very well. I will be here. Grazie, mille grazie, signore," she responded affably.

"Prego. Arrivederci, Signora," Father Damian rang off. The shop proprietor had been off to the side working through some of his paperwork. But he had clearly overheard this priest referring to himself as a fruit peddler. "Oh well," he had thought, "strange things have been happening all over Rome of late. Strange times." It probably had something to do with the underground. The man wanted to have nothing to do with that gang, but he would stay out of the way.

Father Lillard thanked the man and left the hut, looking now for Doctor Narduzzi. He walked toward the black Lancia with a measured pace. Narduzzi stepped out of the vehicle and greeted Lillard, "Buon giorno, Padre," extending his right hand to the priest.

Father Damian shook the doctor's proffered hand and nodded, "Buon giorno, Dottore, it is nice to see you…. again." Lillard leaned in closer to the Italian physician and spoke almost sotto voce, "You are to proceed on to the 'Rose's' residence,'" Rosanna Vallone's code name in the Ambrosia Network, and deliver your fruit packages. She is expecting you." The priest then turned and walked back to his bicycle parked by the station hut. He retrieved it and rode off back to the Vatican.

Doctor Narduzzi directed Alberto to the Contessa's apartment on Via Frattina. He informed Robert Matthews that it was not far from the famous "Spanish Steps." The distance to their destination was actually slightly over a mile. Alberto estimated it would take them ten to fifteen minutes. The black Lancia moved through the largely quiet Roman streets. Soon they were driving across the Ponte Cavour bridge over the Tiber River. Narduzzi explained the sights to Matthews as if he were a tour guide.

Doctor Narduzzi alighted from the Lancia the moment they arrived at the Contessa's door. Just before he had told Matthews, "Maggiore, we have arrived at our destination. You and Sergeant Durval will have to wait just a little while longer, until dusk sets in a little more. Alberto will drive around to a back entrance to the building. When it is safe you men will be taken inside. Okay?"

Matthews gave his muffled assent to the question. Alberto drove around to the back where he encountered a squad of German soldiers. The men were just milling about, as if they were just hanging around with nothing particular to do. Alberto was glad the two Americans had remained in the vehicle. It had been wise to have taken the precaution that Dottore Narduzzi had decided upon.

Matthews was wondering how Durval was doing back in the trunk of the car. "Louis, are you all right?"

"Yeah, I guess so, sir," came back the slow Louisiana drawl.

"Maggiore, there are some German troops about. I think you and the sergeant should wait to converse any further," said Alberto in barely recognizable English.

Thirty minutes later, Narduzzi returned to the car. There was no one about. The German squad had moved off into the now gathering Roman night. "All right, Maggiore, it is safe for you to come out. Alberto will see to Sergeant Durval."

Bob Matthews pushed up on the seat cushion that had rested on his back for all of these past many hours. He blinked his eyes, trying to adjust them to the dim night light. As he emerged from the Lancia he stumbled and nearly fell. Narduzzi caught him by the elbow and helped guide him into the building. The two men went up to the first floor. Matthews remembered that European buildings listed the first flight up as the first floor, not the ground floor as in the states. Narduzzi walked with Matthews until they came to an apartment door with a smiling and attractive woman standing in front of it. He was soon joined by a bent and broken Louis Durval. The ride appeared to have taken more out of him than Matthews. Durval had thought, more than once during the day, that he would go mad.

"Buona sera, gentlemen," Rosanna addressed them, welcome to my home. I know you both have had a very trying and, from your appearance, a painful one as well. In any event, you are safe here. And while you are here I shall require you to follow some simple rules. Some may seem trivial and unnecessary, but I can assure each of you that they must be followed. Is that clear?"

Matthews and Durval simply nodded at this direct and clearly in control Italian woman. Matthews was especially taken by the woman's commanding presence. She would have made a good officer in any man's army. He noted that her English was very good, but he was most intrigued by her attractiveness. It was quite evident to him that it had been a long time since he had last held a woman in his arms.

"Now, as I was saying, these are the rules you are to follow. First, you men cannot use the toilet facilities on an unlimited basis. You are to restrict your use to two times per day for each of you. Second, you must essentially remain in your room during the day. Do not go to the window during the day. Third, bathing will be restricted to once per week. Fourth, you will take your meals with my family. Fifth, you are not to leave the apartment under any circumstances, and, sixth, you are to wear slippers that will be provided to you. I cannot have you men clomping around the floor in your military boots. Do you have any questions at this time?"

"I think that just about covers everything, signora," replied a clearly and fully attentive Robert Matthews. "You wouldn't have any other rules that may have just slipped you mind?" Matthews was attempting to inject some humor into the moment, but it fell completely flat with the Italian noblewoman.

Rosanna looked at the American officer, of whom she could clearly see was a handsome and attractive man, with a sardonic smile. She had noted the attention he had directed at her ample bosom, and the sergeant as well. "I may have one or two more for you men. Let me sleep on it. No, that I believe will be all for now. And now, I would suggest that you clean yourselves up a bit. I will have some food for you. You both must be very hungry."

Matthews quickly found himself becoming infatuated with this woman. Her attractiveness, her figure, her self-assurance, her poise, everything about her. She seemed to possess presence in the right degree, not over the top or overbearing. He and Durval knew of the tremendous risks this woman and her family were taking.

"I do have one question, signora. How should we address you?" queried the now smitten Robert Matthews.

The Contessa looked at Matthews and smiled through owl-hooded eyes, "You may call me signora, at least, for now. For the time being you do not need to know anything else about me or my family. I am sorry if I may sound somewhat uncouth and abrupt, but for the purpose of security that is how it must be," came her reply.

Four

The Jewish Question

By the autumn of 1943, Helmut Kammler had begun adjusting to his role as head of the SS-Sicherheitsdienst and, by extension, the Gestapo in Rome. The entire city was under his thumb, in the figurative sense and the literal one. Kammler would often muse about what his father must be thinking at that moment. Soon, however, he was issued orders form SS Chief, Heinrich Himmler, directing him to turn up the pressure on the Jews living in Rome. Their round-up and deportation was to be his first priority. Privately, Kammler did not agree, just as he had disagreed with the liberation Benito Mussolini by Otto Skorzeny's commandos earlier that fall. He knew Rome better than did those bureaucrats back in Berlin. Deporting the city's Jewish population would garner any sympathy from an Italian populace already angered by the Germans' presence. There was no telling what the reaction might be to a mass round-up.

Kammler did not think he would have enough men for the task, In any event. many of the SS men he did have lacked the necessary experience in the handling of such matters. He had sought the assistance of Field Marshal Albert Kesselring in nearby Frascati. The field marshal had previously dealt with Jews in Tunisia. Kesselring had organized the Tunisian Jews into work groups. Any Jewish leaders who had previously been arrested were set free upon the payment of a fine. Kammler was informed by Kesselring that he would be unable to spare any men for such an operation. "My dear Kammler, I am afraid that I will be unable to provide any men for the round-up operation you have just described for me," Kesselring had said during the two men's last conversation. "And further, I find the concept somewhat appalling."

"I have received my orders from Berlin, Herr Field Marshal. This is a top priority of Reichsfuhrer Himmler. I am sure he does not want to be disappointed," said Kammler.

"He does not want to be disappointed does he, well, perhaps it should be explained to him that I have my own top priorities and obligations to fulfill here in Italy. In case he may not have noticed, the Allies have been making things difficult in a place called Monte Cassino," Kesselring explained patiently to a frustrated Helmut Kammler.

The Allied armies that Kesselring was referring to consisted of a polyglot of soldiers from the United States, Great Britain, Poland, and France. They had been steadily attacking the Benedictine Abbey at Cassino. The two sides had become locked in a mortal combat for months. The Germans trying to block the

Allied troops from penetrating further north. The Americans and British trying to break through and onto Rome itself, and beyond up the Italian boot.

"You have another interesting problem on your hands, Kammler don't you?" questioned Kesselring, who by now had become tired of his conversation with the overbearing SS man.

"What do you mean, Herr Field Marshal?"

"You and I both know about your little situation involving some ... prisoners of war. And, we both know that there is highly rumored involvement of a priest in the Vatican."

Kammler sensed that Kesselring was almost enjoying himself on his side of the desk. "Oh that," Kammler tried to appear dismissive. "Well, it is a matter that my staff and myself are handling. I do not see it as a problem, sir."

"So, you are capable of handling that matter, but you require assistance when it comes to the rounding up of some Jews. By the way, what is the name of this priest? O'Connor, O'something, yes O'Reilly, is that not correct, my dear Kammler?" asked a near smiling Albert Kesselring.

Kammler felt a slow boil rising within himself. Kesselring was clearly mocking him. That accursed priest, O'Reilly, had always been a thorn in his side. The impudence and the arrogance, the outright audacity of this so-called man of the cloth. Kammler nodded his head, but only said, "I have also come here to solicit some advice from you, sir, concerning this.... Jewish matter."

"My advice? What advice can I provide to you and the SS when it comes to Jews?" returned Kesselring with a dismissive look in his eyes.

"Your previous experience with the Tunisian Jews was what I was referring to, Herr Field Marshal."

"Oh, yes. There was that, but I must emphasize the fact that I only had them placed in what could be called protective custody. I did not have them sent to the gas chambers," Kesselring replied in a lecturing tone.

Kammler once again felt the heat rising inside of his head. The Field Marshal had touched another nerve. Here was the army passing judgment on an SS matter. Kesselring and his coterie of proper and sanctimonious Prussians casting aspersions and allegations against the SS, and by extension, the Fuhrer himself.

"I am afraid that I cannot provide any help to you, Kammler, for the moment. General von Vietinghoff and the Tenth Army are fighting for their lives at Monte Cassino. Perhaps, if we should achieve a more satisfactory and dominant position there, than we now possess, then, some personnel can possibly be assigned to your endeavors," said the Field Marshal, with what Kammler took as a finality.

Upon hearing these words, Kammler realized it would do little good to persist with Kesselring. Clearly, his mind had been made up. At least, for the present time. In truth, Kesselring's mind had probably been made up prior to Kammler's visit. He would have to make do with what he had. Kammler thought he might be able to obtain the services of those Fascists who were still loyal to Mussolini and his farcical Republic of Salo government. He knew he would have to tread carefully, asking Italians to participate in his Easter egg hunt for prisoners. He did think that these Fascists might be more receptive to a hunt for Jews. After all, what great love would Catholics have for the safety and well-being of the "Chosen People."

"Very well, Herr Field Marshal. I thank you for having taken the time to receive me and for listening to my special requests. I will now take my leave," said a disappointed and visibly angry Helmut Kammler. "Heil Hitler!"

"You are welcome, Kammler, but try to look at it this way. I am no friend of the Jews. My priority, as of this moment, is to bottle up and destroy the Allies here in Italy. I want to frustrate them, and perhaps, give them pause as to what might well happen to them should they attempt a landing in northern France one day. In any event, good luck to you, Kammler," and with that Kesselring proffered a half stiff-armed salute.

Helmut Kammler returned to Rome a bitter man. He was angry with Kesselring, von Vietinghoff, Hube, that whole gaggle of goose-stepping Prussians. They weren't the real Germans. The SS represented the true Germany. As soon as Kammler had returned to his office he issued orders summoning the Jewish leaders of Rome to a meeting in his office.

* * *

Three days later, Ugo Foa and Dante Almansi stood nervously outside the door of Kammler's office. He greeted them in a pleasant enough manner and with some degree of cordiality. "Good evening, gentlemen. I am so glad that we could meet this evening. I trust that I have not put you men out to any great degree. You know this is one of my favorite times of the year. Especially, to enjoy it in a city as splendid as Rome."

The two men were somewhat mystified by Kammler's remark. The SS man stood behind his desk, now glowering down upon Foa and Almansi. The omnipresent Hitler portrait on the wall behind him. Almansi also noticed other pictures of what looked to have been round-ups conducted by SS troops on another wall. Undoubtedly, involving Jews. Kammler would attempt to bully the two Jewish representatives, despite his reassuring words to the contrary.

They were soon disabused of any further pleasantries on the part of the Obersturmbannfuhrer, and the mailed fist of an ominous threat was soon revealed. "We Germans regard men such as yourselves as only Jews. As such, you represent someone who is at odds with National Socialism and all that it stands for. I have ordered you two men to my office for the purpose of listening to a proposition that I am about to present to you." Kammler spoke these words in an even-handed and non-threatening manner. It was only a prelude. "You are to see to it that the Jewish community of Rome hands over a total of fifty kilograms of gold within the next thirty-six hours. If you should fail to accomplish this task, a total of two hundred Jews will be immediately deported to Germany," he continued. Kammler had no real authorization to do this, but Foa and Almansi did not know this. Kammler was being hopeful that the gold shipment might delay any deportations for the moment.

"Herr Obersturmbannfuhrer, that is a very large amount of gold to obtain, and within such a short period of time," stammered a dumbfounded and shocked Ugo Foa. "I am not sure that it can be done."

"Oh, come now, Signore Foa, you Jews are an enterprising people. Surely, you can all put your heads together for this task. I have great faith in you and your abilities," Kammler replied condescendingly. "You have now been informed and warned by me. Go forth to your 'chosen people' and fulfill my orders."

"Yawohl, Herr Obersturmbannfuhrer. We shall do our best," the two men muttered disappointingly and crestfallen in unison. They both bowed their heads and quietly slinked out of Kammler's office.

After Foa and Almansi's departure, Kammler thought to himself, "Good and good luck to them. A large amount of gold. Indeed." He was reminded of his father and how he and the other village elders would comment on the Jews and their tight-fisted ways. How they were always pleading poverty, and yet, walking about with their noses pointed in the air. As if they were better than the ordinary, hard-working German. Kammler knew Foa and Almansi would find a way to come up with the gold, and then, he might be able to squeeze a little more out of these self-proclaimed 'Chosen People." Who knew, maybe he would go after their diamonds and other valuables.

Ugo Foa and Dante Almansi had left their meeting with Helmut Kammler angry and worried, realizing they would need advice, and likely, some assistance. Both men were well-connected throughout Rome. Their contacts within the Fascist police would, in all probability, be able to do little to help them. They both knew they would have to act and soon.

Kammler's ultimatum for the gold had spread quickly among Rome's twelve-thousand strong Jewish community. Foa and Almansi were hopeful the gold could be raised. They were frightfully unsure as to whether the thirty-six hour deadline could be met. In their office, located beside the central synagogue, the donations were collected. Rings, earrings, chains, pendants, bracelets, even gold fillings that had been removed from teeth. Slowly, the amount of gold began to approach the fifty-kilogram mark. Foa and Almansi twice requested extensions, and both times, Kammler had agreed.

Meanwhile, Vatican operatives had become aware of the SS chieftain's demand of the Jews. His Holiness, Pope Pius XII, offered to lend gold to the Jewish organization should they need it. By early afternoon on September 28th, a Tuesday, the target was reached.

The gold was packed into ten wooden boxes and delivered to Via Wolkonsky. Kammler refused to meet with Foa and Almansi and had them instructed to take the gold to Via Tasso. There they were greeted by a cordial SS Hauptsturmfuhrer, who had the gold weighed. He then informed the men that the gold shipment was short of the fifty kilogram requirement. However, this was quickly cleared up. The SS man who had weighed the gold had made an error.

Foa and Almansi left the SS captain with a feeling of unbridled relief. And Jews throughout Rome allowed themselves the small luxury of relaxing. All across the continent of Europe Jews were being rounded up. In Italy, here in Rome, it seemed as if an exception had been made. There was the sense that the gold payment would forestall and further deportations. The Jews in Rome would not be consigned to the death camps.

* * *

"Krieger, I want you to collect all of the rings and bracelets, and such, and have them placed in boxes. You are to use solid oaken boxes. Have the gold shipped to Obergruppenfuhrer Kaltenbrunner. I will draft a letter which will explain the reason for the gold shipment and my concern over the deporting of Jews from Rome," declared Helmut Kammler.

"Yawohl, Herr Obersturmbannfuhrer, it will be done at once!" replied a bored and resigned Albert Krieger. He knew that Kammler was only trying to placate the SS leadership in Berlin. Krieger did not think the gold would work on a tough nut like Ernst Kaltenbrunner, or even Himmler. These men only wanted blood, in both the literal sense and the figurative one. "Will there be anything else, sir?"

"Nein, that will be all for now," said Kammler as he sat down to compose his letter to Ernst Kaltenbrunner. It began with," Herr Obergruppenfuhrer. I do hope that you are well and in good spirits. I have collected a significant amount of jewelry and gold her in Rome from the Jewish community. The SS has been quite active in the city, I can assure you. We are continuing to put pressure on the Jews. I do have some concerns over planned deportations of Jews from Rome. I believe that such a move could compromise my ability to further exploit the Jewish community, of course, for the primary purpose of intelligence gathering. I might also add that Field Marshal Kesselring has approved of my plans to utilize Jews in labor gangs across the city.

I would also hope that a deportation operation could be delayed in Rome. As always, I will continue to serve you and the Third Reich in whatever capacity you deem necessary."

* * *

Soon after, the gold was received at Ernst Kaltenbrunner's office in Berlin. "What is this, Dannecker?" he demanded.

"I believe it is a gift, Herr Obergruppenfuhrer," replied Hauptsturmfuhrer Theodor Dannecker.

"A gift? For what purpose?" a baffled Kaltenbrunner asked.

"There was this letter attached to the gold shipment, sir." Dannecker handed the note over to Kaltenbrunner.

The SS chieftain scanned the letter with an obvious look of disdain. Dannecker thought the man might have become overcome encountering a foul odor. "Rubbish! This is pure, unadulterated rubbish! Here, look at this." Kaltenbrunner handed the letter back to Dannecker.

"Indeed? Putting the pressure on those God-forsaken Jews and this... This obvious and obsequious attempt to curry favor with me is pathetic. Look, Dannecker, I want you to go to Rome and observe as to what Herr Kammler is doing, or... not doing. You are to leave at once, Now, get Kammler on the phone for me!" he bellowed.

Moments later, "Heil Hitler, Herr Obergruppenfuhrer, it is indeed a pleasure to hear from you once again," gulped a now fearful Helmut Kammler. He was very aware he would have to be most careful in how he dealt with Ernst Kaltenbrunner.

"I am not interested as to whether you find my calling you pleasurable or not. Do not try to placate me, Kammler," the SS chief sneered over the line. "Did you think you could impress me with this gold shipment. Such a trifling amount, surely you and your staff could have done better. And, further, who do you think you are to inform me as to policies and procedures regarding the Jews?" he continued.

"I never meant to deceive you or to do anything untoward, sir," stammered a shaken and now rapidly perspiring Kammler. Even though the two men were separated by more than 500 miles, he felt as if he could picture the hulking Kaltenbrunner glowering into the phone. Kammler was now perspiring heavily within his wool uniform. The patches under his arms had taken on a clammy feel and the insides of his thighs were very uncomfortable as well.

"I know that you were once a protégé of that half-breed, Heydrich, but I run the SS now. Is that clear to you, Kammler? Listen, I am sending Dannecker down to Rome. You are to extend to him every courtesy. Is that clear?"

"Yawohl, sir. Of course," replied an increasingly shaken Helmut Kammler. He thought, "What did this mean? Dannecker? Who was this Dannecker" Probably another one of Kaltenbrunner's hatchet men."

"Kammler, are you there?"

"Yes, sir. I am here. When can I expect Herr Dannecker? I want to be prepared."

"You can expect him to arrive within the next twenty-four to forty-eight hours. And remember, Kammler, every courtesy. You are to consider Hauptsturmfuhrer Dannecker as an extension of myself. In other words, it will be as if I am in Rome personally. Another thing. The deportations must be your highest priority. There is to be no further delay. Have I made myself understood? The immediate and complete eradication of the Jews in Italy is in the special interest of the current political situation and general security of the country. You, Kammler, are not to delay these procedures or to obfuscate them in any way. The more these Jews have an opportunity to move to safe houses of pro-Jewish families, the more they will do so." Kaltenbrunner did not even bother to sign off with the obligatory "Heil Hitler." Instead, he slammed down his phone upon his dark-stained oaken desk, nearly obliterating it.

✳ ✳ ✳

Liam O'Reilly had been watching developments closely. He had become extremely agitated at what he saw was happening to the Jews of Rome. It had filled him with rage and a sense of helplessness. One day he conferred with Father Lillard. "These gentle and unassuming people are being treated like beasts, sub-humans. They have been herded into ghettoes. It is sheer brutality, Damian! The sooner the Germans are defeated the better."

To Father Lillard, this represented a considerable change of attitude for the Monsignor. "You have come a long way in your thinking, Monsignor. I can remember a not-too-distant time when you almost considered the British as bad as the Germans."

"Yes, Damian, I suppose it does. It has been some time in coming, but I cannot just shut my eyes as to what is happening to the Jews. Good God, man! These are flesh and blood people we are talking about. The Nazis view them as cattle and treat them worse. They starve them to death and disease in these ghettoes, and then, they round them up and throw them into unheated cattle cars. They curse at them, they whip them. They set their attack dogs upon them," O'Reilly had worked himself into a fevered state, but he had had to let off steam with someone. As was usually the case, it had fallen on Damian Lillard.

"Yes, Monsignor. I, too, have eyes and has heard many terrible things as well. However, we still have to move with caution. I know you desperately want to help these poor and unfortunate people. I also realize that there is a fine line between not provoking the Germans on the one hand, and on the other hand, acting in some way in trying to help," Father Damian replied carefully and in a low tone of voice.

"Damian, I would like for you to contact Sir D'Arcy Osborne as soon as possible. We are going to have to solicit his support and advice concerning these matters."

"I will do so tomorrow, Monsignor. You have been doing many good things here in Rome, what with the men we have in hiding. I do not think you can afford to extend yourself too much concerning this matter with the Jewish people."

"I know, Damian, I know, but something has to be done. God is watching us, all of us. We must act. We are compelled to act. Yes, as you say, caution must be exercised, but we cannot stand idly by! There, I have worked myself up. Damian, I believe that will be all for now," concluded a now visibly angry and shaking O'Reilly.

* * *

Theodor Dannecker duly arrived in Rome on the following Wednesday, exactly within the forty-eight hour window that Ernst Kaltenbrunner had set. By this time, Kammler's foot-dragging on the Jewish deportations had begun to cause great anxiety and consternation within the corridors of power at SS-Headquarters in Berlin. Heinrich Himmler knew that if the "Final Solution" was the take effect in Rome he might have to have his own personal representative in place. Dannecker was accompanied by a detachment of SS troopers to provide assistance in the proposed upcoming round-ups.

"Heil Hitler, Obersturmbannfuhrer Kammler," said Theodor Dannecker as he stood before Helmut Kammler. He had clicked his jack-booted heels and thrown out the required Hitler salute.

"Yes, Heil Hitler, Dannecker. Please sit down. Now, Captain, how may I be of service?" asked Kammler straightforwardly. He knew he outranked the man, but he also realized that his guest was to be taken seriously. Dannecker was in Rome at Kaltenbrunner's command, and with Himmler's blessing.

"As you know, the deportation issue is the top priority of Herr Kaltenbrunner. It is my job to provide assistance to you in the facilitation of this action. Therefore, it will be necessary for you to obtain the manpower of, at least, one additional battalion. But, this operation must be kept as secretive as possible. I will need the names and addresses of the city's Jewish residents," Dannecker finished, his fingers steepled together in the shape of a tent.

Kammler now realized that he would no longer be able to stall by offering excuses and the need for more time. "Yes, of course, Captain. I have that information right here in my desk," replied Kammler. This should impress the man and attest to Kammler's professionalism. He reached into the top right-hand desk drawer and withdrew the lists that Dannecker wanted. He handed them over.

The Hauptsturmfuhrer looked over the files carefully and said, "Good, good. Then, we should be able to get started fairly quickly, can we not? I think we should be able to commence operations by the weekend. I will notify Obergruppenfuhrer Kaltenbrunner at once. I do believe that should cover things for now. I will confer again with you tomorrow," replied Dannecker, who had been acting as if were Kammler's superior.

"Yes, and now, I will have you taken to your quarters, Captain."

"You don't have to bother, Herr Kammler. I have my own transportation. I expect that you will have things in order for the round-ups. We would not want to disappoint Herr Kaltenbrunner."

Again, the veiled threat. Kammler merely bit his tongue at the implied slight of having been addressed as if the two men were equal in rank. "It will be done, Captain. You can be assured of that."

"Good, Then, I will take my leave," said Dannecker. He'd started to make his way out of Kammler's office when he paused and turned "You know, I never realized how lovely Rome is at this time of year."

Kammler sat down heavily in his chair, once Dannecker had departed. "How will I come up with another battalion," he thought. Kesselring had already turned him down. He sent for Albert Krieger.

"You have sent for me, sir?" asked Krieger.

"Yes, I have, Albert. Sit down. I have just had an audience with Hauptsturmfuhrer Dannecker. He is Kaltenbrunner's personal hatchet man. We are being directed to mount the evacuation of the city's Jewish residents, and by this weekend. Dannecker has been sent here to see that the operation is carried out to the satisfaction of the SS chiefs in Berlin. There is to be no further prevaricating on our part. Dannecker has brought with him a small detachment of SS troopers, but he says we will need an additional battalion of men for the job. I have already been to see Field Marshal Kesselring, but he turned me down flat. Perhaps, we can acquire this battalion from General von Vietinghoff's Tenth Army. We have our connections within the General's staff, do we not? Use them and report directly back to me. Is that clear?"

"Yawohl, sir! I will get right on to it."

"On your way, Krieger. Remember, this needs to be done immediately."

* * *

On Saturday, October 16th, rain was falling. SS men and army troops and military police tore into the Jewish ghetto of Rome along a bend near the Tiber River. The German objective on this day was not to be gold or valuables, but people, men, women, children. Twelve hundred frightened individuals were rousted from their homes, cold and wet, frantically clinging to a few small possessions, and to one another. All that they would be allowed to bring with them to their unknown destination. The arrested were hastily thrown and heaved into waiting army trucks.

Many of the Jews were still in their nightclothes. Children, of all ages, were crying as they were roughly herded out of their homes by burly SS troopers. The younger were screaming in hysteria. Some of the adults, especially amongst the elderly, prayed as they were driven to the Italian Military College, also located along the Tiber River, not too far away.

News of the German raid quickly reached the confines of the Vatican. Contessa Rosanna Vallone had been awakened by a friend of hers, who lived near the Jewish Quarter. The woman informed her of the German action. The Contessa knew she would have to contact Monsignor O'Reilly, but first, she would try and get to as close to the scene as she could.

Rosanna had told her children she would be going out for a short time. When she arrived near the Jewish Quarter what she had fearfully imagined was in fact taking place, right before her eyes. It was indescribable. There was mass chaos as people of all ages could be seen being taken into custody by German troops. Some of the men, particularly the SS, seemed to be taking great delight in the tormenting of their captives. Rosanna spent only a few brief moments witnessing the horrific scenes, but it provided her with more than enough to take to O'Reilly.

"Monsignor, I have just seen the worst possible thing anyone of us could ever imagine. The Germans have been arresting all of the Jewish residents from the Quarter. Old men, children women, all swept up and driven away, as if they were mere cattle," Rosanna explained breathlessly as she sat before

Liam O'Reilly in his simple office at the German College. "Monsignor, something has to be done. It was absolutely horrible. I never imagined that I would witness such a monstrous and terrible thing in my lifetime."

O'Reilly sat back calmly in his chair and took in what Rosanna had just told him. It confirmed the rumors he had already heard. Although, he had remained silent throughout Rosanna's discourse, inwardly, he was raging. The Germans, and especially the SS, just kept jamming their heels into innocent and harmless people. People who were no threat to them. Their actions went beyond simple bullying, they seemed to enjoy inflicting pain and suffering upon their victims. It was pure, savage sadism. O'Reilly steepled his fingers as he continued to sit languidly. "Do you know where these people have been taken, Rosanna?"

"No, Monsignor, but the word on the street is that it is right here in Rome. At least, for the time being. Perhaps, some of your contacts might know. Maybe Signore Foa, that is, if he hasn't already been incarcerated."

"Yes, yes, I will try and find out. Rosanna I do not think that we should take any precipitate action for the moment. It galls me and upsets me to no end. These monsters…. I will see what can be done."

After the Contessa's departure, O'Reilly continued to contemplate what he had just heard. The Germans, be they SS men or Wehrmacht, Luftwaffe, whatever, were simply beasts. He then contacted Cardinal Luigi Maglione, the Vatican's secretary of state, and one of Pope Pius's key aides.

Maglione, in turn, summoned the German Ambassador to the Holy See for an audience and some direct questions. "Ambassador Weizsacker, this is most distressing news about these round-ups of our Jewish brethren. His Holiness is most upset over how these people have been treated by the SS, and by some army personnel" erupted from the outraged voice of Cardinal Maglione. "You must use your influence to put a stop to these round-ups, and from what I have also heard, the ultimate deportation of these people to concentration camps. It is most painful for the Holy Father to see so many people suffering, and just because of their descent."

Ernst von Weizsacker had been listening to the Cardinal in silence. "What would the Holy See do if these actions were to continue?"

"The Holy See would not wish to be placed in such a position where it would be necessary to voice a word of disapproval, or even, one of condemnation."

"Cardinale Maglione, the Reich has been grateful over the fact that the Church has opted to adopt a neutral position concerning the war. I do not believe it would be advisable for the Holy See to make a public protest. That could result in consequences for the Holy Father. Cardinale, these measures that you are condemning have been undertaken under the auspices at the highest level of the German government."

"But Ambassador, I implore you to do something to stop this carnage. My God, I have been told that a man was attempting to help his wife as they were rushed from their building. Apparently, the woman was struggling and was not moving fast enough for the SS troopers. An officer went over to the couple and pulled his pistol out and shot the unfortunate woman in the head. A jetstream of blood erupted from the open wound, splashing all over her husband. These are human beings, sir!" Maglione pleaded.

"Unfounded rumors, my dear Cardinale,"

"Unfounded you say. Ambassador, my source is absolutely reliable. I trust in him implicitly!"

"I am not sure that I am empowered to intervene in any capacity, Cardinale," was all von Weizsacker could reply. "I am very sorry, and now, I have to conclude our meeting. Auf wiedersehn, Cardinale." Von Weizsacker left Maglione's office at a near run.

Maglione had been struck by the Ambassador's words, "the highest level." To him this could only be viewed as a threat. He knew that the Pope did not want to risk a showdown with the Germans. The Vatican had become very nervous over rumors of an impending German takeover of their grounds.

✷ ✷ ✷

British Ambassador, Sir D'Arcy Osborne, met with the Pope that same day, just as the Roman Jews were being transported from Tiburtina Station. They would be on their way to a one-way journey to Auschwitz.

"I am so glad that you could join me here today, Sir D'Arcy. I am in your debt," opened Pope Pius gracefully. "I am most concerned. no, distressed is a better word over what has been happening to our Jewish brethren."

"Holy Father, it has been most distressing for me as well. I may have underestimated my own moral authority, But, you, Holy Father, have, how should I put it, more clout than I possess. Perhaps, you could approach the Germans personally and express your own displeasure most forcefully at their recent actions."

"Yes, Sir D'Arcy, as the chief representative of the Church I do have, as you say, some clout. However, I have to tread carefully in any dealings with the Germans. As you are undoubtedly aware, there have been rumors of a German occupation of the Vatican. That would be disastrous for all of us concerned. I must, and will, do everything in my power to prevent that from happening. You do understand, my first obligation is to the Holy See. We can do far more good by remaining a sovereign entity. Even to the extent of providing assistance to the Jewish people of Rome," replied the pontiff. Pius had been wearing an almost pained expression on his face. The German round-ups and deportations had torn to the very core of his soul. He felt powerless in the face of this abominable action, no doubt performed under the direct supervision of Colonel Helmut Kammler.

"Of course, Your Eminence. I will try to contact Ambassador von Weizsacker and appeal to him. He has always been a reasonable man in my dealings with him in the past. I could inform him that there could be consequences for those who have been committing these obvious crimes against defenseless people. This war will one day come to an end and some Germans will have to account for their actions."

"I am not sure that that will accomplish anything, Sir D'Arcy, despite your best intentions. Cardinale Maglione is meeting with the Ambassador at this very moment. I am not expecting any positive or uplifting news. The Church will continue in its efforts to provide aid and shelter to those who remain in need," replied Pius.

Sir D'Arcy took this as an oblique reference to Monsignor O'Reilly 's operation, but remained silent. "However, I am truly saddened by the number of Roman Jews who have met with their deaths thus far in this war. I was just informed by Monsignor O'Reilly that the number has exceeded one thousand in the recent deportation alone," continued the troubled Holy

Father. He was gripping his prayer beads tightly, in a near strangling motion.

"And I have heard that the Jews who are left in the city are most fearful that there will be more deportations. Many have gone into hiding in Rome and in some of the outlying areas in the countryside," said Sir D'Arcy.

"Yes, it has been brought to my attention that some of these unfortunate victims have sought sanctuary in some of our own parish churches and convents. I cannot let the Germans see that there is any connection between these alleged activities and the Holy See," Pius resumed.

"I quite understand the position you are in, Holy Father. Oh, before I forget, I am to meet with Monsignor O'Reilly about…." started Osborne, but the Pontiff cut him off.

"I do not want to know about any clandestine meetings between yourself and any members of the Vatican. You will do what you have to do. Now, Sir D'Arcy, I must now turn to my own Vatican duties. You do understand?" replied the Pope somewhat imperiously. Pius had not meant to sound abrupt with the British Ambassador. He knew him to be a good man. One who had always been a steadfast and stalwart supporter of the Church.

Osborne gave no indication that he felt he had been offended and replied, "Of course, Your Holiness, but please, I ask you to, perhaps, find some way of expressing your displeasure and concern at these deportations of the Jews. Good-bye, Your Eminence."

* * *

The round-ups of Jews had resulted in its having a significant effect on Liam O'Reilly's growing escape organization. It had become easier to solicit help and funding from average citizens who had previously acted ambivalent to the Nazis. If anything, the raids may have provided for a greater leeway between himself and the Vatican leaders. The Germans had triggered a switch with these men of the cloth. Even though O'Reilly's work had posed a challenge to the Church's so-called neutrality, Church leaders were apparently more willing to look the other way than they ever had previously.

In the wake of the October raids by the SS, some of the Jews began to search out and to find ways to the Monsignor, who was only too glad to offer shelter to those in the most immediate danger. Some of these individuals were being hidden in Church-owned buildings, while others were spirited right out of the country.

One day in November as O'Reilly strolled customarily around the periphery of St. Peter's Basilica, reading from his Bible, he was approached by a young couple.

"Scusi, Padre, would you have a moment?" the man asked. He was short in stature, with black curly hair. He was dressed in rather thread-worn clothes. The woman, that O'Reilly gathered was the man's wife, was equally dressed in a rundown and shabby manner. These people showed all of the signs of having lived for a long time in hiding, and of being on the run. Always looking over their shoulders in fear.

"Yes, of course, young man. What is it that I can help you with?" O'Reilly asked gently in a near soothing manner. He thought he already knew what these people were going to ask him.

"Grazie, mille grazie, Padre. As you can plainly see we do not have much, but we are in desperate need of help. You see, we are Jews and are fearful for our lives. Can you help us? I do not know where else we can go. I am afraid that we can only offer you this gold chain. It has been in my family's possession for many, many years," the young man held out a gold chain with a Star of David attached. He kept looking around furtively and had spoken in a low tone of voice, as if he did not want any passersby to hear that he and his wife were Jews.

"My son, that will not be necessary. I can help you," O'Reilly replied as he slowly shook his head. These young and desperate people were breaking his Irish heart. It was pitiful to have to witness this scene.

"You see, Padre, it has not been much fun for us, but we also have a little boy. He is only seven years-old and we do not want to take a chance that he will be deported to Germany, or somewhere away from us. We have heard and seen, with our own eyes, many bad things on what has befallen on Jews sent to Germany. You know, as part of this 'special handling.'"

O'Reilly guided the couple to a more secluded spot in the shadows of the Cathedral. In a soft voice O'Reilly leaned in close and said, "I will be able to provide the two of you with false papers that will allow you to remain in Rome. Your son will be hidden within the city as well. It will be better if you two are separated from him, but I can assure you that he will be safe. Will that be all right with you both?"

"Grazie, Padre, grazie," the man responded as tears fell down his face. His wife began to sob softly, her body shaking from the emotion that stirred inside of her.

"Please, young man, call me Monsignor," said O'Reilly, clearly moved and emotional himself.

"How much should we pay you, Monsignor? We do have much beyond this gold chain," the young man asked.

O'Reilly shook his head as he said, "You do not have to pay me anything. Let us consider this as an act of God. It is being done because you and your wife need help. As a Christian I am obligated to help anyone who is in need."

"Grazie, Monsignor, we will do as you say," said the young woman. She stood a little taller than her husband and, to this point, had not uttered a word. O'Reilly could see that she was an attractive woman of, perhaps, in her late twenties. Despite her modest and drab attire, and complete lack of make-up, she was clearly very pretty. "Monsignor, we are German Jews. We have been on the run and in hiding for many months. It is our most fervent wish and desire that our little boy be taken care of. Our own lives are not as much of concern to us. We are most grateful to you and the Church. You are truly our last hope. We have heard of some of the fine things that the Holy Father has done, not only for Jews, but for others as well. And even though we are Jews, we are thankful to the Church for what it is doing. Maybe, one day you will be able to convey this to His Eminence," she eventually told O'Reilly. At times, her soft and tender voice had nearly broken. O'Reilly saw that the woman was the rock in the family.

"No, madam. We are all children of God. We all walk with the Lord. He is watching us. And, I can assure that he is watching the Germans very closely."

Again, it was the woman, "But why do you do it, Monsignor? The risks you are taking must be tremendous."

"For me to do nothing would be the greater risk, dear child. I try to follow the dictum of 'Every day is a gift from God. How you live it is your gift to him.' Please return here in two days' time and you will be met by one of my associates. Can you do this?"

The man and the woman nodded simultaneously. O'Reilly nodded his head and walked off after having bid them, "Go with God, my children."

In the days that followed, Rome was a city gripped in fear and a sense of panic. People asked themselves whether the German raids would continue. How many more people would be dragged off and sent to labor camps, or worse? The Germans seemed to be everywhere at once in the streets and alleyways of the sprawling city. Helmut Kammler had directed his men to paint a white line around the Vatican territory in November. The half-foot wide line had been designed to show where the neutral territory of the Holy See ended and where German control began. It was also meant as a direct challenge to Monsignor Liam O'Reilly. It was an implicit message from Kammler to the cleric.

The SS man was saying, "I have my eyes on you, priest. You had better watch your step. One false move, the slightest misstep, and I will swoop down upon you and crush you and all those who are aiding and abetting your nefarious activities."

Helmut Kammler had long been suspicious of the Irish Monsignor, and what he might be up to. Utilizing a string of informants, his own SS-Sicherheitsdienst intelligence apparatus, and other intangibles, the Obersturmbannfuhrer had been slowly and craftily building his case against O'Reilly. Gestapo agents had only recently arrested an Italian deliveryman as he had been transporting supplies from the surrounding countryside to a market in Rome. They had detected that the man had been ferrying money back to families up in the country. Kammler had been able to threaten the poor man into agreeing to engage himself in a scheme to entrap O'Reilly by promising him that his life would be spared.

It was a well-known fact to Kammler that higher-ups in Berlin were watching developments in Rome very closely and with great interest. Himmler and Kaltenbrunner and their lackey, Theodor Dannecker, were tracking the Roman operations most avidly. He was also aware that plans were in place for the Germans to invade the Vatican. Surely, if he could prove that O'Reilly and the Church were behind an escape network of some kind, then, Hitler would undoubtedly order the operation to move forward. The Pope, His Holiness, and all of the Cardinals, "that whole bunch of conniving, duplicitous criminals," would be rounded up and shipped off to the infernal reaches. They would be taught a lesson they would never forget. Then, he, Helmut Kammler would, no doubt, be promoted. Who knew? He might even find himself posted to Berlin. Of course, that would place him closer to that "bastard", Kaltenbrunner! Well, so be it.

Five

Under Surveillance

Helmut Kammler stood on the sidewalk along a piazza that ran off of the Via Del Corso. He looked up at the impressive sixteenth century building in front of him. It was a glorious late-fall morning with hues of yellows and blues in the sky overhead. Inside was the home of the anti-Fascist Prince Filippo Della Massa, an outspoken critic of Benito Mussolini and the Black Shirts. Kammler was aware that the man had been providing assistance to Jewish refugees in and around Rome. Della Massa had been in his sights for some time now. The man was one-half British and had attended Cambridge University. The SS man had also recently obtained fresh evidence that the prince was funding some of Liam O'Reilly's escape organization.

The Obersturmbannfuhrer was visibly excited as his contacts had also informed him that Della Massa was due to be meeting the Irish Monsignor at that very moment. He almost could not contain himself. At long last, he would finally be able to get his hands on this indefatigable priest and, right in the act. Kammler had instructed Untersturmfuhrer Karl Hansen to position SS troopers around the building and to make sure that all approaches had been cut off.

"Hansen! Approach the front door cautiously. Have your men gain entrance to the residence. This is a great opportunity for us. Just think, we are about to catch this 'priest' right in the act. I do not want any mistakes. We have waited far too long for this moment," he explained to Hansen with a cold, almost disdainful manner. Yet, Hansen also detected a gleam in the man's eyes.

Karl Hansen walked up to the front door and knocked firmly, using the Great Dane shaped door knocker. O'Reilly himself had only entered the house moments before. He and Prince Della Massa had been in the middle of a discussion over the money situation of the organization.

"Scusi, Prince Filippo, there are SS men all around the building!" exclaimed an excited Luigi Corlone, Della Massa's long-time secretary as he burst in to the living room, interrupting the two men.

Della Massa stood up at once with a pained look on his face. "Quickly, Monsignor, we must find a way for you to escape," The Prince was a gaunt, tall and thin man, with a dark complexion. This was, no doubt, the result of the man having contracted malaria years before when he had been conducting his farming operations in Libya.

O'Reilly went to one of the windows that overlooked Via Del Corso and saw for himself the SS troopers fanning out as Corlone had just described. Kammler had been most thorough in his preparations, leaving little to chance at the opportunity of his lifetime to finally be able to catch him.

The knocking at the door became more insistent, but the Monsignor had no intention of making it easy for Kammler's men and to simply surrender meekly. He scanned the tapestry laden walls of the living room of the Prince's home and made for the hallway. He also made sure to gather up the 300,000 lire that Della Massa had been about to hand over to him, when they had been so rudely interrupted. O'Reilly turned to the Prince and bid him a hasty good-bye.

Della Massa had acquired an impressive collection of medieval armor over the years, which he proudly displayed throughout his home. Suits were from such places as Augsburg, Venice, Normandy, and many other venues from across Europe. O'Reilly asked one of Della Massa's staff to try and continue to delay the SS men. The Prince then showed the entry to the cellar. As the Irishman went down the creaking steps he felt the closing darkness surround him. At the base of the stairs he heard a rumbling sound. O'Reilly squinted his eyes and he was gradually able to see that coal was being delivered to the home for the upcoming winter.

O'Reilly continued squinting his eyes, and they finally adjusted to the darkness of the dank cellar. He looked out into the yard and saw two coal deliverymen standing beside a parked truck. It suddenly dawned upon him an idea by which he could make his escape. Placing his vestment garments into an empty coal sack, he started to smear his face, arms, and hands with coal dust. O'Reilly, standing in his shirt and pants, then hoisted a sack of coal onto his shoulder and proceeded to propel himself through the cellar window. He was now in the courtyard.

One of the coalmen noticed the preposterous looking O'Reilly and approached him, "Scusi, who are you? What are you doing?"

"Signore, I implore you to help me. I am in hiding from the Germans. I beg you to allow me to join your men, just so that I can make my way away from here."

The man walked over to O'Reilly and reached out for one of his hands. He moved his thumb around the palm and inside the fingers of the priest. Very smooth, with only a slight degree of callousing. O'Reilly was clearly no deliveryman, not even a common laborer. The man continued to view O'Reilly suspiciously, wondering what he should do. Turn him over to the Germans. No doubt, this strange looking character had emerged from the Prince's cellar, so he was probably a friend. If he turned the man in, he might well be indicting Della Massa as well. "All right, you can join us, but you must make your escape as soon as possible. I do not want to get into any trouble."

"Grazie, signore, that is most kind of you. May God be with you," O'Reilly intoned and with well-meant feeling. He then made his way slowly and carefully away from the courtyard. He hoisted the coal sack over his right shoulder and secured the sack containing his vestments to his belt. O'Reilly walked across the courtyard, now in full view of some of the SS soldiers. They paid him no mind. As soon as he had gotten around the corner away from the main street of the Prince's home he stopped and placed his garments back on. No sooner had this been done when he suddenly found himself face to face with an SS trooper.

"Scusi, Padre," the man addressed O'Reilly politely. He continued in a mix of broken Italian and German. "You seem to have gotten yourself rather dirty, haven't you? I did not realize that some men of the cloth also dabbled in coal." The SS man's expression had taken on a hardened tone and, he was not smiling.

O'Reilly stood flat-footed, he had been taken completely by surprise. He tried to think quickly, but his mind just came up blank. He was desperate to come up with something plausible, but what? "Come on, man! Think!" he said to himself. Finally, he said, "Err. I have just brought some coal to a friend. You know how it has been starting to get cold outside."

The SS trooper continued to eye him warily. "A friend you say? I take it that it was nearby. It appears as if you rolled around in it. Well…. I was brought up to trust the word of a priest. But, here, in Rome I am not sure that I should do so."

O'Reilly continued to stand before the German, unsure of what to do or say next. He desperately hoped the man would buy his story and let him go.

"All right, Padre, on your way. We are in the middle of an operation to catch some mucky-muck person," the SS man continued, not realizing to whom he had been speaking to.

"Grazie, grazie, mille grazie, sir. I shall be on my way." O'Reilly then walked back to his office at the German College as quickly as he could. He did not want to arouse any further suspicion. He had endured enough for the day.

Transpiring back at the Palazzo Doria was a scene of confrontation and confusion and suspense. Helmut Kammler stood himself up to his full height and looked down at a frightened and quivering Prince Della Massa. "All right, Prince, where is he?" demanded a furious Kammler.

"Who are you looking for, sir?" Della Massa asked in a querulous voice. He was not at all sure how he should respond to the glowering SS officer. Della Massa was all too well aware of Kammler's reputation.

"Don't try to be coy with me, Prince! Where is he? I know he was here in this very building, in this very room. Now, I will ask you again WHERE IS HE?" Kammler was now screaming, the veins on his neck and forehead were fully inflamed. His face had grown beet-red.

Della Massa thought Kammler would break a blood vessel. He looked down at his hands, then up Kammler and said, "There has been no one here, apart from myself and my staff. Of whom, may I ask are you looking for? I would like to help you if I could, sir. Believe me," Prince Della Massa replied as calmly as he could manage. Inwardly, he could feel himself being twisted into knots. He knew his ulcer would flare up if Colonel Kammler continued to badger him

"I am sure that you would, Prince. I am sure that you would," Kammler leered condescendingly. "You know perfectly well as to whom I am referring to. That priest, the Monsignor. Do I have to spell it out for you any further? ..... Monsignor Liam O'Reilly, Now, once more. Prince Della Massa, where is he?"

"A monsignor?" asked the still quaking Della Massa. "I know of a great many monsignors in Rome, sir. Monsignor O'Reilly? I do not believe that I have seen him for some time."

"Who do you think you are, Prince? You are just an insignificant, sniveling fool. Who do you think you are talking to? One of your lackey staff members? I know all about you and your salacious activities. I could have you taken into custody right now, and interrogated most thoroughly." Kammler continued on in his bellowing tone.

"Then, why don't you, Herr Obersturmbannfuhrer! I do not have to sit here and have you invade my home and impugn my character!" answered a suddenly defiant Prince Della Massa. It was as if Kammler had crossed the Prince's Rubicon.

"Hansen, have your men search the entire house, and I mean to search everywhere. Leave no stone unturned. Question each member of the Prince's staff. Find out anything you can, even if it seems trivial and insignificant," ordered Kammler.

"Yawohl, Herr Obersturmbannfuhrer, at once!" answered the ever compliant Hansen.

As Hansen started to issue his orders, Kammler interrupted, "Oh, Hansen? Have your men question the neighbors, anyone who had been seen on the street. There is no telling what might turn up."

The search of the Prince's home turned up nothing. Kammler pounded his field-gray felt gloves into his hand. He had been so sure that he would catch O'Reilly. He had him. He had him. Once again, "This wily priest" had given him the slip. He then turned on Della Massa and said, "You have a very nice home here, Prince. Very nice, Indeed. I see that having been a critic of il Duce has not compromised your ability to acquire such nice antiquities. And, to live in relative tranquility in the midst of this ghastly and abhorrent war. It would distress me if something untoward were to happen to you or your wife, or even your lovely daughter. I believe she is your only child. Yes…. It would be most unfortunate…." Kammler let the hidden threat lie in his silence.

At that moment, Kammler strolled across the living room floor and picked up one of the priceless antiquities of which the Prince had always been so proud of. "This is most exquisite,

Prince, I must say. It must be worth a vast amount of money." The SS man caressingly turned the vase over in his hands.

Della Massa knew what was about to happen to the vase, and it filled him with dread and foreboding. "Sir, that is an Etruscan vase that has been in my family for many, many years. It dates back to pre-Roman times."

"So! Yes, it is most impressive. How much, would you say, is it worth to you? H-m-m-m Yes, a precious artifact." Suddenly, Kammler dropped the vase on to the tiled floor. It broke into a seeming million pieces. The precious antiquity of the Prince had been reduced to shards of broken pottery and dust. Della Massa's heart sank and he visibly winced. He was on the verge of tears.

"Oh… how clumsy of me. Look at what I have done, Prince. I hope and trust that you are insured?"

Della Massa continued to sit in stunned silence as he gazed at the shattered vase. He was also staring into his shattered world. This Nazi superman was openly threatening him and his family. What could he do? He was powerless, and he knew that Kammler knew this. The Prince had never met the Obersturmbannfuhrer before, but he had the stories that surrounded this horrifying and brutal man, and of his subordinates. It filled the refined and dignified nobleman with a loathing and disgust for all things German. "It is quite all right, Herr Kammler, quite all right, I will have it taken care of," the Prince replied in a muted and anguished voice.

"Listen to me, Prince! I will eventually get to the bottom of this whole operation. I will, and you had better hope that you do not end up swinging from the end of a rope in Regina Coeli Prison. I will teach you and some of your fellow nobility to respect and to fear the SS! So help me God. We will meet again, kind sir. Of that, I can assure you."

Kammler and his men left the Palazzo Doria emptyhanded. The SS man was still baffled as to how O'Reilly had eluded him once again. He had been so sure that this time the cleric would be caught red-handed. Kammler had even allowed himself to envision how he would compose his announcement to Kaltenbrunner. It would have made the loud-mouthed Austrian hack eat his own words. And it would have elevated his standing with Reichsfuhrer Himmler himself.

As Kammler was driven back to his headquarters in the close-topped Kubelwagen, it became clear to him that a new tactic would be required to finally, once and for all, end this cat and mouse game with Monsignor Liam O'Reilly and his entire escape network.

Prince Della Massa and his family and staff were able to eventually resume a somewhat degree of normality in the hours after the departure of Kammler and his men. Suddenly, his telephone rang.

"I have just returned home," said the familiar voice of Liam O'Reilly. "I do hope that you are well, Filppo."

"Well, I am afraid that Obersturmbannfuhrer Kammler is a very angry man right now," replied Della Massa. "He was here for about an hour. His men searched everywhere throughout my home, but apparently found nothing."

O'Reilly subconsciously held up his left hand as he spoke into the phone. "Please, we will have to be brief. There is no telling as to whom may be listening."

"Herr Kammler was certain that you had been here. He did tell me that when I next saw you to inform you that one day he would be entertaining you in Via Tasso," interrupted Della Massa.

O'Reilly chuckled quietly into his phone, "Yes, I can imagine, but listen, today was too close a call. We were extremely lucky. The visits to Palazzo Doria will have to be terminated. I will have you notified when I have come up with an alternate plan. Ciao, for now."

O'Reilly then summoned his assistant, Father Damian Lillard.

"Yes, Monsignor?"

"Yes, Damian. Please, sit down."

"I just found out that you only returned a short time ago," remarked Father Damian, noticing traces of coal smeared on O'Reilly's face and hands.

O'Reilly saw Lillard staring at him and said, "I had to assume the role of a coal handler to affect my escape from Prince Della Massa's home. Our old friend, Herr Kammler, staged a raid for the sole purpose of my capture."

Lillard slowly shook his head, while his face registered a slight grimace, "A coal handler? I suppose you could add that to your repertoire of roles you have played since you first took to the stage here in Rome. Monsignor, pretty soon you are going to be a serious challenge to Sir Laurence Olivier for an Oscar nomination.' Damian had said this all kiddingly, but he was very worried at the seemingly increased risks that O'Reilly had been taking since the whole escape thing had started. And, especially of late.

"I think I will place it up there with my previous role as a clown, don't you think, Damian?" O'Reilly countered in a jocular manner. "I will admit that it was a close call. I was just able to bluff my way past one of Kammler's SS stooges. I had removed my vestments in Prince Della Massa's cellar and spread some coal dust onto my face and hands. Luckily, the Prince had taken receipt of a coal delivery today."

"One day, Monsignor, one day you may go too far. The Germans might often look as if they are pompous buffoons, but they should never be underestimated. You represent a threat to them. You are a direct threat to Colonel Kammler. I believe that you have become a personal target of the man. It has become deeply personal, at least, for him. I hope that the same feeling does not hold true for you."

"I know, I was lucky. I also realize that I cannot take the chance of ever returning to the Palazzo Doria, or even to be found outside of that blasted white line that surrounds the Vatican grounds. No, Damian, I will have to communicate almost solely by way of written correspondence. We will have to employ only our most trusted and reliable couriers. I will, of course, continue to occupy my customary post on the steps of St. Peter's. After all, appearances have to be maintained. We should utilize the minimum number of couriers possible. What do you think, Damian?"

Father Lillard silently envisioned Genevieve Alviano. The young woman could certainly be trusted, and she was always reliable. The Contessa had repeatedly vouched on her behalf on a number of occasions. Lillard, himself, knew the girl possessed a cool and even demeanor and was steady in all situations. "Monsignor, is there anything else you would like for me to do? I do think the precautions you have just mentioned are good and should be implemented straightaway."

"No, Damian. I do believe that will be all for now. Thank you."

* * *

The newly instituted correspondence system seemed to work well until the day O'Reilly received word that Kammler was preparing for another raid on Prince Della Massa. In his office, he had in his possession a variety of forged identity cards. O'Reilly selected those that matched the profiles of the Prince, his wife, and his daughter. He also attached a note addressed to Della Massa, letting him know of the impending raid. The ID cards were then dispatched to Palazzo Doria by Father Damian Lillard.

Just prior to Father Damian leaving on his mission, O'Reilly had instructed him, "Damian, you must hand these cards over to the Prince only or to his wife. Do not entrust them to anyone else, even to members of his household staff."

"It will be done at once, Monsignor."

* * *

The failure to capture Monsignor O'Reilly resulted in Helmut Kammler changing course in his approach. Perhaps, he could reutilize the services of that deliveryman. "What was his name? Gugliemo... something... Cardi. Yes, it was one Gugliemo Cardi. A wormy and weak little man. Kammler would provide Cardi with another opportunity to assist him in the capture of the wily Irish Monsignor.

"Cardi, I have brought you here for the purpose of allowing you another chance to assist me. What do you say? As you have seen for yourself, you have been kept alive. I could just have easily had you disposed of by now. Do you not think that I have been rather generous?" Kammler oozed his comments in his most oily and unctuous way.

Gugliemo Cardi stood in front of Helmut Kammler visibly frightened. His knees practically knocked together. The short, balding, out of shape old man was dressed in what could only be charitably described as rags. He feared for his life, his wretched and near worthless life. He was in fear for the lives of his family as well. What could he do? What should he do? He knew he would buckle under and submit to what this SS man wanted him to do.

Kammler sat across from Cardi, drumming his fingers along the table top. A portrait of Adolf Hitler hung on the wall behind Kammler. "Well? I am waiting. Do not try my patience for too long, Cardi. What will it be? If you should decline my offer, I am afraid that you know what your fate will be. If you should accept, then, you can expect to remain alive. At least, for a little while longer."

Cardi stood mutely and reluctantly agreed. "Si, Herr Kammler, I will do as you have so graciously requested of me."

"Good, Now, this is what I want you to do. Listen, Cardi, and listen very carefully. I want you to personally contact Monsignor O'Reilly. You can easily do this when the man is walking alongside the white boundary demarcation line that surrounds the Vatican. Find some pretext to meet with him. I need for you to get the Monsignor to cross over that line. Do you understand, Cardi?" Kammler was now nearly shouting at the poor and trembling little Italian.

"Pretext, sir? I do not understand this pretext," mumbled Gugliemo Cardi.

Kammler sighed in exasperation. He had not fully realized that this stupid peasant was uneducated and virtually illiterate. "An excuse, Cardi. Tell him that you have an urgent need to seek help for your niece, who is gravely ill. Tell him anything."

"But, sir, I do not have a niece who is sick."

Kammler again raised his eyes to the ceiling. "Do not try my patience, Cardi. It is not unlimited. Just pretend to the good father that she is ill. Now, get out of here before I change my mind and decide to use someone else and cast you out into the nether reaches. One more thing, Cardi. You had better succeed this time. I do not have to tell you what the penalty for failure will be."

The next morning a thoroughly cowed and quivering Gugliemo Cardi stood with Helmut Kammler and other SS men on the first floor of a building located close to Saint Peter's Cathedral. The SS Colonel looked out of the window to see a scene of scurrying people going about their daily activities. In all probability just trying to get by another day during this interminable and unending war. Amongst them were some German soldiers meandering around some of the few remaining market stalls and street-side vendors. The sky was a hazy, leaden gray, so typical in late November in Rome. Kammler continued to gaze outward, when he turned toward Cardi. "Look here, Cardi. You are to make your way to Saint Peter's Cathedral where Monsignor O'Reilly is usually situated. Approach him with the message about your niece. Is that clear? Now, do you understand what you are to say?"

"Si, Herr Kammler. I am to say that my niece is very ill, and could he go and see her. That is correct, is it not?" asked the trembling old man.

"Correct. Now, on your way, Cardi. Remember, you have a lot riding on the success of your assignment," replied Kammler in a baleful manner.

Gugliemo Cardi started to take his first tentative steps when Kammler suddenly turned and said, "Wait, Cardi! I have just been thinking about your message for the Monsignor. I want you to say that your niece is dying. That you are requesting for O'Reilly to visit her personally, so that he may administer last rites. Yes, that is it. Do you understand?"

Cardi stood in front of the glowering German and dolefully nodded his assent.

"Just think. How could the Monsignor turn down a request for last rites? He won't be able to," Kammler mused to himself and his surrounding henchmen. He seemed quite pleased with himself on his sudden inspiration.

Liam O'Reilly was standing just inside of the white demarcation line that was some five hundred feet Saint Peter's front doors. He observed a bent-over old man shambling his way toward the Cathedral. O'Reilly gradually realized that the grizzled old figure was Gugliemo Cardi, the dry goods deliveryman. He was not surprised to Cardi, a man who was frequently seen in and around the Vatican grounds.

Gugliemo Cardi slowly approached the Monsignor and tentatively greeted him. "Buon giorno, Monsignor. Buon giorno."

"And a good day to you as well, Gugliemo, "O'Reilly replied in his still fractured Italian. "What brings you to Saint Peter's today?"

"Oh, Monsignor. I am afraid that I have some bad news. It has been most distressing for me. My niece, Angela, you see, is very, very ill. She has a high fever and, I am afraid, it may be too late. We have tried everything that we could think of, but with the war and everything, we have not been able to do too much. Medicine is just not available. I am so afraid for her," Cardi said in a pitiful and believable way.

"Gugliemo, I am very sorry to hear this about your niece. Would you like for me to visit her? Do you think that I may be able to obtain some of the medicine she needs? I tell you what I will do. I will send Father Damian to see your niece. Where is she now?"

"Near Santa Agnese, Monsignor."

"H-m-m-m...." mused O'Reilly. "That is rather far from here, Gugliemo. You realize that I am not allowed to leave the Vatican grounds. That is why I could send Father Damian. Very discreetly, of course."

The old Italian looked up at O'Reilly with an anguished face and said, "Well, Monsignor, as I have told you, she, Angela, is quite ill. Honestly, I do not think she will make it." Tears were now falling down Cardi's face. He desperately hoped that he looked and sounded convincing to the priest. He hated himself for having to deceive the man, just to save his own miserable life. It was a life that now felt worthless to Cardi. If so, then why was he doing this? "I think she could die at any moment. It would mean so much to me and my family if someone, you perhaps, Monsignor, could administer what will likely be the last rites to Angela."

O'Reilly stood over the diminutive old man and considered his request. It would be wrong and unthinkable for him to refuse such a request as Gugliemo Cardi had just made. "I will try and see your niece as soon as I can. I cannot promise you anything, Gugliemo. As I have said, it would be extremely dangerous for me to leave the Vatican. Return here tomorrow at this time and I will let you know if and when I can visit Angela."

"Grazie, grazie, Monsignor. I am so grateful to you. You are truly a man of God. My family will be so glad to hear this, but...." Cardi said. "I will go now, as I realize that you are a very

116

busy man. Thank you again, Monsignor." Cardi made a slight genuflection in front of O'Reilly. He then moved off, effecting a rather quick gait as he did so. It struck O'Reilly as a little odd. The old man was almost running or, at least, as fast as an old man could run.

"I do not know, Monsignor. I smell a rat, a rat with a big swastika on its back. I see the signature of Herr Kammler all over this," Father Damian expressed in a grave tone to O'Reilly.

"Perhaps, you are right, but I still feel at a loss. After all, it is the man's niece," replied O'Reilly.

"I was not aware that Cardi had a niece living in Rome. From what I have heard it is unclear as to how much of a family he has in the city. In my opinion, it would be a mistake. Should the Germans apprehend you outside of Vatican territory, well, it would be curtains for you and the entire organization. Also, they may not be satisfied with just taking you into custody. They may just kill you outright."

"I don't think so, Damian. I believe they would try to wring out everything I know. It would not be pleasant," said O'Reilly. The two men were standing at the window of the Monsignor's study. Below them could be seen scatterings of individuals going about their daily lives. At that moment, they observed Rosanna Vallone walking hurriedly toward their building.

"Buon giorno, Father Damian, Monsignor O'Reilly. I was hoping you might have a moment so that I could speak with you about the… operation," Rosanna said slightly out of breath.

"Buon giorno to you, my dear Contessa, what has you so concerned?" O'Reilly replied.

"Well, Monsignor, Major Matthews and Sergeant Durval have been in my home for a longer period of time than we had originally anticipated. Not that that has been a problem. They have both been wonderful guests. The two of them have diligently followed every instruction I have given them. Anyway, we are being overwhelmed somewhat, with some of the others. The major and the sergeant are, of course, welcome to stay with me as long as you deem is necessary. My children adore them. The major, err Robert, as even taken on the role of a surrogate father. Nevertheless… I know I am rambling, but something will have to be done soon. If we should get too many men and if we don't have enough safe houses for them, we will wind up in a grave situation."

"I know, Rosanna. I know and I appreciate what you have just told me about your concerns. I fully understand and I am trying to acquire additional funding so that we can obtain more hiding places. For the time being, we will have to do the best that we can," O'Reilly responded sympathetically. He stood against a walnut-stained bookcase which contained many volumes on a whole host of subjects that O'Reilly liked reading about.

"Are you going to tell the Contessa about you most recent proposition, Monsignor?" interjected Father Lillard, who had heretofore been silent in the discussion between O'Reilly and Rosanna Vallone.

"Proposition? What proposition, Monsignor?" questioned a now startled and slightly alarmed Rosanna. Her face reflected her concern.

"What have you gotten yourself into this time? I hope it is not another one of your ridiculous disguises. You know, Monsignor, you are not on the stage performing Shakespeare."

"Yes, Rosanna. It is true that I have only just realized what my true vocation is. To be on stage. Of course, it does not have to be Shakespeare. It might well be Gilbert and Sullivan," mused a smiling O'Reilly. Father Damian could only raise his eyes to the heavens.

"Monsignor, please, what is it?" she pleaded.

Father Damian then proceeded to tell her of the request of Gugliemo Cardi and his supposedly dying niece.

"I wasn't aware that Cardi had any nieces here in Rome. I do not believe that he has much family here. I think, along with Father Damian, that this could be a trap set by our old friend, Colonel Kammler. If it were me, I would not go. Rumor has it that Signore Cardi may have been turned by the Germans," Rosanna continued. "Some time ago he was arrested by the Gestapo. He was held for a short time and, then, suddenly released. It always sounded fishy to me."

"I did not realize that he had been arrested," said a surprised Monsignor O'Reilly.

Rosanna continued, "The word on the street is that Cardi may have provided the Germans with information which very nearly led to your capture by Kammler at Prince Della Massa's home. I would not trust him, Monsignor. Would you like for me ask discreetly more about Signore Cardi's recent activities?"

"No, no, Rosanna. I do not want to set off any possible alarm bells if I can help it. Damian, please leave word with Gugliemo Cardi tomorrow that I will be unable to visit his niece, most regrettably. Tell him that the Holy Father has enlisted my services for a most important task in the Church. Also, tell him that should his niece's condition continue to decline, then, I will arrange for a priest to attend to her spiritual needs," concluded O'Reilly.

"Yes, of course. Is there anything else that I should tell Cardi, Monsignor?"

"No, Damian. That is all. And now, Contessa. Thank you for conveying to us about the housing situation. Father Damian and myself will be working on a solution which I hope will help to alleviate some of the backlog. I will be in touch with you soon. Please try to be patient. I know it is hard. Thank you for all that you and your family are doing, Rosanna."

"Grazie, Monsignor. I know that you have many responsibilities and do not need for a hysterical woman, a contessa no less, to add to your burden," Rosanna said. I will bid you good-bye, Monsignor. Good bye Father Damian," she intoned almost pleadingly. There was anguish in her eyes, her lips were pursed, and she had locked her fingers so tightly together that they had bled. Rosanna rose out of her seat and nodded toward O'Reilly and Lillard and silently left the room.

* * *

In early December the weather in Rome turned colder and the air felt bleaker. The first snow had fallen in the Appenine Mountains. A young US Army lieutenant, Jimmy Cefalo, was hiding in a remote village outside the city. Cefalo had been cold and hungry for several days. He had escaped Italian custody in September and had been on the run since. While holed up in the mountains he had met up with a young Yugoslavian air force officer, Rado Racovic, who himself was now working with the Red Cross. Racovic had been able to get hold of a civilian suit for Cefalo. He had also been able to obtain a train ticket for him, which would enable Cefalo to travel from Caserta to Rome. This had been no mean feat as the distance was more than a hundred miles between the two points.

The American had been moved from church to church, and some convents in between, while in Rome. The Yugoslav officer had been able to place Cefalo in one hiding place for eight days. At that moment, his situation had been brought to the attention of Monsignor O'Reilly. The young American met up with O'Reilly at his then current hiding place at Santo Stefano Church. The parish was located on Plebescito Battista.

"Lieutenant Cefalo, it is a pleasure to meet you. I will not say that I have heard great things about you, yet. That is the usual greeting, or one of them, is it not?" asked O'Reilly in a jovial and friendly way. "Now, let us see how we can help you."

Cefalo was immediately taken by this amiable and outgoing man. He felt as if he could trust him implicitly. "Monsignor, I want express my thanks to you for all that had been done on my behalf. I never could have made it this far. And thank you for meeting with me this evening. I realize that you and many others are taking a chance, but I don't think I have anywhere else to turn to. This was probably my last straw," replied a weary Cefalo.

"No, no, you do not have to concern yourself over my well-being, Lieutenant. However, I would like to ask you a few questions about your background. To establish your bona-fides, if you will."

"Of course, Father, err, excuse me, Monsignor. My name is James Cefalo and I am a First Lieutenant in the US Army. I am from Boston, Massachusetts and I am not married," replied Cefalo evenly.

"Where were you captured, son?"

"My platoon was ambushed just outside of Agrigento by the Adolf Hitler Division. We never had a chance, Monsignor. I feel as if I let my men down. That maybe I was too young to have been placed in command. Some of the men were older than me.

I'm not sure that some of them ever really believed in me, trusted me. Do you know what I mean, Monsignor?"

"My son, age does not necessarily convey leadership," O'Reilly answered gently. The two men were sitting in the pastor's office with a pitcher containing lead-tasting ice water between them. "Lieutenant how old are you?"

I'm twenty-one years old, Monsignor. Perhaps, you are right about age, and the lack of wisdom, and so forth. Anyway, I was taken prisoner and ended up in a makeshift prison camp on the mainland soon after."

"When were you captured, Lieutenant?"

"It was about a week or so, I forget, after we first landed at Gela in July."

O'Reilly had wanted to see whether the dates and events coincided with Cefalo's story. Not that he actually believed that Cefalo was a plant, but he could not afford to be too careful. The Germans, and especially Kammler's SS, were quite resourceful and would employ any means to catch him or any member of the Ambrosia Network. But the lieutenant did not look like a German and he, O'Reilly, had a good feeling about this young man. Some of his associates, such as the Contessa and Father Damian, thought him to be too trusting at times, a little too gullible. In any event, he trusted Mr. Cefalo. "All right, Lieutenant, I believe that you have established sufficient proof of your background. After darkness settles in a little more, we will take a short walk. For the time being, you are to remain here. I will return shortly."

"Okay, Monsignor. I am in your hands," replied a grateful Jimmy Cefalo.

It wasn't until late afternoon that O'Reilly returned to Santo Stefano. He brought with him a plain red cotton shirt, gray trousers, and some clerical garb. This was designed to transform Cefalo into a reasonable facsimile of a priest.

"You see, Lieutenant, now you will look every inch of being a priest, Well, nearly so. As for myself, I will also assume the role of a common everyday priest. I do want to call out too much attention to myself. If we are stopped, I will do the talking. It will be a combination of Irish brogue and street-type Italian. It is rather interesting to hear. Well? What do you think?"

"Looks good and sounds good to me, Monsignor," said Cefalo modestly. He had never imagined he would be required to play the role of a priest. If his own old parish priest, Father Barnard, could see him now. Cefalo had always been a problematic and troublesome child to the elderly cleric.

The two men donned their newly acquired dress and O'Reilly commented to Cefalo, "Good. Now, we can go. After we leave the Vatican grounds we shall have to walk a short way to where transportation will be awaiting us. O'Reilly informed the young American that this had been the result of the Monsignor's good working relationship with a member of the British Legation in Rome.

O'Reilly and Cefalo proceeded to make their way to the rendezvous on Via Cellini. The Irish cleric leaned in toward Cefalo and said in a low voice, "Just pretend that you are engaging in conversation with me. Nod your head, so on." The two walked on without encountering any Germans or Fascists.

The vehicle that was to have taken O'Reilly and Cefalo to the German College was nowhere to be seen. O'Reilly looked up and down Via Cellini, but there was no black Alfa Romeo to be seen. The Irishman knew the pair could not afford to linger about on the streets. They would just have to walk the entire distance of some three miles or so.

As the two men silently trudged their way through the Roman streets, it struck O'Reilly in an amusing way, that the gods were apparently with them on that late afternoon. No one, almost no one was to be found crossing their paths. At long last, for both O'Reilly and for Jimmy Cefalo, they had arrived at the Vatican boundary.

At one of the entrances to the Holy See territory, O'Reilly guided the young American inside. They passed a pair of Swiss guards, dressed as they were in their medieval looking trappings. The Monsignor knew both of the men well and was not requested to provide any type of documentation.

Cefalo followed the priest through the streets and alleyways of the Vatican until they stood in front of the German College. The American thought it was amusing that he was being hidden, at least for a little while, in a building with that name. It was quite ironic.

"Lieutenant, allow yourself to relax, just a little. My assistant. Father Damian, is not here at the moment. I will introduce you to him later. I would like to also introduce you, sometime later this evening, to Sir D'Arcy Osborne of the British Legation here in Rome. Sir D'Arcy has been of invaluable assistance to our efforts. I know you will like him the moment you meet him."

All of this information was running its way around inside of Cefalo's head. It seemed as if he had just sat down and nodded off in the Monsignor's office, then he was being roused by O'Reilly.

"Lt Cefalo, it is time we go and see Sir D'Arcy. I realize that you must be tired, but I think it is important that you meet with this man at this time."

Cefalo nodded his cob-webbed head as he tried to pry open his sleep-induced eyes. He got up from the couch he had been semi-reclined in for the better part of the past three hours and followed the Irishman out of the German College and out past the Holy See itself. Their destination was the British Ambassador's residence located in the Santa Maria Hospice.

The Ambassador had been in the midst of enjoying a scotch and soda that he had just mixed for himself. He had always been so proud of his bartending ability. "Ah-h-h, Monsignor O'Reilly and with a guest. Good to see you. Come in, come in, gentlemen. Won't you both join me in a libation. I just mixed for myself the most exquisite scotch and soda."

"Sir D'Arcy? May I introduce you to Lieutenant James Cefalo of the American Army. Lieutenant, it is my distinct pleasure and honor to introduce you to Sir D'Arcy Osborne of the British Embassy."

"Leftenant, it is my honor to meet you. On behalf of the British Government I would like to express my thanks for you and all of the American chaps who have come over to help us in vanquishing the German armed forces."

Cefalo had not uttered a word yet in the presence of these two impressive men. "Sir D'Arcy, thank you very much for your warm reception and kind words."

"I understand that you have had a rather trying and long journey on your way to Rome. I can only say that you are now in good hands. The Monsignor here is the best! The absolute best! In any event, you are now in Rome. The Eternal City. I only wish that you would be able to take in some of the many wondrous sights this city has to offer. However, unfortunately you are not here as a tourist."

Cefalo continued to be amazed at the Ambassador. He was also somewhat relieved to see that the man was of a relaxed and jovial nature. He was a fun-loving man. Osborne did not give off the air of the stuffy, haughty, and condescending Englishman that he had expected upon his arrival.

"No, Sir D'Arcy. However, on second thought, I would most appreciate some ice-cold mineral water. I have been rather parched throughout the day. Let me also add my thanks and appreciation to you and your staff on behalf of men like myself."

"Not at all, leftenant. Mineral water, ice-cold it shall be. Perhaps, later we can share a scotch and soda," said Sir D'Arcy as he winked at the American.

At that moment, another man had entered the room and joined the little group. Harold Tittman, The US Ambassador to the Vatican, had stepped out of the shadows. Osborne and Tittman began to question Cefalo about conditions and the overall situation in southern Italy. After a while, Cefalo began to find himself falling asleep, with noticeable yawns. He could not help himself. In the past thirty-six hours he had had virtually no sleep. O'Reilly looked over at the man and sensed that Cefalo was probably exhausted after having gone through his gauntlet of travel. He suggested to Osborne and Tittman that they wrap up the meeting for the night. The two ambassadors could resume their discussion with Cefalo the following day.

Liam O'Reilly accompanied Jimmy Cefalo back to his residence at the German College. The two men retired to the Monsignor's room and began to talk about a variety of things. Despite his being tired, Cefalo found his discussion with the priest very stimulating. He couldn't help but notice O'Reilly's golf clubs lying in their bag against a wall. He made a comment to him that he, too, was a golfer. He had been a member of the

Boston College golf team for two years, prior to his enlistment in the army. They both promised one another a game of golf one day after the war was over.

The next day, O'Reilly had Father Damian take the lieutenant to one of the Ambrosia Network's many safe houses. His roommate would be a French Communist from Marseilles. Cefalo knew, almost from the beginning, that the pair were mismatched. He thought the Frenchman was a security risk, and his pompous manner made Cefalo very uncomfortable. Hector Ledoux was a slovenly individual who almost openly flaunted himself in the apartment room the two men shared. Ledoux would often to go to an open window and lean out, apparently attempting to show himself off to passing young women. As if he were God's gift to the world and to them. Cefalo was going to have to get word to the Monsignor that one of them would have to be moved.

O'Reilly, upon receiving word of Jimmy Cefalo's complaint of Ledoux, made the decision to transfer the American to Rosanna Vallone's flat. At least, this would be for a brief time. The move would, of course, necessitate the moving of Sergeant Durval.

"Damian, I need for you to contact the Contessa. Tell her that she is to move Sergeant Durval to another safe house. Apparently, Lieutenant Cefalo and Monsieur Ledoux are incompatible. I am not sure, but perhaps, Mr Cefalo finds the Communist leanings of Ledoux a problem. However, only convey to her that she is to tell Major Matthews that it has become too dangerous for the sergeant to remain together with him. We will move the lieutenant at an appropriate time from Rosanna's apartment," O'Reilly instructed his assistant.

Lillard nodded his assent to his new assignment. "It will be done at once, Monsignor. Do you think that we should continue to disguise some of our charges as priests when we smuggle them into and out of the Vatican and the safe houses?"

"Yes, it seems to have worked successfully for us thus far. We will continue the practice for as long as we have vestments to spare," O'Reilly imparted with a degree of bonhomie. Thus far, he had been able to hide a number of escapees in the North American College within the Vatican. This sector had remained safe and free of German raids. The college grounds contained an old granary and it was there that O'Reilly had been housing a fair number of escaped prisoners and various refugees from across Europe. "Make sure that Major Matthews and Sergeant Durval, and now Lieutenant Cefalo wear vestments whenever they should be walking around on the streets. This activity should be kept to the absolute minimum, in any event. We should also, periodically, impress upon these men the need to minimize their exposure to unseemly elements, i.e. Germans and Fascists. I realize that they must at times feel as if they are being imprisoned once again, but none of us can afford to take any foolish chances. Not at this stage of the game."

"I will pass this information on to the Contessa, and the other handlers, Monsignor. You are right. We have to maintain our vigilance. Colonel Kammler and his SS men would just love to see us all twisting at the ends of long ropes," Damian replied with foreboding. The young cleric was devoted to O'Reilly and to the Church. He had only recently felt himself being more on edge and tense. He went about his daily tasks and duties seeming to be always looking over his shoulder. It could be dangerous, should any sharp-eyed Nazis be lurking around.

"How is our correspondence situation, Damian?" O'Reilly asked, breaking into Father Damian's wandering mind. The Monsignor had set up a new communications network so that families of the men in hiding could send word to loved ones back home. The letters were sent by the men's relatives to the Red Cross in Rome. An elderly widow worked there. The woman had been a good friend of the Monsignor for many years. Letters that she spotted that were addressed to the escaped men were put aside. A courier, such as Genevieve Alviano, would deliver them to O'Reilly's office in the German College.

"I believe it is going along fine, Monsignor. Signora Lucca is doing very good work and, of course, she is always being most discreet."

"That is good to hear, Damian. We may have to cut back on the volume of correspondence. We are not the Royal Mail Service. The number of men has been increasing steadily. Too much of this kind of trafficking could send up a red flag. We do not know if the Red Cross office has been penetrated by Kammler's SS intelligence unit. Please pass the word, Damian."

Liam O'Reilly had good reason for concern as, indeed, the numbers of escapees had been continuously growing, with no apparent end in sight. Word had just been received that, at least, fifty more men, who had once been in the same camp as Robert Matthews and Sergeant Durval, were making their way toward Rome. It was as if everyone knew where to go if they wanted to get out of Italy. And the Vatican was their travel office. Could the Germans fail to possibly know as well? These new men would have to be handled most carefully and discreetly or an opportunity might present itself to Colonel Kammler and his not so merry SS men to crush the Network. And, O'Reilly's neck would be the first in the noose.

The Monsignor had sent word of this development to Sir D'Arcy Osborne. In his note to the British Ambassador, O'Reilly had requested a sum of five thousand lire for the accommodation of these new escapees. The money would be delivered to O'Reilly by Robert Matthews. Matthews would, in turn, become the focal point for this group. The American officer had proven himself to be entirely competent, reliable, and trustworthy. What was more, he showed that he was of an upright character, at least, according to Rosanna Vallone. The Monsignor had begun to suspect that something was possibly brewing between the two. He had noticed the wistful way the woman's face changed whenever Matthews' name was mentioned. Well, that would be only natural. The Contessa was still a vibrant and attractive woman. The major was a strapping and handsome man. Back to business, O'Reilly would see that the money was used to procure additional food, clothing, and miscellaneous articles.

Just to be sure, O'Reilly decided to summon Harold Tittman, the American Charge D'Affaires at the Vatican.

"Yes, Monsignor. I just received your note earlier today. I got here as soon as I could," said a winded Charge.

"I appreciate that, Harold. I have asked you here because I have a request to make of you, and it is most important," O'Reilly began. The grandfather clock struck on the hour of 3:00 PM. The sound reminded the American diplomat as a note with an ominous foreboding.

"Yes, of course, Monsignor. Anything that I can do is yours for the asking."

"Harold, I need for you to find out some background information on Major Matthews. The reason for this is that, before I can entrust this man with what I have planned for him, I would feel better having his, as you might say, his bona-fides confirmed. How long do you think this might take you?"

Tittman sat a little straighter in his chair. "You don't suspect Matthews as being an agent do you, Monsignor? As far as getting the information you want, I am not sure. My communications here in the Vatican are rather limited. I suppose I could request the services of Sir D'Arcy. I will have to get back to you on this, Monsignor," said a surprised and somewhat baffled Harold Tittman. The two men then concluded their business. O'Reilly was still uncertain as to his complete faith and trust in Matthews. He felt ashamed as the major had given no cause in all of his actions involving the escape operation. O'Reilly had, often on impulse, trusted far lesser men in the past. He still fervently believed that the American major was all that he appeared to be, but he had to be absolutely sure.

The Monsignor then went back to his daily review of prayer selections for the remainder of the week. His mind still refused to focus itself on even this simple task.

* * *

At his SS Headquarters on Via Wolkonsky, Helmut Kammler was considering his next plan of action. Twice now, he had come ever so close to nabbing O'Reilly and, twice, the wily priest had slipped the noose. There had to be a way; some way. This chase had long since turned into a personal contest, a duel. One that Kammler was not winning, and that would not do. That would not do at all. Senior SS men in Berlin were watching this contest, this battle of wits, even if they didn't have all the details. And, they would expect results. There was no tolerance for failure. Not in the SS. Should Kammler fail to catch the Irishman, he might expect to have Kaltenbrunner have him shipped to the Russian front.

"Krieger!" he barked. "Come in here!"

"Yawohl, Herr Obersturmbannfuhrer," piped up Albert Krieger in a most farcical and obsequious manner. He always used Kammler's full military title when he sensed that the man was in a bad mood. Today, the clouds were extremely dark. In any event, Krieger felt ridiculous in having to behave in this way. He had his dignity. This was beneath him.

"Krieger, I have been giving the matter of the Irish priest a lot of thought."

"What else was new," thought Krieger.

"Yes. A lot of thought and, perhaps, we have been looking at the problem in the wrong way. Rome is a very large city and we cannot cover every nook and cranny. Not with the manpower we have available to us at the moment," Kammler had continued. "It is likely that O'Reilly would require the assistance from his flocks throughout the city. If we were to concentrate our attention on some of the parishes, something may fall out of the trees. We will raid those churches that are most contiguous with the Vatican. Then, we will expand the effort outward from these points from this inner circle. In other words, we will push outwards in concentric circles."

"One or more of these parish priests must be in league with the man, if even in a secondary role. In addition, I want intensive and close surveillance of the British Ambassador, Sir D'Arcy Osborne, and Mr Harold Tittman, the American Charge D'Affaires. Our sources have Indicated that these three men have been conducting a rather intimate relationship of late. Well? What do you think, Krieger?"

Krieger stood there stunned. He had never expected that Kammler would ever consider asking him for his opinion. He did think that his chief had raised some good points. His plan of action also seemed to be sound. "It looks like a good plan, sir. A good plan. When do you want to commence these raids?"

"I want them to begin by tomorrow evening. Sometime after midnight when little is stirring or should be stirring."

"I will have the surveillance of Sir D'Arcy and Mr Tittman increased immediately."

"Good, Krieger, very good. And now, I have to look forward to having dinner this evening with my wife. I am so looking forward to it," Kammler let drop facetiously. "It might be worthwhile if the woman had anything of even the most remote importance to say."

Krieger had heard this theme a number of times before. He knew that Kammler practically hated his wife; that he could not stand to be in her company for too long a period of time.

Krieger had been introduced to Angela several months before. He had viewed her as a charming and rather beautiful woman. Her blond hair and well-endowed figure had impressed him. Sometimes Krieger would find himself fantasizing about having sex with Angela Kammler.

About two months ago, while attending some meaningless SS function, Albert Krieger had found himself staring at Angela. He had not even realized it until he noticed Angela staring back at him. She had offered him a warm and ingratiating smile, and she had pointed with her eyes as if to say, "Meet me outside." Krieger had felt himself subconsciously hardening, right there in the room full of SS big-shots, including Helmut Kammler.

Krieger had made his excuses and left the party. As he strode through the main hallway he heard a whispered, "S-p-p-p."

Hiding in an alcove was Angela Kammler. As soon as Krieger had leaned into the darkened enclosure he felt himself being pulled in further. Angela attacked Krieger with an assault led by her tongue. She immediately thrust it into his mouth. Krieger brought his hands to her lusty breasts as if by second nature. "We cannot do this, at least, not here," he at last managed to say.

"I want you and I want you right now, not tomorrow," Angela breathed into his ear, when she was not sampling it with her teeth. "I know that you want me. I have seen it in your eyes. You want to sample my breasts. And I want your erect and hardened cock inside of me."

"But what of your husband? If he found out about this he would have me shot, and probably by his own hand." Krieger was torn. On the one hand, he wanted to fuck the shit out of Angela Kammler, and on the other, he did value his life.

"Alright, Albert, you may be right. But I do want you to fuck me in the very near future. I will arrange for us to have a liaison when we can fulfill our sexual fantasies." Angela had backed away a little from Krieger. He could now detect that her breasts were heaving within Angela's chest. He could also see that her nipples were fully aroused.

Angela noted that Krieger was fully hardened. She did want his cock. She wanted it badly, but they would have to be discreet. Very discreet. She knew that she and Helmut were practically finished. They would have to end their sham of a marriage sooner or later. And why shouldn't she indulge herself with another man while she had the chance. Angela vowed that she would give Albert Krieger the sexual adventure of a lifetime.

As Krieger swirled these thoughts around in his brain, he was half-heartedly listening to Kammler carry on. He and Angela had still not yet consummated their sexual mission. It would be good to hump Angela. It would be a real knife in the ribs to Kammler. To think, that he, Albert Krieger, was literally and figuratively fucking the shit out of the man's wife.

"Anyway, that is my problem. That will be all for now, Krieger. Snap to it. I am really tired of all the cat and mouse, cloak and dagger games of this O'Reilly affair. I want to end this thing, and soon!"

In the meantime, Harold Tittman had been able to secure, through the good offices of Sir D'Arcy Osborne, the information that O'Reilly had requested. Satisfied with what Tittman had been able to confirm, Liam O'Reilly now felt reassured that he had found the man he needed to step into the role of director of operations for the Network.

Thursday evening loomed dark for anyone venturing about in the streets of Rome. This would only apply to German troops and Fascist police, and any authorized Roman citizens, with the curfew still in effect. Albert Krieger had been watching the church at Santa Rosaria, located between the Castel Sant'Angelo, the old Roman fortress, and the main hospital in the city. Krieger and his men had been watching the church entrance for some two hours, until he finally gave the order to move in.

An SS sergeant knocked heavily on the main outside door. The noise caused the pastor, Father Alberto Ruggiero, to awaken startled out of a sound sleep. The Father proceeded to make his way forward to see what the disturbance was about. The pounding persisted as Ruggiero, dressed only his nightclothes, hurried to the front door.

Albert Krieger and his men rushed inside the church as soon as Father Ruggiero had opened the door. "What is it that you want, sir?" questioned a frightened and bewildered Ruggiero.

"Stand aside, priest! This is police business," Krieger responded brusquely. "Scharffuhrer Krebs, take some men and go the rectory office and go through the files. Search everything!"

"But, sir, this is Church property. You cannot just barge in and conduct an unwarranted search. Do you have a warrant?" protested a now angry Father Ruggiero.

"Listen, priest. We do not need a search warrant and we don't have to explain anything to you. Who do you think you are and where do you think that you are?" hissed Krieger as he looked at the defiant priest as if he had lost his mind. "You may consider this as inviolate property, but the SS does not!"

Within the hour, Krebs and his men brought forward several wooden boxes of files. "Very good, Krebs. We will take this material back to headquarters, so that we can comb through them more thoroughly," said Krieger. Turning to Ruggiero he spat out, "Let me warn you, priest! You had better watch your step. I warn you! One false step and we will arrest you. I can assure you it will not be a pleasant experience."

Father Ruggiero was left standing with the departure of the SS men. He would have to get word of this outrage to Monsignor O'Reilly as soon as possible. The nerve of that SS officer and his thugs. The Church of Santa Rosaria was everything to him, and to his parishioners. In the midst of this awful and destructive war, in the midst of their crushing and grinding poverty, and in the midst of their absolute despair, the people of Santa Rosaria, at the least, had had something that they could hold on to. Something with which to warm their desolate hearts. Now, all of that might be snatched away soon. Ruggiero had always been aware that he would have to tread carefully in his activities with Monsignor O'Reilly and the Ambrosia Network.

* * *

"What did you come up with, Krieger, on your mission this evening?" inquired a piqued Helmut Kammler.

"Nothing of much significance, I'm afraid, sir. But we did remove several boxes of Santa Rosaria's files. My men are sifting through them at this moment," replied Krieger.

"Who is the pastor at this Santa Rosaria church?"

"A Father Alberto Ruggiero, sir. He has been at the church for the past five years. He hails from the Amalfi coast region. A small town called Positano.

"What else do we know about this priest?" continued Kammler as he sat drumming his fingers on his desk. "Has he been known to have been an activist within the Church? Anything like that?"

"Father Ruggiero comes from an impoverished family, sir. Their great hope in life had always been for the good father to be ordained a priest into the Catholic Church. Apart from that, it is believed that he has always kept his nose clean."

"Harrumph-h-h!" snorted Kammler. "I want twenty-four hour surveillance of this priest and his church. I want to know of his every move. You are to utilize any of our informants to assist in this operation. And, I want to know immediately if anything should turn up from the Santa Rosaria files. Even the smallest, seemingly insignificant detail."

* * *

Several weeks later Angela Kammler was finally able to engineer her rendezvous with Albert Krieger. She had booked a room, under an assumed name, at the Bernini Bristol Hotel. Her husband had unexpectedly received a summons to appear at an SS meeting in Milan three days prior.

On this night Angela would not need a dinner as a preparatory foreplay to her sexual hijinks she would be engaging in with Albert Krieger. Tonight, would be one of raw and passionate sex between a woman desperate for it and a man trying to kill two birds with one stone.

Angela had been waiting for Krieger's arrival at the Bernini Bristol dressed only in the flimsiest of nightgowns. Her breasts poured unhinged, Angela was sure this would get her lover's libido motor humming at first sight.

Krieger walked into the hotel room on the fifth floor, his face slightly flushed. He certainly hoped this night would be worth it. His first sight of the near naked Angela put any doubts to rest. He could feel his penis bulging within his uniform pants. He rushed over to his paramour, but she raised up her arms to halt him.

"Albert, there will be plenty of time for that. I think that we should indulge our palates in an aperitif." Angela indicated a chilled bottle of Lillet on the table next to them. Krieger took the hint and reached for the bottle and poured for both of them into two small brandy glasses. All that were available. He did not care, for as soon as the pair dispensed with their drinks then they could fling themselves at one another with animalistic abandon.

Six

The Contessa

The morning of January 2nd, 1944 dawned cold and crisp. A hazy blue sky lingered over the city of Rome. At precisely 8:00 AM, a black Mercedes-Benz sedan and a six ton Deutz army truck pulled up at the curb of Via Frattina. Stepping out of the sedan was Albert Krieger and Untersturmfuhrer Karl Hansen. Krieger nodded to several of the SS troopers, who had dismounted from the truck, giving them the signal to deploy themselves around the building. Krieger and Hansen led a second detachment of six men into the building.

Krieger led the way through the apartment building and up the stairs to the first floor, stopping in front of the door of the apartment of Rosanna Vallone. He knocked on the door with his gloved right hand.

Inside the apartment, the Contessa was somewhat surprised at the knocking and the accompanying noise of what sounded to her like several men wearing heavy boots. Rosanna looked around the room quickly, making sure that anything compromising had been put away. She had tried to eliminate any indication that she had had any guests in the flat.

Rosanna smoothed out her dress and went to the door and opened it, finding herself facing two SS officers and a squad of troopers. Krieger and Hansen said nothing as they brushed past her and their men fanned out through the apartment.

"What may I ask are you doing, sir? What is wrong?" muttered a startled and frightened Contessa to Albert Krieger.

At first he ignored her. "Your papers, please!" Krieger spat out to her, not even bothering to address her with any kind of courtesy.

"Yes, yes, of course, sir. I have them here in my desk."

Krieger went over to the desk, where Rosanna had retrieved the required paperwork, and was handed them. He scanned them over with only a rudimentary interest and gave them back to her. "How many people live with you?" he demanded.

Rosanna spread her hands toward the table and said, "Three, as you can see here, sir. What, may I ask, is this all about?"

"I see three settings, but only two people, you and what I am assuming is your daughter," Krieger shot back.

"Oh, that. The third place is for my son, who has just stepped out. He is to be back shortly," replied Rosanna defensively. She was trying to sound as convincing as she could possibly muster for this German.

Krieger's men had searched all of the rooms, but had come up with nothing of interest. In the living room, a trooper was browsing his way through of the family's picture albums. Ariana stood nearby trying to contain her growing alarm. She hoped she was not showing that she was perspiring, despite the fact that it was rather cool in the room. Another SS man was flipping through a collection of record albums. One of them was a Mitch Miller record containing the hymns of the US Marine Corps and the US Navy. The SS man might be intrigued to find this, but he, apparently, never noticed the record.

Krieger and Hansen saw that nothing more was to be gained by any further searching. Their men were growing restless. Krieger was aware that they had other apartments to inspect, so he sent the men out. He turned to Rosanna, "I am sorry to have disturbed you Contessa Vallone. I must say that you have a lovely apartment, and a very charming and attractive daughter. She reminds me of my sister, Grete. Unfortunately, she was killed in a British bombing raid last year. She was only sixteen years old. In any event, I bid you both good-bye," Krieger said almost cordially. He then bowed slightly at the waist and headed for the door.

If the SS captain had thought that he might cause Rosanna to feel some degree of guilt concerning his remark about his own sister and her death, it did not, she even doubted that the story might have been true.

The departure of the SS men allowed her and Ariana to breathe a deep sigh of relief. It still took them several minutes before they could finally slow their heart beats down to a more normal level. "Well, that was rather interesting, don't you think, Ariana?"

"No, Mother, I am still shaking like a leaf. Did you happen to notice that one of those Germans was looking through the records, but apparently never noticed the Mitch Miller one. The one with the American marine and army songs. Not to mention the Louis Armstrong one. You know how the Nazis think that jazz music is decadent. That could have been bad for us, would it not have, Mother?" the young woman said.

"Yes, you may be right. It might well have looked suspicious to them. Anyway, they are gone, and we are safe."

"But, Mother, do you think that the Germans suspect anything about Major Matthews and Sergeant Durval?"

"I surely hope not. We will just have to stay strong, Ariana. This is something we have to do. By helping to hide these unfortunate men, we are keeping them out of the clutches of the Germans," answered Rosanna emphatically.

"Yes, Mother, I agree with you, but the risks have been mounting. The Nazis have been rounding up more and more people every day. The whole thing is getting on my nerves. I can't wait for the Allies to get to Rome."

"I know, Ariana. I cannot wait either, but we will just have to remain patient," Rosanna said soothingly.

"Mother, I also suspect that you are anxious so that you and the major can be more open about your relationship," Ariana said to her mother with one arched eyebrow.

Rosanna felt as if cold water had been thrown on her by her daughter's comment. She and Robert had always tried to be most discreet in how they spoke to one another and with their behavior with each other.

"Mother, you cannot be surprised. I do have eyes and I am old enough to be able to interpret the emotions of other human beings. I see the way that the two of you look at one another.

Robert, the major seems to hang on your every word. Mother, I love you dearly, and it is okay. I know that you miss papa greatly, as do Gaetano and myself. But you have to move on. Robert is a fine man. He is a good man. And, he along with many other Americans have come here to help us and Italy."

Rosanna looked at her suddenly mature daughter and realized she was no longer a child. "Ariana, you have grown up before me. I never realized that you possessed such insight. I also did not realize how obvious I have been with Robert. Well, I care for him very much. He is a good and fine man. I am glad you have told me how you feel. I trust that Gaetano feels the same way. As far as moving on, as you have said I am still not sure. At least, not yet."

Rosanna knew that they all had been fortunate to that point in time. Only a late heads-up warning from one of her neighbors, who had been aware of Rosanna's hiding of prisoners of war, some twenty minutes before Albert Krieger and company had arrived at her door. She had been able to move Matthews and Durval out of her building just in the nick of time. The transfer had been facilitated with the assistance of two young women who also lived in Rosanna's building. The girls were part of the Ambrosia Network and served as a stand-by emergency service for just such an occasion. The men, accompanied by the young women, would not attract attention. At least, not as much as if they had traveled alone.

The German raids had been ordered by Helmut Kammler, who also had good reason to believe that a secret radio transmitter was being used in the vicinity of the Contessa's residence. The noblewoman had known that the Germans were working alongside a special Italian police unit called the "Kochel Gang". Pietro Kochel was their charismatic twenty-five year old leader. His men were a ruthless and cutthroat bunch of thugs who traversed Rome often in search of Jews, Communists, anti-Fascists, and escaped Allied prisoners of war.

The month of December 1943 saw a spike in the Underground's resistance activities. A German officer had been shot dead as he had walked out of a hotel on sunny afternoon. Eight soldiers had been killed as a result of a bomb that had been hurled by an Italian operative while riding on a bicycle. None of the perpetrators had been caught by the authorities.

Rosanna Vallone knew that the Germans and, particularly Helmut Kammler, were very angry over these brazen attacks. They saw them as an outright challenge to their authority. She also knew that pressure from the Germans would mount in the coming weeks.

Father Damian Lillard paid a brief visit to Rosanna's home during an afternoon in the immediate aftermath of the SS raid. She told the father of the German operation in great detail. Lillard took the news not unduly alarmed, but he knew this meant that greater precautions would have to be taken in the future. "Contessa, I have some new instructions for you. You will have to move Sergeant Durval to another safe house here in Rome. And it must be done by this Friday."

"Why? Has something gone wrong?" she asked.

"No, not per se, Rosanna. We have just taken in another American officer and we need to relocate him away from the German College, where we have him now."

"What shall I tell Sergeant Durval?" asked a clearly mystified Contessa Vallone. "Do you not think this might look suspicious?"

"You are just to tell him that the situation had become more unsettled. Do not tell him that this new American is to take his place. And you are not to reveal this to Major Matthews, as well. At least, not yet," Father Lillard continued. He was trying not to sound too authoritarian. He felt a great personal admiration and appreciation for Rosanna and her two children. Lillard was all too aware of the danger they had placed themselves in.

"All right, Father, you can inform our friend 'Golf' that I will see to it in regard to the sergeant. I am not sure how much longer myself and my children can continue. Our nerves have been stretched to the breaking point. The recent German raid on my home has only underscored the tension we are under," Rosanna lamented as she twisted her fingers together in her lap. She was clearly agitated, much more so than Lillard had ever seen in her before.

"I understand, Rosanna. We are all under great strain. Hopefully, it will not be for very much longer."

"The Allies do not appear that they will be soon approaching Rome. Do they, Father? They have been hammering away at Monte Cassino to no avail, to this point," she continued wearily. "I am sorry for my outburst, Father. It is rather unlike me. The strong and steady contessa. Forgive me, I just lost my head for a moment. I…. will take care of the sergeant as you have asked."

* * *

The following week, in the midst of a driving rainstorm, Pietro Kochel's men, supported by SS troopers, entered the Lombard Seminary, without warning. Among them was Albert Krieger. The seminary had a sign declaring it was Vatican property and could not be searched. The note had been signed by General Rainer Stahel, the German Army commander of Rome.

The Kochel and SS men fanned out and began an intensive search of the premises. The rector, Monsignor Otto Klabisch, had been in the midst of performing an evening prayer service. He was taken away peremptorily and without explanation. As this scene had unfolded, several hidden Allied prisoners had been able to get away to safety.

Another raid was simultaneously conducted at the Institute of Oriental Studies, where more than twenty Jews had been in hiding. These fortunate individuals had been able to make their getaway through the use of a pre-arranged escape drill.

The searches had continued through the early evening hours. Kochel's men had taken everything and anything of value. They had also arrested eighteen men and women, some of whom were Jews. The raids on the Vatican properties raised alarm bells within the Holy See. The Pope was concerned as to whether Vatican buildings should be continued to be used for housing prisoners. And were the Germans truly planning to occupy Vatican City? His Eminence had learned, through Cardinal Maglione, that the SS was set to increase its force from four hundred men to more than 2,000 in Rome. The source of this information, an Italian colonel, had also informed the cardinal that once these additional men were in place, the Germans would then conduct a gigantic operation to search every building within the city. Even Church properties would be included.

Pope Pius XII had been given repeated assurances by Adolf Hitler himself that the Vatican's sovereignty would be respected. He now wondered how truthful those assurances remained. Pius had also learned of what Hitler had told General Karl Wolff, SS commander in Italy, in July of 1943, that he would one day, "clear out that gang of swine," meaning the Holy See and, no doubt. himself. As yet, nothing had happened. Wolff had told Hitler, later in 1943, that an invasion of the Vatican would draw condemnation throughout Italy and from Catholics throughout the world.

Major Robert Matthews had been observing the entire escape operation and was determined that security would have to be increased within the Ambrosia Network. Too many of the escapees and those persons hiding them had become rather cavalier and complacent about security measures. One day he left Rosanna's apartment accompanied by Genevieve Alviano, and went on a tour of the safe houses. Matthews had constantly stressed to the men the need for memorizing the procedures for an escape drill in the event of a sudden and unexpected raid. Matthews had also enacted a vetting system for newly arrived prisoners, in case the Germans tried to plant spies and informers within the network.

"I don't know. I think the whole thing is getting too big. The Germans will eventually catch on and the whole thing will collapse," exclaimed a worried Robert Matthews.

"I think that you sometimes worry too much, cheri. You shouldn't do that," soothed Rosanna Vallone. "You cannot and should not worry so much. After all, you have to keep your head as you have become the de facto leader."

Rosanna had begun calling Matthews "cheri" of late. The Contessa had clearly softened in her demeanor toward him, and toward Sergeant Durval. He had accepted her explanation of having to move Durval elsewhere. It had not appeared to him to have been unreasonable or unusual. Durval had not been happy about receiving the news, having become a virtual sidekick to Matthews. This attractive and mature woman had become the focus of an increasing desire that had formed within himself. He often wondered if she felt the same way toward him. He did not want to move too fast, but every day he felt his desire mounting within his loins. The Contessa would sometimes be dressed in a casual white blouse with a V-neck, and when she leaned forward, as when she was pointing out something to him on a picture or a map, she would reveal her ample endowment. Matthews would feel himself start to perspire and his penis begin to harden. He would shift his weight as if he could conceal his arousal. He thought that she had been aware of this for a while, and at times he also thought she might have been trying to entice him. Matthews did not believe that Rosanna possessed a mean streak, she was just teasing him in a subtle and seductive manner. She had seemed to welcome his lustful attraction for her.

"Roberto, you are married, are you not? What about your wife back in the states? She must be waiting for you," she interjected plaintively.

"Somehow, I don't think so, Rosanna. Our marriage has been quite strained for several years now and my deployment with the army to North Africa was probably the breaking point. Just before my capture at the Kasserine Pass I received a 'Dear John' letter from her. She said our marriage was over, that she was suing me for divorce. She was claiming abandonment. Doesn't that beat all? Anyway is seems as if she has taken up with an army colonel. I guess you could say she had achieved an increase in pay-grade," he said despondently.

Rosanna leaned in closer to him and placed a hand on top of his left hand. He placed his right hand atop hers, their fingers interlocked. He surprised himself at how fiercely he was gripping her hand. "I am so sorry, cheri. You have not spoken very much about your wife or about your inner feelings. You are dealing with a broken heart. You have been devastated," she said to Robert, desperately wishing she could do something to help ease the man of his pain.

"I suppose, but not really. In a way I had been almost glad to have gotten the letter. Mind you, the timing was not good. I don't think that it caused me to get captured. I do believe that my head was clear…. maybe not. Anyway, what is done is done. What about you, Rosanna? You haven't told me much. I mean you have talked about Ariana and Gaetano, but not very much about yourself or…. your husband."

"He was a very kind and gentle man, a good man. I still miss him deeply. I do not think that I have ever gotten over it, his death. I mean completely over it," Rosanna mused as she looked into Robert's rich brown eyes. She thought she saw the inkling of a tear forming. "I have to think about my children now and about keeping them safe. The war and this…." she waved her free hand into the air, "this, with the Kochel Gang and Kammler and his SS goons."

"Are you a religious person, Rosanna?" he asked.

"Not especially. I mean I have great reverence and respect for Monsignor O'Reilly and Father Lillard, and, of course, the Pope. I suppose you could say that I am not quite a lapsed Catholic. On the other hand, neither am I particularly devout. Before the war, I had seen my share of priests who were not, let me say, taking any vows of poverty. These men lived the good life, while the people struggled to get by. And yet, these priests took as much as they could get from these poor and impoverished people. It was disgusting and shameful. How these so-called men of the cloth could ever live with themselves, I do not know. Forgive me for having gone off on my own personal rant."

Robert looked at her and knew at that exact moment that he wanted her. He wanted her at that very moment. He knew it was going to happen. He would make it happen. It would not be rushed. Rosanna did not deserve that. He felt his desire rising within his pants. Rosanna's chest began to heave, ever so slightly. Robert sensed that she too wanted it to happen.

"You and I have suffered from a broken heart. I would like nothing better than to make mad, passionate love to you," she said most tenderly, still tightly clasping Matthews' hands.

"What about the children, Rosanna?"

"Ariana is at her friend's house, she won't be back for several hours. Gaetano is at one of the safe houses and, he, too, is not due back until later this evening."

"I like you, Rosanna. I like you very much. It has probably been so from the moment I first met you."

Rosanna felt the heat rising within her. The nipples on her breasts had become taut and erect. She was warm and moist in her vulva. She was going to cry out, "Take me, take me! Oh, God in heaven, Robert, please take me! Take me now! Take me hard! I am ready for you." Instead, she said, "I like you very much, cheri, very much," she started to rise and looked down at Matthews. She could see that his shaft was bulging in his pants. "I want you, Roberto, but, please, be gentle with me. It has been a long time and I am afraid that I may be out of practice." And with that she slowly led him to her bedroom.

Rosanna went to the windows and drew the drapes closed, blocking out the mid-day light. They now stood facing one another. She slowly removed her blouse and bra, freeing her breasts. Robert's breath caught in his throat at the sight of her spectacular breasts. They were wondrous to him and larger than he had expected. Her nipples were swollen. Robert's penis was growing harder and harder as he continued to stand in front of her, still not moving. He thought he might burst.

"Aren't you going to get started, cheri?" Rosanna asked with a coquettish smile. She knew she was heightening his sexual arousal and she was enjoying it.

Robert began removing his clothes, flinging them onto the floor. Rosanna resumed her disrobing by dropping her skirt and panties. The two slowly approached one another and lightly embraced. Robert brought his right hand to her left breast, slowly massaging it, while they began French kissing. Their tongues probed one another. She took hold of his throbbing penis.

"Let us go to the bed, cheri." They held hands and settled on to the bed on their knees, French kissing again as they embraced. Robert laid Rosanna down gently on to the bed, her calves lying underneath her. Robert's mouth and tongue continued to devour her own. He went to her ears, gently nibbling on them. Rosanna disengaged her legs and felt Robert's throbbing and rock-hard penis on her stomach. They continued French kissing, more feverishly by the moment. He, then, went to her breasts and licked and fondled them, lightly nipping them with his teeth. Their tongues continued to probe one another. She took hold of his penis and began stroking it. Rosanna felt waves of heated passion rolling over and through her body. It had been so long, so long, since she had made love to a man. So long since she had had a man inside of her. Giuseppe, "Beppe", had been the last. He had been a wonderful and gentle lover. A man who had always sought to be tender and loving to Rosanna. It had been important to him to be able to fulfill her sexual needs, as well as his own.

Robert was of a different frame of mind. How different and refreshing Rosanna was from his own cold and chaste wife. He had taken to calling her the "Ice maiden." Lovemaking for her, after the first few years, had been made to seem like a boring chore. At least, to him, that had been the impression. Mary was nothing like Rosanna at all, not in the least. Robert was now on the throes of a sexual ecstasy that he had never before experienced. "I've dreamt of this moment with you, Rosanna, a million times," he moaned.

"I know, cheri, I know. I, too, have been fantasizing about this for a long time as well," she replied languorously.

Robert slowly slid his way down Rosanna's stomach, licking her skin all over. He then went down to her mound. She opened her legs invitingly. It was as if she were saying, "Go ahead. I am ready for you. I want to feel your hot and piercing tongue penetrating to my vulva and beyond." Robert pushed his tongue into her and slowly started to rotate it around the vulva, over and over. Rosanna began to moan softly in indescribable pleasure. She thought she was undergoing an out of body experience. The hot waves kept enveloping her. A light sheen of perspiration had formed on her forehead and face and along her arms. She achieved orgasm, and then, another, as Robert's tongue continued in its exploration. She brought her thighs up and enveloped his head, embracing it. She stroked his upper back and head with her long fingers. There was a trembling feel to them.

After several moments, Robert rose up and moved himself up along Rosanna's body. His mouth went to hers as he inserted his hardened shaft into her. Rosanna had helped to guide him home.

"Just a taste, Rosanna. I don't want to climax, just yet."

Robert began to drive himself slowly into her. She again brought her smooth thighs up and around his hips, her well-toned calves hooking up and over his plunging buttocks. He then reached under her knees and brought them up and over his shoulders. Maintaining the pace of his thrusting. Rosanna had never experienced this technique before, but it felt wonderful. Robert increased his pace for a while, before withdrawing.

Rosanna then mounted herself atop Robert and slowly impaled herself on his stiff shaft. She screwed her eyes shut, her throat swelled outward, and she arched her back and head. She began to thrust slowly up and down, up and down, and then, she began to increase her own pace, drawing down and grinding on Robert's hard cock.

Robert thought he was going out of his mind. This woman was a sexual goddess. "Good God, I never expected this," he thought. Rosanna's bulbous breasts bounced and swayed above him. She clutched at them with her own hands, massaging them, all the while maintaining her own thrusting motion. Robert brought his calloused hands up to hers and entwined them, continuing the mammary massage.

Rosanna achieved another orgasm during her thrusting. She then extracted herself and leaned forward, her breasts met by Robert's mouth. He took them in, one at a time, left-right, right-left, his tongue lathering her taut, tight nipples, and expanding outward to embrace the aureoles. He bit on them lightly. Rosanna was moaning softly. He massaged them over and over.

Robert placed his index finger inside of Rosanna and began rotating it, along with his tongue, deep into her wet and luscious mound. Rosanna was desperately trying to hold off her climax.

Rosanna shrieked out loud a bellowful howl and immediately extricated herself, rolling onto her back. Robert quickly mounted her, his thick, hard, and fully elongated cock slowly and easily penetrated Rosanna. "Easy, cheri, easy. Let us move a little more slowly and…. then," she cooed into his ear.

Robert began to thrust at a slower pace and did so for a little while. He, too, was trying to maintain himself, to some degree. But his desire for Rosanna overwhelmed him. He began to pick up his pace, Rosanna again brought up her well-muscled thighs to grip his hips. Her calves once again clutched above his increasingly thrusting buttocks. She felt her legs begin to flutter. Rosanna dug her fingernails into Robert's muscled and well-developed back. She stroked her fingers along his spine.

He kept driving himself into her, deeper and deeper, pounding into her. He was pulverizing her. And Rosanna could take it, and she wanted more. "Oh-h-h, cheri, yes. Keep it going Fuck me hard! So hard! Faster, faster," she insisted.

Robert increased his pace and Rosanna met his every thrust. She bit on his ears. They French-kissed hard. She bit into his tongue. He continued to drive himself into her like some kind of out of control machine. She had two more orgasms, but she still wanted his cock to keep pounding into her. She would force herself to meet his every thrust. It went on and on, to the point, where she thought Robert might go well right through her. Rosanna and Robert were rapidly perspiring, but they paid no attention to it as they continued their rabid fornication.

Finally, when neither seemed as if they had nothing left to give, Robert shuddered violently as his hot semen burst forth into Rosanna. He was now howling like a banshee, and she was too. They were like a pair of wild animals attacking one another. Rosanna moaned and screamed as she thrashed beneath the weight of her lover. Robert had let out a roar that practically shook the walls. Rosanna's thighs gripped onto Robert's ribs and she squeezed, and squeezed. It had been unbelievable.

Robert continued to thrust into Rosanna, but he gradually began to slow. "Rosanna. I am going to stay inside of you, but we'll roll over together. You mount me, okay?" he said hoarsely.

"Alright, cheri, all right. I think that you just want to see my heaving breasts above you one more time. Am I not correct?" as she looked up at Robert through her hooded eyes.

"Yes, yes. You have figured me out. I'm such a cad." He then rolled over and Rosanna was on top. She rather liked this position as it allowed her to be in the dominant role. Robert viewed her breasts and her face. His penis still throbbed, still pulsated within Rosanna. She began to bump and grind, her breasts bouncing wildly. She gripped them and shut her eyes, and continued to take in the pleasure of this man.

Robert brought himself up until he was facing her breasts and sucked on them. He took in the nipples and as much of each breast as he could fit into his mouth. Rosanna's hands went through his hair. They French-kissed again. She kept driving herself down onto his still erect penis. She wondered how long he could stay hard. She wouldn't mind finding out.

At last, she was finally forced to give out and collapsed onto Robert's chest. "No more, cheri. No more." Robert, still inside of her, rolled over again and started to penetrate her. Rosanna tried mightily to meet his effort as she brought her legs part way up. "No, no, that is all I have, for the moment, Robert. We can continue things later," she said exhaustedly.

Robert removed himself and plopped onto his back, alongside Rosanna. "I suppose at this point we should indulge in a cigarette. Is that not traditional, cheri?" she asked.

"It seems to be in the movies, anyway," Robert replied.

Rosanna reached over to her nightstand and opened the top drawer. She removed a packet of cigarettes, an Italian brand, and a box of wood-stemmed matches. She extracted one and handed it to Robert. Rosanna then picked one out for herself.

Robert had been impressed by the way Rosanna had removed the cigarettes from the packet. She had deftly tapped the pack against one hand until a couple were protruding. "I didn't know you smoked, Rosanna?"

"I usually don't. Only after special occasions. And this, kind sir, was what I consider to have been a very special occasion. Do you not agree?"

"It was very special for me, too, and it was very tender, Rosanna."

"As it was for me, cheri."

Robert struck a match and lit Rosanna's cigarette first, and then, brought the burning match to his. "Oh, I think we should use an ashtray. We would not want to start a fire. There has been enough smoke in this room already, don't you think, Roberto?" Rosanna commented metaphorically. She lithefully rose from the bed and walked over to a dresser. Robert gazed at her backside, it was lovely, in continued wonder. He was now convinced that he was in love with Contessa Rosanna Vallone. He would not rush in about this with her, not just yet. He would give her time.

Rosanna returned with the ashtray in her hand, her wondrous breasts swaying upon her chest. She sat back down, placing the ashtray between them. They continued smoking in silence. Only the tick of the clock on the nightstand breaking the silence.

"Rosanna, I have noticed during my time here in Italy that some women, especially those in the countryside do not shave under their arms, and some do not even shave their legs," Robert said suddenly.

"And you find this disturbing, my prince? Is that why you wanted to sleep with me just now?"

"Well, uh-h-h, no. That was not it," Robert answered defensively.

"How do you know I did not shave myself just before our lovemaking took place. That I only intended to lure you to my bed," she went on mockingly.

"Rosanna, I think you are pulling my leg."

"I thought that I pulled just about everything else during our escapade. This 'pulling your leg'?" she questioned imperiously.

"It is just a figure of speech that's all. I did not mean anything by it with you," he said, a little defensively.

Rosanna looked over at Robert and gestured with her hand, smoke twirling upward into the air. "I know, cheri. You are right, I was just pulling your leg. How about this?" as she started to fondle him.

Robert began to feel himself start to stiffen again. He put out his cigarette. Rosanna snuffed her' s as well. They placed the butts in the ashtray, and she placed it on the nightstand. He reached for her hand and pulled her over to him until her breasts were resting upon his chest. She felt him begin to grow harder. Rosanna placed her hand and then upon his shaft and started to stroke it lightly. Robert closed his eyes and laid himself back a little more. Rosanna continued to fondle him.

"Now, Rosanna. You continue to amaze me. You really do!" Robert said with a big grin on his face.

"I am just trying to please you, cheri, that is all."

"And you said you may have been out of practice. I might have a problem."

"I don't think you will have any problems, Roberto. None at all. Anyway, we will have to straighten things out before my children come home. Come, we will take a shower." She then led Robert to the bathroom and to one of her pride and joys, the shower unit. It was a fixture that her husband had had installed before the war. The bathtub was surrounded on three sides by treated glass, specially fitted to seal around the tub.

Rosanna, standing naked next to Robert, leaned over to turn on the taps. When she felt she had the temperature about right she walked onto the one-step staircase and sat down on the edge of the tub. She slowly turned herself and set foot into the tub. Robert now did the same. He closed the glass door behind him. Rosanna then turned on the lever to activate the shower. The hot, pulsating water felt heavenly upon their glistening bodies. Almost immediately, Robert began to grow hard again. The sight of the water cascading down Rosanna's body, between her spectacular breasts, drove him wild. His penis had taken on a mind of its own; one that he seemed powerless to stop.

The pair engaged in more fevered French-kissing. Robert caressed her breasts, and, she fondled him. She then guided him down to the tub bottom. She brought her body down until she guided him into her and started to grind herself. She moved very slowly up and down on the shaft. Robert was in the throes of complete and total ecstasy. Rosanna was a sexual goddess, simply unbelievable. Her body and her sexual intensity, even urgency, was something to behold.

Rosanna maintained her humping for several more long minutes and, then, Robert could contain himself no longer. He blew his load in a heated rush. Rosanna felt the liquid flow into her once again. She loved it, simply loved it. She hadn't realized, until her lovemaking with Robert, how much she had enjoyed sex. The raw passion of it. The animal-like intensity of it. She wanted more of it, and she wanted it from Robert. Her cheri. Her lover was strong and skilled in the art of lovemaking to a woman. He knew precisely how to bring her to the moment of ultimate passion.

To Robert, Rosanna was a supreme being. Her body, from her real and spectacular breasts to her long and smooth and well-developed legs. And, to her vulva, and how it received him so perfectly. He felt as if the two of them had achieved the oneness of two people.

After their sex, Rosanna and Robert actually showered. Each then helped the other to dry off. "Roberto, I may be curt with you on one or two occasions this evening. I do not want my children to know of our escapades this afternoon. At least, not just yet."

"I understand, Rosanna. It is all right. Everything will be alright. You do not have to apologize for anything. What we did today is something I will never forget. I was able to give myself to a woman who wanted me, truly wanted me, as I wanted her. The sex was great, but the person that you are, Rosanna, is greater," Robert said with a moving feeling.

Rosanna started to cry, Robert's words were some of the nicest things anyone had said to her. She leaned forward into Robert and whispered, "Cheri, I know now that I have found true love. I did not think that it would ever happen again. Some women do not find love once in their lifetime. I have found two. I know that now, and I know that here," she pointed to her heart. "Come, we still have some time before Ariana comes home. Let us go back to bed and rest. And, I mean rest. We have had enough passion for the time being."

The two trooped their way back to the bedroom. Robert laid himself down onto his left side. Rosanna glided in behind him, her breasts resting along his back. Her nipples started to become aroused and she wondered whether Robert had noticed. She soon had her answer as her lover had fallen into a deep sleep. Rosanna closed her eyes as she clung to Robert and relished about the day they had just had. She had always known that she was a good lover, a very sensual and sexual woman. Now, she also knew that Robert was a very sexual and sensual man. His power and stamina had both impressed and amazed her. Her own power and stamina had amazed her as well. She hoped that there would be more moments of sexual bliss in the future.

Rosanna was at her kitchen counter, preparing the evening meal which would consist of sautéed veal cutlets in tomato sauce, along with some home-made penne pasta. It wouldn't be much for the now four of them, but it was the best she could provide at the moment. Mrs. Ventetuolo, on the third floor, had provided the pasta. The older woman was very warm-hearted and good-natured and had always been willing to help Rosanna out. She knew of the activities of the Contessa and, although never getting directly involved herself, had readily provided food and clothing for the men in hiding.

"Is there anything I can do?" asked Robert as he stood next to Rosanna. He began to nuzzle her hair with his nose.

Rosanna smiled and said, "Ah, cheri, I do not think so. Well… Perhaps, you can help prepare the salad. With what we have here. It is not much, but with the war…."

"I do believe that I can handle that assignment."

"Do you like to cook, Robert?" she asked.

"Not really. Outside of hamburgers and hot dogs on a grill," he answered. "Rosanna, you were a bad girl this afternoon. A very bad girl. Such things I never would have imagined from such a proper woman," Robert exclaimed with a feigned exaggeration.

"Well, you were a rather bad boy yourself, my Roberto," Rosanna fired back. "Taking such advantage of a cultured noblewoman. I enjoyed it. Every minute of it and I would like to do it again, and again."

"And you said that you might have been out of practice. I.... don't think so."

Rosanna accidentally bumped into Robert and their eyes briefly met. It was incredible to her that at that exact moment she could feel herself once again hungering for his body. She could feel the electricity coursing its way through her. This could become dangerous for her, for him, for Ariana and Gaetano. For everyone.

Dinner was a rather subdued affair between Rosanna, Robert and Ariana. Robert looked over at the girl and wondered how much she suspected of anything going on between himself and her mother. Ariana was a bright and perceptive young woman. Robert had picked up on this in the weeks he had been living with the Vallone family.

Midway through the meal, Gaetano burst forth into the apartment. "Buona sera, mother, Ariana, Robert," he greeted them as he sat down at his place at the table. He was a handsome young man of seventeen. He definitely resembled Rosanna, especially in the eyes. They possessed the same hooded effect. The young man was about six feet tall, and Robert estimated, weighed about 150 pounds. He had light auburn colored hair that he maintained in a short, clipped fashion. It was not trimmed in the military manner.

"How nice of you to join us, Gaetano. You could have kissed your mother upon entering the room. You see, Robert, I must apologize for the sometimes lack of manners of my children. Well, they say that times are changing...." Rosanna shook her head in a doleful way.

"Of course, mother. How unthinking of me,' said Gaetano as he got up and went to his mother to kiss her. "I am sorry I was l late. I do have some interesting news. Yes, we are to have another visitor who will arrive later this week."

"Do you know who it will be?" asked Rosanna.

Gaetano shook his head. "No, I only know that he is a young American officer. Nothing more."

"We just had the sergeant moved," interjected the previously silent Ariana.

"Please, Ariana, not now!" said Rosanna.

"But, mother. I feel we are on borrowed time. The Germans and their Fascist lackeys could catch us at any moment. They almost did last week," the girl went on plaintively.

Rosanna did not reply to her daughter, but did say, "Well, it seems, Roberto, you will again have another roommate. How long, Gaetano, will we have to accommodate the young man?"

"I am not sure, mother, but I do not think it will be for more than several days. The leadership wants to move most of the men around, so as to better throw off the Germans. Oh, the young officer is to be escorted from the German College to our apartment by Genevieve Alviano." Gaetano continued.

Rosanna had been aware for quite some time how taken her son had become with the young woman. She thought Gaetano was too young for Genevieve. In addition, she wasn't sure that

162

Gaetano was worldly enough for the girl. She had not spoken of this to her son, hoping it might just be a brief period of infatuation for the young man.

Ariana had noticed from the very first time she had seen Genevieve in the company of Gaetano how her brother had practically openly lusted for the woman. His tongue would almost hang out when Genevieve wore one of her patented low-cut blouses, her breasts tantalizingly revealing themselves. Ariana, in a private moment, had chided her brother about him conceiving of the idea of he and Genevieve becoming a couple. Instead of offering up a snide comment to her brother, she said, "Mother, what do you think about my idea of getting more food for us. You know, what I mentioned the other day?"

Rosanna was staring down at the table, her veal only partially eaten. She did not reply to Ariana.

"Mother, mother? I am asking you a question. And you sit there with a vacant look upon your face." There was a taste of venom in her voice. She knew her mother was having sex with Matthews, she was sure of it. Perhaps, she was bitter about it.

"I am sorry, dear. What was it you were asking. Oh yes, something about the food situation. Yes, well, I think you might have something there. Let me think about it some more."

"Thank you, mother. I am sorry for having snapped at you just now. I did not mean to be cross with you," Ariana responded contritely.

"That is all right, dear. Everyone is uptight these days. Everyone."

Robert had been observing the exchanges between the Vallone family members, but had kept his silence. Rosanna had not even scolded him the entire time. It must have slipped her mind. He knew she would do this playfully, as if this secretly entertained herself by doing it. Robert had always tried very hard not to interfere in the family dynamics.

* * *

There were now more than two thousand escapees in hiding at more than forty sites across the length and breadth of Rome. The Ambrosia Network had grown tremendously from its first days in existence. Administrative help and support had been provided to Liam O'Reilly and Robert Matthews, his de facto second in command, by Messrs. Alan May and Max Salagos. And, of course, by Sir D'Arcy Osborne. Sir D'Arcy had more than once told Matthews, "You must be very careful about what you put in writing. Just because the Vatican has not been raided does not mean it will never be."

The Network needed additional financial inputs. Robert Matthews had, in essence, become the organization's banker. Almost every day he had made his way to and from Rosanna's apartment to Monsignor O'Reilly's office in the German College at the Vatican. He had become a virtual commuter. The money was absolutely essential for the continued procurement of clothing and food and a whole host of other miscellaneous items. Network members were allocated 120 lire per day for their troubles.

D'Arcy Osborne was the veritable money man. The government of Great Britain regularly supplied him funding through an elaborate and carefully crafted arrangement. Additional funding was also being obtained from the efforts of Harold Tittman, the American Charge D'Affaires.

Matthews had also been busy upgrading the Network's security measures. One way that he did so was by devising a code system. Every member of the escape network was assigned a cover name. This was to be used in all communications, written or verbal. O'Reilly became "Golf," Sir D'Acy was "Mount," and Rosanna Vallone became "Mrs. C." It was assumed that all phone calls were being tapped by Kammler's men. Coded language was used as an added precaution. To disguise any references to prisoners, words such as "dispatches" or "parcels were used.

By February of 1944, O'Reilly and Matthews had developed into a smooth and cohesive team. They complemented one another well, often anticipating what the other was thinking of or coming up with a similar solution to a problem. While O'Reilly tended to be impulsive, "Bob" Matthews was more deliberate and rational. He would think through a problem or a situation before making a decision.

Liam O'Reilly held a fundamental belief that there was good in every person. He often took people at face value. Matthews, on the other hand, believed it was the Monsignor's Christian faith that caused him to want to assist anyone possible, regardless of the consequences. Matthews further believed that the cleric's inherent openness rendered the escape network vulnerable to its being penetrated by German and Italian spies.

One day in mid-February, as Matthews was visiting with O'Reilly he was told, "We have a new arrival, Bob. Come in, Joe," said the Monsignor. The man who entered the room was small in stature with a sallow and dark complexion. "Joe, this is Bob. Bob, this is Joe Pollak. He has just arrived."

Matthews remembered seeing the man before, just as he himself had arrived in Rome. The man had said he was a Jew from Czechoslovakia. Pollak had been a medical student before the war. In 1939, he had gone to Palestine and enlisted himself in the Royal Army Medical Corps. He had served in 1941, where he had been taken prisoner.

Matthews had never quite believed Pollak's story when he had first had it told to him by Rosanna. He thought Joe Pollak might well be a Nazi spy.

"I am surprised to see you once again, Joe. I had thought you would be well away from here by now. That is what you had told me when we met briefly several months ago," said Robert.

"Well, you see, Major, I never did quite make it. And that is why you see me now," replied Pollak sheepishly.

"You two have met before? You never told me this, Joe," O'Reilly interrupted in a slightly shocked tone. This duly confirmed to Matthews that Pollak was not one to be trusted. He did not let on to this sentiment in any visible way.

Matthews proceeded to question Pollak, who seemed to provide satisfactory answers, especially concerning the names of escaped prisoners of war. Nevertheless, this man would bear watching.

Soon after the Joe Pollak incident, the Monsignor introduced Bob Matthews to an Italian, one Pietro Tuvellari. He informed Matthews that Tuvellari had brought cash and information to the Network. He was told by O'Reilly that he was to meet this mystery man at the Collinade in St Peter's Square.

"Buon giorno, Signore Matthews. It is indeed a great pleasure to meet with you at last. The Monsignor has told me a great deal about you,' gushed an enthused Pietro Tuvellari.

Matthews looked down at the diminutive Italian and said, "I would advise you not to throw around names so loosely. It could be dangerous for all concerned, secondly," he continued as he evaluated the man standing before him. Tuvellari was dressed in the usual peasant style of clothing, much of it torn or frayed, and it had not been washed in some time. A couple of the man's toes were exposed from his battered shoes as well. "Secondly," Matthews resumed, "we should not meet for too long. You never know who may be watching." Matthews noticed the man's eyes darting about, as if he were a ferret on watch for a mortal enemy.

"I understand, signore, I understand," Tuvellari repeated, bowing slightly at the waist. "I have traveled very far to get here, sir. In fact, I began my journey in Bari."

Matthews was aware that Bari was in the south of Italy. It had once been near the Allied front lines. Why would Tuvellari travel in the opposite direction for more than four hundred miles? The story sounded suspicious to Matthews. Highly suspicious.

"I have in my possession, sir, the sum total of 20,000 lire. I have been instructed to hand it over to you or to some representative of the Vatican," Tuvellari continued.

"Instructed by whom?" questioned an alarmed Matthews.

"By the Monsignor, of course, sir," Tuvellari responded smoothly. He then handed over to Matthews a plain brown envelope. "Is there anything else in which I may be of service to you, sir?" the little Italian asked in an unctuous way.

"No, I don't think so. We appreciate the gift, I will tell the Monsignor. Grazie."

Tuvellari nodded his head demurely and said, "I do what I can to help the cause, sir. I bid you a pleasant arrivederci, kind sir. "The man then turned away and walked very quickly out of the Square.

"I am not sure about Mr. Tuvellari, Monsignor. He could be a German plant. Kammler is still trying to penetrate the

Network," said Robert Matthews as he was once again situated in the German College.

"I think that you are sometimes a bit too skeptical, Robert. I believe in Mr Tuvellari. I admit that I do not know him that well, but I have an innate good feeling about him," said the Monsignor.

"And you, Monsignor, are sometimes a little too trusting in your fellow man. I think that we will have to be very careful in our relationship with this Tuvellari fellow," responded Matthews while he looked the Monsignor in the eye.

"All right, Bob, I will concede that to you. Now, I wanted to discuss another matter with you at this time. It concerns your travels between your living arrangements and this office. I believe this may be putting you at an increased risk. Perhaps, if you were to remain here in the Vatican full-time would be safer."

Robert thought this over for a moment and admitted to himself that O'Reilly's suggestion was sound and made sense. This would, of course, mean his having to leave Rosanna. Their relationship would be forced to take a new turn. Could it survive? Yes, he was convinced of it. "I think that you may be right, Monsignor. Of course, this would force me to leave the Contessa's home She and I have… become rather fond of each other over these past several weeks." Robert had turned his head so that he was facing downward, but it seemed worried and drawn to O'Reilly.

The Monsignor sat back in his chair, looking directly at the American officer. A man he had come to know quite well and a man he respected greatly. He wasn't sure he had ever met a more competent and proud individual. It had been a pleasure to serve alongside this man. O'Reilly had come to trust him implicitly. This trust was not of a questionable nature at all. He well knew that he was, at times, too trusting of those individuals he first met, but of Matthews, there was no doubt. None, whatsoever.

O'Reilly was not surprised by what Matthews had just revealed, concerning himself and Rosanna Vallone. Even though he was a man of the cloth, he was not blind to human emotions between two people. Especially one between a handsome and well-built man and an attractive and voluptuous woman. He nodded as he sat there, facing Matthews. "The Contessa is an attractive woman. She is a good woman. An invaluable member of this organization. I have come to rely on her a great deal. And, despite being a priest, I do understand some of the dynamics between a man and a woman. Would you like for me to tell her?" asked O'Reilly.

Matthews shook his head. "No, Monsignor. This is something I will have to do myself." The American knew that it was best for all concerned. And, yet....

"Good, I think it is best. Now, back to our discussion about Mr Tuvellari. I suggest that we give him a simple assignment, so as to see if he is, indeed, who he claims to be," suggested O'Reilly.

"What do you have in mind, Monsignor?"

"I am not sure, Robert. Do you happen to have an idea?"

"We could ask him to obtain some maps of the area. Maybe those indicating German troop dispositions. If he should pass this test, then perhaps, we could ask him to return to Bari with a list of Allied soldiers who are still on the run in southern Italy. This information may find its way back to the families of these men," said Matthews.

"Yes, yes! I see what you mean, Robert," O'Reilly declared as his face lit up. "All right, let us go forward with this idea. I will instruct Father Damian to have Tuvellari procure these maps and, then…. well, we shall see."

Pietro Tuvellari easily passed the first test. O'Reilly and Matthews then decided to go ahead with the second test relating to the list of names. Robert suggested that the names should be microfilmed. One of Sir D'Arcy Osborne's embassy staff could easily perform this task. The film would then be hidden inside of a loaf of Italian bread. It would then be handed to Tuvellari for the journey south. The Italian would be instructed to use an agreed upon code phrase upon the completion of his message to the British government. This would provide confirmation to Matthews and Osborne that Tuvellari had successfully gotten through.

* * *

That night, Robert took Rosanna in his arms. She knew instinctively that something was wrong. She could almost feel her lover shaking. Robert came right to the point and told her of his having to move full-time into the German College. It had to be done. He just had too many duties and responsibilities, too many tasks, and that, sooner or later, the Germans might catch him on his commuting through the city.

Rosanna, in her heart, knew he was right. But it was still like a body-blow to her solar plexus. The air felt like it was being forced out of her lungs. Her heart was being broken once again. Still, she knew it had to be done. Rosanna knew that she and Robert would be reunited one day. And it would be permanent.

Tears began forming in her eyes, running down her cheeks, as she clung to Matthews. She was gripping him fiercely, as if she could not bear to let him go. He responded in kind. He knew he had found his true love. Matthews also knew that nothing would come between them ever again.

Seven

The Courier

It was mid-afternoon. A light overcast covered the Roman sky. Rosanna and Robert were seated at the dining room table, sipping espresso coffee from elegant demitasse cups. The tea set had been an anniversary gift from her husband some years back. The coffee blend was, in fact, ersatz, for that was all that was available in the wartime city.

"Rosanna, I want you to know how I really feel about you. I love you with all of my heart. I want to be with you, always. When Rome is liberated, and that day will come, I will return here. I do not want to ever lose you," he said with deep feeling.

"I know, cheri. I have known for quite a while how you have felt about me. Our sessions in the bedroom have given me some indication. And I. too, love you very deeply. I would like to believe that you will come back to me, to Rome. But I have heard and seen other men make the same promise. If that were to happen to me, it would break my heart again. After the death of my husband I didn't really know if I could become close to any man again. That is, to be intimate with him. I know now that this of course, has not been true. Our lovemaking has been wonderful and I would like to make love again many times with you in the future, but...." Rosanna struggled with her train of thought.

"No, no, Rosanna. I would never abandon you. You must believe that. I will be here for a few more days, at least, until the new American arrives. I will then probably stay for a couple of more days. And then go to the German College to join the golfer."

Rosanna reached out for his hand and leaned toward him. They kissed lightly. She felt her breasts begin to swell and her loins moisten. She could see that Robert was hardening. Their kissing elevated to the French style. Rosanna rose up from the table and led Robert to the bedroom.

The two tore off their clothes in a frenzy and flung them to the floor. Rosanna flew to Robert and engaged him passionately.

* * *

The young woman was introduced to Lieutenant Jimmy Cefalo in Monsignor O'Reilly's office.

"This is Lieutenant Cefalo of the American army," O'Reilly began. "And Lieutenant, may I have the pleasure of introducing you to Miss Genevieve Alviano. She is one our most trusted couriers in the Network."

"Tenente, it is nice to meet you," Genevieve addressed Cefalo demurely.

172

Jimmy Cefalo stared in wonder at the young woman. Although she wore almost no makeup, she possessed a natural beauty, a presence as well. "It is my pleasure, signorina. And please, call me Jimmy. All of my friends do."

"Okay, Jeemy," she pronounced in her slightly Italian accented English. Genevieve was still hesitant about speaking English. But she had improved to a significant degree of late, having encountered a number of British and American escapees. "Now, I would like to go over a few rules regarding your transfer. It will be tomorrow and in the early afternoon. The journey will a little more than a mile from here. We will be using bicycles as it will be much faster than if we were to walk. You are to play the role of my brother, a deaf-mute. You are not to say anything. I will do all of the talking. We may encounter some German patrols or checkpoints, even some manned by the Fascist police. They may try to trick you. Do not fall for these ruses. Is that clear?"

"Yes, very clear. I will do as you say, signorina. And, thank you. I am very impressed by your attention to details."

"I am not trying to impress you, Tenente. I only want to ensure that I get you to your destination safe and sound. I believe that is how you say it," Genevieve replied in an authoritative voice.

The Monsignor had been sitting quietly behind his desk. There had been no need to interject himself into the discussion. He could see that the young woman had everything under control. Genevieve Alviano was a tried and true veteran of the Ambrosia Network. "Well, then. It seems as if everything is clear. Mr Cefalo. You will be in good hands with Genevieve." "Just one more thing, Mister Cefalo. Can you ride a bicycle?" she asked. It was not done mockingly.

"I believe I can manage, Miss Alviano," Cefalo replied, not at all put off by the question.

"Bene, good. I will meet with you tomorrow afternoon at 1:00 PM."

"I will be here," replied Cefalo.

Genevieve stood, "Monsignor, Tenente, err, Jeemy, I shall go now."

O'Reilly stood, as did Cefalo.

"Go with God, child. Go with God."

Genevieve left the office, quietly closing the door on her way out.

Jimmy Cefalo sat down again and said, "A most impressive and attractive young woman, Monsignor."

"Yes, she certainly is. Genevieve is one of the best at what she does. Our organization could not function without such young men and women. You must follow everything she tells you. Even if it does not make sense to you. She knows what she is doing, believe me. One other thing, Lieutenant, I realize that you find her most attractive, for that is natural. I am not too old to see what can develop between a young man and a young woman. But, you must suppress any amorous thoughts for the time being. It could turn out quite tragic and deadly for all concerned."

The next day, a Friday, dawned bright and crisp over Rome. Jimmy Cefalo had awakened early and was fully dressed, anxiously awaiting his move to new quarters. The Monsignor had instructed Father Damian to have a light breakfast prepared for the American, consisting of rolls and coffee. Cefalo had not been in the mood to eat that much, his stomach turning with butterflies, as his anxiety level kept rising by the minute.

At precisely 1:00 PM, Genevieve Alviano arrived at the German College and Monsignor O'Reilly's office. Today, she was dressed more modestly than she had been the day before. Gone was the suggestive blouse, and in its place, a buttoned-up plaid colored dress. She looked at Cefalo and asked, Are you ready?"

"Yes, I am. I have been quite anxious all morning. I don't think I sat down for more than a minute at a time," Cefalo replied. He was a little disappointed not see Genevieve in another one of her revealing blouses.

"It is just nerves, Jeemy, just nerves. Everything will be fine. Just do as I tell you. One thing. We will travel at a slow, leisurely pace. And I would like for you to stay to the side of me as best you can. I do not want it to look as if you are following me, with no idea as to where you are going. All right?" Genevieve went on, but in a more tender tone. "Oh, Tenente, you know you are assuming the role of a deaf mute. Okay? Of course, do not say anything, but also, if a German tries to trick you by saying or doing anything behind you, you have to ignore it. It could be hard, but I will try and help you. Okay?"

Cefalo nodded his assent.

"Good, Father Damian has procured a bicycle that you will use. And now, we go."

The pair made their way slowly through the Vatican grounds. They passed through a checkpoint just outside the Papal Apartments. Genevieve proceeded cautiously, but in control. Cefalo duly followed alongside, as he had been instructed. There did not seem to be any unusual activity about in the way of German patrols.

Cefalo found himself enjoying the morning sun as he pedaled along through the streets. At times, he felt as if he were daydreaming. Genevieve, perceptive as always, noticed this and she would quickly remind the American to pay attention. This was not the time to play the accidental tourist. It was almost as if it had been the girl who had had the military training and that he was an unaware and carefree tourist.

They had been making good progress, when suddenly, the girl spotted another checkpoint, just past the Castel Sant' Angelo complex. Genevieve saw that it was manned by Germans, but she wasn't sure of what branch they belonged to. They did not look like Gestapo, nor were they army personnel. If she had to hazard a guess, she would have taken them as criminal police, the Kripo. In any event, it could turn out badly for them if they weren't careful.

The two cyclists slowed and proceeded to join a line consisting of other cyclists and some pedestrians. There were ten people in front of them. The German officials did not appear to be checking any of the people too closely. Most were given a perfunctory search and then sent on their way. Genevieve and Cefalo soon found themselves facing a rather ordinary looking official. The man was not very tall, but he did have a Hitler styled brush-like mustache. She hoped this would not portend that the man was a die-hard Nazi, who might well deduce who they really were and what they were up to.

"Papers, fraulein?" the man addressed Genevieve. He had his hands clasped behind his back. He started to bounce up and down on the balls of his feet.

Cefalo observed this and thought to himself, "Look at this guy. Hands behind his back as if were royalty." He associated this gesture as being typical of high-minded European men. He could not stand it. So pretentious.

Genevieve reached into her coat pocket and handed the requisite identity papers to the German. The man perused them rather quickly. "Who is this man?"

"He is my brother. sir," Genevieve replied as calmly as she could manage.

"Does he not speak?"

"No, sir. He cannot. He is a deaf-mute," she answered guardedly.

The official stepped around Cefalo and stood still for several Seconds. He then turned partway around and suddenly snapped his fingers, just behind the ear of the American's head. Genevieve trembled slightly, desperately hoping Cefalo would not flinch, would not move a millimeter. He did not. She let out a low sigh of relief.

"Very well, fraulein. You and …. your brother may proceed." The German stepped aside and waved them on.

They continued on their way along the Tiber River. Cefalo again found himself mesmerized by the famous waterway. He was impressed by the way it cut through the city. As he continued on he took in the fabulous beauty of Rome. It was breathtaking. There was no other way to describe it. At the Hall of Justice building they turned onto the Ponte Umberto bridge. Genevieve led the way to Via Casa, when they were abruptly confronted by a scuffle. Two burly SS men were beating up on an elderly man as he lay curled up in a fetal position on the ground.

"Filthy Jew! Get up! Get up, you pig!" screamed one of the SS men. The pair had been taking turns pummeling the poor old man.

"Please, please, I have done nothing wrong. I am an Italian. I served my country proudly in the First War," the man pleaded with his tormentors. Blood could be seen across his face. His shirt and trousers had been torn as a result of the beating. He whimpered sickeningly as he lay on the ground.

The two troopers continued to thrash the man without letup. Welts and cuts had opened up on the man's face and arms. It looked to Cefalo as if some of the old man's fingers may have been broken as well. The man tried to roll himself on the ground, as if trying to protect himself from further damage, to no apparent avail.

"That is what they all say, right Hans?" snarled the SS trooper who had a long scar along the right side of his face.

"Ja, Fritz. I am only a poor old Italian. I served my country," mimicked the other trooper in an exaggerated falsetto voice. "I am innocent, I tell you. Innocent! I have done nothing. I love il Duce."

"Listen, you filthy Jew. I will tell you what you have done wrong. You are a Jew! A Jew, I tell you!"

Genevieve had observed all of this, along with Cefalo. It was a scene she had witnessed many times in Rome over the past several months. But she knew her companion had not. This was something new to him. And it was shocking. And revolting. Anyone with the least bit of decency would have recoiled at the sight.

The couple had stopped just short of the sight of where the beating was taking place. Cefalo thought to himself, "How could these goons do this to an old man. To anyone. As if that person were a dog in the street. A decent human being wouldn't do this to an animal. "I wish I could do something," he continued in his thoughts.

Genevieve had begun to pedal past, but when she looked back she noticed that Cefalo was still rooted to the ghastly scene.

He continued to watch the beating. Genevieve tried to silently gain his attention.

"Hey you. What are you looking at? Have you never seen a Jew getting what he deserved? What they all deserve," hissed the taller SS man, Hans.

At that moment, Cefalo had forgotten that he was supposed to be a deaf-mute. He quickly started pedaling again, past the two SS men and the fallen Jewish man. He rejoined Genevieve and they moved off.

After they had traveled a bit further, Genevieve paused by the side of the street. "I know what you are thinking, but we cannot react to such a thing. It is hard, but we have to pretend that nothing is happening. That we are not seeing anything out of the ordinary. It has become a way of life for everyone in Rome. I imagine it has become a way of life for anyone living under the yoke of the Nazis."

Cefalo looked at his young and attractive companion. "I have never seen such a thing before in my life." The American had been stunned and shaken to the core of his being.

"That is one of the reasons I am doing what I do. To help rid our city and our country of these vermin. Now, I have had my say. No more philosophizing," Genevieve said with defiance in her voice and upon her face.

"How far are we along?" Cefalo asked in reference to their destination.

"Ah, I would say we have about one-half mile to go. I have to compute this in my head, as we use meters here in Italy. Do not worry, my friend. We shall be there soon," Genevieve answered in her naturally soft and gentle voice. "Andiamo, we go!"

Despite the Monsignor's admonition to him the previous day, Cefalo felt himself falling under the spell of this bewitching young Italian girl.

Soon they were on the main street of Via Del Corso. They arrived at Rosanna Vallone's residence on Via Frattina in the late afternoon. To Cefalo, the journey had not seemed to take as much time as it actually had. Perhaps, that had been the result of having been in the company of Genevieve Alviano.

The couple parked their bicycles around the back of the home, out of sight of any possible prying eyes. Genevieve guided Cefalo into the building. They passed by the apartment of the old hag, Luisa Santagata, a woman that Rosanna Vallone had always regarded as dangerous. Santagata always seemed to make it a habit to monitor all of the comings and goings in the building. Today was no different.

As Genevieve and Cefalo walked by, Santagata had cracked open her door a space and eyed the couple. "H-m-m-m," she thought to herself. "That young woman again, and with another young man. Maybe, she is not as innocent as she appears to be. Maybe, she is one of those kinds of women, And, the Contessa is in reality a madam." To the old woman it was not that wild an idea, given how things had been transpiring in Rome of late. Desperate times spawned desperate measures. Santagata would maintain her own kind of surveillance. The police might well be interested in some of the activities going on inside of this building.

Genevieve knocked lightly on the Contessa's door. It was opened by Robert Matthews. He was dressed in a priest's habit, replete with the requisite collar. Genevieve thought Matthews looked quite authentic, and even, rather dignified. It was almost as if he were a genuine man of the cloth.

"Buon giorno, Genevieve. And this I take is our new guest," he said.

"Si, err, yes, Maggiore. This is Tenente Jimmy Cefalo." She had pronounced his first name correctly. Genevieve was somewhat proud of herself. She had been practicing her English very diligently.

"Welcome. Please come in. Come and relax, you are safe. You are among friends," Matthews said affably.

"Thank you, Major. Thank you," replied Cefalo. He had been looking around at the well-appointed room they were standing in. He found it to be quite elegant. It reflected a genuine woman's touch. A dignified woman.

Matthews gestured for Cefalo to sit in the red easy chair he was standing next to. "Well, I take it everything went smoothly on your way over."

Cefalo nodded. He chose not to mention the scene of the old Jewish man being beaten to a pulp by the two SS thugs.

"Maggiore, we did see one incident on the way. Some SS toughs were in the process of beating up an old man. A Jewish man. It was disgusting!" interjected Genevieve.

"Yes, I imagine it must have been. I have not yet been a witness to this type of thing, but it makes one's blood boil when one hears of such a thing," said Matthews with a pained look on his face.

"Well, Tenente. I have completed my assignment. You have been brought here safe and sound. I will go now."

"Thank you, Genevieve. I am most appreciative of what you have done for me," Cefalo answered gratefully.

"Bene. I go now. Jimmy, Maggiore, arrivederci."

As soon as the girl had left, Matthews and Cefalo engaged in a light conversation. The young man told Robert of the army unit he was from and, where he had been taken prisoner. He also described some of his personal background prior to his joining the army.

An hour later, a blond-haired woman, that Cefalo figured to be in her early forties, entered the apartment. He was immediately intrigued by this attractive woman. She was not Genevieve Alviano, but he could see that she was still good looking and well built.

"Buon giorno. You must be our new guest. I am Contessa Rosanna Vallone. Welcome to my home."

"I am, Contessa. Thank you," said Cefalo, who did not know what else to say.

"Please, Tenente, you may call me Rosanna," the woman said brightly.

"Okay, Rosanna it is."

Matthews had been sitting on the Contessa's beautiful black leather Natuzzi couch, when he decided to break into the conversation, "Rosanna, would you like to inform our new guest about the rules and regulations he is to follow while he is domiciling here?" Matthews had spoken half-mockingly in remembrance of his own introduction to Rosanna.

She paid no attention to his feigned mockery. "Oh, that would Be fine cher.... err, Robert. I must apologize for being a little late. Heavy German patrols. I trust that your journey was not too adventurous, Mr Cefalo."

"No, it was not. It was fine, for the most part. Rosanna, please call me Jimmy."

She nodded at the lean and handsome young American soldier. She had been in admiration of these fine young men for some time. They had come a long way from their homes. Rosanna and her children had come to respect and appreciate them very much. "Jimmy, it is. Now, if you gentlemen will excuse me, I have some things I need to take care of."

"Excuse me, Major. I have to ask you why you are dressed as a priest?" Cefalo asked out of the blue.

"Oh, let me explain, Lieutenant. Whenever I go out on the street, I will sometimes assume the role of a priest. It is merely a cover, a disguise, if you will, to throw off any nosy Germans or Fascist police. It is one of the things I will be briefing you on this afternoon."

* * *

Helmut Kammler was, for one of the few times lately, relaxing at home. If it were at all possible for him to relax in his temporary domicile. It was a Saturday afternoon and the city was in the midst of a warming thaw. For many of the people of Rome it was seen as a possible harbinger of spring. And, hopefully, of the approaching Allies. spring represented a renewal of the human spirit that the season always seemed to promise. Kammler had been considering a new approach to his old problem concerning the escaped prisoners of war and, of course, Monsignor O'Reilly.

In the background, Angela fluttered about, incoherently going on about some stupid thing or other. It did not matter to him. It never did anymore. His son, Peter, had snuck around behind Kammler and, suddenly, pointed the SS man's Lugar pistol at his head.

"Bang, bang! I got you!" the boy shouted triumphantly as if he had finally gotten the better of his father at something.

Kammler whirled around and saw the gun pointed at his head. Peter holding it with a look of glee on his face. He grabbed the weapon from the startled boy's hand and, then, he grabbed

Peter. He was about to strike the boy with his opened right hand when Angela shouted.

"Helmut! What are you doing? Can you not see that he is only a little boy? You were about to strike him. How could you?"

"Little boy? He is almost twelve years old. Young men not much older than Peter are fighting and dying miserable deaths on the battlefront. You have always coddled him, ever since he was a baby."

"Helmut, I sometimes think that I do not know you anymore. You have changed. I am beginning to hate this posting to Rome," Angela fired back indignantly.

"Perhaps, you would prefer residing in Warsaw or Cassino. I hear it is lovely at this time of year." Kammler was growing weary at the prospect of another one of their patented arguments. He had his police duties and that infernal round-up of Jews and prisoners. He did not need for Angela to harp on him once again. "Angela, for the love of God!"

"No!" It was your fault. You should have secured your gun, so that Peter could not gain access to it," she practically screamed into his face. Angela's eyes were flashed out widely.

Kammler looked at his wife in disbelief. In her anger, she looked to him, at least momentarily, seductive. He quickly shook this implausible thought from his head. He took the Lugar and secured it in its holster. He then grabbed his hat and left the room without another word.

Once back in his office on Via Wolkonsky, Kammler sat at his desk and considered his options. He had long been frustrated with his confrontation with the Vatican and against the resistance and the escaped POW situation. It was high time to go to Plan B, in the person of one, Basil Sadasvili, a colorful Georgian personality. The man had been living in Rome for years, working at a variety of odd jobs. Kammler had recently employed Sadasvili as an interpreter. The Georgian had also begun to pass on information to the SS.

The Reich Security Main Office (RSHA) in Berlin had hatched a plan through the creation of the Georgian College of the Vatican. If successful, this could allow for SS Intelligence to infiltrate the Holy See.

Eight

Closing the Ring

It was in late February when the Monsignor received a gold-embossed invitation from the Hungarian Embassy in Rome. It all seemed innocent enough to the cleric as he had attended functions there in the past. He was also aware that social events at the embassy were often attended by German officials.

Liam O'Reilly realized he would be taking a risk by leaving the sanctuary of the Vatican, but he really wanted to go, and so, he did. One of his fellow guests was none other than the German Ambassador to the Holy See, Ernst von Weizsacker. O'Reilly had always found the man to be personable, articulate, and well-mannered. The German was a striking individual with his brilliant white hair and crystal blue eyes.

"Good to see you, Monsignor. It has been awhile," von Weizsacker greeted O'Reilly amiably. "These kinds of get-togethers are good, that is, in view of the war. All of the unpleasantness," the Ambassador had continued on with twisting his nose as if he had suddenly encountered a bad odor.

O'Reilly eyed the man carefully and, although he liked him personally, he was struck by von Weizsacker's choice of words. "Good to see you, Herr Ambassador. Yes, this unpleasantness, as you put it is more than unfortunate. But, in my view, sir, it has been the Germans who have been the root cause of this.... atmosphere." O'Reilly had spread out his arms in a theatrical gesture to the German.

"Well. Monsignor, I was just speaking in a general sense. I have always tried to be open and amiable with his Eminence during my service here in Rome. My good relationship with the Pope has been conveyed to the Fuhrer. Monsignor? May I have a word with you in private?" von Weizsacker leaned in closer to O'Reilly, almost conspiratorially.

"Of course, Herr Ambassador."

The two men stepped into an unoccupied ante-room. "Monsignor, what I am about to convey to you is of the utmost importance, not only to yourself, but to the Vatican as well. German authorities in Rome are aware of your, should I say.... illicit activities. And by authorities, I mean Obersturmbannfuhrer Kammler," Weizsacker intoned gravely. "I have it on good authority that you will be arrested on-sight if you should be caught off of the Vatican grounds. I would think over very carefully what I have just said."

"Your Excellency is most considerate. I will take into serious consideration what you have just told me," O'Reilly replied in his usual genial manner. "But, Herr Weizsacker, you really do not have to worry about me."

And with that the two men parted company for the rest of the evening. O'Reilly made his pleasantries to the Hungarian Ambassador and his wife, as well as to some of the other guests. He then bid them all good night.

The Monsignor had not been totally surprised by what von Weizsacker had revealed to him, but what had been different this time was that the warning had emanated from one of the most senior German representatives in Rome.

* * *

"You asked to see me, Monsignor?" O'Reilly asked tentatively.

"Yes, indeed, I did Liam. Please, come in. Sit down," replied Monsignor Giovanni Montini. The Monsignor served as a deputy at the Secretariat of State in the Vatican. He was also very close to Sir D'Arcy Osborne. "Liam, I have received word that you are being closely watched by the Germans. I do not have any specific details, but what I do know could have serious ramifications not only for you, but for the Holy Father, as well."

O'Reilly sat in front of Montini, but did not immediately reply. What could he possibly say to him?

"Liam, I know how you feel about the war, the Germans, Colonel Kammler, and, believe me, I feel the same way. However, we cannot afford to compromise the Church and the Holy Father himself. That is something that cannot be countenanced. You will have to be extremely careful and quite circumspect from now on," Montini went on at length. It had been difficult for him to have to speak to O'Reilly in this manner. He, too, shared many of the same thoughts as O'Reilly concerning the Fascists, the Nazis, the war. Montini had long been exposed to the poisoned atmosphere that had come about since Benito Mussolini and his Blackshirts had swept into power.

"Thank you, Monsignor. I have always placed great trust and comfort in your words and wisdom. You have been a very good friend to me through our many years here in the Vatican. I promise you that I will take counsel of your advice. You can rest assured I will not conduct any activities that will threaten or compromise the sanctity of the Holy Church."

O'Reilly was soon confronted with more bad news. Major Robert Matthews had been discovered by the rector of the German College to be living within the Vatican grounds. He duly informed the Monsignor that this could not be allowed to continue. Matthews would have to be moved, and immediately. He did not have to go far as O'Reilly was able to place him at Sir D'Arcy Osborne's residence at the British Legation.

German pressure had been mounting against the entire escape Network. Arrests had been on the rise throughout the city. Joe Piszarcik, a key member of the organization, had been arrested by the Gestapo while he had been visiting a friend. This made both O'Reilly and Matthews nervous. Pizsarcik's arrest would undoubtedly lead to others. More operatives could then be collared and tortured for information.

O'Reilly met with Matthews, for one of the last times, in the Monsignor's office. "What do you think Kammler may be up to, Robert?" O'Reilly began haltingly. "How is he gaining the upper hand with us? I suppose we knew it could happen, but still."

"I'm not sure, Monsignor, but we will have to be very cautious in all of our dealings here on out. Any new escapees will have to be thoroughly vetted. We do not have the luxury of having any more slip-ups," replied a pensive and worried Matthews.

"I agree, Robert. I am concerned about what Kammler knows. Joe Pizsarcik's arrest is alarming. He is probably being tortured as we speak. The poor soul. We know that Kammler and his SS thugs will stop at nothing to get what they want. Very well, Robert. It looks as if you will have to go to the British Legation, and soon. The rector has made this quite clear to me."

"I understand, Monsignor. It will make things slightly more difficult, but not impossible. We should still be able to communicate effectively. Sir D'Arcy has a most capable and experienced staff and organization," said Matthews.

* * *

At that moment, Father Lillard came running into the office and stammered, "Monsignor, I am sorry to report that I have devastating news. Father Ruggiero has been arrested by Kammler's men. He was stopped and searched at a checkpoint. It appears that he had on him a great deal of money, and some documents. A witness at the scene saw the whole thing."

"Where has he been taken?" asked an alarmed and visibly shaken O'Reilly.

"Probably to Kammler's headquarters on Via Wolkonsky. I am not sure, Monsignor. What should we do?" continued Lillard in a near hysterical voice.

"We cannot do anything for the moment I'm afraid," murmured O'Reilly. He was sitting upright, closer to his desk, his long fingers steepled upward in front of his drawn and agitated face.

Matthews just sat in stunned silence at the news. Father Ruggiero had been another vital member of the Network. Such a kindly and dignified man. A good man. "Monsignor?" Matthews began guardedly," I know that this is devastating news, but we will have to maintain our poise. We have to pause and take a deep breath. I am confident that the Germans will get nothing from Father Ruggiero."

"I know, Robert. I am very worried for the moment. I believe that we should curtail some of our activities. Not shut down completely, but we should operate at a minimum level of activity. Father Damian, see if any of our people can find out where Father Ruggiero has been taken. I will contact Ambassador von Weizsacker to see if he can do anything, err, provide some kind of assistance."

Father Lillard nodded and swiftly left O'Reilly's office. The Monsignor and Matthews continued to sit in silent contemplation of the recent series of startling events.

At that very moment, Father Alberto Ruggiero found himself strapped to an operating room style of table. Steel bands crossed his chest, making it difficult, if not impossible, to breathe. His legs were secured in a similar fashion. The priest had been stripped of all of his clothing, save for his underpants.

Helmut Kammler stepped into the room and silently observed the man, or what was left of him. Ruggiero's right eye was swollen shut and his nose had been crushed flat. Some of the man's fingers had been broken as well. Kammler stood next to Albert Krieger. "Well? Has he revealed anything, yet?"

"Nein, sir. Not a word. Shall we continue?" questioned Krieger.

Kammler said nothing. He had witnessed and conducted dozens of similar interrogations. He had performed a number of especially gruesome ones himself. Probably his most famous case was the one involving Georg Elsner. The one-time carpenter who had attempted to assassinate Adolf Hitler with a hidden time bomb in 1937 at a Munich beer hall. It was to have been in commemoration of the famous Beer Hall Putsch of 1922.

The Nazi approached Ruggiero and bent down toward the tortured man's right ear. "Well, well, Father Alberto Ruggiero, pastor of Santa Rosaria. Your flock would be shocked to see you like this. They would be absolutely appalled if they knew of your rather nefarious activities. Would they not?"

Ruggiero eyed Kammler out of his one good eye. He knew what be coming, but remained silent.

"Come now, Father. We are all reasonable men here. Tell me what I want to know and this proceeding will be terminated. Surely, you can see that, at least, out of your one good eye," Kammler paused and laughed slightly at his own joke. "You must realize that continued resistance is futile. Tell me what I want to know. I know you really want to tell me. So, go on. Out with it, man. You do not really believe that you have to maintain some sense of honor. Now, do you? Of course not."

Ruggiero tried to twist under his bindings, but any movement caused him unbearable pain. "I do not know anything. I cannot…. tell you…. anything…. sir."

"Fifty thousand lire and those incriminating documents. Come now, Father, you have to be the most endowed bagman I have ever seen," Kammler said soothingly, mockingly.

"I do not know…. anything. I cannot…. tell you any…. thing, sir."

"Such politeness. I am impressed. Very well. Have it your way. I have tried to help you. Really, I have, but you now leave me with no other choice."

Kammler stepped back from the gurney holding Ruggiero's writhing and tortured form, and said to Krieger, "Continue with

192

the interrogation for a few more hours, if he can stand it. If he still doesn't break by then we shall consider using truth serum. And Krieger, if that fails to yield anything, I will have him executed."

The SS chieftain then strode off as Krieger's men began tightening the steel bandings encasing Ruggiero. A blood-curdling scream erupted from the battered man as another one of his fingers was snapped with the use of a pair of electrical pliers.

As Kammler proceeded through the corridors of his SS headquarters, he allowed himself a small smile. This priest, this Father Ruggiero, was finding out that he, Helmut Kammler, was not one to be trifled with. As the poor, wretched man was discovering. The SS would get its way and what it wanted in the end.

In his second floor office, Helmut Kammler stood in front of the map of the street lay-out of Rome. At last, progress, significant progress was being made in his campaign against the escape network. However, he was still a little unsettled about his continuing inability to apprehend Monsignor O'Reilly and his other leading henchmen. Nevertheless, he was pleased with what had been achieved by himself and his men, even Albert Krieger. Kammler was determined to prove to Reichsfuhrer Heinrich Himmler and the Austrian brute, Ernst Kaltenbrunner, that he was still the man for the job in the Eternal City.

Kammler sat down at his desk and calmly retrieved some of the case files that required his personal attention. His eye focused on the file containing the arrest and interrogation of a Communist operative, one Josef Almontini. The man had been apprehended in January. Almontini had been brutally beaten, at times with spiked mallets. And yet, the man had not revealed anything.

Kammler had then instructed his men to visit Almontini's mother. Dressed in dark trench-coats and fedoras, the SS men had pretended to be fellow resistance members of her son. They told the old woman that they wanted to free her son. The frightened Anna Maria Almontini offered up names of those in the resistance who might be able to assist these erstwhile friends of her son.

The information Kammler's men had obtained led two Gestapo agents to an apartment building in the Parioli district. The building was part of O'Reilly's network of safe houses. As it happened, a man named Caruso lived in the apartment, and he was an underground leader. The two agents were able to quickly gain the Italian's confidence. "We appreciate your letting us talk with you, Signore Caruso," one of the two agents gushed. "I see that you have some guests. I do hope that we haven't disturbed you."

"No, no, we have just been conversing amongst ourselves. You know, just whiling away the time," replied an evasive and concerned Caruso. He looked over at his two guests, British Army lieutenants Stanley and Wolfson. He continued on with his new visitors. "Perhaps, you gentlemen would like to join us for lunch. I have just prepared a simple repast of cheeses and some cold cuts."

"That is most kind of you, sir, most kind," replied Enrico, aka Heinrich Dorfman. He and his colleague, Hans Brunner, proceeded to help themselves to some of the food Caruso had presented.

The time passed slowly, until Dorfman and Brunner thanked Caruso for the lunch and left.

"I think you have just made a big mistake by allowing those two men in," said a clearly upset William Stanley. "it was a big risk. You don't even know them. You may have compromised our security, Caruso. Even more, you may have threatened the entire network."

"But what was I to do? They seemed like two nice gentlemen to me," Caruso replied weakly.

"They seemed like German agents to me," countered the until then silent Wolfson. "I do hope that nothing comes of it."

Not two hours later, the two German agents returned. This time they were accompanied by armed SS men. "Gentlemen, I am afraid that I have to inform you that you are to be taken into custody," a no longer polite and friendly Dorfman bellowed. "Take them away! And you there, yes, you. What is your name?"

"I am just a cook, sir. I just cook for Signore Caruso and any of his guests. I know nothing," stammered a frightened and shaking Federico Gugliemo. A small, wistful man with tufts of graying and white hair sprouting from his head.

"Hans, isn't it amazing that every Italian we run into knows nothing. Absolutely nothing. No wonder they have been so useless to us and our cause. They know nothing. Come here, now!" a boiling Dorfman commanded and pointed at the old Italian. "What do you know of? Come now, old man, you must surely know something."

"Sir, I beg of you. I am just a cook. Nothing more. What could I know," said the now rapidly perspiring Gugliemo.

"If you wish to join our recently departed guests, you had better start talking."

"All right, sir, all right. I do know of some Englishmen and some Americans who have been hiding out in various buildings in the area."

"Name them!" Dorfman commanded.

Federico Gugliemo then proceeded to identify some of the safe houses in the neighborhood and surrounding areas.

* * *

The two women were seated at the coffee table enjoying an afternoon tea. It was a habit they had followed for many years before the war. For the past couple of years, the routine had, at times, become almost non-existent. Rosanna Vallone and Lady Barbara Daniella sat in the two matching red-brocaded armchairs.

"It has been far too long, Rosanna. I wish we could have had tea far more often these last few years," said Barbara Daniella. The woman was dressed in a pink chiffon dress, with a pearl accented amulet dropping into her fulsome cleavage. Lady Barbara was rather tall for an Italian woman and with her frizzled style flowing blond hair, she was clearly not from the southern regions of Italy. In fact, she hailed from near Trieste, quite close to the Yugoslavian border.

"Yes, I wish it too, Barbara. But…. with the war and my loss of Giuseppe. Well…." replied Rosanna.

"He was a good man, Rosanna. And, he was always faithful to you. God only knows how many times I attempted to seduce him, but to no effect. I am only kidding, Rosanna," Barbara replied as she playfully touched Rosanna's sleeve. She knew of the Contessa's activities in the Escape Network. Daniella, herself, had never directly participated in any of its operations. She had been active in funneling ample amounts of money to help fuel its operations. "Rosanna, what is on your mind? Something seems to be troubling you. What is it? You can tell me, we have been friends for too long."

"Si, grazie, Barbara. I asked you over today to ask a favor of you. You do not have to do it."

"What is it, Rosanna? You do not have to be circumspect with me."

"I know, but still…."

Rosanna looked down at the floor as she spoke. "As you may know, or suspect, things have been getting rather intense here in Rome. You and I have never spoken directly of such things. The Germans have been quite active of late. Many people have been rounded up…. God only knows what has happened to them while in the hands of the Gestapo or the Kochel Gang."

"I know, Rosanna. It is true, you and I have never spoken about…. these certain things. Nevertheless, I have always known or had a pretty good idea of what you do in your…. spare time. I have always admired you for it. So courageous. So daring. I do not believe that I possess such skills."

"I think you underestimate yourself, Barbara."

"What is it that you would like me to do for you?" pressed Barbara.

"Well, you know Bruno Bettinelli rather well, do you not?"

"Si, I do. He has always been and…. remains a friend of mine. What has he to do with your request?"

"We know that he works closely with the remaining members of the Fascist Grand Council. Perhaps, he may know of certain things that are about…. to happen in the city," Rosanna continued.

"Things?" queried Lady Barbara.

"Si. Such things as…. impending raids, those persons suspected by the Gestapo, you know. That kind of thing."

"And you believe, or your friends believe, that Bruno may have some knowledge of such activities."

"We... err, certain individuals are under great pressure and if there is anything we can learn, anything that may help us...."

"You would like me to seduce him, is that it? At my age, Rosanna?" Barbara exhaled with a feigned exaggeration and a degree of indignation.

"You do not look your age, Barbara. And, heaven knows, you certainly do not act like a sixty year-old woman."

"Why, thank you, Rosanna. I appreciate the compliment. All right, I will contact Bruno, When?"

"As soon as possible, but you cannot make it look as if you are too anxious."

"Leave it to me, Rosanna. I know just how to appeal to Bruno. I know that he has sought some kind of companionship with me for some time. Even though he is more than fifteen years my junior, he has long coveted these," as Barbara cupped her large breasts in her hands. "How should I.... extract this information?"

"I will that to your discretion, Barbara."

"You would like for me to hump his brains out, wouldn't you?" Barbara asked with her bright blue eyes aflame.

Rosanna smiled, "You have always gotten straight to the point. I have always appreciated your way of thinking, Barbara. If you believe you can accomplish your mission by utilizing some of your feminine whiles, then, by all means, go ahead. You know you have never changed. You have always been rather avant-garde. I sometimes wish I could be like you."

"All right, Rosanna. I will give my body for Italy. In any event, it is one of my trademarks. Lady Barbara Daniella, doyen of Roman nobility." She looked intently at Rosanna and intoned, "I will do as you wish, and it may be rather fun to engage

Signore Bettinelli. I have always liked him. I know that he is not and never has been a hardliner. A Bible thumper for il Duce."

Rosanna cut in, "Barbara, this is not to be taken lightly. The matter before us is quite urgent. You cannot let yourself take a personal involvement in this…. this…. endeavor."

Barbara looked at Rosanna, the golden sun framing and highlighting her hair, and leaned forward, taking the younger woman's hands into hers. Rosanna could see and feel how the other woman could seduce anyone. She felt an electricity pulse its way through her body.

"I realize that, Rosanna. I know this will not be a light-hearted lark. We do, however, have to lighten things up once in a while, or we could likely go mad. Lovemaking, the telling or hearing of a joke, is necessary if life is to go on."

"Thank you, Barbara. Oh, there is one more thing. I almost forgot. On the off chance, if you could find out anything as to where the Germans have taken Father Alberto Ruggiero, it would be most appreciated. He was arrested at a checkpoint recently. We fear that he is being tortured by the Gestapo right now. He may even have been killed by this point."

"This bastards! The filthy swine! That tears it! I will do whatever I can to help you, Rosanna. To help all of the others in your association."

"Thank you, Barbara. On behalf of all of us," Rosanna replied to her good friend.

* * *

Later that very day, Barbara Daniella placed a telephone call to Signore Bruno Bettinelli.

"Lady Barbara, what a pleasure it is to hear from you. It has been awhile," said a clearly enthused and welcoming Bettinelli into the phone.

"Oh, Bruno. You know how it is, with the war and everything," said Barbara. How have you been? I hope well...."

"Oh, fairly well. I hope that you have been as well. You know I have been very busy with my work with the Grand Council. All in all, pretty fair."

"Bruno, I was wondering.... Oh.... you will think of me of being rather forward, but....", Barbara could feel her heart begin to flutter. It was silly to feel this way, after all, she was to talking to Bruno.

"Yes, what is it, Barbara? And, no, I would not consider you as being forward. I know you to be a decent and honorable woman."

"Well?" she resumed coyly. "I would like to see you some time. You know, just to talk, that is, more freely than we can over the phone. One does not know of whom may be listening."

"That would be a splendid idea, Barbara. It has been far too long since we have been able to speak to one another in a.... heart to heart manner. I am tied up for the next couple of days. I do have Saturday open. How does that sound? Say about 7:00 PM? Where would you like to meet?"

"Oh, well. There isn't much to pick from these days, at least, from the restaurants that are still open. And my place is such a dreadful mess. Perhaps...."

Bruno was right on cue, as Barbara had dearly hoped. "I have a superb idea, Barbara. Why not come over to my place. I will cook for you a marvelous dinner of veal scaloppini alla Bettinelli."

"I love it, Bruno. It sounds so divine and.... romantic," Barbara practically cooed into the phone. "What, may I ask, is the alla Bettinelli part?"

"That is a surprise that will only be revealed on Saturday evening. Should I have my car sent over to get you?"

"Oh, that is so kind of you, Bruno. But no, I can make my own way and, besides, I like to walk. It is part of my fitness program. Can I bring anything? What should I wear?"

"No, dear. Just bring yourself. As to what you should wear, I leave that to your tasteful discretion," Bettinelli was anticipating Barbara in one of her patented revealing black dresses. It would likely be the one that revealed her magnificent and fulsome breasts. He had long dreamed of encountering them, along with the rest of this dazzling woman. Bettinelli felt himself hardening at these continuing thoughts.

"My discretion?" Barbara thought to herself. "I think I will wear that stunning royal blue shift with the open front. It will reveal so much of my cleavage that Bruno's eyes may well pop right out of his head."

"Well, Bruno, dear. I will sign off now. I know that you are a very busy man. And thank you again for the dinner invitation. I am so looking forward to it. It has been wonderful just talking to you again. I will see you on Saturday. Ciao, Bruno."

"It has been my pleasure, Lady Barbara. I will see you on Saturday evening, Ciao, Barbara."

Barbara Daniella left her palatial home on Via Vittoria at 7:00 PM. It was only a short walk to Bruno Bettinelli's residence on Via CondorIa, a scant three blocks away. She would take her time, as it was still rather fashionable to arrive slightly late. Ahead of or on-schedule arrivals had never been considered proper etiquette in Italian high society circles. Besides, it might heighten Bruno's passion for her.

The early evening was pleasantly mild as Barbara strolled languidly along Via Crozetta. Spring was unmistakably in the air, and with it, hopefully, would see the arrival of the Allied armies. Mammoth battles were still going on at nearby Anzio and at Monte Cassino.

Barbara came across two German officers on her walk over to Bettinelli's. The two soldiers were just drawing abreast of her as she approached them. Her light coat was unbuttoned down to her waist, her revealing dress giving the Germans an eye-view of her impressive physique. It seemed as if one of the two was going to make some remark to her. It would probably have been something crude or vulgar. Barbara hurried past the men as quickly as he could on her heeled Salvatore Ferragamo shoes.

Around 7:30 PM, Lady Barbara knocked lightly on the front door of Bruno Bettinelli's house. After a moment's pause, the door opened and Bettinelli stood and welcomed her inside. She extended her right hand, as Bettinelli bowed imperceptibly forward, taking her hand and kissing it softly.

"Lady Barbara, welcome to my home," said an enthused Bruno.

"A pleasure, Bruno, a pleasure, indeed," replied Barbara. "You have an adorable and lovely home," she continued as she gazed around the living room area. The man possessed some fine artwork and, she guessed, rather expensive artifacts as well. In addition, she noticed some impressive looking tapestries and draperies in the room. The lovely accenting furniture was dark and unmistakably nineteenth century.

"How remiss of me. Let me take your coat," said Bettinelli as he moved to help Barbara to remove it. As he stood before her, Bruno was momentarily stunned speechless. The woman was wearing her royal blue dress. And to say it was revealing, would have been an understatement for Bettinelli. He could see that Barbara was not wearing a bra. Her breasts stood out so firmly, it was simply remarkable.

"Grazie, Barbara, grazie," stammered Bettinelli as he had been able to find his voice again." Now, please, sit yourself down and relax. Dinner is almost ready. I am afraid it is not quite what I had hoped to have prepared for you. I do think you will find it satisfying and…. filling. I have some reasonably fresh Italian bread and some homemade ravioli, as an appetizer. Home-made, that is, courtesy of Mrs. Bellini two doors down. And the piece de resistance, the veal scaloppini alla Bettinelli," the Italian continued in a near soliloquy.

"It all sounds and smells wonderful, Bruno," Barbara replied enthusiastically.

"Thank you. But you are too kind. Please allow me to attend to the veal and, then, we can begin."

The meal went by uneventfully. Barbara did compliment Bruno on the veal and the bread. She also thought he had chosen a rather good vintage of chianti wine.

She had also been struck by how, at first, Bettinelli seemed to have little appetite. But, of course, he had been staring at her chest off and on throughout the meal. Oh, he had tried to be coy about it. Barbara knew the dress and herself were arousing the man, which had been her intention from the beginning. The wine had seemed to relax her, to loosen her up for the night ahead, and her…. mission.

"Bruno? Are you not hungry? You haven't touched much of your meal. I must compliment you on the veal. It was superb. Wherever did you learn to cook like that?" The veal had not been that good, but she wanted to butter him up as much as possible, without going too far over the top.

"It is nothing, Barbara. Thank you for the compliment. I have always had a flair for cooking. It is in my blood. Both my mother and father were good and avid cooks," Bettinelli responded in a demure fashion. He was glad, though, that Barbara had seemed to enjoy the meal. He then began to dig into his own veal scaloppini. He had hardly touched his ravioli. Mrs. Bellini would have been disappointed.

"Bruno, you simply have to tell me all about the alla Bettinelli part of the veal dish."

"Oh, that is nothing special. It only consists of the tender loving I have devoted to preparing the meal for you, my special guest," he replied. His voice had risen a half-octave.

"How quaint and charming, Bruno. Thank you," Barbara replied as she thought the man was laying it on a bit too thick. So be it.

"And now. For dessert. I have some cannolis and an aperitif you simply have to try. It is called Crema Mandorla. I first came across it years ago, while in the midst of traveling through the Naples area.

"I can't wait, Bruno," Barbara responded brightly. She had indeed heard of and was well-familiar with Cream Mandorla. It was a pleasing liqueur made from fermented almonds. "Oh, well," she thought to herself," I won't spoil the man's delight."

Bettinelli had briefly gone to the kitchen for the cannolis and had returned. He poured some of the liqueur into two cut-glass tumblers. He handed one over to Barbara. "Here is to us and…. to a wonderful evening. And, to Italy!" he proclaimed.

Barbara clinked her glass with Bruno's and said, "Indeed, Bruno. To a wonderful still young yet evening." Her blue eyes were focused squarely on her companion's.

Bettinelli could feel himself becoming aroused at the woman's words and at the tone of her voice. He proceeded to consume some of his own liqueur. He brought two fingers to his mouth in the classic Italian gesture for something great, magnificent. "Magnifique, do you not agree, Barbara?"

"I do indeed," said Barbara as she began inching her way closer to Bettinelli. He had been sitting at the other end of the sofa. "Bruno, this has been a truly wonderful evening. You have been too kind. It has been a night where there have been too few and too far in between, with the war and everything. I have been rather…. how can I put it? Rather lonely. I do not have a man around. Marco has been dead for, I do not how many years it has been now. Oh, look at me, burdening you with my problems. I am sure that you have many of your own, as well."

Bettinelli looked over at Barbara with compassion. "You are not burdening me, Barbara. I appreciate that you have felt free to have me into your confidence." He himself had moved closer to Barbara. He could feel himself growing harder in his lower extremity.

The two looked at one another, silently, for a while. Barbara thought this was the moment for her to make her move. It was the moment of seduction. Bruno and Barbara almost simultaneously put down their drinks. In a flash they were at each other's mouths. It began with soft kisses, then, proceeded to their tongues probing one another. His left hand went to one of her breasts. Bruno could feel her erect nipple through her sheer dress. One of Barbara's hands went to his crotch, and she let it linger there.

Barbara made to stand as if to lead him to his bedroom, but she was not sure where it was. Seeming to understand her quandary, Bruno stood and guided her to his boudoir. It was a moment he had long desired. It was a moment he had fantasized about many times. And now, he would engage this attractive and enigmatic older woman in passionate and rabid sex.

As soon as they had entered the bedroom, they began to disrobe, slowly. Barbara easily removed her dress and let it drop to the floor in a lingering motion. She stood wearing only her silk panties. Bettinelli observed her and marveled at the woman's spectacular and firm breasts. She did not even need a bra. Barbara peeled off her panties and then went and reclined herself, facing Bruno.

Bruno had more clothing to remove. His shaft was by now very hard and erect. He went to the bed and moved in alongside Barbara. They began kissing feverishly, soon proceeding to the French style. Her tongue found its way to his ears. He returned in kind. He cupped her breasts and suckled them, slightly biting down on her taut and bulging nipples. Barbara fondled his throbbing penis. Her hand deftly stroking the rod as if she were playing a Stradivarius violin.

Barbara looked up at the ceiling and thought to herself, "I am probably going to have to hump him again, so as to make sure to put him under. This will enable me to try and find the information I need."

A couple of hours later, Barbara awakened in a rather groggy state. Her sexual workout with Bruno had been strenuous and, yet, fulfilling. He was still asleep next to her. Barbara began to wonder if she could get him to be able to perform again. She would soon have her answer as Bruno rolled over and faced her.

"It seems as if I dozed off," he said rather groggily himself.

"We both did, lover boy. It was wonderful Bruno. You know just how to satisfy a woman's needs," she continued artfully. Barbara looked down and could see that Bruno was becoming aroused again. She reached down and took his elongating penis into her hand. She carefully and tenderly stroked it. It was getting harder.

Barbara went onto her stomach and slightly raised her body on her knees and lower legs. This would allow Bruno entry to her from the rear. There was to be no foreplay this time.

Bruno silently understood and positioned himself to enter Barbara as she wished. He guided his engorged penis into her and slowly began to thrust. His upper body was now resting, as he moved, on her back.

After several minutes, Bruno could no longer contain himself and his raging semen poured its way into Barbara one more time. She was spinning around in her mind, as if she were experiencing an out of body episode. She could see herself standing next to the bed and watching Bruno ravage her. Barbara could picture the look on her face as she was being fucked like no other time in her life. Bruno's thrusting began to slow and he removed himself from Barbara.

Finally, the two were spent. Barbara was now sure she would be able to accomplish her task. No man of Bruno's age could emerge from the following sleep for a few hours, at least. She rolled off of Bruno and lay by his side, taking his right hand into hers. Almost immediately, he had fallen into a deep sleep. Barbara would wait awhile and then begin her search for any upcoming German activity, and for any information as to where Father Ruggiero was being held.

Barbara checked her wristwatch, it read 2:00 AM and Bruno was still sleeping restfully. She thought he indeed should. Less than a half hour had elapsed from when he had first fallen asleep. Barbara silently left the bed, desperately hoping she would not awaken Bruno. She remained naked. She thought she should remain so, for if Bruno should awaken and he found her clothed and flitting about the house he might become suspicious.

Barbara left the bedroom and padded her way to the study. If Bruno had any pertinent material, it would surely be in there. She made her way to the large oaken desk in the center of the room. None of the drawers seemed to be locked as she tried to open one of them. A good sign, she thought. Her breasts slapped together from side to side as she moved about. She dearly loved them and what they did for her when she was engaged sexually with men, but at the moment, they were a hindrance to her. Maybe she should have worn a bra, but then, her breasts may not have distracted and mesmerized Bruno to the full effect she had intended all along.

At the desk, she paused, then, slowly opened the top center drawer. She rummaged through it, but found nothing of interest. Only some pens and notes. The usual paraphernalia typically found in a desk drawer. She next tried the top right drawer, and again found nothing. The same held true in her search of the lower right-hand drawer. Barbara started to break out into a cold sweat. She felt moisture rolling down her chest and in between her breasts.

Barbara stopped her search and went out of the door of the bedroom to check on her lover. Bruno was still fast asleep, only now he was snoring loudly. That was good, she thought.

She returned to the study, to resume her search, her breasts heaving and swaying against her chest. She now proceeded to the left-hand drawers of the desk. The top left-hand drawer yielded nothing of interest. She asked herself, "Where we would he have any information? Perhaps, Bruno did not even have it in his home." No matter, she continued looking. When Barbara opened the lower left-hand drawer she found some blank stationery paper, embossed with the Bettinelli letterhead family crest. It was lion's head above two crossed swords. A lion, indeed, was Bruno. At least in bed.

Her mind went back to their recent passionate and frenzied lovemaking. His humping of her for all he was worth. How she had impaled herself upon his hardened and throbbing penis. Barbara broke her reverie as she lifted the stationery. And, voila! There it was. A small, leather-bound notebook with the Fascist Grand Council seal on top. She lifted the notebook, her heart beating faster and faster, and opened it slowly. It contained a letter stating that the Germans were, indeed planning to occupy the Vatican. The invasion was dated to commence on 01 April 1944.

Another letter contained a list of names of whom would be apprehended. Near the top of the list, after the Pope and some Cardinals, was the name of Liam O'Reilly. And there was more. Barbara spied a three by five-inch notecard tucked into the corner of the bottom of the drawer. She read the note and immediately turned pale. It revealed that SS chief, Helmut Kammler, was planning to have O'Reilly shot by a sniper if he even should come close to that notorious white line that ringed the Vatican.

Barbara tried to find any information as to the whereabouts of Father Ruggiero, but failed to come up with anything at all that might provide a clue. She quickly put back everything the way it had been and returned the leather notebook to its rightful place in the drawer. She placed the stationery paper back on top of the notebook and closed the drawer.

Barbara hurried from the study. The cold tiles of the stone floor beneath her feet. Those damned breasts of hers were on their usual wild joyride.

She moved into the bedroom. Bruno was still sleeping peacefully. She allowed herself a brief moment to relax and bring her pulse back down. Quietly, she began to get herself dressed. As she was penning a note to Bruno to thank him for the wonderful evening, a thought came to her. Why not just ask the man if he knew anything about Father Ruggiero? This would mean a change in her plans, as she had decided previously to leave her Romeo that night and to return home. Of course, that would have meant her moving about in the middle of the night. She might run into Germans, or worse, Kochel Gang members. One of them might decide he wanted to engage Barbara. No. She would undress and return to bed next to Bruno. In the morning they might indulge themselves in more sexual pleasure.

Barbara was awakened around 8:00 AM. Bruno was not in the bed, but she could hear him moving about in the kitchen. She stretched and got up. She walked into the kitchen, naked. Bruno looked over at her and smiled.

"I am just making some breakfast for us. You wouldn't have something else on your mind, would you?" Bruno asked with an arched eyebrow. Already, his penis was moving to an erection. He stopped what he had been doing and removed his apron.

Barbara could see the bulge in Bruno's pants and she smiled. How would she perform for him this time? She decided they would go through the usual foreplay, but when they both reached the point of complete arousal she would mount him. She would drive him completely out of his mind. Barbara was literally going to fuck his brains right out of his skull.

And that was precisely what she did. Barbara knew that Bruno could not, could never, get enough of seeing her atop him, her large breasts knocking themselves about. His hands reaching for them, fondling them. Barbara indeed took him hard.

Afterward, as Barbara lay curled up along Bruno's back, her breasts resting seductively on it, she asked, "Bruno, dear? I have a question for you. It is rather important, and somewhat sensitive to me."

"Yes, dearest. What is it? You can ask me anything."

"Well, I have this friend. A dear friend and no one has seen him for several days," Barbara continued on. She knew she would have to tread her way carefully with her line of questioning.

"Who is it, Barbara? Anyone that I know?"

"No. This person is a priest. His name is Father Alberto Ruggiero. He has not been seen anywhere, as I said, for the past several days. He is the pastor of Santa Rosaria Church. I have known him for many years. He is a most kind man. Very dignified, and I am most concerned about his well-being. As you know, the Germans and their Fa...." she stopped herself in mid-sentence as she had been about to utter Fascist lackeys. "Well, there have been many arrests of late and there is no telling what may have happened to him. I would very much appreciate it if you could look into this…. for me. Discreetly, of course."

Bruno well understood what Barbara had meant to say only a moment before, but he did not react to it. He knew that Barbara had not meant to offend him, but still, the term lackey wounded him. Bettinelli had been a lonely man for many years. His wife of more than twenty-one years had one night suddenly left him. Anna Maria had run off with an army general. Apparently, Bruno's own position on the Fascist Grand Council and his law work had not been enough for the woman.

Bettinelli turned himself around to face Barbara, "For you, dearest, I will do what I can to meet your request. Barbara, not all of us believe implicitly or, at least, did believe in il Duce or some of the other blowhard members of the government. I want you to know that I have done what I could to…. minimize or, at least, mitigate, the toxicity level in the city. I would like for you to believe me."

Barbara looked at Bruno, with her crystal-blue eyes, not as a lover or as an operative of the Ambrosia Network, but now as a woman. She was struck by the man's sincerity and tenderness. She knew of his own personal pain. His wife running off with some Fascist goose-stepper. She placed a hand to his face to caress it and then to his lips. "Thank you, Bruno. It means a lot to me."

"Bene. Let us now have some rolls and coffee, at least, ersatz coffee. I will then drive you home."

* * *

Later that morning, Barbara Daniella called Rosanna Vallone and suggested that the two women have a late afternoon tea at her apartment. Barbara did not want to reveal any of the information she had learned at Bruno's in which some undesirable person might overhear. Rosanna had quickly agreed to the meeting.

Barbara sat back in couch and contemplated what she had done the night before with Bruno Bettinelli. What might happen to her if someone should discover that she had slept with a Fascist, one who worked closely with the Grand Council, no less. She knew the penalty she would be forced to pay. A shaved head and being forced to wear a sign around her neck proclaiming, 'I am a Fascist whore!' or 'I sleep with Fascists!" Barbara dropped this line of thought from her head.

* * *

Liam O'Reilly received word of Barbara Daniella's findings through Rosanna that same night. He would immediately pass on the news of the proposed German occupation of the Vatican to the Holy Father. He would add word of the wanted list of persons to be arrested. O'Reilly would keep to himself, for the time being, the item concerning Kammler placing snipers around the Vatican grounds for the purpose of assassinating him. The Monsignor had been disappointed to learn that Lady Barbara had been unable to ascertain the whereabouts of Father Ruggiero. The poor man was undoubtedly suffering at the bloody hands of the SS thugs. He harbored the distant hope that Bruno Bettinelli might be able to learn where the Nazis were holding his friend, before it was too late.

"The arrests have been mounting, Monsignor," a nervous Father Lillard said to Liam O'Reilly.

"I know, Damian. I know."

"It was very close in January when the Germans took into custody Renzo Luccelli and his stepson. It was a miracle that Harvey and O'Lawlor weren't arrested as well." Father Damian had referenced two British escapees who had been hiding out with the noted filmmaker Renzo Luccelli and his family. "And even though we have implemented the cell system, arrests are still being made by Kammler's men." The new security system consisted of each person having knowledge of only the three to four people in their own particular cell.

"Well, Damian, I must say that the new clearing process has helped to improve the security of our entire operation. New men are being evaluated much more closely than ever before. You are right, though. Herr Kammler has been ramping up the pressure. He must be getting great joy out of this. The Nazi juggernaut, the purveyors of pure evil are about to extinguish a group of people who represent what is good and decent," O'Reilly quietly thundered in his righteous indignation.

* * *

Crosstown in Rome, Helmut Kammler continued to feel well— pleased with himself. The arrests of escape line operatives had continued to increase. The Jewish round-ups were continuing., to Kaltenbrunner's delight. And his most recent ordering of a mass dragnet of Italian men of all ages had proven to be very successful.

Kammler's presence at this operation reflected its importance to all of the higher German authorities who had been watching the situation closely. In February and March his SS men, assisted by Wehrmacht infantrymen and SIPO police had swept off the streets of Rome any man between the ages of sixteen and sixty. Individuals had been dragged off of trains, buses, wagons, virtually anything of conveyance. The detained men and boys were then press-ganged into helping construct military defense works around the Anzio region. Others were destined to end up in labor camps across the continent of

Europe. And some would be sent to the death camps of Auschwitz and Treblinka.

The round-up operation had secured several thousand men and had sent shock waves throughout Rome. Many shops and businesses simply shut down. Most Romans were too frightened to even be seen on the streets.

Kammler's various operations had also been ably assisted by the appointment of Pietro Caruso, as Chief of Police in the city. Caruso, an ardent Fascist and die-hard supporter of Mussolini, would bring great zeal and enthusiasm to the mission. It had amused Kammler to learn of Caruso stepping out of his office one day to observe a round-up operation, only to find himself being arrested by one of Kammler's own SS men. The man had been released soon after, but only after having undergone much embarrassment and humiliation.

The round-ups had been working as Kammler could clearly see. In February his men had rushed an apartment on Via Giulia and found two resistance men, Gianni Mattei and Carlo Lalo. In their possession had been a large cache of explosives. Mattei had later hanged himself in his cell at Regina Coeli, after having been brutally tortured. Lalo had been summarily executed at the hand of Albert Krieger.

Kammler gave his tacit approval of a plan devised by Pietro Caruso and Pietro Kochel to have Church extra-territorial properties searched. The two Italian Fascists had found that the Basilica de San Paolo le Mara had been sheltering several categories of fugitives. A raid in mid-February had turned up several young Italians who had been evading service in the armed forces. It had also been discovered that a number of Jews had been in hiding. They would be shipped forthwith to Auschwitz.

The German raids on the Church properties angered Vatican officials, who duly protested to the German and Italian authorities. Orders were then issued by the Vatican for the removal of all non-clerics from their buildings. A schism soon erupted between those of whom opposed the move, who saw the Church sending many people to a certain death, and those who had been in favor. These officials saw the move as the Church protecting and preserving its independence and neutrality.

* * *

He was looking into the mirror and he was filled with distaste. Monsignor Liam O'Reilly had just donned the uniform of an SS Hauptsturmfuhrer. He took in the peaked cap, adorned with skull badge, and winced. O'Reilly was preparing himself to visit Father Alberto Ruggiero. He would go the man so as to hear his last confession.

Ruggiero had been confined to Rome's notorious Regina Coeli Prison for the past few weeks. It hadn't seemed possible that he could have survived for this long. He was barely clinging to life following the savage beatings and tortures at the hands of Kammler's SS monsters. The Monsignor knew that Ruggiero would likely not have uttered a word to the Germans. They would get nothing from this proud and dignified man.

O'Reilly was forced to make his visit on this particular evening as he had learned that Ruggiero was scheduled to be executed at dawn on the following day. The information had been gained from Bruno Bettinelli, who had come through for Barbara Daniella and The Network. The assignment was to be carried out by a firing squad of Republic of Salo soldiers. The

Republic was the rump state created for Benito Mussolini by his comrade and friend, Adolf Hitler.

The Monsignor chided himself one final time. Everything was ready. It was now time for him to go to perform one last service for Alberto Ruggiero. He left his quarters in the German College and proceeded on his way to Regina Coeli.

O'Reilly walked for nearly two miles and had yet to encounter any German patrols or checkpoints. He was becoming concerned that it was all looking too easy. Surely, some Germans must be about. At last, he stood in front of the infamous jail. Its reputation one of dread and of immense suffering. He was quickly able to bluff his way through the prison security by using his forged pass. Guards had been instructed that O'Reilly, the erstwhile SS captain, was to be allowed admittance to the prisoner Ruggiero. O'Reilly had told officials at Regina Coeli that he had just arrived in Rome and that he was under the personal orders of SS General Kaltenbrunner to interrogate the Italian priest more thoroughly.

The Monsignor was let into Father Ruggiero' s cell. The light in the room was very dim, the only illumination provided by a single candle set upon one of the cell's walls. What he saw shocked him to his core. There lay Alberto Ruggiero, or what was left of him. Both of the man's eyes had been blackened shut. Ruggiero's nose had been broken, smashed would have been a more fitting description. His jaw looked to have been broken as well. O'Reilly could see that some of the man's fingers and toes had been broken. Blood and pus had mixed together in a nauseating dehumanizing ooze. Traces of blood had bled through the prison garb that had been issued to Ruggiero. The cloth was torn and hacked along the wretched looking man's body.

O'Reilly steeled himself after several minutes and approached Alberto Ruggiero. He bent over the man and then took a knee on the blood-spattered cell floor. He reached out and very tenderly took hold of one of Ruggiero's hands. "Father, it is Monsignor O'Reilly. I have come to you in your hour of need. I am here to listen to your last confession. Do not try to speak. If you can hear me, squeeze my hand."

Ruggiero was only barely conscious, but he did hear O'Reilly, and he did understand what had been spoken to him. He closed his hand on the Monsignor's hand with as much pressure as he could.

"Do not speak, Father. I know what God wants you to say. He can read your thoughts. He knows what is in your heart. You have lived a good life. You have done good and noble service for your flock, your Church, and to your God. He knows, he understands. You may rest in peace. God will see to it," O'Reilly spoke softly, barely above a whisper. He did not want to take the chance that an SS man might be listening.

The Monsignor removed a bottle of Holy Water from his tunic. He took out his rosary beads and a prayer shawl. He sprinkled some of the Holy Water upon Father Ruggiero's prostrate body and began to silently recite prayers. He then quickly put the articles away and slowly raised himself over the beaten and battered man before him. He thought, "As God is my witness, the men who have done this to you. I swear it! God will make them pay one day! He will see to it."

O'Reilly went over to the cell door and knocked. An SS trooper let him out. He was soon back out on the street. He was not paying any particular attention as his mind was still reeling from what he had just witnessed with Father Ruggiero. He suddenly heard the voices of several men. Germans? Most likely. Who else would be on the streets at this hour. Before O'Reilly knew it, several SS man were hardly more than ten yards away from him. As he saw them, they, in turn, saw him. The men were approaching him. He recognized one of them as Albert Krieger. Krieger would surely recognize him and the game would be up.

Tensing his body, he bolted from the spot on the sidewalk. O'Reilly was not exactly she where he was. The SS men shouted at him to stop. He ignored them and kept running and soon found that he had run several blocks. O'Reilly could hear that the SS troopers were still behind him. He was now in a narrow alley when he was confronted by a fairly high fence. He quickly estimated it to be about five feet high and looked to be constructed of wooden panels. O'Reilly tried to pick up as much speed as he could and, then, he leapt as high as he could. He was able to get himself atop the fence and then he pushed himself off. He landed heavily on his right shoulder. He winced in pain and remained on the ground for what seemed like several minutes. He had been stunned, but he didn't think he had broken anything. Slowly, he got to his feet and dusted himself off. He reached down for his cap and secured it on his head. He then cautiously and gingerly made his way back to the Vatican compound, and safety.

✳ ✳ ✳

At promptly 6:00 AM on the following day, Father Alberto Ruggiero was rousted from his cell. His Fascist guards handled his battered body as carefully as they could manage. After all, in their view, he was still a priest, despite what the Germans thought. Ruggiero was offered some water to drink, but he was unable to swallow anything. The SS torturers had seen to that. The guards left him in the cell momentarily.

At 6:45 AM, Ruggiero was brought out to the courtyard of Regina Coeli. It was dawning on what would turn out to be a fine spring day. It was only mid-March, but spring was rapidly approaching. Ruggiero could not see the emerging sunlight. He did feel it upon his face. He was devoid of almost all thoughts in his pummeled head. He only knew he had always done his best. He had always thought of others before himself.

The guards brought him over to a lone chair located in front of one of the courtyard's walls, and placed him in it. They secured his arms and legs with a thick rope. One of the soldiers placed a black hood over Ruggiero's battered head. He hardly needed it now. There was no way he could see what was about to happen to him. But he instinctively knew.

Opposite the forlorn figure of Father Ruggiero stood a ten man firing squad of Fascist soldiers. They were commanded by Tenente Eugenio Rota. Next to him stood Unterstrurmfuhrer Kurt Lang, one of Helmut Kammler's SS underlings.

"You know what to do, Tenente. Do your duty!" hissed Lang.

"Si, Tenente. I know what my duty is," responded a heartbroken Rota. He hated what the Germans were forcing him to do. He hated them with every fiber of his being. He could not wait for the Allies to arrive and chase the verminous Germans out of Rome and Italy for good. Still, he hesitated. A priest.... a priest....

"Well?" Lang barked at Rota. "What are you waiting for? Now, do it!"

Rota silently nodded and commanded, "Squad! Attention!" The ten man squad stood now at attention. "Ready!" The squad brought their rifles to bear on the target. "Aim!" The squad focused on the priest. "Fire!" came the command from Rota.

Ten rifles fired in near perfect unison. It had been an impressive display of teamwork. Even il Duce might well have been proud of these men. And yet, not a single bullet had hit Father Ruggiero. Some had not even come close.

Kurt Lang looked on in stunned disbelief. How could they have missed a man sitting in a chair not twenty feet away? "Tenente Rota! What is the meaning of this?" Lang screamed. Rota thought the man's head might pop right off. "How could you men miss the target?"

Rota, looking on, could only counter with, "But, he is a priest! How can you expect these men to cold-bloodedly execute a priest? A man of God!"

"A priest, indeed," Lang hissed through his clenched teeth. Whereupon he strode over to Ruggiero, simultaneously removing his Walther PPK pistol from its holster. He checked the slide and then placed the gun to Ruggiero's head. He paused for only a second before he pulled the trigger. A geyser of blood shot out from the priest's skull in a wide arc. Rota and his men watched the scene unfold slackjawed. Most of them made the sign of the cross as Lang had pulled the trigger.

Kurt Lang stepped back to avoid the jetstream of blood and to admire his handiwork. As he strode off, he looked over at Eugenio Rota and his men and muttered disgustedly, "Italians…. Useless…. Useless."

𝕹ine

Resistance Aflame

Liam O'Reilly had just concluded his evening prayers when he allowed himself another moment of silent contemplation. It was true that the German pressure had been increasing of late and that the raids and arrests had not abated. But on this day the Monsignor had just received some rare good news. There had been almost nothing of the sort recently. John Foreman, one of O' Reilly's good friends and associate in the Ambrosia Network, had managed to escape from his German captors. The British Army captain had been caught up in a German dragnet in February. Foreman had then been taken to a derelict complex of buildings on the outskirts of Rome. The area had once been the site of a glassworks factory, long since fallen into disuse.

The next day, O'Reilly shared this uplifting news with Robert Matthews. Matthews read the note from Foreman and handed it back to the Monsignor.

"Back in Rome. Where the hell are you? The sole consolation from my sore arse will be when I see your smiling face. John."

Foreman had escaped from his German captors by leaping from a prison train. He had then spent the next several days bicycling his way around Rome.

It was then that Foreman reunited with O'Reilly in a joyous reunion. Amidst a series of hugs and backslaps, the Monsignor had exclaimed, "In the name of God! It is so good to see you back, John. You do look a bit paler and thinner, but the important thing is that you are all in one piece. This is a most happy day for all of us."

The two men had then spoken for several hours about the network, the arrests, and the overall war situation in Italy. In February at Monte Cassino, a scant one hundred miles from Rome, The Benedictine Monastery had been obliterated under an avalanche of Allied bombs. It was estimated that five hundred tons of explosives had been dropped on the abbey. The air attack had been the direct result of the New Zealand general, Bernard Freyburg. The general had insisted to US commander, Mark Clark, and to the overall Allied commander, Sir Harold Alexander, that he would not order his troops to advance until the abbey had been bombed. Freyburg had been convinced that the Germans had been using the monastery all along as an observation post for calling in artillery strikes against Allied troops. The monastery had stood on that very site for hundreds of years.

The destruction of the abbey angered the Roman Catholic Church. Many refugees who had been hiding there had been killed in the bombings. Cardinal Luigi Maglione, the Vatican secretary of state, called the attack," a blunder and a piece of gross stupidity."

Pope Pius XII and the College of Cardinals saw something more in the abbey's destruction. They had always viewed Rome as an historic and cultured city that should have been immune from destruction. The attack had ended that assumption. The Holy Father now feared that the Eternal City itself might well come under direct attack.

Against this backdrop, Helmut Kammler continued to step up SS efforts to penetrate and ultimately squash the Vatican and O'Reilly, and his dastardly Escape Network. Kammler had recently mounted a new operation to gain access into the Vatican. It involved the just recently formed Georgian College in Rome.

Father Michael Tukavili had just been introduced to the first six students who would become part of his new College. The priest hoped to begin operations in the near future. The six young men had just arrived from Germany. Tukavili had only been told that the men were all considered good Catholics, and who all wanted to become Catholic priests.

Father Michael soon deduced that the men had been recommended to him by one Basil Sadavili, a Gestapo informant of Helmut Kammler. Sadasvili's was to have been the College's administrator. The two confronted one another and angry words were exchanged. Tukavili was able to quash the admittance of the six Germans, who were immediately dispatched back to Germany.

The Obersturmbannfuhrer would not be deterred. At Albert Krieger's suggestion, a new operative was brought to this real life stage of intrigue. Giorgio Grossi was well-known to Liam O'Reilly, as he had oftentimes provided rooms for a number of escapees. Krieger had discovered this and when Kammler proposed money and the threat of physical violence upon his person, Grossi caved in and accepted. He would become an informant, as repugnant as this was to Grossi. He knew he was a weak man in spirit and would be unable to tolerate the least bit of torture.

On March 15, 1944, O'Reilly secretly met the turncoat Grossi in his office in the Vatican. He had no reason to suspect any subversive motives from the man.

"Monsignor, there are six escapees in hiding not far from Rome. They are off somewhere in the countryside. One of them, I gather, is rather sick. I was wondering if you, Monsignor, could provide some assistance to these poor men? There is no one else to turn to," said the gray-haired, forlorn-looking older man.

"I am always willing to help, Giorgio. You know that. That is, when I can," mused an apprehensive O'Reilly. "Perhaps, I could say mass for these men where they are in hiding. And, the ill man could be brought here into Rome."

"Grazie, Monsignor, mille grazie. I knew I could count on you. I will go then and convey this to the men," gushed Grossi, his face breaking out into a cold-sweat.

St Patrick's Day dawned bright and clear. O'Reilly, joined by Father James Buckley and John May, was singing a loud rendition of "*Aghador*," an old Irish rebel ballad. They were interrupted by a telephone call. O'Reilly answered the phone and a dark frown crossed over his face. His fellow balladeers took this as more bad news.

"All right, I understand. May God forgive him." He hung up the phone and turned to his two colleagues. "Gentlemen, it seems as if our friend, Signore Giorgio Grossi, has betrayed us. That was a call from one of my informants warning me not to go out to these supposed escapees this Sunday. It is a trap set by the Germans and, I suspect it has been laid out by my old adversary, Colonel Kammler."

The concern of the Vatican over possible new offensive Allied military actions was soon confirmed. In the first three weeks of March, Rome was attacked by American and British bombers nearly every day. The Ostia tram station was heavily damaged, as were the gasworks. Numerous churches had also been destroyed including a partial destruction of Santa Rosaria. The war that had once seemed to have been so far away was now at the very doorstep of the city.

* * *

Elena Mello was having her way with her husband, Alfredo. In fact, she was dominating him, and Alfredo loved every moment of it. Elena had mounted herself atop her husband, bumping and grinding away on his hardened shaft.

She kept up her bucking as her well-formed. modestly sized breasts were swaying above Alfredo. He reached for them with his calloused hands. He massaged them with an increasing fervor. He absolutely loved them. He marveled at the way Elena's nipples were now rock-hard to his touch. He was driving himself into his wife with increasing power with each of his upward thrusts.

Elena felt a white-heat as she increased her own fevered pace atop her husband. Until Alfredo fired a molten burst of semen into her. "O-h-h-h-h, that feels so good," she thought.

"We have not had enough sex over the past few months. But not tonight." Elena kept up with her humping. She looked down at Alfredo, his face stretched into a taut grimace, but a pleasurable one.

Suddenly, the telephone rang. "What is it at this time of night? Who could it be?" Elena mumbled to herself. She had wanted to go on and have more sex with Alfredo. She reluctantly removed herself and went to the phone.

"Pronto. Si, si. I understand. I will be there as soon as I can. Ciao." She hung up the phone.

"Who was that? And at this time? What could be so important?' questioned a now unhappy Alfredo Mello.

Elena only shook her auburn shaded head. "I have to go now."

"Now? In the middle of the night?" asked Alfredo with a dark scowl creasing his weather-beaten face.

"Si. Now. It is very important," she replied in a worried tone.

"It's that bloody network, isn't it?" Alfredo replied venomously. "They are like leeches. They never let go."

Elena, who had resumed sitting in the bed, looked straight ahead, but had turned her eyes toward Alfredo. "You too have been a part of the network, or do I have to remind you?" She was referring to the work the both of them had done for Monsignor O'Reilly's organization. Elena did not mention her other work on behalf of the Resistance group of Rome.

"I know, I know, Elena. But really. This is getting to be too much. What do they want from you this time?"

"I cannot tell you that. You well know that should anyone of us should fall into the wrong hands we could be made to reveal things. I have to go!" Elena rose up and padded over to the bathroom.

Alfredo watched as her hips wiggled in that seductive way as she walked. It was a real feminine walk. When Elena turned her body slightly he took in her wondrous breasts. He had never tired of fondling them, cupping them, pinching her nipples.

Once she was in the bathroom, Elena proceeded to wash up sparingly. She began with her face and hands. She then took out a small cloth and wet it along with some soap. She went to her crotch and gently cleaned herself out. Elena looked at herself in the mirror.

Elena stepped back into the bedroom and began to dress. She would wear peasant styled clothing, so as to not attract any attention to herself. She would have to proceed very cautiously as the time was now past the curfew hour.

"Elena, I beg of you! Do not go! Why do you have to? Why put yourself at such risk?" Alfredo pleaded with his wife. "What have these people done for you, for us?"

"Done? And the Germans and Fascists are your friends, Alfredo? Do I have to remind you that our two sons have had to go into hiding or else face the distinct prospect of being deported to Germany to be confined in a work camp or labor camp. Or worse, the possibility of a death camp. No. I am committed to helping out in any way that I can. You cannot stop me."

Alfredo knew that he was beaten. He knew that when his wife made up her mind, that that was it. "Elena, please be careful. That is all that I ask."

"Alfredo, dear, you know that I will. Do not worry. I shall not be too long," Elena said to her husband as she caressed his face. She looked over at the rest of Alfredo, who had remained naked. How she longed to be able to go back to bed and engage in more passionate lovemaking, but that would have to wait. Elena took two fingers of her right hand and touched them to his lips and then brought them down to Alfredo's rising penis. She placed her fingers on the cap. "Ciao. Alfredo."

Elena Mello left her apartment on Via Margulta and turned into the pleasantly warm Roman night. She continued onto Via del Corso, the main street in her neighborhood. There, she paused for a moment. She had not observed any German patrols about anywhere. Elena could not afford to be seen, as she was out well after the curfew hour.

The Germans were rather strict about its enforcement. No one was allowed on the streets. She soon left Via del Corso and was making her way through some of the back streets toward the Ponte Cavour. Her rendezvous would not be there. The Germans were always present at bridge crossings. No, the meet was to be off of Via Brunetti.

Just as Elena was turning off to head to Via Brunetti, she spotted two Germans. The men were languidly walking along the street. They appeared, to Elena, to be chatting aimlessly, most likely about nothing. How the war kept going on. How they missed their families and so on. "Well?" she thought. "You can end the war and go home. And leave us Italians alone."

Elena managed to find an enclosed doorway to a building. She ducked inside and held her breath, as if the very act of breathing would give her away. She did not think the Germans had seen her. They had not called out in alarm, but still…. The two men continued on their walk just about to the point where Elena was hiding. She tried to withdraw further into the enclosure as the tension kept building. "Why can't they just walk faster? Oh, please. Just hurry. Sure, during the daytime you are always strutting around, goose-stepping your way throughout Rome," her mind pleaded.

The two were just about to pass by Elena, when they suddenly stopped. "Oh, no. They know I am here!" Elena screamed into her head. She felt her knees knocking themselves together. She could almost hear them as well. She began to tremble. "Will I ever see Alfredo and my two sons again?"

The Germans had only stopped to light cigarettes for each other. They never saw or suspected Elena. They then continued on their way down Via Brunetti. Elena was finally able to relax and she exhaled, still slightly trembling. Her knees were still shaking.

After several minutes had elapsed, Elena was finally able to regain some degree of composure. She slowly peered her head out of the alcove doorway. The coast was clear. She stepped out and walked to the address of 112 Via Brunetti.

There was no one about at the address, so Elena stopped and went down several steps to a cellar doorway. She tried turning the handle on the rustic and worn wooden door. It gave way with a creaking, almost tormented sound. Elena looked over her shoulder and grimaced at the haunting sound of the door. It was as if the door did not want to allow Elena admittance to what was within. Maybe she should just go home.

After Elena was finally able to enter the room, she closed the door behind her. She could see nothing, it was pitch black. She could, however, smell the old and damp mustiness of the enclosed space. She went to her handbag and removed a packet of Players cigarettes. Elena fumbled with the pack in the darkness and managed to tear a corner of it open. She carefully removed one cigarette, taking care not to break it as her hands trembled. Although, Elena rarely smoked, particularly now, during the war, she was not totally averse to the practice. She would not turn green upon lighting one up. Elena continued to rummage through her handbag, the box of wooden stemmed matches somewhere within. At last, she located them and removed one match from the box. She struck the match against the side of the box. A flame flared out and Elena brought it up to the cigarette she had placed in her mouth.

"Very good, signora. Molto bene. I am glad to see that you could carry out your instructions," a hidden male voice called out.

Elena, at first, did not recognize the man's voice, but it sounded familiar. He sounded Italian and of the local dialect, but she was not sure. After all, this man could be a German who spoke faultless Italian. Nor could she see this mystery man. "Who are you?" Elena asked in a halting manner.

"You do not have a need to know for the moment," the shadowy man replied. There was something in his voice, his inflection, that was familiar to her.

"But, what? Are you not with the Escape Network. I assumed the call was from them?"

"You assumed incorrectly, signora. I am not with the 'Network'" he emphasized the last word. "No. I am not with that pedantic and amateurish operation. What you were told over the phone was a pretext, an excuse......"

"I know what it means. I am not stupid!" Elena snapped off with fire. She resented the man's condescending tone and imperious manner. She had had to cut him off at his knees.

"No, no, of course not. I apologize, signora. I did not mean to offend you." The man was backpedaling, but he liked the venom he had heard in Elena's voice. He had an intuitive feel that this woman would be the right choice for the proposed mission. "No, I am not with that group. I am with another organization. One that is equally determined to remove the Germans, and others, from Rome. What we have in mind is a bit different than hiding prisoners of war and helping them evade the Nazis," he went on.

It was now slowly dawning on Elena. Yes, she had begun to recognize the man's voice. It was…. it began with a P-a-a—a, P- Paolo. Paolo, what is it? She knew it. It was on the tip of her tongue. Cardi… Paolo Cardi. Yes, that was it. She did not know him, but knew of him, and his reputation. A ladies' man, a raconteur. A man who rather enjoyed his way in fulfilling and satisfying women's carnal desires.

"I have asked you here this evening for the purpose of soliciting your assistance."

"My assistance?"

"Si. Your help if you will. Would you agree to help on our mission?" the man named Cardi asked.

"That would depend. What are your plans, if I may ask?" Elena probed.

"What we have in mind is something that will be so shocking, so profound, that it will shake the very foundation of the German occupation of Rome. Well? What do you have to say about that?" Cardi concluded, impressed with himself.

"You mean violence, don't you?" Elena asked.

"Si. Violence. My question to you, here and now, is are you in or are you to be on the outside?"

Elena Mello thought the question over for several moments. This would be very different from helping POWs. Should she? Or not?

"I do not have all day or night, signora," Cardi interjected into her thoughts.

"Why do you... need me?"

"At this time, you do not need to know. If your answer is no, we shall move onto someone else. Someone with more fortitude. Someone who sees the need to drive the accursed Germans out of Rome. Elena Mello we know that your two teenaged sons are in hiding. If they should be seen on the streets, they may well be dragooned off to Germany or Austria." Cardi suddenly stopped, as if to let the words sink in for Elena's consumption.

Elena sat deep in thought, Cardi's words resonating in her brain. His argument made sense, it had struck the right chord within her. Cardi was right. The Italians had to strike back. They had to, and that moment was at hand in Rome. Elena knew she had to give some kind of answer that night.

* * *

Across town at Via Volpa, near Piazza Navona, three men were engaged in a heated discussion.

"What are you afraid of, Enrico? Can you not make a decision?" implored an exasperated and clearly frustrated Mario Casso.

"I just do not know, Mario. To do such a thing. The killing it would involve. Has there not been enough of that in Rome of late?" replied a frightened and shaking Enrico Visconti.

"Killing? Killing? You speak of their having been enough killing lately. Has it not been the Germans and their Kochel Gang associates who have been doing a great deal of the killing. Besides these killings, let us not forget the hideous tortures many of these poor victims have suffered while on the way to their maker." Casso was in full combat mode as his voice began to rise. He understood and sympathized with his long-time friend, but for the life of him he could not comprehend his friend's obstinate reticence.

"But what you are planning. It seems so.... so...... senseless," Visconti started to get up from his seat on an old wine barrel. Lucca Bianchini placed a hand on Visconti's shoulder.

"No, Lucca. Let the coward go. It seems as if he thinks the Germans and their Mussolini lapdogs are more trustworthy than us," Casso said with ferocity and venom in his voice. His rage was building its way to the boiling point. He had always known Visconti would have no stomach, no heart for the operation they were planning.

Casso and Visconti had known each other since the First War when both had served as infantrymen during the disastrous Caporetto battle. Neither man had since spoken of their experiences at Caporetto, but both well knew in their hearts what had happened there.

Casso vividly recalled Visconti cowering in a trench, waiting to be killed by German shock troops. The man had been completely paralyzed by fear. He had been frozen at the very spot for only several minutes, but it had seemed like hours. Casso, a sergeant, had taken pity on Private Visconti and had helped him get through the battle. Visconti had been just another man who simply could not function in combat. These men, no matter how hard they tried, just could never get over their nerves. They were always taking counsel of their own fears. In battle this could have fatal consequences not only for themselves, but for those men around them.

"Mario, perhaps we should not place so much pressure on Enrico, eh?" Lucca Bianchini said, breaking Casso's daydream. He was playing good cop opposite Casso's bad cop role.

"Pressure? Pressure, you say? No. He has to make a decision. Make it, Enrico, or you and I are through," snarled Casso.

At that moment, Visconti suddenly broke down into tears. He was visibly shaking, his shoulders heaving. He knew that deep inside himself he was a coward. He knew and accepted the fact that he was not and never could be like that famous American actor, John Wayne. He could never stand tall when the chips were down. "Casso is right," he thought. "I am just a quivering coward. A man who is afraid of his own shadow."

Mario Casso looked down at his old friend and just shook his head. He wished that for just once the man could grow some balls. Something. Anything! As he had given up, Visconti rose to his feet.

"All right. All right. You win. I will join your merry band of troubadours and we shall go forth together to smite the German devils!"

Both Casso and Bianchini gave out quizzical expressions as if to say, was Visconti putting them on?

"Are you sure, Visconti? This is not the time to be flippant or to fool around," insisted Casso.

"I think he is on the level, Mario," said Lucca Bianchini. Casso looked at the man. He was one that Casso could trust. Bianchini was twenty-five years old and had known Mario for only two years. Like Visconti, Bianchini was a member of Casso's street-sweeping crew. Lucca possessed nerve and daring. He would always be a good man in the clutch.

"All right, then. Glad to have you aboard, Enrico," Casso replied, almost sarcastically.

"Mario, will the bomb be ready, and in time?" Lucca suddenly asked urgently.

"Cardelli has assured me that he will have everything ready, and it will be on time. He is one of the best," Casso stated firmly. In truth, he was not really sure about Gianni Cardelli, reputed explosives expert. He knew of him only by reputation. Cardelli had been a demolitions and explosives man in the First World War. Casso could not be certain if Cardelli still possessed the nerve required for such a task. He would not reveal his qualms to Visconti or Bianchini.

"This will really be something, eh, Mario?" enthused Bianchini.

"Indeed. Just imagine fifty pounds of TNT packed into a sweep cart. And it will be done on 23rd March 1944," continued a now excited Mario Casso. All present knew what the date stood for. In 1919, Fascism was born in Italy when Benito Mussolini had joined together several rival factions in Milan.

"Who will place the cart into position?" again it was Bianchini. Visconti remained silent as he stared down at the floor.

"That is being arranged now by one of our colleagues. Can you just imagine the SS police regiment, two hundred men strong, proudly marching up Via Rasella, and then...... Boom! Finito! This will strike a blow for Rome and for Italy."

Enrico Visconti wished he could share in the enthusiasm of Mario Casso and Lucca Bianchini, but he well knew there would be reprisals forthcoming from the Germans. Terrible reprisals and they would be swift.

* * *

"Well, signora. I believe you have been given sufficient time to think through the proposal made to you. Do you have an answer? Are you willing to step forward for Italy? For Rome?

For your own family?" spoke Paolo Cardi. He was now sitting across from Elena Mello in the basement of his dingy apartment house.

"I have given much thought for the past several days. My answer is........ yes...... Yes! I will do it. I am ready to step forward," a defiant Elena Mello exclaimed as she slammed her right fist onto the table set before them. The force of her blow surprised Cardi.

"What is it that you want me to do?"

Paolo Cardi then proceeded to tell her in great detail. Elena was taken aback at what she heard. She had been selected to be the one who would place the bomb on Via Rasella. Cardi explained that having Elena serving in the role of a street-sweeper would be even more innocuous and non-threatening as any man. Women, desperate women, had been serving as sweepers for some time.

The bomb would be completed by Cardelli and ready within the week. Right on time for the Mussolini commemoration. Elena knew she could not reveal to Alfredo her assignment. He would be furious and would forbid her any further involvement with these terrorists.

Paolo Cardi did not hide from Elena the fact that the bomb could detonate prematurely. But not to worry, there would not be much left of her, and she would not feel a thing.

For the next week, Elena absentmindedly busied herself in a variety of mundane domestic chores around the house. She tried to be more attentive to Alfredo. They made passionate love on several occasions. This might be the last time she would able to enjoy any pleasures of the flesh. She also attempted to have a message delivered to her sons in hiding somewhere in the vicinity of the city. In her note, she had expressed how much she missed them and how much she loved them. God willing, soon they would all be reunited.

The night of 22nd March arrived with a finality for Elena Mello. Tomorrow afternoon she would place the rubbish cart onto Via Rasella, and inside would be contained the fifty pounds of dynamite. She desperately hoped she would able to pull it off. She knew that Mario Casso and Lucca Bianchini were convinced she was the right person for the job. She could do it. She would do it!

Elena had been given final instructions by Casso on how she was to act as a street-sweeper on his crew. She would join his team at 8:00 AM the next morning. It would be arranged for them to be at work on Via Rasella by the early afternoon. There would be other women cleaning the streets, as well, to further ward off any suspicion on the part of the Germans. Security measures were still rather lax.

Elena has been briefed as to exactly where she was to place her explosives laden cart where it would do the most damage. She now only hoped to God that she could maintain her nerve. She felt perspiration break out along her entire body.

There had been other recent attacks that Elena was aware of. A German here or there, but they had been mere pinpricks. What was more, German reprisals had been swift and vicious. Ten Italians chosen at random had been shot for every German killed.

Noontime was approaching as Casso's crew worked on. It had been a very hot and humid morning and the afternoon was predicted to be even warmer. The crew broke for a brief lunch.

Elena could not bring herself to eat anything. She knew she would be unable to keep anything solid down. She only drank some bitter tasting water. The hour, her moment, was rapidly approaching.

The Casso crew resumed their work and at approximately 2:00 Elena pushed her cart up the narrow and cobbled street of Via Rasella. She struggled to wedge it up against the curb so as to keep it from rolling away.

It was just before 3:00 PM when the men of the 11th Company, 3rd Battalion of the SS Police Regiment arrived on Via Rasella. Their singing voices and marching boots rang out across the alley. Nearly two hundred men were arrayed in their battle dress.

Elena Mello first heard, and then saw, the Germans approaching her position. She had been smoking a cigarette, from the same John Player's pack she had used when she had first met Paolo Cardi. "Too late to have changed brands," she thought. She bent into the cart and with the lit cigarette ignited the bomb's fuse. She then placed her cap back on her head, as had been arranged for her watching accomplices. She calmly walked away, being careful not to run.

Elena just had enough time to make her getaway. As the SS men passed by the cart, a massive explosion tore through the alley. About thirty soldiers took the brunt of the blast and were killed instantly. Dozens more lay grievously wounded. Many of these men would not survive the night.

Elena's cart had been virtually vaporized, leaving a huge crater in the street. Leaking pipes from burst water mains mixed with the blood and gore of body parts. Pieces of arms, legs, and heads had been scattered along Via Rasella and the adjoining buildings. Two civilians had also become victims. Large chunks of masonry had been blown from numerous buildings. Via Rasella, usually among the quietest streets in Rome, was in total chaos. Mario Casso and Paolo Cardi and their associates had struck in the biggest, most visible, and most defiant attack yet.

The Underground was not yet through on this day, at least not just yet. Upon seeing the successful detonation of Elena's bomb, several more operatives tossed four mortar bombs at the surviving SS men. Firing erupted from Germans who had been uninjured from the blast. These men had assumed that they were under fire from the surrounding buildings. Bullets ripped across their fronts, doors, and windows.

Rushing to the scene was Rome's police chief, Pietro Caruso. He had been attending the twenty-fifth anniversary Fascist ceremony nearby. He was stunned by what he saw: blood, lots of blood, dismembered bodies, moaning and crying. He could not believe it. "Who could have done this? Who could have done this?" screamed into his head. "Those swines in the Underground!"

Joining Caruso was General Kurt Malzer, German Armed Forces Commander in Rome. Malzer, a chronic alcoholic, had been drinking heavily during his just concluded luncheon with Helmut Kammler. "Pietro, what had just happened here?" Malzer screamed out.

"I do not know. I cannot comprehend it," stammered a still shaken Caruso.

"Pietro! Have your men start rounding up every resident of Via Rasella. I will have reinforcements sent in. We will get to the bottom of this massacre," Malzer shouted through his inebriation. "I swear to God!"

It did not take long for many of the most powerful men in Rome to descend upon the scene. Guido Buffarini-Guidi, Interior Minister, and Consul General Friedrich Mollhausen, and Colonel Eugen Dollmann among them.

At gunpoint, entire families were rousted from their homes and into the street. They were then taken to the gates of Palazzo Barberina, where they were ordered to stand with their hands raised into the air.

Meanwhile, the rage and fury had been building within the volatile and unstable Kurt Malzer. His alcohol filled brain fueled a burning desire for immediate revenge. These bloody Italian swine could not be allowed to get away with this. In front of the others he said, "I will have every building on Via Rasella blown up, razed to the ground! This street shall be leveled. Nothing is to be left standing!"

The young diplomat, Friedrich Mollhausen, was stunned by Malzer's words. "General, you cannot be serious. You don't even have all of the facts. I dare say, we do not have many facts at all. There has been no investigation."

"I do not need facts, Mollhausen. I only know what I see before me. I see that vengeance must be sought for what has been done to these brave German soldiers. Look, Mollhausen, what has been done to them," Malzer hurled back his venomous retort.

* * *

"Colonel Kammler! Colonel Kammler!" an excited Albert Krieger stammered as he ran into Helmut Kammler's office.

"Yes, Krieger, what is it?" Kammler replied wearily.

"Sir, a bomb was just detonated in Via Rasella. It was devastating. There are many dead and wounded," Krieger continued on breathlessly.

Kammler sat stunned at the news. He had just finished his lunch with Kurt Malzer only a short time before.

"Sir, an SS police detachment had been marching up the street when a massive explosion tore through their ranks. It was terrible."

Kammler continued to say nothing. He had thought, no, he had assumed that he had had a thumb on the accursed underground movement. It was more than likely that they had been the ones who had set off this bomb. "All right, Krieger. Summon my car and driver. We are going to Via Rasella now," he commanded.

"Yawohl, sir." Krieger then clicked his heels and gave out the one-armed Hitler salute. Kammler merely flicked out his right arm in what Krieger though resembled a casual 'Heil.'

As Kammler and Krieger approached Via Rasella in their staff car, they ran into Mollhausen and Dollmann. Helmut Kammler had never cared for the phlegmatic Dollmann, and he had never concealed his feelings toward the man. Dollmann, in turn, had always considered Kammler as narrow-minded and mean-spirited.

"This is unbelievable! All of these bodies, the carnage. Do we have any idea who did this?" Kammler threw out at the assembled men.

"Indeed, sir. No, we do not yet know who is responsible for this attack. We do think that we have a pretty good idea," Dollmann offered matter of factly.

Kammler nodded his head, he knew of whom Dollmann was referring to. He turned to Krieger, "Krieger. Get me General Malzer on the car phone.

Mollhausen interjected, "Excuse me, Colonel, but I believe the general is still in the area."

Kammler ignored him, waiting to be put through to Malzer. "General, Colonel Kammler. Heil Hitler," said Kammler.

"Heil Hitler, Colonel.," replied a still shaken Kurt Malzer. "it is just terrible. Just terrible. What has happened? I swear to you, Kammler, I will wipe them out. To do such a dastardly thing to our men and in broad daylight here in Rome, and under our very noses," Malzer continued on in his highly exaggerated state.

Kammler listened as Malzer bellowed on. He thought his colleague sounded as if he were slurring some of his words. That wouldn't have been a surprise to Kammler. He knew Malzer to be an inveterate lush, even in the middle of the day. The Via Rasella attack would probably send him on a one week bender. Kammler realized he would, at least, have to remain calm.

"I tell you, Kammler. They are all to be shot! Every last one of them! And, I will do it. I will.

"Sir," Kammler finally cut in. "I am prepared to take control of the situation." Kammler was trying to get Malzer to simmer down, at least to a low boil. This was not the time to be running around as if one's head had been cut off. "Leave it to me, sir. I will get to the bottom of this outrage. That, I can assure you." Kammler was finally able to ring off from the drunken Malzer. He then directed his attention to the chaotic scene playing out on Via Rasella.

"Stop that shooting!" Kammler commanded the SS men upon his arrival at the scene of the attack. The troopers had continued hosing down doorways and windows along the street in the wake of the blast. "Krieger, arrange for transport for the wounded. Those men must be taken care of quickly or the else the death toll will mount even higher. Find out how many have actually been killed."

Kammler began walking along Via Rasella. He took in the full impact of what had just occurred. He stopped and picked up some pieces of mortar shells that had been hurled at the marching SS men. He spotted the left arm of a little girl and visibly recoiled. "Yes!" he thought defiantly. "I will get to the very bottom of this treacherous attack. I will find out who is responsible and I will make them pay dearly. Very dearly."

Later that same day, Kammler had been able to put together what had happened on Via Rasella. He was in no doubt at all that the Resistance had been behind the attack. He then went to Kurt Malzer's headquarters.

"General, I believe that the main bomb and the mortar bombs were thrown from the roofs of buildings along Via Rasella. The death toll now stands at twenty-eight men. I suspect that the count will increase. Many of the survivors were very badly wounded and I do not think some of them will survive."

Kurt Malzer had finally been able to calm himself down. In fact, he hadn't even had a drink in several hours. Kammler was surprised at Malzer's apparent recent sobriety. There might be hope for this lush yet. "I do not care...... err, Kammler. Do whatever it takes to bring the swine responsible to justice!" he barked out.

* * *

Upon receiving word of the attack in Rome, Adolf Hitler had reacted predictably. He was overheard telling one of his aides, "I want those responsible for this atrocity to pay dearly! I want reprisals! I will see to it that every building on that accursed street is blown up. For every German who was killed, I want thirty Italians shot!"

* * *

In Rome, high level German officials were convening on how best to handle the crisis. Kurt Malzer and General Eberhard von Mackensen, Fourteenth Army commander, and Helmut Kammler conferred via telephone.

Von Mackensen, "Kammler, what experience do you have on the matter of reprisals?"

To which Kammler replied, "Herr General, I once discussed the subject with General Harster in Vienna."

"And what did the general suggest, Kammler?"

"Sir, he said that if a reprisal is called for, that persons already in custody should be shot."

"That sounds interesting and quite reasonable, Kammler. All right, this is what I propose. For every German who was killed in the Via Rasella attack, and for those who will expire from their wounds, ten Italians should be executed. Do you and Malzer have any objections or any suggestions?" asked von Mackensen.

"None, Herr General," replied Kammler and Malzer in near unison.

"Good. Then we shall proceed. You men know what to do. Heil Hitler!" as von Mackensen cut off the call.

Kammler and Malzer continued discussion on their own on the subject.

"You know, General, it may be difficult to rope in so many Italians to meet this quota. I certainly don't have the number in my custody at the present time. And, besides, we can assume that the death toll will undoubtedly rise."

Malzer, for once, had nothing to offer. He only nodded his head lamentably. He felt as if he could use some sleep in his present condition.

* * *

At the German College within the Vatican, Liam O'Reilly had been informed of the Via Rasella attack. Many of the details were still missing, but he had gotten the gist of what had transpired. He knew that German reprisals would be swift and severe. He was now worried about the increased vulnerability of the escapees the Network still had in hiding. O'Reilly was most concerned for such key operatives as Rosanna Vallone and Robert Matthews. And there were others, such as himself and Father Damian Lillard.

The Monsignor quickly ordered Matthews to move, temporarily, as many Allied servicemen as possible from their current safe houses to new locations. If people, like Rosanna, were caught by the Germans to be hiding these men, then, they too, would likely be shot as well.

* * *

Helmut Kammler was sitting in his office at SS Headquarters on Via Wolkonsky with Albert Krieger. It was late morning, a Wednesday. The two men were putting together a list. "We don't have enough, Krieger. Seven more of our men have just died. That now brings the total to thirty-five casualties."

"Perhaps, sir, you can approach the police chief, Pietro Caruso. He may be able to help us augment our own list," suggested Krieger.

"That is a good idea, Krieger. Get me Caruso on the phone."

Kammler then proceeded to instruct the Italian as to what he needed in the way of prisoners for his count. He also contacted his old mentor from Vienna, SS General Harster, for additional advice on how he should proceed in the matter of the executions.

Helmut Kammler called his entire staff together in the afternoon. Among them was one, Hauptsturmfuhrer Erich Priebke. "I want all of the records in the office to be searched. All of the prisoners who have been sentenced to death for offenses against German troops. Any at all, are to be executed!"

Just as Kammler was completing his briefing he received a visitor. It was none other than Consul-General Mollhausen. The Consul had gotten word as to what Kammler and his men had been up to. He was horrified.

"You cannot be serious, Kammler! This would mean the execution of more than three hundred people. More, should the present death toll rise. This goes beyond the norm of patriotism. It is beyond all reason. Remember," the diplomat pointed his hand at Kammler, "you may have to answer for this action. And, not only to any possible tribunals, but to God."

"I have my orders, Mollhausen. I have my orders. As to the possibility of future military tribunals, as you say, so be it. As to God, what do I care. I serve the Fuhrer and Germany," Kammler said evenly.

* * *

Rosanna Vallone was seated upon her couch, silently contemplating the news of the Via Rasella attack. She had learned that the bomb had killed and wounded many Germans. Two Italians had also been killed. Innocent, harmless people. One of them a young girl, her left arm blown off at the shoulder. "Terrible, so terrible," she thought to herself She knew that German retribution would not be long in coming and it would be savage. Already, mass raids and arrests were going on all over the city. The Nazis had virtually emptied out Via Rasella of all of its residents. Rosanna had also heard of executions of civilians as payback for the bombing. She wondered what impact this would have on the Escape Network, on Monsignor O'Reilly, and on the escapees themselves. What about the effect on herself, and her family?

The Contessa was, at that moment, hiding three escapees, two Americans and a soldier from New Zealand. His name was Preston. He was constantly telling jokes amongst the three men. And with his pronounced accent, they always sounded especially funny. He was a natural-born comedian.

Rosanna clutched her hands and thought wistfully of Robert. She remembered quite clearly their mad and passionate lovemaking. She longed for it again. She wanted to feel his manhood inside of her body again. Absentmindedly, she began massaging her ample breasts. She felt her nipples fill and harden. Suddenly, she stopped. "I cannot allow myself to conjure up such past memories, even if they kindle pleasure within myself," she thought ruefully.

Across Rome, Jimmy Cefalo had remained confined to Genevieve Alviano's apartment. The two of them had adjusted themselves to one another and had settled into a comfortable routine. Often they had sat together for hours just talking about themselves, or about Italy, or Boston, or the war.

To pass the time on this day, Cefalo had been intently studying Italian. He was determined to be able to converse with Genevieve in her own native language. He had also begun to enjoy the language itself. It was easy to learn, at least, in comparison to English, as there were virtually no silent letters. Almost everything was sounded out.

Cefalo had been thumbing through an Italian-English dictionary Genevieve had given to him off and on throughout the day. Suddenly, the girl burst through the front door of the apartment. She was breathing hard. Cefalo could clearly see that she was excited and angry. He watched her chest rise and fall.

"What is it, Genevieve? You look as if you have just seen a ghost."

"They've done it! They have really done it!" she called out loudly, as to not only at Cefalo, but to the whole of Rome.

"Done what? What are you talking about?" replied a mystified and fearful Cefalo.

"The underground. They...... set off a bomb...... err, several bombs on Via Rasella. Many Germans were killed and wounded. Even two Italians were killed. One of them was a little girl, her arm had been severed. They said there was blood and gore all over the street and on the buildings nearby," Genevieve went on without pause.

Cefalo did not know how or if he should respond. Should he go to her? Of course, he had to.

"This is terrible! Why did they have to do it? And, why now? This will only bring the Germans to full boil. They will destroy the city. It is just.... terrible! Why?" she continued wailing.

Cefalo went to her and gently embraced Genevieve. It was the very first time he had seen her cry. The young woman had always been such a rock. The tears were flowing unchecked. Genevieve did not resist his touch. In fact, she squeezed his arms with her hands. "It will be all right, Gen, all right," he said softly into her ear.

Genevieve turned her face to meet his gaze. The two of them could feel what had been building between then for some time.

"Gen, I am here for you. Don't worry. I will protect you," Cefalo said with deep sincerity and feeling.

Genevieve brought her lips to meet his and they kissed for the first time, tenderly. They continued and she slowly slid her tongue into Cefalo's mouth. He responded with his own.

"Genevieve, are you there? Can you hear me?" came the excited voice of Rosetta Cacci, her upstairs neighbor. "Please open up. The Germans are conducting another raid through the neighborhood."

Genevieve and Cefalo looked at one another, as if in stunned disbelief. It couldn't be. The girl reacted first and strode to the door. Upon opening it, Rosetta burst inside. She was highly agitated and breathing heavily.

"Genevieve, the Germans are over on the next block. They will be here soon," Rosetta gushed forth, her chest heaving. A cold sweat bathed her pale and angelic face.

"All right. All right. Jimmy, you will have to be moved, and quickly," Genevieve halted in mid-sentence.

Rosetta picked up her thread. "Do not worry, I will guide Mr. Cefalo out of the building."

"Right. Bene. Jimmy," she turned to the American, "you will go with Rosetta. She knows what to do. Do not worry. She will get you away from here safely. Now, quickly, gather up all of your things. I will straighten out the apartment so that if the Germans do come here they will find nothing. Now, go quickly, subito!"

Cefalo's mind was now in a whirl of conflicting and turbulent thoughts. He began to gather up his things. Every article of clothing he possessed. Everything, right down to his toothbrush. As he moved about, he began to calm himself down. Out of the corner of his eye he observed Genevieve and Rosetta quietly picking things up and checking everywhere. They even checked the bed-sheets and pillowcase covers for any of his hair.

Cefalo was ready within minutes. He had stuffed his belongings into an old Italian army duffel bag Genevieve had given to him. Once again his heart began to flutter with uncertainty and fear. Not knowing what might lie ahead began to unnerve him.

"Right, now Jimmy. You will follow Rosetta. Do whatever she says. Understood?" Genevieve directed.

Cefalo nodded his head. What would happen to him? What would happen to Genevieve? Would he ever see her again? He would just have to trust in these two remarkable women. Everything would work out for the best.

Finally, Cefalo and Genevieve stood in front of one another. Even thou Rosetta stood only a few feet away, it was as if she were not in the room. He moved to her first, but she ran to him. They embraced for one last time and gave one another a brief kiss. Tears started to fall down Genevieve's cheeks. Cefalo, himself, felt a tear well up in his eyes.

"Genevieve, thank you. Thank you for all that you have done for me. I will come back. This is not the end. Believe me, I will return." Genevieve nodded as she looked down at the floor. She was too choked up to even speak. Softly, she said, "I know, Jimmy. But you have to go now. The Germans may well be here at any moment."

Wordlessly, Cefalo broke his embrace and with one last look at Genevieve he left with Rosetta. As the door slowly closed, Genevieve collapsed onto her threadbare armchair. She gripped her forearms tightly together in her lap and wept. The war had become too much for her. How much could any human being endure before they could no longer go on.

Genevieve did not have the luxury of wallowing in her own pity for too long. Less than an hour after Cefalo's escape, the Germans arrived at her apartment. She let them in and was confronted by a sneering, self-obsessed SS lieutenant. He directed his men to search every square inch of each room while he looked her up and down. The young woman began to feel as if she were being violated. Apparently satisfied, the SS officer turned on his heel and led his men out. Genevieve let out a slow breath of relief and let her thoughts drift back to Lieutenant James Cefalo.

* * *

"Kochel, I have just been in contact with your colleague, Pietro Caruso. I need for you to supplement Caruso's effort to procure a sufficient number of names. I expect results, Kochel, results!" Helmut Kammler virtually shouted into his phone.

An exasperated Pietro Kochel could not bring himself to tell the Nazi chieftain that he thought his objective was not worth it. Instead, he said, "I understand Colonel Kammler. My staff is doing all it can to provide assistance to your, your.... endeavor."

"Bullshit, Kochel! You and Caruso had better get a move on, if you both know what is good for you," Kammler spat back at the Italian Fascist. He then peremptorily slammed down his phone on his desk.

The following day Kammler met with Kurt Malzer and Sturmbannfuhrer Karl Dobleck, the commander of the now decimated Third SS Police Battalion. Kammler informed the men that he and Albert Krieger had made significant progress in the compilation of the list of prisoners to be shot. He also told them that he was waiting for a list with fifty names on it. It was to be provided by Pietro Caruso within the hour.

"Dobleck, I want you and your men to carry out the executions," said Kammler. Malzer endorsed the order on the spot.

"I am not sure Herr General, Herr Obersturmbannfuhrer," replied a hesitating Dobleck to the two senior officers. "My men are tired, many are old, and some of them are very religious. They could not, I believe, in good conscience carry out an order of this kind."

"Excuses, Dobleck. You are only offering us excuses," hissed a once again inebriated Kurt Malzer. "It will simply not do in the SS to so openly prevaricate and delay! Go, Dobleck, get out!" Malzer looked over at Kammler. "Listen, Kammler. I will contact General von Mackensen. Maybe, he can provide some additional manpower. You would think that Dobleck whose command was just obliterated, would eagerly look forward to such a task."

Kammler did not bother to reply, but only shook his head dolefully.

"I am sorry, General Malzer, but General von Mackensen is not available at the moment," responded his chief of staff Colonel Wolfgang Hauser.

"Listen, Hauser, this is most important. Colonel Kammler needs personnel for a most important assignment," Malzer continued on angrily. "He needs to assemble an execution team for the purpose of retribution for the Via Rasella massacre."

"Speaking on behalf of the General, I am afraid he will be unable to accede to your, excuse me, Herr Kammler's request for more men. By the way, the attack was perpetrated on SS men, was it not? Then, shouldn't it be the SS that carries out the reprisal?" Hauser replied to a now stupefied and absolutely furious Kurt Malzer. The chief of staff was able to terminate the call with dispatch.

Meanwhile, Kammler's list of names had gradually begun to rise. Listed among the unfortunates were shop workers, plumbers, butchers, and shoemakers of all ages. Catholics and Jews, and some of no-declared faith were included as well. Two of Liam O'Reilly's operatives, Andrea Casadei and Vittorio Fantini, had only recently been arrested. They had been picked up along with Brother Robert Place, when he had gone out to bring in new members of the Escape Line.

The growing list had encompassed some former members of the Italian military. Some of these men had been actively involved in the overthrow of Benito Mussolini the previous July. There was one significant name among those dragooned by the SS and his name was Colonelo Giuseppe Cordero Lanzo de Montezumo. Helmut Kammler had known that the colonel had created a front designed to oppose the Nazis and the Fascists. Montezumo had also established a clandestine radio network, known as Centro X. Information was transmitted over it on German troop movements to the Allies.

The SS had arrested Montezumo in January. He had been duly tortured by Kammler's men. The SS Colonel had personally observed some of the interrogations, offering suggestions on occasion. Montezumo's jaw had been broken, his eyes battered shut, and his legs and face had been pummeled as well. Kammler had hoped the man would lead him to other members of the Resistance and to the Escape Network. And, of course, to Monsignor Liam O'Reilly.

* * *

Word of the Via Rasella attack and the subsequent Nazi reprisals had gotten back to the Vatican and to Liam O'Reilly. The Monsignor had been informed of a private audience between Giuseppe Montezumo's cousin and the Pope. The Marchioness Fulvia de Mento begged the Pontiff to help her cousin in any way that he could. The poor man was in desperate straits. There was no telling how long he could hold out while at the hands of those inhuman German beasts. He may have been dead already.

"He is in Colonel Kammler's bloody hands as we speak?" the Holy Father asked the Marchioness with defiance in his voice.

"Si, he is, your Holiness, and we know what that means."

Pius XII winced visibly and then said, "I can only promise you that we will do all that we can. Unfortunately, I cannot guarantee you anything. Marchioness, I will pray for your cousin. That, I can guarantee."

* * *

Liam O'Reilly knew, felt that the moment of truth, the moment of denouement was at hand. He wondered and worried how much longer he and the members of his eclectic band would remain free.

Ten

Slaughter and Clampdown

elmut Kammler stood watching as the prisoners were pushed, kicked, and dragged into the waiting trucks. Those like Colonel Montezumo, who had been so badly tortured and brutalized, that they were barely conscious. Many of them had suffered through the excruciating pain of having toe and finger nails ripped out. Hands and feet had been smashed. These poor souls were barely recognizable now.

Included in this group were two men, Paolo Cardi and his father, Umberto. Upon learning that his father had been swept up in a German raid, Paolo had gone berserk. His participation in the Via Rasella bomb attack had, in effect, condemned his own father to death. To atone for this, Paolo had felt that he had to join his father on what would be his last journey. His mind drifted back to several days before.

"Paolo, you cannot do anything! You can't!" pleaded a desperate Elena Mello. She and Paolo were seated in the same dingy underground room where they had first met.

"I cannot believe it! I cannot, Elena! The Germans have got my father. He is to be executed in reprisal for our attack on Via Rasella. Do you realize that I have condemned my own father to death?" wailed an inconsolable Paolo Cardi. His face was contorted into a nearly unrecognizable mask of pain.

Elena did not know what to do or what to say to this man in his agony. Tears were now streaming down his face. She, too, had been experiencing her own internal anguish and mental torture. She had been overcome and grief-stricken when she had learned that two Italians had been killed as a result of the bomb she had set off. Elena did not think that God would ever forgive her for what she had done.

She went over to Paolo and placed her arms around his neck. With a tissue she tried to dry away some of his tears. Then, she bent down and brought her lips to his. She kissed him with a soft caress, and he responded in kind. Elena inserted her tongue into his mouth and, again, he followed suit. She would offer her body to him. She knew Paolo would find a way to join his father. To join him in death.

Elena began to remove her clothes, he did not. She now stood before him, naked, her breasts mounted proudly upon her heaving chest. Her nipples stood out like bright orbs. Paolo noticed that she possessed a superb body. Her arms and legs had good muscular definition. Elena's stomach was flat and defined. She was ready for him. She was begging for him.

Cardi stood slowly. He began to disrobe. Elena patiently waited, her libido building within her. When Cardi, at last, dropped his underwear, she was surprised. The man was rather well-endowed in his own right. She silently marveled at the length and breadth of Cardi's shaft as it assumed its full and erect shape. Elena hoped she would be able to accommodate him.

The couple engaged themselves in, at first, soft kissing, but this soon progressed to fevered French-style kissing. He explored her body tenderly. Elena had never before betrayed her husband, Alfredo but, this time, this was only thing she could think of to help assuage her own guilt and to help Paolo face his own nightmare.

At the very moment of her extreme sexual arousal and pleasure, and his, Paolo Cardi climaxed into Elena. He maintained his incredible thrusting and Elena still gripped his body tightly. Paolo had marveled at the strength he had felt in Elena's legs as she had squeezed them against him.

The two of them then lay entwined in each other's arms Both realized it would be the last time they would ever see each other.

"Paolo? Are you all right?" Elena asked tentatiely.

Cardi barely heard her voice, his mind was already drifting away from the present and he was imagining what tomorrow would behold. He would join his father and together they would go forward to meet their maker. He knew he had to do it. He was obligated to do it.

"Paolo?" Elena asked softly.

"Si, I hear you, Elena," Paolo responded in a dry and husky voice, laboring with his emotions. "Elena, I want to thank you for what you have done for me. I mean not only for what we just did, but for everything."

"I could not think of anything else that I could do. I feel so guilty. I sometimes wish I had never gotten involved," Elena said through her building tears.

"Sh-h-h, do not blame yourself. After all, it was I who convinced you to join our cause. You, me, Casso, Visconti. We have all virtually pulled the trigger on my father's life." Cardi soon drifted off to sleep in Elena's arms.

* * *

"Schutz!" barked Helmut Kammler. "Tell your men what is to be expected of them. If any should choose to refuse to take part in the executions, then, they will be shot for refusing to obey a direct order."

"Yawohl, Herr Obersturmbannfuhrer!" responded an excited Hans Schutz, one of Kammler's subordinates.

Helmut Kammler looked on the gathering scene as it unfolded and was satisfied. He directed his driver to move on. Schutz, meanwhile, got into his kubelwagen command car and ordered the convoy containing the frazzled and dispirited prisoners to move out.

It was dark and foreboding inside each of the army trucks, but the prisoners were able to catch glimpses of some of the familiar landmarks, such as the churches and the ancient ruins. The condemned seemed to know that this would be the last time they would see them again.

The convoy kept moving until it took a pronounced right-hand turn. They had reached the entrance to the Ardeatine Caves. The trucks pulled up to a stop, air-breaks squealing in the gathering night. The prisoners were roughly rousted out of the trucks and into the darkness.

Gathered near Colonel Montezumo were the two Cardis, father and son. Paolo had managed to find a way to join his father when the older man had been taken from Promesi Jail. In the confusion of the prisoners being organized by their handlers, the younger Cardi had inserted himself within the small group that contained Umberto.

All over Rome, prisoners had been taken from their cells. Elenora Lavoretti, a lawyer who had been assisting in the hiding and movement of prisoners of the Ambrosia Network, had been arrested for this very work.

Umberto San Lucena, a doctor, had been arrested and tortured for his role in the network. He had operated a radio for the Centro X group. Not an intimate, but known to O'Reilly and Matthews. San Lucena was hustled out of his cell. He thought he had a feeling about what was to happen to him and the others. He had, at last, met his fate and it would not be pleasant.

The prisoner count had climbed to more than three hundred Italians who would never see the light of day again. At the caves, Kammler knew he would have about five hours in which to complete the executions. Strangely, he felt himself becoming emotional and, almost tearful, as he addressed his subordinates. Krieger, Schutz and Erich Priebke observed this and wondered what to make of it. Krieger thought, "Now, we shall see how tough you are, Kammler. It is always easy when you are fighting the war from behind your desk, but here, now...."

Schutz and Priebke held no thoughts. Both of them realized, in his own way, that men react differently when faced with great and emotional stress. They continued to listen impassively to Kammler's instructions.

Hauptsturmfuhrer Erich Priebke went over to the convoy of trucks and began to check a list of "Todeskandedalin." He asked each of the condemned their names and crossed them off with his pen. The first five men were taken into the caves, torches lit the way. The men were ordered to take to their knees. They did so and bowed their heads. They knew this was the end. Nothing could be done or would be done for them. Schutz ordered his SS men to fire and five shots rang out, the echo reverberating throughout the cave complex. It was precisely 1530 hours.

Helmut Kammler had been standing outside of the caves. He wanted the executions to be carried out swiftly. There was to be no dallying about this task. After the start of the killings he walked over to one of the Mercedes trucks from the convoy. He selected a prisoner at random, as did each of his junior officers, and they then went back into the cave. Kammler joined Albert Krieger, and Schutz, and Priebke, in opening fire on their own personal group of prisoners. There would be no going back for him. Blood was on his hands.

The murder rampage continued as the two Cardis, father and son approached, awaiting their turn. Cardi senior was whimpering and had to be helped along by his son. Paolo Cardi tried desperately to maintain a stoic face, but it was almost impossible for him. Paolo thought of his mother and what their deaths would do to her. She would be devastated and probably never recover from the shock. His two sisters, Margareta and Sophia, would declare their undying desire for revenge, vendetta. He knew their temperaments. After all, they were

Italian women and would do all in their power to seek vengeance.

"Who are you?" asked a startled Erich Priebke as he encountered the two Cardis.

"I am Umberto Cardi," stammered the elder one, hardly able to get the words out of his trembling mouth.

"No, not you. I mean you!" as Priebke pointed to Paolo.

"I am Paolo Cardi, sir. I have chosen to be with my father. I did not want to have him face this alone."

Priebke looked from one to the other and shook his head. "Well," he thought, "if he wants to die, he can die." He made a notation to his list. He would inform Kammler later about the list and the change in the count. "All right, you two can go on," as he motioned Paolo and his father to join the other condemned prisoners.

Cardi senior and Cardi junior were then forced to kneel down along with three other men. Paolo found himself starting to recite the 'Hail Mary', while his father had resumed his whimpering. The old man began weeping openly. He knew he was not a courageous man and never had been. The command was given and five more shots rang out in the cave. Both Cardis had been executed with bullets fired into the backs of their skulls. Paolo and Umberto Cardi pitched forward into the previously dug pit, joining the other poor victims and entered martyrhood. Their names would be long remembered in the Roman community.

The killings went on and the bodies kept piling up in the Ardeatine Caves. One of Kammler's junior officers, an Untersturmfuhrer Wotzen, at first, had refused to take part in the shootings. Kammler went over to the young SS man. "Wotzen, do you think you can carry out your duty?"

"I am afraid I cannot, sir," the young man replied with a tremor in his voice.

"You know that being afraid is not in the lexicon of the SS. You do realize that, do you not?" Kammler continued on calmly, as if he were merely discussing a routine office matter. It was strange, but as the executions had gone on, Kammler had felt himself becoming calmer himself and more accepting of the task at hand. "Wotzen, I know that you can do it and I will help you," as he then took out his Luger sidearm so that Wotzen could see it. He guided the young SS man over to the next set of prisoners scheduled to be shot. Wotzen silently understood and he, too, removed his own pistol. Both men raised their guns.

"Ready, Wotzen?" Kammler asked.

Wotzen nodded as a lump took shape in his ever tightening throat.

"All right, then. On the count of three we will fire together. Ein... zwei... drei... Feuer!"

Wotzen hesitated for a fleeting second, but fired his weapon just after Kammler had discharged his own. Two heads exploded before them. One of them a rare woman prisoner. It was the person that Wotzen had himself executed. A young woman with what had once been soft auburn colored hair. Blood and brain matter cascaded outward in bright arcs. Kammler quickly turned to Wotzen as if to shield him from the gruesome scene before them. The SS officer started to lose his composure and vomited. An SS scarffuhrer guided him out of the cave complex.

By 1600 hours, prisoners from Via Tasso and Regina Coeli who had been on Kammler's list had nearly all been executed. The SS chieftain was still unhappy. "Krieger!" he commanded. "Where is Caruso's list?"

"It has not arrived yet, sir."

"Go and get Caruso. Personally, if you have to. Drag him out from wherever he is hiding. That worm! Find him! I want that list. I need those men. In fact, do not bother if you cannot find him. Just go ahead and take fifteen to twenty people, men or women, it does not matter. That should bring us to the total we need to reach," Kammler concluded.

Albert Krieger was soon on his way to Trestevere Prison. He never even bothered to try and locate Pietro Caruso. He merely commandeered the first group of prisoners he could find. They were hustled out of their cells and pushed into a waiting army truck. The men, who had expected to have been released that very day were, instead, to be used to augment the reprisal total.

The sun had now gone down and the Ardeatine Caves were now bathed in darkness. The massacre was approaching its conclusion as well. A total of 335 people had been put to death by Helmut Kammler's SS men.

"Krieger, Priebke. I want the entire cave complex to be blown up. See to it, that it is done. I want it done right away!" commanded Kammler.

Moments later, prepared charges of explosives were set off and the grim day had at last reached its grisly and murderous conclusion.

The SS chief then returned to the Hotel Excelsior and met with senior military personnel. Among them was Gruppenfuhrer Karl Wolff, the senior SS man in Italy.

"Tell me what happened at the Ardeatine Caves," Wolff began.

Helmut Kammler gave a detailed recounting of the day's events. "A total of 335 prisoners were executed in reprisal for the dastardly Via Rasella attack."

"I am not sure that will be a sufficient number, Kammler. I think you may have been a little too lenient with these.... these Roman citizens. These people are not entitled to any special or favored treatment. Believe me," Wolff continued as he fidgeted with one of the medals pinned to his tunic. "All right, Kammler. Have a communiqué issued which will cast blame for our military action on the activities of the Resistance. No, wait, make that justifying our military action."

"Yawohl, Herr Gruppenfuhrer!" piped back Kammler.

"And Kammler, we must contain this increase in anti-German feeling here in Rome. I also want the city to be ridden of all of the remaining Jews and anti-Fascists."

Kammler continued to listen to Wolff impassively and in silence. Privately, he was not all happy at what Wolff was saying. "Hadn't there been enough killings already? How much blood did men like Wolff want before they would ever be satisfied? Does he not know or care about how many men will be required to root out these others, these Jews......?"

Key Vatican representatives were now trying to piece together what had taken place at the Caves. One report from Monsignor Nunzio Rotta, a regular visitor at Regina Coeli, revealed that inmates had told him of fellow prisoners being taken out and, then, shot. It had been unclear as to where the shootings had taken place. Other stories and rumors abounded. Some were rather grisly and difficult to listen to.

At the German College within the Vatican, and at the British Ambassador's residence, a state of high anxiety was in the air for Liam O'Reilly and Robert Matthews. More than forty escapees and Italians had been jailed in the wake of the last German dragnets. O'Reilly had been most anxious to find out if any of them had been included in the Ardeatine attack. The Monsignor would later learn that a number of Escape Line personnel had been shot in the caves. Matthews was deeply traumatized by the news of the Cardi's deaths. He had met the younger Cardi briefly and thought he had been a man of great courage and charisma.

"Monsignor, I think that you may have to consider yourself rather lucky," said Matthews.

"I suppose you could say that," responded O'Reilly, sitting in his spartan office with the ever-present grandfather clock chiming in the background. "It could have easily happened that I could have been pulled in during one of Kammler's interminable raids. If I had been arrested, undoubtedly, I would have been on the Nazis' hit list and shot along with those other poor and unfortunate people."

Matthews looked at the Irish priest, but remained silent. Every day he had come to admire this remarkable man more and more. He was truly what was good in a world that had almost disappeared in this dark and brutal chapter of it.

"Good God, man! How much more blood will have to be spilled? How many more will have to be tortured and suffer hideous deaths? And, and.... when will the Allies finally get here, Bob? When?"

* * *

The Saturday following the attack on Via Rasella the Germans buried their dead. All of the top Nazis in Rome: Kammler, Mollhausen Dollmann, and Wolff were in attendance. Kammler again listened as Wolff promised more in the way of retaliation. More Jews and other undesirables were to be rounded up. It was a repeat of the same litany of the upper SS leadership. Kammler even thought that it had started to sound tedious and boring.

Local people who lived near the Ardeatine caves began to detect strange and unpleasant odors escaping from the tunnels. Complaints were soon forthcoming to local civic authorities and the German occupation forces.

"Colonel Kammler, people are starting to complain about the smells emanating from the Ardeatine area. We will have to do something," cried an excited Pietro Caruso, the erstwhile Police Chief of Rome.

"Let the people complain. What do I care," responded Helmut Kammler flippantly as he shuffled through some papers. "Listen, Caruso, if you want to do something, then, do it! However, do not attempt to have any of the bodies removed. Oh, and by the way, Caruso, nice work on that list of prisoners you were supposed to have provided," Kammler sneered as he could not resist a dig at the Fascist policeman.

"But, Colonel, I did provide you with a list," protested a chastened Caruso.

"Yes, you did. When it was too late, Caruso!" as Kammler cut off the Italian. "In any event, do not trouble me any further about some unpleasant odors. Blame the weather. The Allies. I do not care!" as Kammler slammed down his phone.

* * *

Father Damian Lillard had long grown used to these rants of Monsignor O'Reilly, and today was another one. Their number had been increasing of late.

"Damian, Father Giorgio managed to gain access to the Ardeatine Caves. He and Father Valentino were able to find a way inside. They say the smell they encountered was overpowering. They saw piles of bodies stacked up and scattered about. Disgusting! They also saw that a number of victims had had their hands tied behind their backs. Good God, man!"

"Father Giorgio has been a good friend of yours, Monsignor. What can we do? Is the Vatican going to formally protest this, this… massacre to the German High Command?" Lillard replied as he spread his arms in a gesture of hopelessness. His voice had started to pitch higher in his growing excitement and building outrage.

"I am not sure, Damian. I'm just not sure, at least, at this point. I do know that what the Germans have done will stay with me for years, likely, forever. I do not think I will ever get over this. This outright bloodletting. This carnage," O'Reilly mused on, while thinking, if he himself, had somehow contributed to the massacre. His activities with the Escape Network. His continual frustrating of Colonel Kammler and his plans to crush O'Reilly. This may have all spilled over in the SS's massacre at Ardeatine.

"Monsignor, are you worried about the bounty Kammler has placed on your head?" Father Lillard asked, referring to the 30,000 lire reward the German had created for the capture or killing of Liam O'Reilly.

"Well, of course, Damian, but I cannot worry or obsess over it, can I?"

"What about the snipers Kammler has placed around the Vatican perimeter? I fear that he only wants to have you shot. He does not care at all about arresting you. Rumor has it that

Kammler himself is sometimes stationed at these posts. A high-powered rifle with a sniper scope, as if he personally wants to do the deed....," Lillard continued.

"Yes, there is that, too. But....

"And Monsignor, I don't think it to be a good idea to tease the Germans on some of your daily walks." Father Lillard was now referring to O'Reilly periodically straddling the ubiquitous white line the Germans had painted alongside the Vatican boundary. The Monsignor, while opened to a passage in the Bible, could be seen walking just to the inside of the line in full view of any of the hidden snipers. He would almost, at times, appear to be about to step over it and, then, suddenly pull his raised foot back. "Oh, Damian, do not be so concerned over my welfare. I just like to have a fun once in a while. Just a little tease," chortled a suddenly upbeat O'Reilly. He was, however, not finding these reminders of Lillard as amusing as he outwardly presented to his assistant.

"Yes, but I do think that you might be just stretching things a bit, don't you? You know, Monsignor, when the Contessa heard about one of your escapades, well, I thought she was going to have heart failure."

"Tell her that she worries too much over me. Please reassure her, and yourself, that I will be extremely careful in all of my future endeavors. I am a big boy and what I have done are small things. They have just been ways to get back at the Germans, Damian."

"And in a way that may well provoke them, Monsignor," Father Lillard answered.

Monsignor O'Reilly and Father Lillard well realized the invaluable assistance that had been rendered to the Escape Network by the British legation and the American consul in

Rome. The escapees within their charge were in the main British, but also included a smattering of Americans, South Africans, and even some Russians and Greeks. Across the city of Rome, the Network operated some two hundred hiding places. The Monsignor had always considered that, perhaps, the organization had grown too big, thus providing for more opportunities for Kammler and his SS to penetrate it.

The Via Rasella attack had resulted in the Germans bringing more troops into Rome. They seemed to be everywhere at once. The city was in a tense state of affairs, as if it were sitting on a tinderbox. Then, out of nowhere, came what seemed might be deliverance.

"What would you say to being able to get hold of routine orders as they originate from the SS and their Fascist lackeys?" asked John Mayberry, the British legation butler to a stunned Robert Matthews.

"What are you talking about? Do not try to make jokes. Not at a time like this," scolded Matthews.

"Robert, this is not a joke. I am deadly serious."

"Go on."

"I have a contact who has access to these orders, almost from the moment they are drafted. What do you say to that?" continued Mayberry patiently. The Brit was juggling his silver-plated pocket watch as he spoke to the American.

"Who is it?" Matthews pressed.

"I cannot reveal that at this time. Are you still interested?"

The American officer was pondering the proposition. "What if this contact is a hoax? A German plant. And, how much will this information cost us, John? As you well know, money is tight. Food, transport, and so on will still be required," Matthews continued, eying the British butler. He knew the

Network was going through more than 180,000 lire per month in expenses. Donors, such as Lady Barbara Daniella, had obligingly increased their donations, but still…. And money continued to flow in from the British government to Sir D'Arcy Osborne.

"My contact is willing to provide his information for 1,000 lire, Bob. Is that doable for you?"

Matthews continued with his pensive thinking, but finally decided to agree to Mayberry's proposal. It just might be the very break they so desperately needed at this moment.

In a matter of days Matthews was sifting through detailed SS and police order transcripts. The new information would provide the Network with solid leads, not haphazard guesswork, as to German intentions and actions. He now knew of specific houses the Germans were planning to search. He would often know of planned raids by noontime of the days in question. Matthews and O'Reilly were usually given about a five hour window in which to give out warnings and to arrange for new accommodations. The priest had also established a courier / messenger system in which to warn householders of an impending raid. Mayberry's source of information had proven to be a gold mine.

* * *

Helmut Kammler had been asleep at his post within the SS headquarters on Via Wolkonsky. He was aware of what O'Reilly and his cohorts had been up to. In early April, he thought he had struck true gold. His men had been carefully watching the San Roberto Bellarmine Church, Kammler had known that the church and its priests had been helping Allied escapees by offering then food and shelter. Don Pietro Perfetto was one of these so-called priests. Although he dressed as a cleric, he was not in any actual shape or form. Arrested by Pietro Kochel's men in late March, he had quickly revealed who in fact he really was.

Perfetto had been performing a variety of tasks in several safe houses for Monsignor O'Reilly. He had also served in the role of a courier for the Escape Network. O'Reilly had been informed of these turn of events by Francois de Riall, who had been entrusted with the supervision of the French escapees in Rome.

De Riall had informed Robert Matthews that Perfetto had only revealed information to Kammler after undergoing severe and unremitting torture. The man had been broken, literally as well as figuratively, in body and spirit. Matthews was also told that after his release, Perfetto had been seen about Rome in the company of well-known Gestapo agents. This had caused O'Reilly and Matthews to move a number of escapees from hiding places that Perfetto had had knowledge of two new ones that would have been unknown to him. Still, Kammler had been able to arrest a considerable number of men, twenty-one in all.

"Robert, Perfetto's betrayal has had enormous consequences for us. It has placed even greater pressure on us to find new houses in which to hide our men," exclaimed an agitated O'Reilly.

"We will have to keep these men completely hidden. I mean air-tight. We cannot take the chance of having them being caught out of doors on the streets," responded an equally vexed Robert Matthews.

"You are quite right, Robert. We ourselves will also have to remain out of circulation, if you will, for the time being," O'Reilly continued as the grandfather clock imposed its chime in the background of his spartan office.

Matthews glanced over at the giant timepiece and realized, for the first time, that the clock was a truly impressive instrument. He broke his reverie when he said, "Well, Monsignor, Kammler has not yet put us out of business. He has placed a severe crimp on our maneuvering, but we are still alive and still viable."

"Yes, Robert, but for how long? Every day I pray for the Allies to break out of Anzio and for their forces at Monte Cassino to break through as well. Deliverance has to come to the Holy City! It has to!"

"We are now confronted with another problem, Monsignor. The Germans have severely curtailed the city's bread ration. Many people are barely able to stay alive. Protests have broken out as hungry and frustrated men and women feel as if they are at the end of their rope," Matthews went on.

"And things have also turned violent. Looting has broken out. I heard that the SS just arrested ten women. They then shot them and proceeded to dump their bodies into the Tiber," O'Reilly finished Matthews's thoughts, a pained look on his face.

* * *

Helmut Kammler reacted to the ration crisis with his typical cruelty and harshness. He directed Krieger to set up an organized flying squad of SS agents and troopers. On Easter Sunday, three more Germans were killed in yet another Resistance attack. Kammler saw this as his chance to seize the initiative, once again, by having the Quadaro district surrounded. The working-class neighborhood was home to several of the Underground groups. A raid on this area might well lead to his being able to finally crack O'Reilly and his blasted Escape Network.

Kammler and his SS men struck on a bright April morning in the largest round-up in Rome since the previous September. Some 2,000 men and boys were gathered in and held for questioning. Seven hundred and fifty of them were then immediately deported to Germany and Austria. Among them was one of Elena Mello's teen-aged sons.

More raids followed in the ensuing days in the Spogna and Navona districts of Rome. Not as large as the Quadaro operation, it was, perhaps, the most devastating. Several key Escape Line operatives, men like William O'Flynn and Bill Simpson, had been seized. Simpson had tried to claim that he was Irish and, therefore, should not have been arrested. The SS scharfuhrer who had listened to his plea had been unmoved.

At Regina Coeli prison, Simpson maintained his innocence. "Listen, I tell you I am in the employ of the Vatican. You will have to provide some answers tomorrow morning if I do not show up for work."

"Really? You still wish to maintain this preposterous story of you being Irish. We know that you are, in fact, American. Your feeble and pathetic attempt at an Irish brogue sounds more Scottish to me," leered an unimpressed Albert Krieger. "Now, why don't you drop all of this pretense and admit as to who you really are."

"I have nothing further to say to you."

"Very well, as you wish. Take him away! Later, we shall see if you still have nothing to say," said Krieger as he indicated to his men to remove Simpson.

Bill Simpson's disappearance caused great concern for both Liam O'Reilly and Robert Matthews. By late April, the two men realized that the Germans now knew how the Escape Network was being supported financially. Kammler had been able to connect the funding to Sir D'Arcy Osborne, the British Ambassador. Friends of the German in the Swiss embassy had provided the key information unwittingly. Ernst von Weizsacker had learned, through one of his informants, of the lavish Swiss funding operation to the Network. While the Ambassador had secretly informed the Vatican that this practice would have to cease, he had also told Helmut Kammler of the development.

Meanwhile, Kammler increased the pressure on O'Reilly. He barred all public access to the German College. All non-Vatican personnel, such as Rosanna Vallone and Genevieve Alviano, could no longer visit the Monsignor in his office.

The ban also forced O'Reilly to devise new ways in which to conduct Escape Line business. He would now arrange to meet Matthews within the confines of St Peter's Cathedral. He was even able to persuade the head of the Swiss Guards to allow him to use of their guardroom for private discussions.

A new Allied offensive had opened in the south of Italy in May. This kindled optimism about an impending liberation of Rome. Would the Allies finally be able to make it? Could they break through the tough German defenses at Monte Cassino?

Helmut Kammler renewed his efforts to break up and destroy the Network. He directed his men to increase their surveillance of Rosanna Vallone, her attractiveness notwithstanding.

"Ariana, have you noticed anything strange lately? I mean have you seen anything odd or unusual around our home?" asked the Contessa of her daughter.

"No, mother. At least, I don't think so. Why do you ask?"

"I'm not sure, dear, but I am leery about some of our new neighbors that have moved in across the street. Maria believes they are not to be trusted."

"Does she have any idea as to who they are?" asked Ariana in a now concerned manner.

"She says she believes they are two German men and an Italian woman," continued Rosanna.

"It is probably nothing, mother. On the other hand, it could be just a liaison point for the purpose of carnal relations."

"Carnal relations, Ariana?" Rosanna replied, somewhat shocked at her daughter's verbiage.

"Mother, really! I am nineteen and am aware of such things between men and women," Ariana replied somewhat testily. "In any event, it might do well for us to be more careful in the future."

It was an accurate assessment. The very next day two men knocked at the Contessa's door. They were Allied prisoners who had been on the run for weeks.

"I am afraid you men will not be able to stay here. I fear that I am being watched," said a shaken Rosanna Vallone to the unwashed and worn-down men standing before her.

The two crestfallen men left and walked back out onto the street. They were immediately picked up by a Gestapo tail, but were able to soon elude them in the warren of streets and alleys surrounding the Contessa's home.

Rosanna sent word right away of this event to O'Reilly and to Robert Matthews. They all knew what this meant. The Contessa and her family were now in grave danger. Their involvement with the Ambrosia Network had come to a sudden and definitive end. The Monsignor surreptitiously arranged for the Vallone family to be spirited out of Rome and out to a farm in the countryside. Rosanna feared as to whether she would ever see Robert Matthews again.

Matthews was soon made aware of another startling turn of events by Father Lillard. The two men were sitting in an ante-room at the British Legation. Lillard was defying the German edict of not leaving the Vatican grounds. "Robert, I just received word that Father Masters has been taken into custody by the Gestapo. It seems as if they just dragged him off to the Via Tasso Jail. They picked him up, despite the fact that he was on the grounds of Santa Maria Maggiore," Lillard gasped breathlessly.

"I am sorry to hear of this. It is just more bad and distressing news. It's not good news at all," replied a no longer shocked Matthews. "How did they get him? And why?"

"Apparently, he had been tailed by a Gestapo agent who questioned him. It seems as if Father Masters then attempted to make a break for it to the church, when he was then clubbed in the head by the German. Father managed to reach the church, but the SS seized him anyway. They have been interrogating him since," Father Damian continued.

"The Germans will stop at nothing in their quest to break us. They think nothing at abusing, even torturing a priest. Look at what Kammler had done to Father Ruggiero," Matthews felt his anger rising within himself.

"Robert, we can only hope and pray that Kammler and his thugs do not torture him too badly, or kill him outright."

"Father, it may be better for him, and for us, if they do kill him," concluded Matthews. He truly hoped that he would be proven wrong.

* * *

"You would not believe it, Monsignor. I have just received two messages, one from Pietro Kochel, and the other from your old friend, Hauptsturmfuhrer Krieger, Kammler's lapdog," exclaimed an agitated Damian Lillard as he handed the messages to O'Reilly.

The Monsignor read Krieger's note first and then proceeded to slam his fist down upon his desk. The drapes had been drawn across the windows of the room, lending a foreboding presence to the discussion between the two men." The sheer audacity of this man! I simply cannot believe it!"

"Of whom, Monsignor?"

"Kammler. Would you believe that he wishes, wishes mind you, to arrange for a covert meeting with me? He says it is a matter of grave importance to discuss. It seems as if he is now concerned with the recent Allied offensives underway at Anzio and Cassino. It looks as if, at last, the Americans and the British will break through. Quite possibly all the way to Rome and beyond. And Damian do you know what he wants?"

Father Damian mutely stood there and shook his head.

"He would like for me to arrange safekeeping and passage of his wife and children to Germany. Of all the…. Can you imagine, Damian? It is preposterous after all this man has done. The killings, the tortures, the abject quaking fear that he and his men have inflicted on the Holy Church, Rome, its citizens, and to our very own organization." O'Reilly stood up from his desk, the notes shaking in his hands.

Father Lillard thought that he detected a wisp of steam rising up from the Monsignor's head. "How do you plan to help him, Monsignor?" Damian asked quietly.

O'Reilly looked at the younger man, at first., with what looked to be one of contempt, but turned into an enigmatic smile. "You do know me so well, Damian. Despite all that I have just said. You knew I would, at the least, hear the man out. Yes, it may be possible to get Herr Kammler's family safely to Germany."

O'Reilly then read the note from Pietro Kochel. "It seems as if Mr Kochel is of the same frame of mind as that of Colonel Kammler. He, too, is growing concerned over the present military situation. Undoubtedly, he is probably trying to save his own neck. Good God, man! Can you believe these two men? Men who have been trying to annihilate us for so long. Now, they are appealing for our assistance, for our help. Our mercy."

"What is Kochel proposing, Monsignor?"

"He wants to make a deal with me. If I can place his wife and mother in a religious home when he is evacuated from Rome, then, he will ensure that our colleagues in Regina Coeli shall remain there. They will not be harmed. He will personally see to it that they are not sent to Germany."

* * *

One week later, on a dark and moonless night, Monsignor Liam O'Reilly waited near the gate to the Vatican grounds along Via lo Vaticano. He was secretly wondering if he hadn't made a mistake in agreeing to meet with Helmut Kammler. He could be kidnapped by the Nazi's thugs and never heard from again. Likely, he would be tortured unmercifully and, perhaps, even by Kammler himself.

"I knew you would come, priest. I just knew it," a cold and impassioned voice called out to O'Reilly in the dank night.

O'Reilly looked about, but could not locate the voice. He knew who it was. "What do you want, Colonel?"

"Ironic, is it not? The commander of all SS forces in all of Rome seeking aid from a man of the cloth. They say that politics makes for strange bedfellows," Kammler continued.

"What is that you seek, Colonel? And why from me? I do not have the time, nor the inclination, to engage with you in a casual conversation over philosophy," O'Reilly fired back figuratively at the SS man.

"No, of course, you didn't. I was just attempting to, as the Americans say, 'Break the ice.' Please, you must indulge me that much."

"I do not have to indulge you in anything, Colonel! Now, I am a busy man."

"Busy? Indeed, priest. I have been trying to crack you and your gang for some time now. You and that infernal network, but to no avail. I must commend you. You have been a most worthy adversary. I have truly enjoyed our little chess match, if you will," Kammler went on laconically.

"This has not been a game or a chess match, Colonel. Perhaps, for you it has been. It has not been so for the thousands of Rome's citizens. The odiousness and the downright cruelty of you and your men's actions have been disgusting and immoral. You will have to answer for your actions one day," said O'Reilly as he felt the venom building within his own throat.

"Indeed, I undoubtedly will, Monsignor. For now, though, I have a request of you. I will come straight to the point. We know what the implications are for the immediate future. The Allies will soon arrive in Rome. It could be within a few weeks or even days. Our gallant German forces will be unable to hold back against the enemy any longer. I, along with all of the German forces in the city, will be evacuated. There is, however, no provision in place concerning dependents. That is where you come in, Monsignor. My wife and children will require safe passage back to Germany. There are many people who would dearly love to get their hands on them. I know that a man with your vast talents and expertise and organization can perform this task. What do you say?" Kammler asked as he concluded his self-righteous monologue.

O'Reilly could now see the German a little more clearly, standing in his field-gray SS uniform. The Monsignor simply stared back at Kammler with a feeling of revulsion and disgust. "You have the gall, the nerve, to stand before me and ask that I help you and your family. Good God, man! You would stoop so low, such as this? Have you no shame, Colonel?"

"You and your Church were most fortunate that the Fuhrer did not go through with the planned occupation of the Vatican that had been planned for April 1st. That cabal in the Holy See that you serve has been most fortunate," said Kammler as if he were lecturing a schoolboy.

"Colonel, you now stand here and proceed to lecture me. I truly will never understand the logic men like you employ. You go around strutting that silly and stupid goosestep and barking out commands. You hold simple and innocent people in a grip of mortal fear. You torture and kill these same people without compunction and without a shred of mercy. And now, you, you Colonel Helmut Kammler want me to help you!" responded a defiant and angry O'Reilly.

"Will you help me, or not?"

Liam O'Reilly stood up to his full height of six feet two inches and faced the Nazi officer. The surrounding night seemed to grow darker and colder around him. It felt as if it were closing in on him. "I cannot promise you anything, Colonel. I just cannot promise anything."

Kammler nodded, the SS runes on his collar tabs flashed. "Thank you, Monsignor. That is all I can ask for." He then turned on his heel and vanished into the night.

All of Rome knew it and felt it. Liberation. Deliverance was finally, agonizingly at hand. The German occupation of their beloved city, the Eternal City, was about to end. It was June 3rd, 1944 on the calendar, but it felt as if a holiday were about to take place.

Ernst von Weizsacker visited the Vatican, for what would be the last time, and met with Monsignors Tardini and Montini. He confirmed with them about the imminent German evacuation. He, too, had a request of them in the form of having them serve as brokers with the Allied forces, so as to obtain the safe passage of any German nationals leaving Rome. The city would be declared an "open city." There would be no military action to be taken by either side. And, historic buildings would be preserved, untouched for posterity. The Vatican, weary of the war and the suffering of the Italian people, agreed to pass the proposal on to the Allies.

The Germans were now clearing out of Rome quickly. Men like Eugen Dollmann took in the sights of the city for what would be the last time. Kammler, Krieger, and Priebke left hurriedly, but before they had been able to take the time to destroy incriminating documents. Documents which detailed their murderous activities in Rome.

Pietro Kochel and his Fascist band, and Pietro Caruso, the Fascist Police Chief, could not have gotten out fast enough to suit them. They were well aware of what awaited them should they be caught by the Americans or, worse, if they were to be apprehended by the Resistance.

The city was deluged in a blizzard of leaflets dropped by Allied aircraft. The leaflets bore the message General Sir Harold Alexander, proclaiming that the liberation of Rome was at hand. The citizenry was encouraged to maintain civil order and not to conduct drumhead trials and executions of those individuals having or suspected of having collaborated with the Germans.

One man who would not experience the joy of liberation was Captain John Armstrong. The British Army officer was to have been a part of the deal worked out between O'Reilly and Pietro Kochel. The Monsignor had fervently hoped Armstrong would be released. Instead, the truck bearing the captain out of Rome pulled off to the side of a country road. Several prisoners with Armstrong, their hands bound behind their backs, were ordered out of the truck. They were then commanded to drop to their knees. Each man was shot once in the back of the head. It was yet another horrific act that reflected once again the brutality of the Ardeatine Caves massacre.

Eleven

Liberation and Wedding Bells

onsignor O'Reilly was on his knees deep in prayer. He was expressing his thanks to his Lord God for having delivered peace to Rome and to her long-suffering citizenry. Her people were finally free. He also realized that he had survived Helmut Kammler and his Nazi accomplices. And yet, he also realized that he had lost many close and dear friends, such as Father Alberto Ruggiero. Although Rome had suffered some damage from the Allied bombings, he had been relieved that the city had largely been spared major damage and any significant loss of life.

American tanks and troops first rolled into Rome on June 3rd. Civilians of all ranks: men, women, even children climbed aboard those same tanks. They were no longer afraid as they had been just a short time before, when German tanks and armored vehicles openly tried to intimidate them.

During the first night of liberation the city was hit with a power outage. It did not seem to matter as the people just stayed out on the streets in a delirious outpouring of thanks.

The next day, General Mark Clark, the US Fifth Army commander, led the way into the city in its first full day of freedom. The general was given his own personal tour of the city. It was a moment he had anticipated and planned for, for months.

Mark Clark was driven over to St Peter's Cathedral, where he paused momentarily for pictures. Liam O'Reilly was standing in the square, as he usually did nearly every morning of each day. He had been reading from his Bible, and thinking. Upon seeing the arrival of Clark and his entourage he went over and introduced himself. "Welcome to Rome, sir! Is there anything that I can do for you?"

"Good day to you, Monsignor. It is indeed a fine day for Rome, is it not?" replied an energized Mark Clark.

"Indeed, it is, General."

"If I may, Monsignor, could I impose upon you to allow me to visit the Campidoglio? I do not want to put you through too much trouble," Clark continued.

O'Reilly was visibly impressed with the American general. He was a tall and imposing man. His hawk-like nose lent him more of the quality of a natural-born leader. "It would be my pleasure, sir. I will arrange for someone to guide you and your men there."

"Thank you, Monsignor. By the way, what is your name?"

"Monsignor Liam O'Reilly at your service, General," snapped out O'Reilly brightly.

As General Clark set off for the Campidoglio, O'Reilly thought to himself, "What took you so long in coming?" He also realized that he was now free to go about anywhere throughout his beloved city. That infernal white line would soon be obliterated, its symbolization no longer staining the Vatican. O'Reilly was no longer a prisoner within its very grounds. No longer was he threatened by Helmut Kammler or any other Germans.

* * *

Meanwhile, another group of individuals were also now free to emerge from their places of hiding. The Vallone family wasted no time in returning to the Eternal City and their home. They went immediately there to find their abandoned apartment untouched from when they had hurriedly left it only a short time before.

Rosanna Vallone was very grateful for this, but she was anxious to make contact with her old friends, Genevieve Alviano and Barbara Daniella and, of course, Monsignor O'Reilly. And, there was her reuniting with her lover, Robert Matthews.

Rosanna and Genevieve had become very close in the preceding months of tension and both had shared many thoughts and secrets. The Contessa had known of the young woman's budding relationship with Lieutenant Cefalo. She was aware that things had developed to a certain degree between the two young people. Of course, Rosanna wanted to find Matthews quickly and desperately hoped that he was well and had not been captured by the Germans. He probably would have been shipped off to some place like Germany and to an uncertain fate. Rosanna felt as if she could almost see him and touch him.

Two days after Rome's liberation, Rosanna Vallone and Genevieve Alviano entered the German College and proceeded directly to the office of Monsignor O'Reilly. They did not have an appointment, but they did not think he would mind seeing them at this impromptu meeting. They were rather sure he would be delighted to hear of their requests.

"Rosanna and Genevieve, how delightful to see the two of you again. And, under such different and pleasant circumstances," O'Reilly enthused as he rose from behind his desk in greeting the two women. He briefly shook their hands and exchanged air kisses as well. "Now, to what do I owe this visit from the two of you?"

"Well?" the Contessa began haltingly, "well, Monsignor, both Genevieve and myself would like to ask a special favor. We would like your blessing.... your blessing." Rosanna again hesitated. She did not think she could go through with it. She looked down at the floor as she clutched her hands tightly together.

"Rosanna, my dear. What are you struggling so mightily with? You have a request, but you hesitate," O'Reilly responded soothingly. "I have never known you before to be unable to speak about what was on your mind."

Genevieve had remained silent to this point, but now felt it was time to speak. She knew what her friend was struggling with. Rosanna wanted to be able to marry Robert Matthews, should she find out that he was safe. However, he was a recent, or was about to be, divorcee. His wife had long been trying to divorce him.

Rosanna well knew the Church's view toward this type of situation. If she were to marry Matthews, the Catholic Church would not recognize her union. In fact, it would excommunicate her. This fact had been tormenting and torturing her.

"Monsignor," Genevieve began gently," I think Rosanna knows what she would like to ask you, but she is fearful as to what your reply will be."

Rosanna looked over at the mature, beyond her years, young woman and reached for her hands. Genevieve took them and the two women almost simultaneously began to generate tears. This tore at O'Reilly's heart as though he knew as to what Rosanna was so terrified of.

"It is all right, Genevieve. I am all right," said Rosanna as she had regained her voice. "I am a grown woman and I will just have to come right out with it." She picked up her head and looked right at O'Reilly. "You see, Monsignor, I have fallen in love with Robert and I would like to marry him. However, as you well know, he is about to be divorced by his wife. The Church would not recognize our marriage. It would have no meaning. I.... do not know what we can do."

O'Reilly sat back and steepled his fingers together in his trademark fashion. "I understand your dilemma, Rosanna. There is a way that can be used that would obviate your problem of being able to marry Robert. And it would be accepted and recognized by the Church."

"What can we.... or you do, Monsignor?"

"Robert could request an annulment to his marriage to his ex-wife. They do not have any children, correct? So he wouldn't have to renounce them or disown them, if you will. Robert could try that approach," O'Reilly said gently.

The cascade of falling tears on Rosanna's face began to slow. She attempted a halting smile. "That would be good, Monsignor. When could we begin this process of…. annulment?"

"It could commence right away. I will meet with Robert and get Father Lillard involved, as well. Now, as to you Genevieve. Do you have something to request of me?"

"I do, Monsignor. I do. I, too, have developed very strong feelings for Lieutenant, err, Jimmy Cefalo. You see, we have also fallen in love with one another and we wish to marry. We would consider it an honor and a blessing if you could officiate our nuptials. We would also deeply appreciate it if we could have the ceremony performed in Santa Rosaria Church."

"Well, I see. Let me say that nothing would please me more than to accede to the wishes of the both of you fine women. Genevieve, do you and Mr Cefalo have a date planned?"

"No, Monsignor. Of course, it would be after the war. Also, both Rosanna and myself would like to have our marriages performed at the same time," Genevieve had continued on as she maintained her grip on Rosanna's fingers.

"I think that that is a most remarkable suggestion. Yes! Quite remarkable," O'Reilly boomed out volubly.

Rosanna and Genevieve both burst into tears and fervently embraced each other. The friendship and love between these two remarkable women was deep.

O'Reilly looked at the two amazing women. Both of them had experienced great personal loss. Both of them had lived and worked through the terrible German occupation. It was truly a moment of redemption and a moment of rekindled hope and renewal for the future of Rome, and of Italy.

* * *

Rosanna Vallone was at home with Gaetano and Ariana when she heard a knock on the front door. Ariana got up to answer it and when she opened the door she saw standing before her a smiling Robert Matthews. She ran into his arms and he embraced her. Ariana knew of her mother's love for this man and that she wanted to marry him. Besides, Ariana herself, liked Robert very much. He could not take the place of her father, but she knew Matthews to be a good, kind, and caring man.

"Ariana, for goodness sake, who is it?" asked a now curious Rosanna.

"I think it is someone you will want to see, mother." Ariana trailed Matthews as he entered the room.

Rosanna looked up and saw her lover, her man, and became slightly light-headed. This was the man she desperately loved and wanted to spend the rest of her life with. Although she had very briefly seen him several days before, he had been gone soon again, taken from her. Matthews had had to be reprocessed by army authorities and undergo a medical examination.

Rosanna ran to Robert and felt his powerful arms embrace her body. They kissed somewhat passionately, seemingly unmindful of Gaetano and Ariana's presence. Gaetano added his own joy to the moment. Rosanna and Robert sat next to one another on her leather brocaded couch, holding hands and staring into each other's eyes.

"It is so good to be back here and amongst the people I most care about. It really feels good. We are all safe now," Robert exhaled excitedly. "I've really missed all of you!"

"Si, err, yes. It is over and we can now start to get on with our lives. Robert, what will happen to you, now? I mean, will you have to go back with the army? You know what I mean. Will you have to leave me.... us and be sent to a new unit? Will you have to go back to the war?" questioned a now crestfallen Rosanna.

"Well, I probably won't be thrown right back into the fire, at least, not right away. I will likely be sent to Sicily or North Africa and, then, be sent to a new outfit."

"So! You will be leaving me again? Is that what you are saying?" said a now, at once, an angry and despondent Rosanna.

"Mother, please. I do not think that is what Robert is saying," Ariana interrupted.

"Ariana, please! I ask you to stay out of this. It is between myself and Robert. It does not involve you or Gaetano."

"Rosanna, please. I beg of you. Do not make it sound as if I am abandoning you. I am still in the army, you know," Robert replied in an almost pleading voice.

"I know, cheri. I know. I am sorry. I did not mean to be curt with you. Ariana? I apologize. Robert, I know you have been through so much. Well, let us enjoy the time we will have with one another while you are still in Rome," Rosanna said as she had suddenly softened and brightened simultaneously.

Ariana and Gaetano knew that their mother would like to spend some time alone with Robert. They said good-bye to the two of them and quietly left the apartment. The couple would not make love that afternoon. That would come later that night, when the mood would be softer and more receptive to their intimacy. For now, Rosanna and Robert would just enjoy each other's company. They would take in the lovely day that had now filled the newly liberated city.

* * *

For SS man Helmut Kammler the Germans' flight from Rome had been a complete and degrading humiliation. They had been chased out with their tails between their legs. It was difficult for him to have to resign himself to these stark and real facts.

Kammler did not immediately rejoin his family in Germany. He was not all anxious to see his wife, Angela, but he did miss his children. At first. He had been able to vacation in Venice for a brief time. Kammler took in all of the sights of this beautiful, canalled city on the Adriatic Sea. He even found time for a gondola ride through the canals, in the feminine company of one of Venice's young women. The gondolier was an older gentleman who hadn't seemed particularly keen on taking the German on to his craft. The man had even refused a tip from Kammler, as if to say, "I do not want your money, German!"

Helmut Kammler was next posted to Moderno, in the north of Italy. There he would work in concert with the local Italian chief of police. He was to act strictly in the role of an advisor. Kammler considered this work to be a comedown from the duties he had been entrusted with in Rome. It may have been a way for what Ernst Kaltenbrunner considered payback. After all, Kammler never did catch the wily Monsignor Liam O'Reilly. And, what was more, he had never rolled up the priest's band of intrepid subordinates.

* * *

Liam O'Reilly was now heavily involved with looking after the local families who had so ably and bravely assisted the Ambrosia Escape Network during the occupation. He also provided assistance and support to the few remaining Jews that had survived in Rome. O'Reilly had given many of the frightened Jews places of shelter away from the prying eyes of the Germans.

The Monsignor, Robert Matthews, and Sir D'Arcy Osborne one day sat down together to discuss how best they could help those people who had provided invaluable assistance to the Escape Line. They decided that each person should be recognized for his or her own contribution.

The situation in Rome had taken a turn to the subject of justice or for some people retribution and revenge. The families who had lost loved ones in the Ardeatine Caves massacre sought to recover the bodies that were still contained within. Nearly every day a seemingly never ending procession of mourners made their way to the site of the massacre. Many of them carried lit candles and flowers. Some brought pieces of jewelry or little trinkets. Something of which to help them remember their deceased loved ones. In the blazing summer sun, they stood and prayed, surrounded all the while by the overpowering smell from the decaying bodies.

In late June, the US Army established a commission to begin an inquest into the Ardeatine massacre and other dastardly acts committed by the Germans and Fascists during the occupation. Pietro Caruso, who had escaped from Rome just before the arrival of the Allied troops, was among the first of those to be held accountable. Caruso was indicted for having provided a list of prison inmates to the Germans whom were later killed. The man did repent for his actions and was often to be found reading from his Bible while he awaited trial for his crimes. During his subsequent trial, the court found him guilty and Caruso was sentenced to death. He would die before an Italian firing squad. All ten men of the unit would hit their target.

More arrests and trials followed in the weeks ahead for such men as Aldo Zambardi and Pasqua Perfetto. These men had outrightly betrayed the Ambrosia Network. They had been originally recruited by Liam O'Reilly himself and they had, in fact, helped an innumerable number of escaped prisoners. Another identified was Dottore Carlo Cipolla, who had served in the role of a double agent for none other than Helmut Kammler. All of these men were fortunate to have gotten away with their lives as each was sentenced to lengthy prison terms.

Monsignor O'Reilly and his erstwhile assistant, Damian Lillard, were in the process of discussing the matter of retribution in the midst of their daily workload in their offices in the German College.

"How could these men, Perfetto and Cipolla, have betrayed us, Damian?" O'Reilly lamented as he worked his way through files listing destitute people who were in urgent need of assistance from the Vatican. "It is inconceivable to me how these men could have done this. I had trusted them and what did they do? They violated their code of honor and loyalty."

"I guess one can never know how someone will act or react when they are faced with great pressure, great strain," responded Father Damian. "Do you think they should be condemned and put to death, Monsignor?"

O'Reilly thought to himself for a moment and then answered, "No, I do not think so. These men have indeed sinned and God will punish them in his own way. It is not for us mere mortals to invoke condemnation upon them. They did wrong, but in every man there is good. At least, some good."

"Would that extend to someone like.... Colonel Kammler, Monsignor?"

O'Reilly struggled to formulate a reply to the question. "I can only hope that God, in his divine mercy, can forgive that man for what he has done. I do not think that I can."

"On a different note, Monsignor, it seems as if your work with the Escape Network has gained you some recognition. The Allied Control Commission has cited you for your work. And the Holy Father has commended you for this work as well," enthused Father Damian.

"I would trade all of the honors in the world and all of the accolades I have been receiving since the liberation if I could have saved even one more victim, such as Father Ruggiero. A man like him was more worthy than myself."

The authorities in the now Allied controlled Rome continued their round-ups and punishments of those who had been deemed responsible for war crimes. One of the criminals who failed to get away was none other than Pietro Kochel, the notorious leader of his pack of Fascist killers. Kochel had been apprehended by an American Counter-Intelligence Command (CIC) unit and thrown into Regina Coeli Prison.

Kochel freely admitted to having the blood of Roman citizens drenched upon his hands, in the literal and the figurative senses. During a hazy and overcast afternoon Kochel was executed by yet another Italian-manned firing squad. Some of its members having lost family members or friends at the hands of Pietro Kochel.

In the days that followed, Rosanna Vallone and Robert Matthews spent time wandering around her neighborhood. No longer were they in fear of the Germans or of Fascists, such as Pietro Kochel. The very air that they breathed seemed cleaner and fresher than just a short time ago. Rosanna and Robert discussed their futures together.

"Robert, I am starting to get a little anxious about us. I wish there was a way for the annulment to be speeded up."

"Patience, Rosanna. You must have a little patience. Things will work out for us. I am confident. I have complete faith in the Monsignor. He will see to it that it gets done," Robert replied evenly, although he was trying to give Rosanna's hopes a boost, he, too, had had some misgivings of late.

"You are not having any second thoughts are you, cheri? After all, I am nearly ten years your senior."

"No, I am not having second thoughts. I like a mature woman. Our being together was meant to be. It was meant for me to have to travel across the Atlantic Ocean and everything that has happened in between and to meet you and your family. It was written in the stars. And besides, if you were even just five years younger I fear that I might not be able to satisfy you in bed."

"I think that you still could, cheri. Of that, I am not concerned. I do not know, my mind feels as if it is going in ten directions at once" Rosanna continued on nervously.

The couple was sitting on a park bench along the Piazza Mignanelli. It was a lovely and warm summer day in Rome. The notorious humidity had abated somewhat for the day. It was perfect for the two lovers. After the chill experienced during the German occupation, this type of weather was nothing to complain about.

"You know, I was little concerned as to how Ariana and Gaetano would take the news about us. I could never take the place of their father, and I would never, ever, think about doing that. But I will love them and care for them as if they were my very own," said Robert as he looked into Rosanna's hazel-colored eyes.

"I know, cheri. I know that, said Rosanna as she tenderly took hold of his right hand. She felt a heat building inside of her. She was becoming physically aroused.

Robert, too, was feeling passion building within himself. He admitted that sometimes he could not control himself when he was in Rosanna's presence. The woman positively oozed sexuality. He would often picture Rosanna naked and mounted above him. Her full breasts heaving over him as his hardened penis drove itself into her body. The look of complete and total passion written all over her grimacing face. Robert could never get enough sex from this woman. He would have to contain himself for the moment. Later, when he could take Rosanna and engage her in intense and passionate lovemaking.

"Rosanna, I have been informed that I will probably be sent to North Africa. Then, it's likely I will be sent on to my old division, the First. They are now in Normandy.

"When will you have to leave, cheri?" she asked, a slightly higher octave in her voice.

"Probably not for another two weeks or so is my guess. I will just be hanging around Rome in the meantime. I do think I should be able to stay with you a good amount of the time. That's good news, right?"

Rosanna looked down at the ground as she nodded her head. She realized that his returning to action could get Robert killed. She could not bear the loss of him, she just couldn't. Not on top of the loss of her husband and the deaths she had only recently witnessed in Rome. She would just have to wait and hope and pray that the good Lord would look over him and safely bring him back to her.

"Rosanna, honey. I think that we should wait to get married. We are still waiting for the annulment to go through. I promise you that I will return. I will!" Robert said with an intensity that Rosanna could tangibly feel.

"Si, no, you are right. It would be better to wait," said Rosanna. Rosanna had not told him that she had spoken about marriage to Genevieve Alviano and Monsignor O'Reilly and about having a double wedding.

"I love you, Rosanna. I love you with all of my heart. I want to spend the rest of my life with you."

"I love you, too, Robert. We will have many years together," she said. Rosanna well knew that much could happen until the war was finally over.

* * *

Across Rome, another couple was contemplating their future and what might be lying in store for them. Genevieve Alviano and Jimmy Cefalo were walking along the streets of the newly liberated and revitalized city. Genevieve had been able to secure a job with the American occupation forces. She would be performing translation and interpretative services for ordinary Italians in their dealings with the new authorities. There was much work to be done in regard to the interrogations of former Fascists, and also in the provision of basic services for the average citizen. Genevieve loved her new work. She began each day with a feeling of anticipation and optimism.

Genevieve was aware that Jimmy would eventually be forced to leave her there in Rome. She desperately did not want it to happen, but she knew it was inevitable. "Rosanna and myself spoke with Monsignor O'Reilly. He said he would be overjoyed to officiate our wedding. And, also, Rosanna's to Major Matthews."

Cefalo held Genevieve's hands in his. "That's great, Gen. Really great. But when do you think we should get married?"

"Well, I am not sure. Rosanna is still waiting for the major's annulment to go through. The Monsignor is trying to have it, how would you? have it," she halted in mid-sentence.

"Expedited?" Cefalo offered to her.

"Si, err, yes. Expedited. No one is quite sure how long it might take. In any event, Rosanna and me both feel that we should wait until the war is over. What do you think?"

"Well," Cefalo said carefully, "there is no need to rush things. We will wait until we win the war."

"No need to rush things? You say," Genevieve replied with a playful pout on her angelic face. "A fine thing to say to the woman you profess to love so deeply."

"You know what I mean, Gen. You are just...."

"Pulling your leg?" she kidded him, using the correct idiomatic expression.

Cefalo found that she was catching on quickly to American colloquialisms. "I can see that you are picking up on American expressions. I am impressed," he replied in mock horror and good naturedly. The two of them were becoming quite used to one another.

All around the young couple people could be seen scurrying to and fro while immersed in their daily activities. They seemed to move at a more upbeat pace than they did just a short time before. The presence of freedom, true freedom, and the onset of summer contributed to this ebullient feeling, to the doubts of no one.

Genevieve and Jimmy drank in all of the sights and sounds of the glorious city that was Rome. Of course, any itinerary had to include the Colosseum, St Peter's Cathedral, the Sistine

Chapel, and the famous Spanish Steps. There was so much more for them, or more specifically for Cefalo to see. There was the Palatine Hill, the Arch of Constantine, and the Victor Emmanuel Monument, including its Tomb of the Unknown Soldier.

Genevieve had, of course, seen all of these things before, but this time she was sharing their wonder and mystique with a man who would become her husband. She was seeing these breathtaking landmarks in a new light. She would have to wait for her betrothed to return from his upcoming renewed service with the US Army. Genevieve would pray for his safety like she had never prayed before, and she would trust in God to make her, no, their dream come true. "I wish you didn't have to leave, Jimmy. I know that will not happen, but still...." she said softly as tears started to course their way down her golden colored cheeks.

The couple had paused for a moment to snap some pictures of Genevieve in the exquisite, he thought, romantic Farnese Gardens. The glow from the young woman was something for him to behold. He was glad that he had had the foresight to borrow the well-used and worn Ansco camera from Father Lillard.

"Genevieve, there is nothing in this world that can or will stop me from coming back to you. You must believe that," Cefalo intoned deeply.

"I know, I know, but when you do go back into action, something could happen. I just could not bear it," the young woman felt as if her heart was breaking. The tears continued to fall.

"You must not think like that, Gen. You cannot. There is always the chance that something could happen to me. I

300

wouldn't lie to you. But we will have to trust that bad things will not."

"You know that amidst all of the excitement that has been going around, I almost forgot to tell you that I was finally able to contact my father in Anzio. He says that he is well, thank God. The whole town has been devastated with the fighting that raged there for so long. I must go to see him as soon as possible. Would you like to go with me? I think he would be most impressed with you, even if you are not a genuine Italian man."

"That would be a great idea, Gen.! Just great! In fact, I do believe I just might be able to obtain the services of a vehicle and driver," said Cefalo, hardly able to contain himself. "Let me get to work on it. We might be able to go in a day or two. How does that sound?"

"It sounds wonderful. And, thank you," Genevieve replied as she embraced herself in Cefalo's waiting arms.

* * *

The newly freed city of Rome was welcomed by many other individuals. None more so than Mario Casso, the erstwhile street-sweeper chieftain. He had been at the very heart of the bomb attack on Via Rasella, along with Pietro Cardi and Elena Mello. In the latter half of June, he had one day wandered into Giuseppe Prato's bar. He had inadvertently stumbled into a reunion of sorts of some of the Resistance members who had participated in the planning and execution of the attack. Lucca Bianchini was there, but Enrico Visconti would not be joining the group that day, or any day soon thereafter.

In the wake of the Via Rasella bombing and with the news of the death of a young girl among the victims and, then, the German reprisals, Visconti had decided he could no longer live with the guilt that had consumed him. One day, not long after the Ardeatine Cave massacre, he affixed a rope with a noose around a wooden beam in the basement of his home and hanged himself. Visconti had been unable to go on living and he had cursed the names of Mario Casso and Lucca Bianchini and others of their so-called noble Resistance as his life slowly ebbed out of his body.

Elena Mello stared wistfully out through the front window of Prato's, not really focusing on anything in particular. Ordinary people were going about their daily activities, and most them could be seen to have a smile on their faces. Or they had, at least, a look of contentment and peacefulness.

Elena had been having trouble concentrating on a number of things since the bombing. She had never revealed her role to her husband. She knew she never could, ever.

"Elena, are you alright?" asked Casso, while he sipped on a double espresso. "You seem as if you are a million miles away."

"I sometimes wish I were a million miles away from here, Mario. I do not think that things will ever be the same for me ever again."

"You realize we had to do it. We had to!" implored Casso to her. "We had to strike back at the Germans. All of Italy compelled us to do so!"

"Did we, Mario? Was it all really necessary? Was it worth the price of a little girl losing her life or the hundreds who were later massacred at the Ardeatine Caves?" Elena replied with a heartbreaking anguish. "I keep trying to tell myself that it was the right thing to do, but now I don't really believe it. I do not thing I will ever...... ever get over it."

"We are at war, Elena! At war! It had to be done! One day you will look back on this and realize that the attack was justified. One day."

"Perhaps, Mario, perhaps, but I am a woman. I am not a combatant. I am woman with a husband and two children. One of them is now somewhere in Germany. We do not know if he is even still alive. Do you realize how they would feel, how they would see me if my role were to be revealed to them? I shudder to think. They might very well reject me, turn me into an outcast," she continued with a bitterness in her voice.

The sun outside the bar was now shining brightly. It was another truly glorious day in Rome. Elena only wished she could feel some of the sun's warmth, as inside of her she felt very cold. Very cold indeed.

Lucca Bianchini was seated at the same table as Mario Casso and Elena Mello. He had listened intently to Elena's wounded words and her breaking heart. He deeply empathized with her as he, too, had felt consumed by guilt and remorse. He had also been directly involved with the bomb plot. He, too, could not shake the dark thoughts that had engulfed his brain. A child, a little girl who had only been ten years old. Her whole life should have been ahead of her. She should have been able to grow up, to have played with her friends and, eventually, she may have married and had children of her own. But not now. Bianchini and his colleagues had seen to that. He extended his right hand to one of Elena's and covered it. He met her gaze as she looked over at him. Bianchini slowly nodded his head, as if he understood her thoughts. He was telling her that he felt her pain.

"Elena, I won't try to say things to you just so you will feel better. I understand as I, too, have been complicit in the attack. I only want to say that you are not alone. Please, feel free to speak to me at any time that you think you may need to. I will always be there for you."

"Thank you, Lucca. That is very kind of you. I think I will just have to bring myself to accept what I have done in time. That time may never come, but I will try. I have to for my family and for myself."

* * *

"Monsignor, I got here as soon as I could. You have news for me?" questioned Rosanna Vallone in a fearful tone. She was afraid of what she might hear from O'Reilly.

"I do indeed, Rosanna. Please, sit down. I have just received word concerning Robert's request for an annulment. It has been granted. It even received the Holy Father's approval and blessing as well," said a jovial O'Reilly as he looked at Rosanna's heaving chest. Although he was a man of the cloth and had always been faithful and dedicated to his vows, he, nevertheless, could not help but notice the woman's impressive frontal physique. He continued. "There was some trepidation about Robert not being a Catholic, but the powers that be were finally able to look past it. I am very pleased and most happy for you. For both you and Robert."

"Oh, Monsignor, that is the news I have been waiting for, for so long," Rosanna replied in an almost hypnotic state of mind. For the time was now nearing the end of 1944. The war in Europe was about to enter its final stages. The Russians had been steadily driving the Germans back toward Germany in the east. The Americans and the British were at the western border of the country. Her beloved Robert was with the liberating American forces, serving once again with the First Infantry Division, the "Big Red One." Thankfully, he had not been killed in action, but had been only slightly wounded while he was at the Falaise Gap in France.

The Contessa and the Monsignor both realized that things could still go wrong. The Germans had just launched a massive surprise attack in the Ardennes Forest in Belgium and were driving back a number of American units. A large number of panzer and infantry divisions had caught several unprepared American divisions completely by surprise. If the Germans could penetrate through to the Channel coast, they could then divide the Allied forces in two. And quite possibly extend the war indefinitely.

"How is Robert, Rosanna?" Have you heard from him lately?"

"I have, Monsignor. He is well, thank God. He was slightly wounded somewhere in France, but that was some time ago during August. I am not quite sure where he is at the moment. He probably does not want me to worry. I still do. Thank you for asking, Monsignor."

"I am so glad to hear that, Rosanna. I truly am. It is only natural for you to be concerned about his welfare, but I do believe that God is watching over him and his men. Now, I do realize that it may be still too early. Have you and Robert been able to set a date for......?"

"No, Monsignor. We have decided that it might be better if we were to wait until the war is over, and Robert comes back safely, of course," she said.

"Yes, that would be the prudent thing to do. All right. By the way, how is Lieutenant Cefalo? Has Genevieve had any word from him?"

"She has, Monsignor. Jimmy is also serving in France. He is well. Genevieve and myself are most happy about this. They have also decided to wait for the war's end. Of course, we all would like to be married at the same time."

"Splendid, Rosanna! It will give me great satisfaction and joy to be able to perform this double wedding ceremony. The four of you are most deserving of it."

"I would have to agree with you, Monsignor. We are definitely looking to the future," gushed a thankful Rosanna Vallone.

* * *

The war in Europe officially ended on May 8th, 1945 with the German surrender to the Allies. The war for Benito Mussolini had ended one week previously, when the German convoy he was traveling in was stopped by Italian partisans in northern Italy. The former dictator, along with his mistress, Claretta Petacci, were gunned down alongside a wall-lined road. The next day their bullet riddled bodies were strung up outside a Milan gas station. It was an ignominious and grisly end to the Fascist chapter in Italian history. Italy had finally freed herself of the man who had promised its people an empire, but in the end had led her down the road to ruin and defeat.

Major Robert Matthews and now Captain James Cefalo both emerged from combat in France and Germany virtually unscathed. After clearing up some of the inevitable army red tape, both men had been able to secure leave and were soon on their way to Rome. Matthews, by this time, had also been promoted to the rank of Lieutenant Colonel.

Upon their arrival at the massive Termini Train Station in Rome, they stepped out onto a platform absolutely swarming with people. Despite the day being overcast, with a definite hint of rain looming, the two men noticed that no one seemed to care. The war was over now. Good days would be ahead for all.

Robert called Rosanna's apartment with the news of their arrival in the city. He and Cefalo then hired a taxi and directed the driver to the Contessa's residence on Via Frattina. Waiting there would be Rosanna and Genevieve Alviano. The young woman had been unable to contain herself when Rosanna had given her the news of Jimmy Cefalo's arrival.

Monsignor Liam O'Reilly had been able to obtain Church permission for the double wedding and to schedule it for the last week in June. It would be performed at the Church of Santa Rosaria, in honor and in memory of the late Father Alberto Ruggiero.

* * *

Saturday morning dawned bright and warm in Rome. There were few clouds in the sky overhead. Rosanna Vallone and Genevieve Alviano had been able to procure wedding gowns from the not-so-famous Monsieur Russo, a couturier located in the Old Quarter of Rome. Russo was in fact a Frenchman who had moved to the city many years before from his native Marseilles. The Russo name he had adopted was derived from the French Rousseau. The rather doddering man strongly resembled the veteran character actor, Vito Scotti.

The two women had gone to Russo after Rosanna had unsuccessfully tried to squeeze herself into her original wedding dress. The tailor had done a remarkable job of fashioning gowns out of what was then available in Rome.

The two women alighted on to the curb outside of Santa Rosaria from their makeshift US Army limousine. Both of them looked stunning to all who had gathered to witness the nuptials.

Rosanna's gown was certainly not ostentatious. It was a simply designed and functional piece of clothing that fit her perfectly. Genevieve was wearing a gown similar to the one on Rosanna. Her dress was white. Rosanna had selected a light peach color. Both of them wore rose garlands in their hair.

Monsignor O'Reilly patiently waited for Rosanna and Genevieve to make their way down the center aisle of Santa Rosaria. Robert Matthews and Jimmy Cefalo waited for the procession as they stood in front of the altar. Escorting Rosanna was Sergeant Louis Durval and escorting Genevieve was her proud and beaming father.

At precisely 10:00 AM, the holy sacrament of marriage commenced for the two couples. Both Matthews and Cefalo had been awestruck at the sight of Rosanna and Genevieve. It was a moment they would remember for the rest of their lives.

The two women took their places by their soon to be significant others. Monsignor O'Reilly began. He had been thinking of all that had transpired over the past two years. All of the trials and tribulations. The many people who had suffered, those who had been tortured, and those who had been killed. Today represented renewal and hope for all of those in attendance at this wondrous ceremony set before God.

Standing among those in witness was the widow of Pietro Cardi, and the mother of Paolo Cardi. Maria Cardi would not be defeated by what had happened to her husband and son. She would endure and go on, for them.

As O'Reilly proceeded along, Rosanna could not contain the immense joy she felt and tears welled up in her eyes and began to run down her cheeks. Genevieve saw this, but kept the radiant smile on her own face. She tightened her grip on Jimmy Cefalo's hand.

"By the powers vested in me by the Holy Catholic Church, I now pronounce you husbands and wives. You may now kiss your brides," O'Reilly intoned with one of his broadest smiles.

Gaetano and Ariana Vallone both wept and embraced one another. It was good for their mother to have found Robert Matthews. And it would be good for them as well.

Robert turned to fully face Rosanna, he framed his hands around her now smiling face and gently kissed her. Jimmy Cefalo looked into Genevieve's hazel-colored, almond shaped eyes and leaned toward her. Their lips met in perfect synchrony as they embraced each other.

Twelve

Conviction/Conversion

elmut Kammler gazed at the crucifix hanging on the courtroom wall in silent contemplation. Gone was the formerly imposing field-gray SS uniform of the Obersturmbannfuhrer he was once. He was now dressed in a non-descript and ill-fitting dark suit. The one-time feared SS man seemed to have been transformed, Secretly, he hoped it might help his cause in the war-crime trial he was about to experience.

In the public gallery were seated relatives and friends of those lost in the Ardeatine Caves massacre. They wanted to see and hear about how their loved ones had suffered and died. They wanted to see the man who had played the central and pivotal role in the killings. They wanted to see the monster in the flesh.

Helmut Kammler had already provided his Allied interrogators a detailed account of the role he had played in the massacre. The SS man had given testimony in 1946 of his part during the trials of Kurt Malzer and General Eberhard von Mackensen. The two men had tried to foist all blame for the killings on Kammler. He, in turn, had calmly replied that he had shown the list of prisoners to be killed to Malzer and von Mackensen. And, that both had concurred with all of the names on the List.

After the war, Helmut Kammler had been held at the notorious Dachau concentration camp, just outside of Munich. Allied authorities had then handed him over to Italian control. Ironically, he was then placed in the equally notorious and sinister Regina Coeli Prison. During his incarceration, Kammler turned himself into a prolific letter writer to his lawyers, family members, and friends, and to one man in particular, Liam O'Reilly.

The Monsignor took possession of Helmut Kammler's first note and read through it. After consultation with Father Lillard, he began to write back to the German. Kammler soon became more open and forthright in his comments and thoughts. He informed O'Reilly that he was seriously considering converting to Catholicism.

Liam O'Reilly eventually reached a point where he felt he must visit the former SS officer, his one-time nemesis, in his prison cell. Forgiveness was at the core of his being and beliefs, and the root of his faith in the Church.

"Thank you for coming to see me, Monsignor. It is most kind and considerate of you," Helmut Kammler said with noted deference and humility to O'Reilly. "I was hoping that we could be open and frank with one another."

"I agreed to see you Herr Kammler, in part, because I am obligated to by the Holy Church. Also, because I am a man, by nature, who has always believed in giving people a second chance, or even a third chance at redemption."

"I appreciate that, Monsignor. I am struck by the juxtaposition that we now find ourselves in. What I mean is if our positions or roles were to be reversed, do you think I would visit you to discuss, oh, say, human nature or......" Kammler let his words trail off.

"It is not important for you to know what is in my heart, Herr Kammler. It is important to know what is in your heart."

"Yes, indeed. If you do not mind, Monsignor O'Reilly, perhaps, we could discuss, oh, I don't know... literature? Have you read anything good of late?" asked Kammler, trying to lighten the cloying mood that had fallen over the two men.

For the next two hours, O'Reilly and Kammler talked about a number of things, including art and religion, and literature. The two men agreed to see each other again.

O'Reilly soon began to bring books to Regina Coeli for Kammler to read. In a bizarre twist of fate, the two war-time rivals had become peacetime friends.

One day in 1947, Rosanna Matthews stopped by the Vatican to visit with her old friend, Monsignor O'Reilly. During the course of their afternoon conversation O'Reilly declared, "You know, Rosanna, I have actually begun to enjoy the company of Herr Kammler. Imagine, here I am a man who once had a 30,000 lire bounty on his head and, now, we have become pals."

Rosanna had drawn a cold look across her face. She loved and deeply respected Liam O'Reilly, but she could not, would not, countenance herself to being able to adapt to this kind of new-found feeling, and she promptly said so. "Monsignor, I just cannot share your enthusiasm over your new friend. I could try to, within my heart, but I cannot. There are just too many memories, painful memories, too much pain. Emotional pain to ever or even remotely contemplate any degree of camaraderie or compassion where Colonel Kammler is concerned. I hope you understand, Monsignor," Rosanna spoke movingly and from the heart.

"Of course, Rosanna. I never meant to offend you. It is just that part of me, in my role for the Church, wants to…. has to…. welcome someone even someone as distasteful as a Colonel Kammler, into the fold of the Catholic Church. I have an obligation to forgive, not forget, but to forgive."

"Monsignor, you have that right and I respect that. But I cannot forget, nor forgive, that man. I just do not have it in me to do so. You are disappointed in me?" she asked softly.

"No, no, I am not, Rosanna. It is just that I have listened to this man for some time now. In fact, Helmut has even broached the subject of converting to the Catholic Church. Could you even imagine that just a short time ago?" O'Reilly continued on as if the Contessa was not even in the same room.

Rosanna felt another cold chill wash over her. How could the Monsignor, her old and dear friend, speak almost reverentially about this brute of a man? Sure, Kammler now looked far different and much more benign than when he ruled over Rome with an iron fist in his sharply pressed SS field-gray uniform. Rosanna decided she would have to leave before she said something to her friend that she would later regret.

Helmut Kammler went on trial for war-crimes in May of 1948. The prosecution outlined its case against the former SS officer. One hundred relatives of the dead Ardeatine victims stood witness in the courtroom. As the charges were read aloud, several of them broke down and openly wept. A woman in the gallery shouted down at Kammler. "I'd like to tear out those eyes that ordered what was done to my father and brother!"

In his defense, Kammler related the events of the massacre in a clinical and detached manner. His account was precise and he displayed no emotion. He further told the court that he had forbidden religious assistance to the condemned because he had thought it would have only slowed down the timetable. This was simply too much for many of the spectators. Some shouted out, "Schweinehund!" Kammler paid no mind and proceeded to explain that the killings had been a legitimate act of war. An atrocity had been perpetrated against German troops. Someone had had to pay for it.

The Italian military tribunal determined that, in fact, the killings had not been legitimate and did constitute a war crime. Helmut Kammler was sentenced to life in prison. Many in the courtroom were outraged as their relatives had gotten death, while Kammler would be allowed to live.

Monsignor O'Reilly and Kammler stayed in contact through 1949. The German felt that he had grown very close to the Irish priest. He continued his quest to become a Roman Catholic. Late in the year, Liam O'Reilly, in a response to a letter he had received from Kammler, visited Regina Coeli. This time he received Helmut Kammler, the one-time Nazi, into the Catholic Church.

Liam O'Reilly was appointed a Domestic Prelate in 1953 by Pope Pius XII. It was in honor of what the Monsignor had done on behalf of the Church. He resumed his daily tasks and responsibilities within the Vatican. It was difficult for him to adapt to an anonymous life. After all, he had become a celebrity of sorts. He had also gained some enemies within the Vatican, those who felt that he had gotten too full of himself. O'Reilly had become aware of this, but he also knew that was a price he had had to pay.

Robert and Rosanna Matthews settled into a comfortable, yet challenging lifestyle in post-war Rome. Matthews had been able to secure a position with the Allied Military government in Italy. His main area of responsibility was to assist in the tracking down and arrest of former Fascist officials for criminal acts, including some for war crimes.

Rosanna and her two children accepted Robert wholeheartedly. He was even able to improve upon his Italian. Often he and Rosanna would switch from English to Italian, and back, as if it were second nature. They would maintain a good and fulfilling life and share an unbreakable bond of love.

The Contessa eventually reconciled her conscience with the Monsignor. She would devote herself to the rebuilding of Italy. Rosanna would also maintain her close ties to Genevieve Alviano and her new husband.

*** * ***

The war's end was not too unkind for either Bruno Bettinelli or Lady Barbara Daniella. Bruno did have to suffer through the indignity of not being able to serve in the new post-war government of Italy for a period of five years. This was because of his previous ties to Mussolini's Fascist rule. Bettinelli immersed himself in the reconstruction efforts required in the rebuilding of his shattered country.

Lady Barbara did not have to suffer through the shame and humiliation of having her head shaved for having slept with the enemy. She had not been forced to wear a placard around her neck proclaiming that she had been a Fascist whore.

Barbara and Bruno were quietly married in a private ceremony in Rome in 1946. The man who presided over their wedding was none other than Monsignor Liam O'Reilly. Rosanna, her old friend, was in attendance along with Robert Matthews.

Barbara always retained her bright outlook and zest for life. She and Bruno shared a deep appreciation for all that Italy represented, and for one another. She remained ardent and passionate in the boudoir, as well. Barbara was well aware that many women past the age of fifty did not possess the sexual libido they once had, but she still did.

On Barbara's 65th birthday she greeted Bruno at the door of their home, naked. Bruno stood in front of Barbara and took in the full measure of his still remarkable wife. Her frizzled blond hair had begun to turn gray. Those bright blue and vibrant eyes were still inviting. Her breasts, although they had started to sag a bit, were still very real and spectacular. The stomach was not quite as flat as it once was. Barbara's arms and thighs were still well-defined and muscled. The hips had thickened a little, but, oh well, whatever.

Bruno advanced toward Barbara and took her into his arms. They kissed tenderly, but rapidly proceeded to intensive French kissing. He bent and picked her up and carried her to the bedroom, where he gently placed her on their bed. Barbara was ready for him; she had made sure to lubricate herself before Bruno had arrived home.

Bettinelli eyed Barbara the entire time as he slowly stripped off his clothing. His penis was rapidly engorging itself and was at full attention by the time he dropped his underpants to the floor.

"Bruno, do you remember that time we made love in 1944? The night I came over for dinner. The night I seduced you."

316

"I remember it quite well, my dear. How could I ever forget such a night? I recall it as the night that you rather took advantage of me," he replied.

"Yes, I did do that, didn't I? But I felt it was something I had to do for Rosanna and her colleagues," Barbara responded tenderly to her husband.

"I know, dear, I know. And I have come to accept it. It was a little different at first." Bruno sounded wounded and Barbara felt it.

"I know, Bruno. I know. It has hurt me and bothered me ever since. I want you to know that the passion and desire I had for you that night was real. I never faked anything during our lovemaking. Anything. I gave to you all that I had," she went on almost pleadingly.

"You do not have to apologize, dear. It is all right. We are together now."

"Thank you, dear. Bruno?"

"Yes, dear?"

"Do you remember how we made love that night?"

"Yes. We had a lovely dinner, some light conversation and, then, you allowed me to ravage you. It was wonderful. You on top of me. You squirming beneath me. I well remember the feel of your powerful legs gripping my body. Your feet tucked tightly over my thrusting buttocks. You were relentless."

"Yes, I was. But no. I mean the second time we made love that evening. Do you remember?"

I do indeed. And you now wish for an encore?" Bruno asked teasingly.

"Yes, I do," Barbara replied as she rolled off of the bed and onto the floor on her stomach.

"No foreplay?" Bruno again teased his wife. He was still growing harder. He wanted so badly to plunge his penis into Barbara.

"No foreplay, Bruno. Just a straight shot right into me."

Barbara was enjoying their sex immensely, as much as she ever had. Her husband was now thrusting himself deeper and deeper into her. Bruno was picking up speed, his hands squeezed Barbara's breasts tighter. Waves of orgasms swept through Barbara's body. She could not remember how many she had had already. She was thankful she could still achieve them. Even younger women did not always have the luxury of enjoying them anymore.

At last, the couple was spent. They laid side by side to one another. Her left hand caressing his right. "Bruno, we have been lucky. My years with you have been the happiest of my life. Thank you, dear."

"You are welcome, my dear. And I feel the same way about you."

Barbara and Bruno would continue lovemaking in the years that followed, almost to the day she passed away at the age of ninety. It was March 23, 1974. Her beloved Bruno would live for only another five years. His heart had been shattered by Barbara's death. But how they had lived, and loved.

* * *

The war's end was not as kind or as forgiving for Elena Mello. She could never shake from herself the guilt she had felt ever since that fateful March day in 1944 on the Via Rasella. Elena had followed the war crimes trials in Italy with a disinterested view. She had not paid especial attention to the trial of Helmut Kammler.

Post-war Italy for the rest of the Mello family was more a means of adjustment in going back to a peacetime existence. Elena never revealed to her husband or to her two sons her role in the bombing. She felt they would never understand as to why she had agreed to be such a willing participant in such a sordid and deadly act. No, it could never be disclosed to them. Elena Mello would take her secret to the grave.

* * *

Genevieve and Jimmy Cefalo remained in Rome until 1946. Cefalo was still in the army, serving for a time under Robert Matthews in the continuing hunt for Fascists and some Nazis who had gone underground. Genevieve, in the meantime, had brought her father to live with them in Rome. Her brother, Pietro, had been repatriated back to Italy. The young man had emerged from his German prison camp deeply embittered. He hated the Germans for what they had done to him, with an absolute and burning passion. Pietro felt as if he had been robbed of his soul. And he had come to dislike his sister because he had it in his head that she had experienced a soft and easy life when Rome was occupied.

Genevieve and Jimmy then decided they should move to the United States, specifically to Springfield, MA. Cefalo had relations in the city and thought it was a good place to settle down with Gen. After some fierce arguments, they managed to convince Genevieve's father to move with them. It was time to leave Italy.

The couple would welcome two children into their new world, a boy and a girl.

Pietro Alviano refused to join his sister and father in the US. He would remain in Rome and drift from job to job and one political cause to another. And he would always feel embittered.

* * *

Liam O'Reilly was celebrating mass in Rome in 1960, when he suffered a serious and debilitating stroke. This forced him to have to retire back to his native Ireland. The Monsignor lived with his sister in the small town of Cahersween until the day of his passing on October 30, 1963. He was sixty-five years old. The man had truly lived a rich and rewarding life. He had been able to help so many people, enabling them to live their own rich and fulfilling lives.

* * *

The final denouement for Helmut Kammler arrived on February 9, 1978, when he finally lost his long and agonizing battle with cancer. He was seventy-one years old. Following his conversion to Catholicism Kammler had been confined to the fortress jail at Gaeta. Walter Reder, himself a former SS Sturmbannfuhrer, was another inmate at the jail. Reder had been convicted and sentenced for having ordered the deaths of hundreds of civilians in Marzabotto, a village located near Bologna in September of 1944. Among the victims had been many women and children, some had been only a few months old.

The Italian government saw the two ex-Nazis as having been cut from the same cloth. Reder and Kammler had had similar backgrounds. They were both serving life sentences. The two men were often to be found spending much time together, talking, sharing meals, and exercising in the prison yard.

Helmut Kammler was able to find love again while he was in prison, in the person of Anneliese Wagner. This divorcee hailed from Soltau in what had become West Germany. During the course of her job as a refugee assistant, Kammler's plight had been brought to her attention. Wagner began to make discreet inquiries of the former SS man. Soon, she began to correspond with Kammler. Anneliese also began sending packages containing clothes and food to the jail in Gaeta.

Their relationship started to grow to the point that this lonely German woman felt herself developing romantic feelings for the incarcerated ex-Nazi officer. The couple wrote to one another over the course of the next several years. Many of the letters from each of them were many pages in length. Kammler and Wagner poured out every thought and feeling that the both of them possessed.

Helmut Kammler had long been divorced from the petulant and demanding Angela. Anneliese Wagner was, herself, long divorced from her drunken and mean-spirited husband. A man who had caused her almost nothing but pain throughout their empty marriage. Anneliese had been able to convince Italian authorities to allow her periodic visits to see Kammler. In 1972, the couple was secretly married in the jail at Gaeta. Kammler was to remain in the prison. Anneliese could only visit him from time to time. Conjugal liaisons were not allowed.

Helmut Kammler had resigned himself to the fact that he would likely remain in prison for the rest of his life. In 1975, while undergoing a routine physical examination he learned that he had stomach cancer. The Italians then transferred him to Celio Military Hospital in Rome.

Following numerous attempts to gain her husband's release, Anneliese made the decision to abduct Kammler from the hospital he was confined in. That Wagner would be able to pull it off could well be attributed to the fact that security at Celio was quite lax, if not downright lazy. Anneliese bluffed her way into Kammler and then basically walked right out with him and to freedom. The SS man was spirited over the Italian border with West Germany with the assistance of Wagner's son. They had concealed Kammler in the trunk of their car.

Once they were back in Germany, Anneliese and Helmut Kammler settled in Soltau. The end was fast approaching for Kammler, and he knew it.

In his final moments, Helmut Kammler thought that it had been ironic that he had lived longer than his one-time nemesis, Liam O'Reilly. He began to see, in his mind, the faces of some of his victims in the Ardeatine Caves. He saw the bruised and battered face of Father Alberto Ruggiero. And there were others. So many others. He had tried to atone, in some small way, for the pain and suffering that he had personally inflicted. Kammler was unsure as to whether he had succeeded. Only God would know.

Helmut Kammler was sure of one thing. When Liam O'Reilly had come to the end of his life he would not have had to atone for anything. The Monsignor had lived a good and noble life. He had served his God and his Church well. Kammler, himself, had lived an empty life and he had served a black and evil regime.

About the Author

George Banks was employed for more than 30 years by the Defense Department as an analyst of private defense contractors. He has degrees from the University of Rhode Island and Michigan State University. The subject of World War II and, in particular the Italian campaign have long held his interest. The author resides in the Providence, RI area.

www.ingramcontent.com/pod-product-compliance
Lightning Source LLC
Chambersburg PA
CBHW060947030726
47503CB00003B/761